MRS. SPRING FRAGRANCE

broadview editions
series editor: L.W. Conolly

Portrait of Edith Maude Eaton/Sui Sin Far, n.d., photograph courtesy of Diana Birchall.

MRS. SPRING FRAGRANCE

Edith Maude Eaton/Sui Sin Far

edited by Hsuan L. Hsu

broadview editions

Library and Archives Canada Cataloguing in Publication

Sui Sin Far, 1865-1914
  Mrs. Spring Fragrance / Edith Maude Eaton/Sui Sin Far ;
edited by Hsuan L. Hsu.

(Broadview editions)
Includes bibliographical references.
ISBN 978-1-55481-027-7

  I. Hsu, Hsuan L., 1976- II. Title. III. Series: Broadview editions

PS8487.U44M77 2011   C813'.52   C2011-905378-0

Broadview Editions
The Broadview Editions series represents the ever-changing canon of literature in English by bringing together texts long regarded as classics with valuable lesser-known works.

Advisory editor for this volume: Juliet Sutcliffe

Broadview Press is an independent, international publishing house, incorporated in 1985.

We welcome comments and suggestions regarding any aspect of our publications— please feel free to contact us at the addresses below or at broadview@broadviewpress.com.

North America
Post Office Box 1243, Peterborough, Ontario, Canada K9J 7H5
2215 Kenmore Avenue, Buffalo, NY, USA 14207
Tel: (705) 743-8990; Fax: (705) 743-8353
email: customerservice@broadviewpress.com

UK, Europe, Central Asia, Middle East, Africa, India, and Southeast Asia
Eurospan Group, 3 Henrietta St., London WC2E 8LU, United Kingdom
Tel: 44 (0) 1767 604972; Fax: 44 (0) 1767 601640
email: eurospan@turpin-distribution.com

Australia and New Zealand
NewSouth Books
c/o TL Distribution, 15-23 Helles Ave., Moorebank, NSW, Australia 2170
Tel: (02) 8778 9999; Fax: (02) 8778 9944
email: orders@tldistribution.com.au

www.broadviewpress.com

This book is printed on paper containing 100% post-consumer fibre.

Typesetting and assembly: True to Type Inc.,
Claremont, Canada.

PRINTED IN CANADA

Contents

Acknowledgements

My research on Sui Sin Far and her historical contexts has been supported by fellowships from Yale University and the University of California at Davis, and by conversations with Hoang Phan, Edlie Wong, Miriam Thaggert, and Arnold Pan. I am also grateful to Grace Wang, Dominika Ferens, and Martha Lincoln for generously reading drafts of the introduction. Kang, Hsiang-Lin, Kang Jr., Lin, Cristina, Kile, Kalissa, and Martha have kept me on my toes and taken me on informative trips to west-coast Chinatowns. This book has also benefited greatly from classroom discussions with undergraduates and graduate students at both Yale and UC Davis, and from rigorous questions asked by audiences at the University of Chicago's Reproduction of Race and Racial Ideologies Workshop, UC Santa Cruz's Asia-Pacific-Americas Research Cluster, and the Asian American Cultural Center at Yale.

Amy Ling and Annette White-Parks's edition of *Mrs. Spring Fragrance and Other Writings* has been indispensable to scholarship on Sui Sin Far, and in preparing this complete edition of *Mrs. Spring Fragrance* I have attempted as far as possible to avoid overlap with the important supplementary texts included in their collection. I have also drawn liberally from scholarship on Sui Sin Far and am particularly indebted to the illuminating book-length studies of her work and life by Annette White-Parks and Dominika Ferens. Thanks, also, to Kevin Bryant, Cara Shipe, and Kristian Jensen for their assistance with preparing and proofreading the typescript. And, of course, I am grateful to Marjorie Mather, Leonard Conolly, and the anonymous reviewers at Broadview Press for providing encouraging and demanding feedback towards revising and rounding out this teaching edition.

The supplementary materials in this volume have benefited from scholarship by Mary Lui, Annette White-Parks, and Dominika Ferens. The Comparative Ethnic Studies Library, Asian American Special Collection, Bancroft Library at UC Berkeley, and Diana Birchall have been generous in helping me locate documents, produce reproductions, and acquire the necessary permissions.

Introduction

Writing under the pen name Sui Sin Far ("Water Lily"), Edith Maude Eaton (1867–1914) published dozens of stories, articles, and essays focusing on the inhabitants of America's "Chinatown" settlements. Although her magazine stories responded to specific times and places over approximately twenty years spent traveling throughout Canada, the United States, and Jamaica, Sui Sin Far attempted to create a unified picture of the Chinese in North America by reprinting many of her stories in one volume, *Mrs. Spring Fragrance*. The earliest book of fiction published in the United States by an author of mixed Chinese and white descent, *Mrs. Spring Fragrance* presents a complex and sympathetic picture of the racial, religious, and socio-economic tensions that characterized life in Chinatown during the period of Asian exclusion.

Because both her own life and the subject matter of her writings are marginal to conventional literary histories (which usually associate the turn of the century with realist or naturalist novelists such as Henry James, William Dean Howells, Edith Wharton, Jack London, and Frank Norris), Far was not initially viewed as a significant author. Her writings went unnoticed for decades, until emerging Asian-American writers recovered her as an important precursor in 1974. Since then, critics have viewed her stories and essays as complex expressions of antiracist, feminist, and cosmopolitan views, as well as important ethnographic documents written by a mixed-race woman who, although she could perhaps have "passed" as a non-Chinese, devoted herself to understanding—and improving public opinion about—Chinese communities in the Western hemisphere, as well as to connecting and mixing the supposedly different spheres of Chinese and Western culture.

This introductory essay will provide overviews of Far's life, the reception of *Mrs. Spring Fragrance* since its first publication in 1912, the historical conditions and inequalities underlying America's Chinatown settlements (in which most of the stories take place), and the formal strategies that Far's stories use to sway her readers toward more sympathetic understandings of the Chinese. Throughout, I will emphasize how *Mrs. Spring Fragrance* responds to public debates about whether or not the Chinese could be "civilized" by creatively incorporating sentimental and

Christian conventions that Far would have been familiar with from working at mission homes and Chinese Sunday schools.

Edith Maude Eaton/Sui Sin Far:
The "Connecting Link"

Edith was the second of fourteen children born to the English merchant Edward Eaton and Grace "Lotus Blossom" Trefusis, a Chinese woman who had been adopted by English missionaries. Although Edith was born in England, her family relocated to New York and then Montreal in the early 1870s. Around this time, the Eatons became impoverished as Edward struggled to find stable employment. When she was eleven years old, Edith and her siblings withdrew from school to help support the family: "My sisters are apprenticed to a dressmaker; my brother is entered in an office. I tramp around and sell my father's pictures, also some lace which I make myself" (Appendix A1, p. 225).

For much of her career, Eaton supported herself by working as a stenographer. While typing for the Montreal law firm Archibald and McCormick in the mid-1880s, she began publishing humorous articles and verses "in the radical U.S. newspapers *Peck's Sun, Texas Liftings*, and *Detroit Free Press*."[1] Devoting what free time she had to working on her writing, forming relationships with Chinese communities throughout North America, and looking after her younger sisters, Eaton remained single throughout her life. She may have identified with a "Eurasian" woman she mentions who eventually cancelled an engagement that she had consented to as a result of social pressure: "Joy, oh, joy! I'm free once more.... Never again will I allow any one to 'hound' or 'sneer' me into matrimony" (Appendix A1, p. 232).

In her memoir, "Leaves from the Mental Portfolio of an Eurasian" (Appendix A1), Far details the gradual process of coming to terms with her Chinese racial and cultural ties—a process that included whispered insinuations, fights with neighborhood children, and a profound sense of isolation from both her English father and her Chinese mother ("I am different to both of them—a stranger, tho their own child" [p. 225]). According to her biographer, the turning point in Far's writing career occurred when, in the early 1890s, she accompanied her mother on a visit to a young Chinese woman newly arrived in Montreal. This visit

---

1 Annette White-Parks, *Sui Sin Far/Edith Maude Eaton: A Literary Biography*, 26.

intensified Far's longstanding interest in the lives of Chinese migrants: she soon began doing "most of the local Chinese reporting" for Montreal newspapers and visiting Chinese settlements throughout North America; in 1896, she began publishing stories about Chinese characters under the pen name "Sui Seen Far."

This commitment to writing about sympathetic Chinese characters for Anglophone readers may have limited popular interest in Far's writings, since Americans had "for many years manifested a much higher regard for the Japanese than for the Chinese" (p. 231). Far reports that many Chinese and Chinese Eurasians "passed" as Japanese in order to leverage this interest: her sister Winnifred Eaton, for example, published several bestselling novels by writing exotic Japanese romances under the pen name Onoto Watanna. By contrast, Far represents herself as an uncompromising writer who draws on journalistic experience and first-hand conversations with Chinese migrants while refusing to pander to conventions that exoticized or denigrated the Chinese. As she put it in a letter to the associate editor of *Century*, she aimed "to depict as well as I can what I know and see about the Chinese people in America."[1]

Despite decades of struggle with sickness, poverty, catastrophe (in 1907 all her manuscripts and scrap books were destroyed in a train wreck), job instability, public opinion, and the preferences of white male editors, Far eventually achieved a degree of literary reputation in January 1909 with the publication of her autobiographical piece, "Leaves from the Mental Portfolio of an Eurasian," in *The Independent*. Written from the position of a "Eurasian," the article forcefully presented its author as a spokesperson for the Chinese in North America and a "connecting link" between "Occidentals" and "Orientals" (Appendix A1, p. 233). Subsequently, Far moved to Boston and devoted herself to writing, publishing nine stories in 1910 and completing the manuscript of her first and only published book the following year. In June 1912, A.C. McClurg published 2,500 copies of *Mrs. Spring Fragrance*.

The Reception of *Mrs. Spring Fragrance*

The acknowledgements page of *Mrs. Spring Fragrance* (p. 34) provides some clues about the kinds of readers Sui Sin Far intended to reach. Most of the magazines in which Far's stories

---

1 Quoted in White-Parks, 44.

first appeared fit into four groups: those addressed to middle-class women (*American Motherhood, Gentlewoman, Good House-keeping, Housekeeper, Ladies' Home Journal*), magazines for children (*Children's, Little Folks, Youth's Companion*), magazines focusing on regional topics (*Out West, Overland, Westerner*), and publications aimed at a general, educated readership (*The Independent, New York Evening Post, Short Stories*). While these audience groupings reflect characteristics of Far's stories, the metaphor of motherhood—and the recovery of dear "children [sent] out into the world" (p. 34)—in the book's acknowledgements suggest that *Mrs. Spring Fragrance* is most prominently concerned with sentimental themes of motherhood, reproduction, and childrearing. Although this engagement with sentimentalism as a strategy for social change is crucial to the organization of *Mrs. Spring Fragrance* as a book-length collection, critics have often focused more on individual stories that develop themes such as the inequity of anti-Chinese legislation, the empowerment of women, the picturesque (or "local color") characteristics of Chinatown communities, and the social and familial tensions attendant upon cultural assimilation.

Initial responses to *Mrs. Spring Fragrance* had little to say about the stories' aesthetic qualities, instead emphasizing the book's exotic subject matter and, in some cases, its critical attitude toward anti-Chinese legislation. For example, *The Independent* introduces Sui Sin Far as an author of "dainty stories of Chinese life" before presenting a more nuanced assessment of her writing: "The conflict between occidental and oriental ideals and the hardships of the American immigration laws furnish the theme for most of the tales ..." (Appendix A4, p. 235). A reviewer for the *New York Times* bemoans Far's "lack of artistic skill" while noting that her presentation of "the lives, feelings, [and] sentiments" of Chinatown's inhabitants strikes "a new note in American fiction" (see Appendix A6, p. 236). A more favorable review, published in *The American Antiquarian and Oriental Journal*, describes her stories as "so true and so natural that they might easily be based on fact ... written by a woman who knows Chinese character intimately and appreciates the romance and tragedy of Chinatown" (Appendix A8, p. 238). Praising the book's "fine spirit," novelty, and capacity to "arouse sympathy," the reviewer concludes that "The book deserves a wide reading." In a rave review for *The New England Magazine*, Frederick Burrows declares that "Such a book justifies the printing press," only to end with a description of the book's exotic bamboo decorations and the "daintiness" of its characters (Appendix A7, p. 237). Despite receiving positive reviews, however, *Mrs. Spring Fragrance* was not widely read in the decades following its publication: its sentimental plots, ethnographic descriptions, and pro-Chinese subject matter perhaps appeared outmoded in the contexts of the Great War, literary modernism, and continuing legislation targeting Asian immigrants.

The resurgence of interest in Far's writing can be traced to the introduction to *Aiiieeeee! An Anthology of Asian-American Writers* (1974), a foundational document of Asian-American literature. Frank Chin, Jeffery Paul Chan, Lawson Fusao Inada, and Shawn Wong open their anthology by identifying Far as "one of the first to speak for an Asian-American sensibility that was neither Asian nor white American" (p. 3). While Far's stories were occasionally cited in the 1980s and reprinted in anthologies throughout the 1990s, the reception of her work has been most influenced by Amy Ling's and Annette White-Parks's carefully edited volume, *Mrs. Spring Fragrance and Other Writings* (1995). Calling Far's work "the first expression of the Chinese experience in the United States and Canada and the first fiction in English by any Asian North American," Ling and White-Parks present generous selections from *Mrs. Spring Fragrance* alongside Far's other stories and journalistic essays about Chinatown published between 1890 and 1913. Much scholarly work on Far has continued to emphasize her ambivalent status as an advocate for the Chinese in America who was neither of full Chinese descent nor a US citizen. Although her writings present sympathetic portraits of Chinese characters, Far writes that on account of her language and appearance "the Chinese merchants and people generally are inclined to regard me with suspicion" (Appendix A1, p. 230). While it would be anachronistic to entirely subsume Far's writings to contemporary identity categories such as "Asian American" and "hapa"[1] (she referred to herself as "Eurasian"), her situation roughly parallels these groups' ambivalent positions with respect to conventional ethnic and national identities.

Rather than embracing any particular identity, Far's writings espouse a cosmopolitan sensibility that resonates with contemporary interests in transnational migrations and cultural mixture. From Mr. Spring Fragrance's comic yet artful misquotations of Tennyson to the "motley throng made up of all nationalities" that streams through Chinatown's streets (p. 68), from the Eurasian

---

1 Mixed-race with some Asian or Pacific Islander ancestry.

heroine of "'Its Wavering Image'" to a Chinese schoolboy's reen-
actment of Christ's sacrifice in "The Gift of Little Me," Far presents positive images of national, racial, and cultural mixture.
Such depictions of middle-class Chinese merchants and American missionaries forging economic and sentimental ties across
the Pacific, however, are complicated by the uneven experiences
of migration—particularly those of women and children—featured in "The Wisdom of the New," "In the Land of the Free,"
"The Americanizing of Pau Tsu," and "The Sing Song Woman."

Providing an interesting alternative to this focus on Far's relationship to Chinese or Asian identity, Marjorie Pryse and Judith
Fetterley propose that we read her stories as works of literary
regionalism focused more on a place than a particular race. In
stories such as "'Its Wavering Image,'" they argue, Far criticizes
"local color" literature—embodied in the self-serving reporter
Mark Carson—that offers up exoticized depictions of Chinatown
and its Chinese inhabitants. By contrast, Far's own representations of Chinese communities acknowledge place-based com-
plexities such as internal tensions within groups and the well-
intended but often troubling interactions between white
missionaries and Chinese locals. Although urban Chinatowns are
distinct from more conventional literary regions such as Willa
Cather's Southwest or Sarah Orne Jewett's coastal Maine villages, several of the stories that established Far's literary reputation appeared in the regional magazine *Land of Sunshine: A Magazine of California and the Southwest.* Pryse and Fetterley's
approach helpfully highlights the ways in which Far's techniques
of ethnographic description and cultural translation reflect a
widespread interest in literary descriptions of eccentric places.

Although they are often set in Chinese settlements, Far's writings focus not on the "bachelor community" of single men that
comprised most of the population of Chinese living in the US,
but on the experiences of white and Chinese women and Chinese
children. The nuanced depiction of conflicts and alliances
between Chinese women, white women, and Chinese men—
often in the context of struggles over how to raise Chinese children—in stories such as "Mrs. Spring Fragrance," "The Inferior
Woman," and "The Story of One White Woman Who Married a
Chinese" has led feminist critics to claim that Far often identified
with her independent white characters—such as Adah Charleton,
Adah Raymond, and Miss McLeod—who worked to benefit the
Chinese community. Though she acknowledged that "the world
is so cruel and sneering to a single woman" (p. 231), Far chose

not to marry, and thus aligned herself with the single women in her stories who sacrifice their own happiness to work against anti-Chinese legislation and public opinion. Although Far did not directly engage in political activism, critic Mary Chapman notes that "Sui Sin Far styles a more directly and privately contoured model of political agency for women than the progressive ideal of suffrage" (978).

While scholars have noted Far's depictions of independent female characters, they have had less to say about the role of children in *Mrs. Spring Fragrance*. Structurally divided between sentimental stories for adults (the section titled "Mrs. Spring Fragrance") and shorter "Tales of Chinese Children"—the book is implicitly addressed to white, middle-class women and children. Perhaps Far imagined that mothers would read the opening stories of romance, tragedy, and adventure to themselves, and read the fables in the second section aloud to their children. In addition to stories for children, the book also includes many stories—such as "In the Land of the Free," "The Gift of Little Me," "A Chinese Boy-Girl," and "Pat and Pan"—whose plots feature struggles over the education and socialization of children. Far from presenting "dainty" stories about Chinese homes and families, *Mrs. Spring Fragrance* charts the domestic struggles that made the homes, schools, and Christian missions of Chinatown key sites for the work of biological and social reproduction.

Representing Chinatown

Sui Sin Far's fictional treatments of distressed and (in some cases) reconstituted Chinese families responded to local conflicts and troubled living conditions in Pacific coast Chinatowns. At first welcomed to the US as railroad workers, Chinese laborers settled throughout the western states following the completion of the Transcontinental Railroad in 1869. Though they worked in mines, laundries, restaurants, factories, farms, and as domestic servants, Chinese immigrants were soon targeted by disaffected white workers, who blamed them for keeping wages down. Anti-Chinese agitation by the Workingmen's Party and other groups led to a series of laws excluding Chinese women and laborers from the US (see Appendix B), as well as widespread conceptions of the Chinese as a stoic, mechanical, effeminate, and unassimilable group. This public sentiment against Chinese workers was expressed in dozens of often violent purges of Chinese settlers from towns throughout the western US in the 1880s. Driven out of rural settlements, thousands of Chinese resettled in the urban Chinatowns featured in *Mrs. Spring Fragrance*.

Although writers frequently viewed Chinatown as a "bit of the Orient set down in the heart of a Western metropolis" in which there "throbbed the pulse of China,"[1] US Chinatowns were entirely unprecedented communities configured by racial persecution, immigration laws, and economic forces. Legal restrictions on Chinese immigration such as the Page Act Law of 1875 and the Chinese Exclusion Act of 1882 specifically targeted women and laborers, creating a "bachelor community" of older men unable to bring existing or potential Chinese wives to the US. The gender imbalance among the Chinese in the US reached its highest point—"nearly twenty-seven men to every woman"—in 1897; in San Francisco's Chinatown, where there was a higher concentration of Chinese merchants exempt from exclusion laws, the ratio was approximately six men to each woman in 1900. Chinese men developed alternative domestic practices including multiple-family households headed by Chinese women, positions as live-in servants, extended kinship networks, and the cross-racial forms of "social communion" facilitated by opium dens.[2] The historian Nayan Shah has documented how writers, planners, and health experts denigrated such forms of "queer domesticity" as contagious threats to white, middle-class domesticity. Laws regulating hygiene and public safety disproportionately affected Chinese residents: for example, the San Francisco Cubic Air Ordinance of 1870, which required at least five hundred cubic feet of living space for each adult, led to a raid on Chinatown tenements and over one hundred arrests.[3] However, middle-class Chinese couples did establish families in the US: "According to the 1900 census, there were 1,435 Chinese children in [San Francisco], constituting about 10 percent of the total Chinese American population"; that same year, 72 per cent of Chinese children were in two-parent Chinese families, compared to considerably less than half in previous census data.[4] Because the anti-Chinese movement frequently depicted the

---

1 Arnold Genthe, *As I Remember*, 32.
2 Nayan Shah, *Contagious Divides: Epidemics and Race in San Francisco's Chinatown*, 93.
3 Jean Pfaelzer, *Driven Out: The Forgotten War Against Chinese Americans*, 75.
4 Wendy Rouse Jorae, *The Children of Chinatown: Growing Up Chinese American in San Francisco*, 47, 50.

Chinese as unable or unwilling to establish normative families in the US, Wendy Rouse Jorae points out that "Women and children, though rare, were ... critical to the Chinese community's effort to establish a more respectable image of Chinese family life in America."[1]

While much hostility against the Chinese can be attributed to white labor organizers who blamed Chinese workers—rather than the corporations who hired them—for inadequate wages and deteriorating working conditions, literary and visual texts also played a significant role in framing public perceptions of the Chinese. Influenced by popular dystopian accounts—such as Pierton W. Dooner's *Last Days of the Republic* (1880)—of how Americans would fare if they allowed the Chinese to overrun and conquer the US, Bret Harte and Frank Norris depicted the Chinese as secretive and cunning in "Plain Language from Truthful James" and "The Third Circle" (see Appendices B1, D5). As Far noted, even "clever and interesting Chinese stories written by American writers" tended to "stand afar off from the Chinaman—in most cases treating him as a 'joke'" (Letter to Robert Underwood Johnson, quoted in White-Parks 44–45). Arnold Genthe's photographs of San Francisco's Chinatown reaffirmed these stereotypes by depicting mysterious Chinese figures half-hidden amid dark cellars, shadowy doorways, and unkempt streets (see Appendices D2, D3). Political cartoons and illustrated periodicals went even further, depicting well-intentioned white women leered at by Chinese sexual predators, unhygienic Chinese workers eating rats and using spit to iron clothing, and undifferentiated hordes of Chinese immigrants flooding into California's ports (see Appendices C5, C6).

Even missionaries—culture workers who intended to help the Chinese—often had detrimental effects on Chinatown communities. While institutions such as San Francisco's Presbyterian Mission Home—run by its well-known superintendent, Donaldina Cameron—undoubtedly helped combat the trade in prostitutes and slave girls, their widely publicized "rescues" of enslaved girls also helped bolster the legitimacy of racist immigration laws (see Appendices C2, C3, D6). Cameron worked closely with authorities, often breaking into Chinese homes with the San Francisco police to track down thousands of enslaved and abused children, and sometimes allowing immigration officials to use the Mission Home as a detention center for undocumented immi-

---

1   Jorae, *The Children of Chinatown*, 16.

grants captured in raids. Although mission teachers educated rescued girls "using a highly structured schedule of tasks and activities," the ultimate disposition of these educated girls was uncertain: the Mission Home arranged middle-class marriages for some, but others were placed as domestic servants in white households, or sent to families or missionaries in China (Donovan 118). Mission schools thus transferred the labor of domestic servants from recently established Chinese households into Christian, middle-class homes, while bolstering anti-Chinese discourses that blamed Chinese family structures—rather than gendered immigration laws and state prohibitions on intermarriage—for prostitution and involuntary child labor.

Although Far herself worked in a mission school, she represents her relationship to Chinese students as one of mutual identification (note the play on the word "far," which echoes the author's pen name): "Occasionally I taught in a Chinese mission school, as I do here in Boston, but learned far more from my scholars than I could ever impart to them."[1] The tense and intimate relations between missionaries and Chinese immigrants figure prominently in *Mrs. Spring Fragrance* and Far's other writings. Unlike Christian-authored texts and pamphlets such as Lu Wheat's *Third Chinese Daughter* (1906) and the Pacific Presbyterian Publishing Company's *Dragon Stories* (see Appendix C3), however, Far's stories focus on unintended consequences of conversion including the pangs of assimilation, struggles over the custody of children, accidental death, and even infanticide. By foregrounding relations between mothers and children, Far strategically draws on a long and rich tradition of Christian-influenced sentimental literature, which the following section will discuss in detail.

"My Heart is Unusually Large": Far's Sentimental Fiction

Far was not alone in criticizing missionaries' denigrating depictions of Chinese home life. In a controversial *North American Review* article entitled "Why Am I a Heathen?" (1887), the freelance writer Wong Chin Foo defends Chinese marriage practices and critically parses the political economy underlying missionary "love": "So Christians love the heathen; yes, the heathen's possessions; and in proportion to these the Christian's love grows in

---

1   Far, "Sui Sin Far, the Half Chinese Writer," 294.

intensity. When the English wanted the Chinamen's gold and trade, they said they wanted 'to open China for their missionaries.' And opium was the chief, in fact, only, missionary they looked after, when they forced the ports open" (Appendix C8). Mary Austin's "The Conversion of Ah Lew Sing" (1897) and Willa Cather's "The Conversion of Sum Loo" (1900) also satirize the conventions of missionary rescue narratives, showing how both Chinese students and white teachers utilized the mission home to serve personal rather than civilizational ends (see Appendix C7).

Even as a child, Far recalls, the scale of her feelings was disproportionately large: "I am small, but my feelings are big" (p. 225). This excessive sentimentalism contradicts stereotypes about the Chinese, who are "said to be the most stolid and insensible to feeling of all races" (p. 224). At the same time, her inordinate sensitivity to the suffering of others makes Far eminently qualified for her vocation as sentimental author: "If there is any trouble in the house in the way of a difference between my father and mother, or if any child is punished, how I suffer!" (p. 224). Fashioning herself as a Christ-like martyr, Far connects her sentimentality with her mixed-race status: "The doctor says that my heart is unusually large; but in the light of the present I know that the cross of the Eurasian bore too heavily upon my childish shoulders" (p. 224). The "cross of the Eurasian" invokes both the crucifix and the biological crossing of blood that marginalizes the author from both Chinese and white communities. In an exemplary instance of the interest in salvation through Christ's martyrdom that Min Hyoung Song has traced through Sui Sin Far's writings, Far here both confesses her suffering and—in an act of sentimental self-empowerment—leverages it to claim an "unusually large" capacity for feeling and suffering which makes her akin to Christ himself.

Far's fiction extends this strategy of refashioning—instead of satirizing or entirely rejecting sentimental Christian motifs. As a professional writer struggling to sell stories to the only magazines that paid well for "women's" literature, the daughter of a Chinese woman "stolen" by a missionary school, and an occasional teacher in San Francisco and Boston's Chinatown mission schools, Far was ambivalent about missionary ideals of domesticity and religious conversion (p. 225). Several stories express Far's skepticism about the assimilation of Chinese children. "In the Land of the Free" and "A Chinese Boy-Girl" show how mission homes collude with the government to deprive parents of both custody and cultural influence over their children. In "The Wisdom of the New," the threat of losing the capacity to reproduce a culturally Chinese child leads Pau Lin to commit infanticide. Sacrificing her child to "save" him from assimilation, Pau Lin ironically invokes the classic Christian formula of solace at a dead child's bedside: "The child is happy. The butterfly mourns not o'er the shed cocoon" (p. 80). In a striking revision of the death scene of the innocent Little Eva in *Uncle Tom's Cabin* (1852)—who famously passes "from death unto life"—this child's soul is saved from Christianity itself.

· While missionary representations of Chinese children almost exclusively featured the education of Chinese orphans by Christian (and often white) parental figures, stories such as "Children of Peace" and "The Banishment of Ming and Mai" feature Chinese immigrants and even intelligent animals rearing orphans. "The Story of One White Woman Who Married a Chinese" entirely inverts the standard trajectory of missionary adoption by depicting a caring Chinese man who marries a struggling white divorcee, promising her that "Your child shall be as my own." "The Gift of Little Me" offers a more egalitarian model of adoption, in which the Scottish schoolteacher becomes assimilated to the Chinese community to the same extent that she teaches Western ideas to their children. For the virtually kinless teacher, adoption runs in both directions: "Had she not adopted [these Chinese people] as her own when kinfolk had failed her?" (p. 90). Although "The Gift of Little Me" raises the specter of kidnapping and forcible adoption that Far explored in other stories, Miss McLeod is ultimately proven innocent of stealing an infant by Little Me's confession that he had attempted to give his only brother to his teacher as a Christmas present. The story thus ends on a comic note with Little Me's misunderstanding (or too literal understanding) of the story of Christ in which God "[gave] a darling and only Son to a loved people" (p. 87).

Little Me's idiosyncratic assimilation of the story of Christ has its counterpart in the fables or "Tales of Chinese Children" that comprise the second section of *Mrs. Spring Fragrance*. Apparently addressed to children as well as adult readers, this section includes both stories about missionaries attempting to assimilate white, Chinese, and mixed-race schoolchildren and simple fables designed to inculcate an appreciation of honesty, piety, and hard work. In her essay on the "Tales of Chinese Children," Martha Cutter suggests that these stories "[utilize] the mind of the child, with its less rigid racial categorizations and hierarchies, to show

how adult readers might reconfigure their own limited concepts of racial, cultural, and sexual 'identity.'"[1] In addition to producing sympathetic feelings between white readers and Chinese child characters, however, the "Tales of Chinese Children" convey moral lessons. Whereas the assimilative project of the mission school plays a prominent role in many of Far's stories, fables such as "The Dreams that Failed," "The Deceptive Mat," and "The Crocodile Pagoda" invert the scene of assimilation by using ostensibly Chinese tales to discipline their audience of middle-class and primarily white children. If these tales—many of which had previously appeared in children's magazines—were meant to be read aloud by mothers and children, then they used Chinese characters, stories, and values to consolidate white family ties and to educate white children. By teaching Chinese morals to Western children, the concluding section of *Mrs. Spring Fragrance* suggests that integrity of character is not "Chinese" or "American" but universal.

If her emphasis on supposedly universal traits of good character succeeded in making Far's readers more sympathetic towards the Chinese (as several of the book's reviewers indicated), it did so by reinforcing US and Eurocentric norms of behavior. Far's strong preference for plots involving interracial and intercultural understanding suggests that the Chinese may achieve equity within the US and international community simply through good behavior, hard work, and self-discipline. As critics Sean McCann and Arnold Pan have pointed out, Far's stories often feature merchants or missionaries learning to empathize across racial lines while eschewing the progressive political activism of characters such as the "Superior Woman" (in "The Inferior Woman") and the first husband in "The Story of a White Woman Who Married a Chinese," who is described as being too busy with politics to attend to his wife. Ironically, by taking individual self-sacrifice as a moral standard, Far avoids representing the Chinese working masses whose rights have already been sacrificed by US laws.

Yet even the moralistic "Tales of Chinese Children" include stories that do not neatly conform to universally applicable lessons. For example, "What About the Cat?"—an apparently innocent story about the pleasures of storytelling and one of the few stories in *Mrs. Spring Fragrance* that devotes significant space to servants—subtly shows how storytelling may protect the

---

1   Martha Cutter, "Empire and the Mind of the Child: Sui Sin Far's 'Tales of Chinese Children,'" 32.

socially disempowered from blame and unwanted attention. When the princess asks two maids, a chamberlain, and a gardener about the cat, each tells her it is somewhere else. When she discovers they have been lying to her, they "trembled and paled" at her anger, but the chamberlain's claim that the stories were designed to amuse pleases her and the servants are spared from punishment. There is not one moral here but two: for the princess, stories are a source of entertainment; for the servants, they can be used to both deceive and entertain the princess and thus stave off her "severity." The last of the book's longer stories, "Pat and Pan," presents a more historically contextualized critique of universalism. Disadvantaged by age, race, and gender, Pan is "not supposed to learn, only to play" when she is allowed to attend the mission school along with her adopted white brother Pat. Although Pan learns the English language and Christian hymns with much greater facility than Pat, she ends up rejected by Pat and his white friends for purely racial reasons. The story thus indicates the tension between the universal values of a Christian education and racial codes that qualify or negate the humanity of non-white subjects. This tension between universal, cosmopolitan modes of thinking and feeling and racial particularization extends through the whole of *Mrs. Spring Fragrance* and makes it not only a unique document in the history of US Chinatowns, but an original and significant contribution to US literature.

★★★

The sheer range of issues and contexts covered by her stories as well as their critical reception indicates that Far's contemporary significance encompasses numerous fields and questions. Along with writers such as Wong Chin Foo and the anonymous detainees who carved Chinese verses into the walls of the Angel Island Immigration Station, Far is one of the earliest authors to bring the techniques of literary realism to bear on Chinese American communities—and particularly on the experiences of Chinese women and children. At the same time, her fiction engages with conventions drawn from sentimental fiction, missionary reports, fables, journalism, and children's literature in order to intervene in how these discourses imagine Chinese "character." But the significance of Far's writings transcends their historical interest and their origins among North America's Chinese settlements: Far's philosophical interest in cosmopolitanism ("After all I have no nationality and am not anxious to claim any," p. 233), along with her interest in racially and culturally mixed characters, link the racial tensions of her era to contemporary problems of transnationalism, racial hybridity, and cultural pluralism.

Edith Maude Eaton/Sui Sin Far: A Brief Chronology[1]

1865   Edith Eaton is born in Macclesfield, England, to Edward and Grace Eaton. She is the second of their fourteen children. Edward worked as a representative for Eaton Silk Company. Grace was born in China, adopted by Scottish missionaries, and (reportedly) educated at the Home and Colonial School in London.

1870   Moves with her family to Montreal, Canada, where Edward Eaton hopes to find more lucrative employment.

1875   Page Act Law is passed, prohibiting the immigration of contract laborers, convicts, and women intending to be prostitutes from China.

1882   Chinese Exclusion Act prohibits the immigration of all Chinese laborers to the US, denies US citizenship to Chinese already living in the US, and imposes restrictions on Chinese returning to the US after leaving the country. The Exclusion Act would be renewed and revised until its repeal in 1943.

1889–90   Publishes poems and short stories in the *Dominion Illustrated*.

1894   Begins writing for the *Montreal Daily Star* and *Daily Witness*. Joins a Chinatown mission society with her mother and teaches English in the Sunday school.

1896   Publishes stories in *Fly Leaf*, *Lotus*, and *The Land of Sunshine*. Begins an influential correspondence with *Land of Sunshine*'s editor, Charles Lummis.

1896–97   Moves to Kingston, Jamaica, in December 1896 to work as a reporter for *Gall's Daily News Letter*. Publishes short articles under the pseudonym Fire Fly.

---

1   This chronology is indebted (with her permission) to Dominika Ferens, "Appendix: Chronology of the Eatons' Lives" (185–87).

1898	Moves to San Francisco and then Seattle, volunteering at Chinatown missions. Works as a stenographer and typist to support her writing career.
1898–1901	The Boxer Uprising in China attempts to counteract the influence of western merchants, missionaries, and diplomacy in China. The US contributes troops to the Eight-Nation Alliance that suppressed the Boxers.
1898–1903	Publishes stories in *Land of Sunshine*, *Overland Monthly*, and *Youth's Companion*.
1900	Edith's sister Winnifred, writing under the pseudonym Onoto Watanna, publishes the popular romantic novel *A Japanese Nightingale*.
1903	Spends several months in Los Angeles and writes a series of articles about Chinatown for the *Los Angeles Express*.
1904	"A Chinese Boy-Girl" is published in *Century Magazine*.
1906	San Francisco earthquake and fire destroys much of Chinatown; the Chinese quickly rebuild in an "oriental" style more accommodating to tourists and public health officials. The earthquake also destroys immigration records, opening the way for "paper sons" to immigrate under assumed identities.
1908–09	Publishes children's stories in *Good Housekeeping*.
1909	Publishes "Leaves from the Mental Portfolio of an Eurasian" and three stories in *The Independent*. The *Westerner* commissions a series of essays on "The Chinese in America."
1910	US Bureau of Immigration opens detention facility on Angel Island, where over 175,000 arriving Chinese immigrants will be processed over the next 30 years.
1910	Moves to Boston, where she remains until 1913. Publishes in *Hampton's*, *The Independent*, *Good Housekeeping*, *New England Magazine*, and *Delineator*.
1911–12	A.C. McClurg declines to publish Sui Sin Far's novel, the manuscript of which has never been located.

1912	*Mrs. Spring Fragrance*, a collection of stories, is published by A.C. McClurg and receives favorable reviews.
1914	Dies in Montreal after moving back there in 1913.

A Note on the Text

This Broadview edition has been reproduced from the first edition of *Mrs. Spring Fragrance* (Chicago: A.C. McClurg, 1912). I am grateful to Kristian Jensen and Cara Shipe for their assistance with preparing and checking the typescript. The text of this edition reproduces that of the first edition, except for typographical errors, which have been corrected. Because Eaton referred to herself as "Sui Sin Far" in her correspondence and because she consistently adopted it as a pen name, I have generally chosen to follow most scholars in referring to her as "Sui Sin Far" or "Far."

Like all Broadview titles in this series, this edition situates *Mrs. Spring Fragrance* in historical and discursive contexts by including appendices of contemporary documents. These documents have been arranged to convey different viewpoints, often in conversation with one another concerning prominent issues of the era.

MRS. SPRING FRAGRANCE

CONTENTS

MRS. SPRING FRAGRANCE

TALES OF CHINESE CHILDREN

ACKNOWLEDGMENT

I have to thank the Editors of The Independent, Out West, Hampton's, The Century, Delineator, Ladies' Home Journal, Designer, New Idea, Short Stories, Traveler, Good Housekeeping, Housekeeper, Gentlewoman, New York Evening Post, Holland's, Little Folks, American Motherhood, New England, Youth's Companion, Montreal Witness, Children's, Overland, Sunset, and Westerner magazines, who were kind enough to care for my children when I sent them out into the world, for permitting the dear ones to return to me to be grouped together within this volume.

SUI SIN FAR

MRS. SPRING FRAGRANCE

Mrs. Spring Fragrance

I

WHEN MRS. SPRING FRAGRANCE first arrived in Seattle, she was unacquainted with even one word of the American language. Five years later her husband, speaking of her, said: "There are no more American words for her learning." And everyone who knew Mrs. Spring Fragrance agreed with Mr. Spring Fragrance.

Mr. Spring Fragrance, whose business name was Sing Yook, was a young curio[1] merchant. Though conservatively Chinese in many respects, he was at the same time what is called by the Westerners, "Americanized." Mrs. Spring Fragrance was even more "Americanized."

Next door to the Spring Fragrances lived the Chin Yuens. Mrs. Chin Yuen was much older than Mrs. Spring Fragrance; but she had a daughter of eighteen with whom Mrs. Spring Fragrance was on terms of great friendship. The daughter was a pretty girl whose Chinese name was Mai Gwi Far (a rose) and whose American name was Laura. Nearly everybody called her Laura, even her parents and Chinese friends. Laura had a sweetheart, a youth named Kai Tzu. Kai Tzu, who was American-born, and as ruddy and stalwart as any young Westerner, was noted amongst baseball players as one of the finest pitchers on the Coast. He could also sing, "Drink to me only with thine eyes,"[2] to Laura's piano accompaniment.

Now the only person who knew that Kai Tzu loved Laura and that Laura loved Kai Tzu, was Mrs. Spring Fragrance. The reason for this was that, although the Chin Yuen parents lived in a house furnished in American style, and wore American clothes, yet they religiously observed many Chinese customs, and their ideals of life were the ideals of their Chinese forefathers. Therefore, they had betrothed their daughter, Laura, at the age of fifteen, to the

---

1 Derived from the word "curiosity," curios were exotic items intended to attract non-Chinese visitors to Chinatown.
2 A popular English song with lyrics drawn from Ben Jonson's poem "Song to Celia" (1616).

eldest son of the Chinese Government school-teacher[1] in San Francisco. The time for the consummation of the betrothal was approaching.

Laura was with Mrs. Spring Fragrance and Mrs. Spring Fragrance was trying to cheer her.

"I had such a pretty walk today," said she. "I crossed the banks above the beach and came back by the long road. In the green grass the daffodils were blowing, in the cottage gardens the currant bushes were flowering, and in the air was the perfume of the wallflower. I wished, Laura, that you were with me."

Laura burst into tears. "That is the walk," she sobbed, "Kai Tzu and I so love; but never, ah, never, can we take it together again."

"Now, Little Sister," comforted Mrs. Spring Fragrance "you really must not grieve like that. Is there not a beautiful American poem written by a noble American named Tennyson,[2] which says:

"'Tis better to have loved and lost.
Than never to have loved at all?"[3]

Mrs. Spring Fragrance was unaware that Mr. Spring Fragrance, having returned from the city, tired with the day's business, had thrown himself down on the bamboo settee on the veranda, and that although his eyes were engaged in scanning the pages of the *Chinese World*,[4] his ears could not help receiving the words which were borne to him through the open window.

"'Tis better to have loved and lost,
Than never to have loved at all,"

---

1 Possibly the San Francisco Chinese-Western School, established on Sacramento St. in San Francisco's Chinatown in 1888 under the direction of China's Consul General. For some years, the Manchu government helped arrange for teachers and contributed some funds to locally funded Chinese schools in the US.

2 Alfred, Lord Tennyson (1809–92) was poet laureate of Britain.

3 These famous lines are from Tennyson's "In Memoriam A.H.H." (1849), a requiem for his friend Arthur Henry Hallam.

4 Founded as the weekly *Mon Hing Bo* in 1891 and converted to a daily in 1901, *The Chinese World* was a San Francisco-based Chinese-language newspaper.

repeated Mr. Spring Fragrance. Not wishing to hear more of the secret talk of women, he arose and sauntered around the veranda to the other side of the house. Two pigeons circled around his head. He felt in his pocket for a li-chi[1] which he usually carried for their pecking. His fingers touched a little box. It contained a jadestone pendant, which Mrs. Spring Fragrance had particularly admired the last time she was down town. It was the fifth anniversary of Mr. and Mrs. Spring Fragrance's wedding day.

Mr. Spring Fragrance pressed the little box down into the depths of his pocket.

A young man came out of the back door of the house at Mr. Spring Fragrance's left. The Chin Yuen house was at his right.

"Good evening," said the young man. "Good evening," returned Mr. Spring Fragrance. He stepped down from his porch and went and leaned over the railing which separated this yard from the yard in which stood the young man.

"Will you please tell me," said Mr. Spring Fragrance, "the meaning of two lines of an American verse which I have heard?"

"Certainly," returned the young man with a genial smile. He was a star student at the University of Washington, and had not the slightest doubt that he could explain the meaning of all things in the universe.

"Well," said Mr. Spring Fragrance, "it is this:

"'Tis better to have loved and lost,
Than never to have loved at all."

"Ah!" responded the young man with an air of profound wisdom. "That, Mr. Spring Fragrance, means that it is a good thing to love anyway—even if we can't get what we love, or, as the poet tells us, lose what we love. Of course, one needs experience to feel the truth of this teaching."

The young man smiled pensively and reminiscently. More than a dozen young maidens "loved and lost" were passing before his mind's eye.

"The truth of the teaching!" echoed Mr. Spring Fragrance, a little testily. "There is no truth in it whatever. It is disobedient to reason. Is it not better to have what you do not love than to love what you do not have?"

"That depends," answered the young man, "upon temperament."

---

1   The lychee is a fruit native to China.

"I thank you. Good evening," said Mr. Spring Fragrance. He turned away to muse upon the unwisdom of the American way of looking at things.

Meanwhile, inside the house, Laura was refusing to be comforted.

"Ah, no! no!" cried she. "If I had not gone to school with Kai Tzu, nor talked nor walked with him, nor played the accompaniments to his songs, then I might consider with complacency, or at least without horror, my approaching marriage with the son of Man You. But as it is—oh, as it is—!"

The girl rocked herself to and fro in heartfelt grief.

Mrs. Spring Fragrance knelt down beside her, and clasping her arms around her neck, cried in sympathy:

"Little Sister, oh, Little Sister! Dry your tears—do not despair. A moon has yet to pass before the marriage can take place. Who knows what the stars may have to say to one another during its passing? A little bird has whispered to me—"

For a long time Mrs. Spring Fragrance talked. For a long time Laura listened. When the girl arose to go, there was a bright light in her eyes.

II

MRS. SPRING FRAGRANCE, in San Francisco on a visit to her cousin, the wife of the herb doctor of Clay Street, was having a good time. She was invited everywhere that the wife of an honorable Chinese merchant could go. There was much to see and hear, including more than a dozen babies who had been born in the families of her friends since she last visited the city of the Golden Gate. Mrs. Spring Fragrance loved babies. She had had two herself, but both had been transplanted into the spirit land before the completion of even one moon. There were also many dinners and theatre-parties given in her honor. It was at one of the theatre-parties that Mrs. Spring Fragrance met Ah Oi, a young girl who had the reputation of being the prettiest Chinese girl in San Francisco, and the naughtiest. In spite of gossip, however, Mrs. Spring Fragrance took a great fancy to Ah Oi and invited her to a tête-à-tête[1] picnic on the following day. This invitation Ah Oi joyfully accepted. She was a sort of bird girl and never felt so happy as when out in the park or woods.

---

1 Private, one-on-one conversation (French).

On the day after the picnic Mrs. Spring Fragrance wrote to Laura Chin Yuen thus:

MY PRECIOUS LAURA,—May the bamboo ever wave. Next week I accompany Ah Oi to the beauteous town of San Jose. There will we be met by the son of the Illustrious Teacher, and in a little Mission, presided over by a benevolent American priest, the little Ah Oi and the son of the Illustrious Teacher will be joined together in love and harmony—two pieces of music made to complete one another.

The Son of the Illustrious Teacher, having been through an American Hall of Learning, is well able to provide for his orphan bride and fears not the displeasure of his parents, now that he is assured that your grief at his loss will not be inconsolable. He wishes me to waft to you and to Kai Tzu—and the little Ah Oi joins with him—ten thousand rainbow wishes for your happiness.

My respects to your honorable parents, and to yourself, the heart of your loving friend,

JADE SPRING FRAGRANCE

To Mr. Spring Fragrance, Mrs. Spring Fragrance also indited a letter:

GREAT AND HONORED MAN,—Greeting from your plum blossom,[1] who is desirous of hiding herself from the sun of your presence for a week of seven days more. My honorable cousin is preparing for the Fifth Moon Festival,[2] and wishes me to compound for the occasion some American "fudge," for which delectable sweet, made by my clumsy hands, you have sometimes shown a slight prejudice. I am enjoying a most agreeable visit, and American friends, as also our own, strive benevolently for the accomplishment of my pleasure. Mrs. Samuel Smith, an American lady, known to my cousin, asked for my accompaniment to a magniloquent lecture the other evening. The subject was "America, the Protector of China!" It was most exhilarating, and

---

1 The plum blossom is the Chinese flower of virtue. It has been adopted by the Japanese, just in the same way as they have adopted the Chinese national flower, the chrysanthemum. [Sui Sin Far's note]

2 Celebrated on the fifth day of the fifth moon of the lunar calendar, the Fifth Moon or Duanwu Festival commemorates the Chinese scholar and minister Qu Yuan, who drowned himself in exile in 278 BCE.

the effect of so much expression of benevolence leads me to beg of you to forget to remember that the barber charges you one dollar for a shave while he humbly submits to the American man a bill of fifteen cents. And murmur no more because your honored elder brother, on a visit to this country, is detained under the roof-tree of this great Government instead of under your own humble roof. Console him with the reflection that he is protected under the wing of the Eagle, the Emblem of Liberty. What is the loss of ten hundred years or ten thousand times ten dollars compared with the happiness of knowing oneself so securely sheltered? All of this I have learned from Mrs. Samuel Smith, who is as brilliant and great of mind as one of your own superior sex.

For me it is sufficient to know that the Golden Gate Park is most enchanting, and the seals on the rock at the Cliff House extremely entertaining and amiable. There is much feasting and merrymaking under the lanterns in honor of your Stupid Thorn.

I have purchased for your smoking a pipe with an amber mouth. It is said to be very sweet to the lips and to emit a cloud of smoke fit for the gods to inhale.

Awaiting, by the wonderful wire of the telegram message, your gracious permission to remain for the celebration of the Fifth Moon Festival and the making of American "fudge," I continue for ten thousand times ten thousand years,

Your ever loving and obedient woman,

JADE

P.S. Forget not to care for the cat, the birds, and the flowers. Do not eat too quickly nor fan too vigorously now that the weather is warming.

Mrs. Spring Fragrance smiled as she folded this last epistle. Even if he were old-fashioned, there was never a husband so good and kind as hers. Only on one occasion since their marriage had he slighted her wishes. That was when, on the last anniversary of their wedding, she had signified a desire for a certain jadestone pendant, and he had failed to satisfy that desire.

But Mrs. Spring Fragrance, being of a happy nature, and disposed to look upon the bright side of things, did not allow her mind to dwell upon the jadestone pendant. Instead, she gazed complacently down upon her bejeweled fingers and folded in with her letter to Mr. Spring Fragrance a bright little sheaf of condensed love.

III

MR. SPRING FRAGRANCE sat on his doorstep. He had been reading two letters, one from Mrs. Spring Fragrance, and the other from an elderly bachelor cousin in San Francisco. The one from the elderly bachelor cousin was a business letter, but contained the following postscript:

Tsen Hing, the son of the Government schoolmaster, seems to be much in the company of your young wife. He is a good-looking youth, and pardon me, my dear cousin; but if women are allowed to stray at will from under their husbands' mulberry roofs, what is to prevent them from becoming butterflies?

"Sing Foon is old and cynical," said Mr. Spring Fragrance to himself. "Why should I pay any attention to him? This is America, where a man may speak to a woman, and a woman listen, without any thought of evil."

He destroyed his cousin's letter and re-read his wife's. Then he became very thoughtful. Was the making of American fudge sufficient reason for a wife to wish to remain a week longer in a city where her husband was not?

The young man who lived in the next house came out to water the lawn. "Good evening," said he. "Any news from Mrs. Spring Fragrance?"

"She is having a very good time," returned Mr. Spring Fragrance.

"Glad to hear it. I think you told me she was to return the end of this week."

"I have changed my mind about her," said Mr. Spring Fragrance. "I am bidding her remain a week longer, as I wish to give a smoking party during her absence. I hope I may have the pleasure of your company."

"I shall be delighted," returned the young fellow. "But, Mr. Spring Fragrance, don't invite any other white fellows. If you do not I shall be able to get in a scoop. You know, I'm a sort of honorary reporter for the *Gleaner*."

"Very well," absently answered Mr. Spring Fragrance.

"Of course, your friend the Consul will be present. I shall call it 'A high-class Chinese stag party!'"

In spite of his melancholy mood, Mr. Spring Fragrance smiled.

"Everything is 'high-class' in America," he observed.

"Sure!" cheerfully assented the young man. "Haven't you ever heard that all Americans are princes and princesses, and just as soon as a foreigner puts his foot upon our shores, he also becomes of the nobility—I mean, the royal family."

"What about my brother in the Detention Pen?"[1] dryly inquired Mr. Spring Fragrance.

"Now, you've got me," said the young man, rubbing his head. "Well, that is a shame—'a beastly shame,' as the Englishman says. But understand, old fellow, we that are real Americans are up against that—even more than you. It is against our principles."

"I offer the real Americans my consolations that they should be compelled to do that which is against their principles."

"Oh, well, it will all come right some day. We're not a bad sort, you know. Think of the indemnity money returned to the Dragon by Uncle Sam."[2]

Mr. Spring Fragrance puffed his pipe in silence for some moments. More than politics was troubling his mind.

At last he spoke. "Love," said he, slowly and distinctly, "comes before the wedding in this country, does it not?"

"Yes, certainly."

Young Carman knew Mr. Spring Fragrance well enough to receive with calmness his most astounding queries.

"Presuming," continued Mr. Spring Fragrance—"presuming that some friend of your father's, living—presuming—in England—has a daughter that he arranges with your father to be your wife. Presuming that you have never seen that daughter, but that you marry her, knowing her not. Presuming that she marries you, knowing you not.—After she marries you and knows you, will that woman love you?"

"Emphatically, no," answered the young man.

---

1   From 1907 to 1916, the US Immigration Bureau ran a detention center for Chinese, Japanese, and Asian Indians in Elliott Bay in Seattle; Chinese were detained at the Angel Island immigration station in San Francisco Bay beginning in 1910.

2   A reference to the indemnity money that China paid to the victorious Western Eight-Nation Alliance following the 1899–1900 Boxer Rebellion. The US decided in 1907 to return part of its indemnity money by using it to set up scholarships for Chinese students to study in the US.

"That is the way it would be in America—that the woman who marries the man like that—would not love him?"

"Yes, that is the way it would be in America. Love, in this country, must be free, or it is not love at all."

"In China, it is different!" mused Mr. Spring Fragrance.

"Oh, yes, I have no doubt that in China it is different."

"But the love is in the heart all the same," went on Mr. Spring Fragrance.

"Yes, all the same. Everybody falls in love some time or another. Some"—pensively—"many times."

Mr. Spring Fragrance arose.

"I must go down town," said he.

As he walked down the street he recalled the remark of a business acquaintance who had met his wife and had had some conversation with her: "She is just like an American woman."

He had felt somewhat flattered when this remark had been made. He looked upon it as a compliment to his wife's cleverness; but it rankled in his mind as he entered the telegraph office. If his wife was becoming as an American woman, would it not be possible for her to love as an American woman—a man to whom she was not married?

There also floated in his memory the verse which his wife had quoted to the daughter of Chin Yuen. When the telegraph clerk handed him a blank, he wrote this message:

Remain as you wish, but remember that "'Tis better to have loved and lost, than never to have loved at all."

When Mrs. Spring Fragrance received this message, her laughter tinkled like falling water. How droll! How delightful! Here was her husband quoting American poetry in a telegram. Perhaps he had been reading her American poetry books since she had left him! She hoped so. They would lead him to understand her sympathy for her dear Laura and Kai Tzu. She need no longer keep from him their secret. How joyful! It had been such a hardship to refrain from confiding in him before. But discreetness had been most necessary, seeing that Mr. Spring Fragrance entertained as old-fashioned notions concerning marriage as did the Chin Yuen parents. Strange that that should be so, since he had fallen in love with her picture before *ever* he had seen her, just as she had fallen in love with his! And when the marriage veil was lifted and each beheld the other for the first time in the flesh, there had been no disillusion—no lessening of the respect and affection, which those who had brought about the marriage had inspired in each young heart.

Mrs. Spring Fragrance began to wish she could fall asleep and wake to find the week flown, and she in her own little home pouring tea for Mr. Spring Fragrance.

IV

MR. SPRING FRAGRANCE was walking to business with Mr. Chin Yuen. As they walked they talked.

"Yes," said Mr. Chin Yuen, "the old order is passing away, and the new order is taking its place, even with us who are Chinese. I have finally consented to give my daughter in marriage to young Kai Tzu."

Mr. Spring Fragrance expressed surprise. He had understood that the marriage between his neighbor's daughter and the San Francisco school-teacher's son was all arranged.

"So 'twas," answered Mr. Chin Yuen; "but it seems the young renegade, without consultation or advice, has placed his affections upon some untrustworthy female, and is so under her influence that he refuses to fulfill his parents' promise to me for him."

"So!" said Mr. Spring Fragrance. The shadow on his brow deepened.

"But," said Mr. Chin Yuen, with affable resignation, "it is all ordained by Heaven. Our daughter, as the wife of Kai Tzu, for whom she has long had a loving feeling, will not now be compelled to dwell with a mother-in-law and where her own mother is not. For that, we are thankful, as she is our only one and the conditions of life in this Western country are not as in China. Moreover, Kai Tzu, though not so much of a scholar as the teacher's son, has a keen eye for business and that, in America, is certainly much more desirable than scholarship. What do you think?"

"Eh! What!" exclaimed Mr. Spring Fragrance. The latter part of his companion's remarks had been lost upon him.

That day the shadow which had been following Mr. Spring Fragrance ever since he had heard his wife quote, "'Tis better to have loved," etc., became so heavy and deep that he quite lost himself within it.

At home in the evening he fed the cat, the bird, and the flowers. Then, seating himself in a carved black chair—a present from his wife on his last birthday—he took out his pipe and smoked. The cat jumped into his lap. He stroked it softly and tenderly. It had been much fondled by Mrs. Spring Fragrance, and Mr. Spring Fragrance was under the impression that it missed her. "Poor thing!" said he. "I suppose you want her back!" When he arose to go to bed he placed the animal carefully on the floor, and thus apostrophized it:

"O Wise and Silent One, your mistress returns to you, but her heart she leaves behind her, with the Tommies[1] in San Francisco."

The Wise and Silent One made no reply. He was not a jealous cat.

Mr. Spring Fragrance slept not that night; the next morning he ate not. Three days and three nights without sleep and food went by.

There was a springlike freshness in the air on the day that Mrs. Spring Fragrance came home. The skies overhead were as blue as Puget Sound stretching its gleaming length toward the mighty Pacific, and all the beautiful green world seemed to be throbbing with springing life.

Mrs. Spring Fragrance was never so radiant.

"Oh," she cried light-heartedly, "is it not lovely to see the sun shining so clear, and everything so bright to welcome me?" Mr. Spring Fragrance made no response. It was the morning after the fourth sleepless night.

Mrs. Spring Fragrance noticed his silence, also his grave face.

"Everything—everyone is glad to see me but you," she declared, half seriously, half jestingly.

Mr. Spring Fragrance set down her valise. They had just entered the house.

"If my wife is glad to see me," he quietly replied, "I also am glad to see her!"

Summoning their servant boy, he bade him look after Mrs. Spring Fragrance's comfort.

"I must be at the store in half an hour," said he, looking at his watch. "There is some very important business requiring attention."

"What is the business?" inquired Mrs. Spring Fragrance, her lip quivering with disappointment.

"I cannot just explain to you," answered her husband.

Mrs. Spring Fragrance looked up into his face with honest and earnest eyes. There was something in his manner, in the tone of her husband's voice, which touched her.

---

1   Slang for a young man whose name is unknown.

"Yen," said she, "you do not look well. You are not well. What is it?"

Something arose in Mr. Spring Fragrance's throat which prevented him from replying.

"O darling one! O sweetest one!" cried a girl's joyous voice. Laura Chin Yuen ran into the room and threw her arms around Mrs. Spring Fragrance's neck.

"I spied you from the window," said Laura, "and I couldn't rest until I told you. We are to be married next week, Kai Tzu and I. And all through you, all through you—the sweetest jade jewel in the world!"

Mr. Spring Fragrance passed out of the room.

"So the son of the Government teacher and little Happy Love are already married," Laura went on, relieving Mrs. Spring Fragrance of her cloak, her hat, and her folding fan.

Mr. Spring Fragrance paused upon the doorstep.

"Sit down, Little Sister, and I will tell you all about it," said Mrs. Spring Fragrance, forgetting her husband for a moment.

When Laura Chin Yuen had danced away, Mr. Spring Fragrance came in and hung up his hat.

"You got back very soon," said Mrs. Spring Fragrance, covertly wiping away the tears which had begun to fall as soon as she thought herself alone.

"I did not go," answered Mr. Spring Fragrance. "I have been listening to you and Laura."

"But if the business is very important, do not you think you should attend to it?" anxiously queried Mrs. Spring Fragrance.

"It is not important to me now," returned Mr. Spring Fragrance. "I would prefer to hear again about Ah Oi and Man You and Laura and Kai Tzu."

"How lovely of you to say that!" exclaimed Mrs. Spring Fragrance, who was easily made happy. And she began to chat away to her husband in the friendliest and wifeliest fashion possible. When she had finished she asked him if he were not glad to hear that those who loved as did the young lovers whose secrets she had been keeping, were to be united; and he replied that indeed he was; that he would like every man to be as happy with a wife as he himself had ever been and ever would be.

"You did not always talk like that," said Mrs. Spring Fragrance slyly. "You must have been reading my American poetry books!"

"American poetry!" ejaculated Mr. Spring Fragrance almost fiercely, "American poetry is detestable, *abhorrable*!"

"Why! why!" exclaimed Mrs. Spring Fragrance, more and more surprised.

But the only explanation which Mr. Spring Fragrance vouchsafed was a jadestone pendant.

The Inferior Woman

I

MRS. SPRING FRAGRANCE walked through the leafy alleys of the park, admiring the flowers and listening to the birds singing. It was a beautiful afternoon with the warmth from the sun cooled by a refreshing breeze. As she walked along she meditated upon a book which she had some notion of writing. Many American women wrote books. Why should not a Chinese? She would write a book about Americans for her Chinese women friends.[1] The American people were so interesting and mysterious. Something of pride and pleasure crept into Mrs. Spring Fragrance's heart as she pictured Fei and Sie and Mai Gwi Far listening to Lae-Choo reading her illuminating paragraphs.

As she turned down a by-path she saw Will Carman, her American neighbor's son, coming towards her, and by his side a young girl who seemed to belong to the sweet air and brightness of all the things around her. They were talking very earnestly and the eyes of the young man were on the girl's face.

"Ah!" murmured Mrs. Spring Fragrance, after one swift glance. "It is love."

She retreated behind a syringa bush, which completely screened her from view.

Up the winding path went the young couple.

"It is love," repeated Mrs. Spring Fragrance, "and it is the 'Inferior Woman.'"

She had heard about the Inferior Woman from the mother of Will Carman.

After tea that evening Mrs. Spring Fragrance stood musing at her front window. The sun hovered over the Olympic mountains like a great, golden red-bird with dark purple wings, its long tail of light trailing underneath in the waters of Puget Sound.

---

1   Compare with Appendix A3.

"How very beautiful!" exclaimed Mrs. Spring Fragrance; then she sighed.

"Why do you sigh?" asked Mr. Spring Fragrance.

"My heart is sad," answered his wife.

"Is the cat sick?" inquired Mr. Spring Fragrance.

Mrs. Spring Fragrance shook her head. "It is not our Wise One who troubles me today," she replied. "It is our neighbors. The sorrow of the Carman household is that the mother desires for her son the Superior Woman, and his heart enshrines but the Inferior. I have seen them together today, and I know."

"What do you know?"

"That the Inferior Woman is the mate for young Carman."

Mr. Spring Fragrance elevated his brows. Only the day before, his wife's arguments had all been in favor of the Superior Woman. He uttered some words expressive of surprise, to which Mrs. Spring Fragrance retorted:

"Yesterday, O Great Man, I was a caterpillar!"

Just then young Carman came strolling up the path. Mr. Spring Fragrance opened the door to him. "Come in, neighbor," said he. "I have received some new books from Shanghai."

"Good," replied young Carman, who was interested in Chinese literature. While he and Mr. Spring Fragrance discussed the "Odes of Chow" and the "Sorrows of Han,"[1] Mrs. Spring Fragrance, sitting in a low easy chair of rose-colored silk, covertly studied her visitor's countenance. Why was his expression so much more grave than gay? It had not been so a year ago—before he had known the Inferior Woman. Mrs. Spring Fragrance noted other changes, also, both in speech and manner. "He is no longer a boy," mused she. "He is a man, and it is the work of the Inferior Woman."

"And when, Mr. Carman," she inquired, "will you bring home a daughter to your mother?"

"And when, Mrs. Spring Fragrance, do you think I should?" returned the young man.

Mrs. Spring Fragrance spread wide her fan and gazed thoughtfully over its silver edge.

---

1 These classic Chinese texts—a collection of odes and a tragic play—were both available in English translation in the anthology *Oriental Literature: The Literature of China*, ed. Richard James, Horatio Gottheil, and Epiphanius Wilson (New York: The Colonial Press, 1900), 125–30, 281–302.

"The summer moons will soon be over," said she. "You should not wait until the grass is yellow."

"The woodmen's blows responsive ring,
As on the trees they fall,
And when the birds their sweet notes sing,
They to each other call.
From the dark valley comes a bird,
And seeks the lofty tree,
Ying goes its voice, and thus it cries:
'Companion, come to me.'
The bird, although a creature small
Upon its mate depends,
And shall we men, who rank o'er all,
Not seek to have our friends?"[1]

quoted Mr. Spring Fragrance.

Mrs. Spring Fragrance tapped his shoulder approvingly with her fan.

"I perceive," said young Carman, "that you are both allied against my peace."

"It is for your mother," replied Mrs. Spring Fragrance soothingly. "She will be happy when she knows that your affections are fixed by marriage."

There was a slight gleam of amusement in the young man's eyes as he answered: "But if my mother has no wish for a daughter—at least, no wish for the daughter I would want to give her?"

"When I first came to America," returned Mrs. Spring Fragrance, "my husband desired me to wear the American dress. I protested and declared that never would I so appear. But one day he brought home a gown fit for a fairy, and ever since then I have worn and adored the American dress."

"Mrs. Spring Fragrance," declared young Carman, "your argument is incontrovertible."

II

A YOUNG man with a determined set to his shoulders stood outside the door of a little cottage perched upon a bluff over-

---

1 From "The Value of Friendship," an ode anthologized by Confucius in
  The Shi-King, trans. James Legge. This translation would have been
  available to Sui Sin Far in James, Gottheil, and Wilson, 167.

looking the Sound. The chill sea air was sweet with the scent of roses and he drew in a deep breath of inspiration before he knocked.

"Are you not surprised to see me?" he inquired of the young person who opened the door.

"Not at all," replied the young person demurely.

He gave her a quick almost fierce look. At their last parting he had declared that he would not come again unless she requested him, and that she assuredly had not done.

"I wish I could make you feel," said he.

She laughed—a pretty infectious laugh which exorcised all his gloom. He looked down upon her as they stood together under the cluster of electric lights in her cozy little sitting-room. Such a slender, girlish figure! Such a soft cheek, red mouth, and firm little chin! Often in his dreams of her he had taken her into his arms and coaxed her into a good humor. But, alas! dreams are not realities and the calm friendliness of this young person made any demonstration of tenderness well-nigh impossible. But for the shy regard of her eyes, you might have thought that he was no more to her than a friendly acquaintance.

"I hear," said she, taking up some needlework, "that your Welland case comes on tomorrow."

"Yes," answered the young lawyer, "and I have all my witnesses ready."

"So, I hear, has Mr. Greaves," she retorted. "You are going to have a hard fight."

"What of that, when in the end I'll win."

He looked over at her with a bright gleam in his eyes.

"I wouldn't be too sure," she warned demurely. "You may lose on a technicality."

He drew his chair a little nearer to her side and turned over the pages of a book lying on her work-table. On the fly-leaf was inscribed in a man's writing: "To the dear little woman whose friendship is worth a fortune."

Another book beside it bore the inscription: "With the love of all the firm, including the boys," and a volume of poems above it was dedicated to the young person "with the high regards and stanch affection" of some other masculine person.

Will Carman pushed aside these evidences of his sweetheart's popularity with his own kind and leaned across the table.

"Alice," said he, "once upon a time you admitted that you loved me."

A blush suffused the young person's countenance.

"Did I?" she queried.

"You did, indeed."

"Well?"

"Well! If you love me and I love you—"

"Oh, please!" protested the girl, covering her ears with her hands.

"I will please," asserted the young man. "I have come here tonight, Alice, to ask you to marry me—and at once."

"Deary me!" exclaimed the young person; but she let her needlework fall into her lap as her lover, approaching nearer, laid his arm around her shoulders and, bending his face close to hers, pleaded his most important case.

If for a moment the small mouth quivered, the firm little chin lost its firmness, and the proud little head yielded to the pressure of a lover's arm, it was only for a moment so brief and fleeting that Will Carman had hardly become aware of it before it had passed.

"No," said the young person sorrowfully but decidedly. She had arisen and was standing on the other side of the table facing him. "I cannot marry you while your mother regards me as beneath you."

"When she knows you she will acknowledge you are above me. But I am not asking you to come to my mother, I am asking you to come to me, dear. If you will put your hand in mine and trust to me through all the coming years, no man or woman born can come between us."

But the young person shook her head.

"No," she repeated. "I will not be your wife unless your mother welcomes me with pride and with pleasure."

The night air was still sweet with the perfume of roses as Will Carman passed out of the little cottage door; but he drew in no deep breath of inspiration. His impetuous Irish heart was too heavy with disappointment. It might have been a little lighter, however, had he known that the eyes of the young person who gazed after him were misty with a love and yearning beyond expression.

III

"WILL CARMAN has failed to snare his bird," said Mr. Spring Fragrance to Mrs. Spring Fragrance.

Their neighbor's son had just passed their veranda without turning to bestow upon them his usual cheerful greeting.

"It is too bad," sighed Mrs. Spring Fragrance sympathetically. She clasped her hands together and exclaimed:

"Ah, these Americans! These mysterious, inscrutable, incomprehensible Americans! Had I the divine right of learning I would put them into an immortal book!"

"The divine right of learning," echoed Mr. Spring Fragrance, "Humph!"

Mrs. Spring Fragrance looked up into her husband's face in wonderment.

"Is not the authority of the scholar, the student, almost divine?" she queried.

"So 'tis said," responded he. "So it seems."

The evening before, Mr. Spring Fragrance, together with several Seattle and San Francisco merchants, had given a dinner to a number of young students who had just arrived from China. The morning papers had devoted several columns to laudation of the students, prophecies as to their future, and the great influence which they would exercise over the destiny of their nation; but no comment whatever was made on the givers of the feast, and Mr. Spring Fragrance was therefore feeling somewhat unappreciated. Were not he and his brother merchants worthy of a little attention? If the students had come to learn things in America, they, the merchants, had accomplished things. There were those amongst them who had been instrumental in bringing several of the students to America. One of the boys was Mr. Spring Fragrance's own young brother, for whose maintenance and education he had himself sent the wherewithal every year for many years. Mr. Spring Fragrance, though well read in the Chinese classics, was not himself a scholar. As a boy he had come to the shores of America, worked his way up, and by dint of painstaking study after working hours acquired the Western language and Western business ideas. He had made money, saved money, and sent money home. The years had flown, his business had grown. Through his efforts trade between his native town and the port city in which he lived had greatly increased. A school in Canton was being builded in part with funds furnished by him, and a railway syndicate, for the purpose of constructing a line of railway from the big city of Canton to his own native town, was under process of formation, with the name of Spring Fragrance at its head.

No wonder then that Mr. Spring Fragrance muttered "Humph!" when Mrs. Spring Fragrance dilated upon the "divine right of learning," and that he should feel irritated and humiliated, when, after explaining to her his grievances, she should quote in the words of Confutze: "Be not concerned that men do not know you; be only concerned that you do not know them."[1] And he had expected wifely sympathy.

He was about to leave the room in a somewhat chilled state of mind when she surprised him again by pattering across to him and following up a low curtsy with these words:

"I bow to you as the grass bends to the wind. Allow me to detain you for just one moment."

Mr. Spring Fragrance eyed her for a moment with suspicion.

"As I have told you, O Great Man," continued Mrs. Spring Fragrance, "I desire to write an immortal book, and now that I have learned from you that it is not necessary to acquire the 'divine right of learning' in order to accomplish things, I will begin the work without delay. My first subject will be 'The Inferior Woman of America.' Please advise me how I shall best inform myself concerning her."

Mr. Spring Fragrance, perceiving that his wife was now serious, and being easily mollified, sat himself down and rubbed his head. After thinking for a few moments he replied:

"It is the way in America, when a person is to be illustrated, for the illustrator to interview the person's friends. Perhaps, my dear, you had better confer with the Superior Woman."

"Surely," cried Mrs. Spring Fragrance, "no sage was ever so wise as my Great Man."

"But I lack the 'divine right of learning,'" dryly deplored Mr. Spring Fragrance.

"I am happy to hear it," answered Mrs. Spring Fragrance. "If you were a scholar you would have no time to read American poetry and American newspapers."

Mr. Spring Fragrance laughed heartily.

"You are no Chinese woman," he teased. "You are an American."

"Please bring me my parasol and my folding fan," said Mrs. Spring Fragrance. "I am going out for a walk."

And Mr. Spring Fragrance obeyed her.

---

1 "'It does not greatly concern me,' said the master, 'that men do not know me; my great concern is, my not knowing them'" (Confucius, *The Analects*, trans. William Jennings, in James, Gottheil, and Wilson, eds., 9).

IV

"THIS is from Mary Carman, who is in Portland," said the mother of the Superior Woman, looking up from the reading of a letter, as her daughter came in from the garden.

"Indeed," carelessly responded Miss Evebrook.

"Yes, it's chiefly about Will."

"Oh, is it? Well, read it then, dear. I'm interested in Will Carman, because of Alice Winthrop."

"I had hoped, Ethel, at one time that you would have been interested in him for his own sake. However, this is what she writes:

"I came here chiefly to rid myself of a melancholy mood which has taken possession of me lately, and also because I cannot bear to see my boy so changed towards me, owing to his infatuation for Alice Winthrop. It is incomprehensible to me how a son of mine can find any pleasure whatever in the society of such a girl. I have traced her history, and find that she is not only uneducated in the ordinary sense, but her environment, from childhood up, has been the sordid and demoralizing one of extreme poverty and ignorance. This girl, Alice, entered a law office at the age of fourteen, supposedly to do the work of an office boy. Now, after seven years in business, through the friendship and influence of men far above her socially, she holds the position of private secretary to the most influential man in Washington—a position which by rights belongs only to a well-educated young woman of good family. Many such applied. I myself sought to have Jane Walker appointed. Is it not disheartening to our woman's cause to be compelled to realize that girls such as this one can win men over to be their friends and lovers, when there are so many splendid young women who have been carefully trained to be companions and comrades of educated men?"

"Pardon me, mother," interrupted Miss Evebrook, "but I have heard enough. Mrs. Carman is your friend and a well-meaning woman sometimes; but a woman suffragist, in the true sense, she certainly is not. Mark my words: If any young man had accomplished for himself what Alice Winthrop has accomplished, Mrs. Carman could not have said enough in his praise. It is women such as Alice Winthrop who, in spite of every drawback, have raised themselves to the level of those who have had every advantage, who are the pride and glory of America. There are thousands of them, all over this land: women who have been of service to others all their years and who have graduated from the university of life with honor. Women such as I, who are called the Superior Women of America, are after all nothing but schoolgirls in comparison.

Mrs. Evebrook eyed her daughter mutinously. "I don't see why you should feel like that," said she. "Alice is a dear bright child, and it is prejudice engendered by Mary Carman's disappointment about you and Will which is the real cause of poor Mary's bitterness towards her; but to my mind, Alice does not compare with my daughter. She would be frightened to death if she had to make a speech."

"You foolish mother!" rallied Miss Evebrook. "To stand upon a platform at woman suffrage meetings and exploit myself is certainly a great recompense to you and father for all the sacrifices you have made in my behalf. But since it pleases you, I do it with pleasure even on the nights when my beau should 'come a courting.'"

"There is many a one who would like to come, Ethel. You're the handsomest girl in this Western town—and you know it."

"Stop that, mother. You know very well I have set my mind upon having ten years' freedom; ten years in which to love, live, suffer, see the world, and learn about men (not schoolboys) before I choose one."

"Alice Winthrop is the same age as you are, and looks like a child beside you."

"Physically, maybe; but her heart and mind are better developed. She has been out in the world all her life, I only a few months."

"Your lecture last week on 'The Opposite Sex' was splendid."

"Of course. I have studied one hundred books on the subject and attended fifty lectures. All that was necessary was to repeat in an original manner what was not by any means original."

Miss Evebrook went over to a desk and took a paper therefrom.

"This," said she, "is what Alice has written me in reply to my note suggesting that she attend next week the suffrage meeting, and give some of the experiences of her business career. The object I had in view when I requested the relation of her experiences was to use them as illustrations of the suppression and oppression of women by men. Strange to say, Alice and I have never conversed on this particular subject. If we had I would not have made this request of her nor written her as I did. Listen:

"I should dearly love to please you, but I am afraid that my experiences if related, would not help the cause. It may be, as you say, that men prevent women from rising to their level; but if there are such men, I have not met them. Ever since, when a little girl, I walked into a law office and asked for work, and the senior member kindly looked me over through his spectacles and inquired if I thought I could learn to index books, and the junior member glanced under my hat and said: 'This is a pretty little girl and we must be pretty to her,' I have loved and respected the men amongst whom I have worked and wherever I have worked. I may have been exceptionally fortunate, but I know this: the men for whom I have worked and amongst whom I have spent my life, whether they have been business or professional men, students or great lawyers and politicians, all alike have upheld me, inspired me, advised me, taught me, given me a broad outlook upon life for a woman; interested me in themselves and in their work. As to corrupting my mind and my morals, as you say so many men do, when they have young and innocent girls to deal with: As a woman I look back over my years spent amongst business and professional men, and see myself, as I was at first, an impressionable, ignorant little girl, born a Bohemian, easy to lead and easy to win, but borne aloft and morally supported by the goodness of my brother men, the men amongst whom I worked. That is why, dear Ethel, you will have to forgive me, because I cannot carry out your design, and help your work, as otherwise I would like to do."

"That, mother," declared Miss Evebrook, "answers all Mrs. Carman's insinuations, and should make her ashamed of herself. Can anyone know the sentiments which little Alice entertains toward men and wonder at her winning out as she has?"

Mrs. Evebrook was about to make reply, when her glance happening to stray out of the window, she noticed a pink parasol.

"Mrs. Spring Fragrance!" she ejaculated, while her daughter went to the door and invited in the owner of the pink parasol, who was seated in a veranda rocker calmly writing in a notebook.

"I'm so sorry that we did not hear your ring, Mrs. Spring Fragrance," said she.

"There is no necessity for you to sorrow," replied the little Chinese woman. "I did not expect you to hear a ring which rang not. I failed to pull the bell."

"You forgot, I suppose," suggested Ethel Evebrook.

"Is it wise to tell secrets?" ingenuously inquired Mrs. Spring Fragrance.

"Yes, to your friends. Oh, Mrs. Spring Fragrance, you are so refreshing."

"I have pleasure, then, in confiding to you. I have an ambition to accomplish an immortal book about the Americans, and the conversation I heard through the window was so interesting to me that I thought I would take some of it down for my book before I intruded myself. With your kind permission I will translate for your correction."

"I shall be delighted—honored," said Miss Evebrook, her cheeks glowing and her laugh rippling, "if you will promise me that you will also translate for our friend, Mrs. Carman."

"Ah, yes, poor Mrs. Carman! My heart is so sad for her," murmured the little Chinese woman.

V

WHEN the mother of Will Carman returned from Portland, the first person upon whom she called was Mrs. Spring Fragrance. Having lived in China while her late husband was in the customs service there, Mrs. Carman's prejudices did not extend to the Chinese, and ever since the Spring Fragrances had become the occupants of the villa beside the Carmans, there had been social good feeling between the American and Chinese families. Indeed, Mrs. Carman was wont to declare that amongst all her acquaintances there was not one more congenial and interesting than little Mrs. Spring Fragrance. So after she had sipped a cup of delicious tea, tasted some piquant candied limes, and told Mrs. Spring Fragrance all about her visit to the Oregon city and the Chinese people she had met there, she reverted to a personal trouble confided to Mrs. Spring Fragrance some months before and dwelt upon it for more than half an hour. Then she checked herself and gazed at Mrs. Spring Fragrance in surprise. Hitherto she had found the little Chinese woman sympathetic and consoling. Chinese ideas of filial duty chimed in with her own. But today Mrs. Spring Fragrance seemed strangely uninterested and unresponsive.

"Perhaps," gently suggested the American woman, who was nothing if not sensitive, "you have some trouble yourself. If so, my dear, tell me all about it."

"Oh, no!" answered Mrs. Spring Fragrance brightly. "I have

no troubles to tell; but all the while I am thinking about the book I am writing."

"A book!"

"Yes, a book about Americans, an immortal book."

"My dear Mrs. Spring Fragrance!" exclaimed her visitor in amazement.

"The American woman writes books about the Chinese. Why not a Chinese woman write books about the Americans?"

"I see what you mean. Why, yes, of course. What an original idea!"

"Yes, I think that is what it is. My book I shall take from the words of others."

"What do you mean, my dear?"

"I listen to what is said, I apprehend, I write it down. Let me illustrate by the 'Inferior Woman' subject. The Inferior Woman is most interesting to me because you have told me that your son is in much love with her. My husband advised me to learn about the Inferior Woman from the Superior Woman. I go to see the Superior Woman. I sit on the veranda of the Superior Woman's house. I listen to her converse with her mother about the Inferior Woman. With the speed of flames I write down all I hear. When I enter the house the Superior Woman advises me that what I write is correct. May I read to you?"

"I shall be pleased to hear what you have written; but I do not think you were wise in your choice of subject," returned Mrs. Carman somewhat primly.

"I am sorry I am not wise. Perhaps I had better not read?" said Mrs. Spring Fragrance with humility.

"Yes, yes, do, please."

There was eagerness in Mrs. Carman's voice. What could Ethel Evebrook have to say about that girl!

When Mrs. Spring Fragrance had finished reading, she looked up into the face of her American friend—a face in which there was nothing now but tenderness.

"Mrs. Mary Carman," said she, "you are so good as to admire my husband because he is what the Americans call 'a man who has made himself.' Why then do you not admire the Inferior Woman who is a woman who has made herself?"

"I think I do," said Mrs. Carman slowly.

VI

IT was an evening that invited to reverie. The far stretches of the sea were gray with mist, and the city itself, lying around the sweep of the Bay, seemed dusky and distant. From her cottage window Alice Winthrop looked silently at the open world around her. It seemed a long time since she had heard Will Carman's whistle. She wondered if he were still angry with her. She was sorry that he had left her in anger, and yet not sorry. If she had not made him believe that she was proud and selfish, the parting would have been much harder; and perhaps had he known the truth and realized that it was for his sake, and not for her own, that she was sending him away from her, he might have refused to leave her at all. His was such an imperious nature. And then they would have married—right away. Alice caught her breath a little, and then she sighed. But they would not have been happy. No, that could not have been possible if his mother did not like her. When a gulf of prejudice lies between the wife and mother of a man, that man's life is not what it should be. And even supposing she and Will could have lost themselves in each other, and been able to imagine themselves perfectly satisfied with life together, would it have been right? The question of right and wrong was a very real one to Alice Winthrop. She put herself in the place of the mother of her lover—a lonely elderly woman, a widow with an only son, upon whom she had expended all her love and care ever since, in her early youth, she had been bereaved of his father. What anguish of heart would be hers if that son deserted her for one whom she, his mother, deemed unworthy! Prejudices are prejudices. They are like diseases.

The poor, pale, elderly woman, who cherished bitter and resentful feelings towards the girl whom her son loved, was more an object of pity than condemnation to the girl herself.

She lifted her eyes to the undulating line of hills beyond the water.

From behind them came a silver light. "Yes," said she aloud to herself and, though she knew it not, there was an infinite pathos in such philosophy from one so young—"if life cannot be bright and beautiful for me, at least it can be peaceful and contented."

The light behind the hills died away; darkness crept over the sea. Alice withdrew from the window and went and knelt before the open fire in her sitting-room. Her cottage companion, the young woman who rented the place with her, had not yet returned from town.

Alice did not turn on the light. She was seeing pictures in the fire, and in every picture was the same face and form—the face and form of a fine, handsome young man with love and hope in his eyes. No, not always love and hope. In the last picture of all there was an expression which she wished she could forget. And yet she would remember ever—always—and with it, these words: "Is it nothing to you—nothing—to tell a man that you love him, and then to bid him go?"

Yes, but when she had told him she loved him she had not dreamed that her love for him and his for her would estrange him from one who, before ever she had come to this world, had pillowed his head on her breast.

Suddenly this girl, so practical, so humorous, so clever in every-day life, covered her face with her hands and sobbed like a child. Two roads of life had lain before her and she had chosen the hardest.

The warning bell of an automobile passing the cross-roads checked her tears. That reminded her that Nellie Blake would soon be home. She turned on the light and went to the bedroom and bathed her eyes. Nellie must have forgotten her key. There she was knocking.

The chill sea air was sweet with the scent of roses as Mary Carman stood upon the threshold of the little cottage, and beheld in the illumination from within the young girl whom she had called "the Inferior Woman."

"I have come, Miss Winthrop," said she, "to beg of you to return home with me. Will, reckless boy, met with a slight accident while out shooting, so could not come for you himself. He has told me that he loves you, and if you love him, I want to arrange for the prettiest wedding of the season. Come, dear!"

"I am so glad," said Mrs. Spring Fragrance, "that Will Carman's bird is in his nest and his felicity is assured."

"What about the Superior Woman?" asked Mr. Spring Fragrance.

"Ah, the Superior Woman! Radiantly beautiful, and gifted with the divine right of learning! I love well the Inferior Woman; but, O Great Man, when we have a daughter, may Heaven ordain that she walk in the groove of the Superior Woman."

The Wisdom of the New

I

OLD Li Wang, the peddler, who had lived in the land beyond the sea, was wont to declare: "For every cent that a man makes here, he can make one hundred there."

"Then, why," would ask Sankwei, "do you now have to move from door to door to fill your bowl with rice?"

And the old man would sigh and answer:

"Because where one learns how to make gold, one also learns how to lose it."

"How to lose it!" echoed Wou Sankwei. "Tell me all about it."

So the old man would tell stories about the winning and the losing, and the stories of the losing were even more fascinating than the stories of the winning.

"Yes, that was life," he would conclude. "Life, life."

At such times the boy would gaze across the water with wistful eyes. The land beyond the sea was calling to him.

The place was a sleepy little south coast town where the years slipped by monotonously. The boy was the only son of the man who had been the town magistrate.

Had his father lived, Wou Sankwei would have been sent to complete his schooling in another province. As it was he did nothing but sleep, dream, and occasionally get into mischief. What else was there to do? His mother and sister waited upon him hand and foot. Was he not the son of the house? The family income was small, scarcely sufficient for their needs; but there was no way by which he could add to it, unless, indeed, he disgraced the name of Wou by becoming a common fisherman. The great green waves lifted white arms of foam to him, and the fishes gleaming and lurking in the waters seemed to beseech him to draw them from the deep; but his mother shook her head.

"Should you become a fisherman," said she, "your family would lose face. Remember that your father was a magistrate."

When he was about nineteen there returned to the town one who had been absent for many years. Ching Kee, like old Li Wang, had also lived in the land beyond the sea; but unlike old Li Wang he had accumulated a small fortune.

"'Tis a hard life over there," said he, "but 'tis worth while. At least one can be a man, and can work at what work comes his way without losing face." Then he laughed at Wou Sankwei's flabby muscles, at his soft, dark eyes, and plump, white hands.

"If you lived in America," said he, "you would learn to be ashamed of such beauty."

Whereupon Wou Sankwei made up his mind that he would go to America, the land beyond the sea. Better any life than that of a woman man.

He talked long and earnestly with his mother. "Give me your blessing," said he. "I will work and save money. What I send home will bring you many a comfort, and when I come back to China, it may be that I shall be able to complete my studies and obtain a degree. If not, my knowledge of the foreign language which I shall acquire, will enable me to take a position which will not disgrace the name of Wou."

His mother listened and thought. She was ambitious for her son whom she loved beyond all things on earth. Moreover, had not Sik Ping, a Canton merchant, who had visited the little town two moons ago, declared to Hum Wah, who traded in palm leaves, that the signs of the times were that the son of a cobbler, returned from America with the foreign language, could easier command a position of consequence than the son of a school-teacher unacquainted with any tongue but that of his mother-land?

"Very well," she acquiesced; "but before you go I must find you a wife. Only your son, my son, can comfort me for your loss."

II

WOU SANKWEI stood behind his desk, busily entering figures in a long yellow book. Now and then he would thrust the hair pencil[1] with which he worked behind his ears and manipulate with deft fingers a Chinese counting machine.[2] Wou Sankwei was the junior partner and bookkeeper of the firm of Leung Tang Wou & Co. of San Francisco. He had been in America seven years and had made good use of his time. Self-improvement had been his object and ambition, even more than the acquirement of a fortune, and who, looking at his fine, intelligent face and listening to his careful English, could say that he had failed?

One of his partners called his name. Some ladies wished to speak to him. Wou Sankwei hastened to the front of the store. One of his callers, a motherly looking woman, was the friend who had taken him under her wing shortly after his arrival in America.

---

1   A fine paintbrush.
2   An abacus.

She had come to invite him to spend the evening with her and her niece, the young girl who accompanied her.

After his callers had left, Sankwei returned to his desk and worked steadily until the hour for his evening meal, which he took in the Chinese restaurant across the street from the bazaar. He hurried through with this, as before going to his friend's house, he had a somewhat important letter to write and mail. His mother had died a year before, and the uncle, to whom he was writing, had taken his wife and son into his home until such time as his nephew could send for them. Now the time had come.

Wou Sankwei's memory of the woman who was his wife was very faint. How could it be otherwise? She had come to him but three weeks before the sailing of the vessel which had brought him to America, and until then he had not seen her face. But she was his wife and the mother of his son. Ever since he had worked in America he had sent money for her support, and she had proved a good daughter to his mother.

As he sat down to write he decided that he would welcome her with a big dinner to his countrymen.

"Yes," he replied to Mrs. Dean, later on in the evening, "I have sent for my wife."

"I am so glad," said the lady. "Mr. Wou"—turning to her niece—"has not seen his wife for seven years."

"Deary me!" exclaimed the young girl. "What a lot of letters you must have written!"

"I have not written her one," returned the young man somewhat stiffly.

Adah[1] Charlton looked up in surprise. "Why—" she began.

"Mr. Wou used to be such a studious boy when I first knew him," interrupted Mrs. Dean, laying her hand affectionately upon the young man's shoulder. "Now, it is all business. But you won't forget the concert on Saturday evening."

"No, I will not forget," answered Wou Sankwei.

"He has never written to his wife," explained Mrs. Dean when she and her niece were alone, "because his wife can neither read nor write."

---

1 "Adah" is a name with which Edith Eaton/Sui Sin Far appears to have identified: her sister Winnifred uses the name Ada to refer to Edith in *Marion: The Story of an Artist's Model.* Later, Sankwei also connects Adah with the pen name Sui Sin Far by describing her as a "water-flower—a lily!" (p. 70).

"Oh, isn't that sad!" murmured Adah Charlton, her own winsome face becoming pensive.

"They don't seem to think so. It is the Chinese custom to educate only the boys. At least it has been so in the past. Sankwei himself is unusually bright. Poor boy! He began life here as a laundryman, and you may be sure that it must have been hard on him, for, as the son of a petty Chinese Government official, he had not been accustomed to manual labor. But Chinese character is wonderful; and now after seven years in this country, he enjoys a reputation as a business man amongst his countrymen, and is as up to date as any young American."

"But, Auntie, isn't it dreadful to think that a man should live away from his wife for so many years without any communication between them whatsoever except through others."

"It is dreadful to our minds, but not to theirs. Everything with them is a matter of duty. Sankwei married his wife as a matter of duty. He sends for her as a matter of duty."

"I wonder if it is all duty on her side," mused the girl.

Mrs. Dean smiled. "You are too romantic, Adah," said she. "I hope, however, that when she does come, they will be happy together. I think almost as much of Sankwei as I do of my own boy."

III

PAU LIN, the wife of Wou Sankwei, sat in a corner of the deck of the big steamer, awaiting the coming of her husband. Beside her, leaning his little queued[1] head against her shoulder, stood her six-year-old son. He had been ailing throughout the voyage, and his small face was pinched with pain. His mother, who had been nursing him every night since the ship had left port, appeared very worn and tired. This, despite the fact that with a feminine desire to make herself fair to see in the eyes of her husband, she had arrayed herself in a heavily embroidered purple costume, whitened her forehead and cheeks with powder, and tinted her lips with carmine.

He came at last, looking over and beyond her. There were two others of her countrywomen awaiting the men who had sent for them, and each had a child, so that for a moment he seemed

---

1 A queue is a long, braided pigtail. This hairstyle was imposed on all the Chinese as a sign of subjection during the Qing Dynasty (1644–1911).

somewhat bewildered. Only when the ship's officer pointed out and named her, did he know her as his. Then he came forward, spoke a few words of formal welcome, and, lifting the child in his arms, began questioning her as to its health.

She answered in low monosyllables. At his greeting she had raised her patient eyes to his face—the face of the husband whom she had not seen for seven long years—then the eager look of expectancy which had crossed her own faded away, her eyelids drooped, and her countenance assumed an almost sullen expression.

"Ah, poor Sankwei!" exclaimed Mrs. Dean, who with Adah Charlton stood some little distance apart from the family group.

"Poor wife!" murmured the young girl. She moved forward and would have taken in her own white hands the ringed ones of the Chinese woman, but the young man gently restrained her. "She cannot understand you," said he. As the young girl fell back, he explained to his wife the presence of the stranger women. They were there to bid her welcome; they were kind and good and wished to be her friends as well as his.

Pau Lin looked away. Adah Charlton's bright face, and the tone in her husband's voice when he spoke to the young girl, aroused a suspicion in her mind—a suspicion natural to one who had come from a land where friendship between a man and woman is almost unknown.

"Poor little thing! How shy she is!" exclaimed Mrs. Dean.

Sankwei was glad that neither she nor the young girl understood the meaning of the averted face.

Thus began Wou Sankwei's life in America as a family man. He soon became accustomed to the change, which was not such a great one after all. Pau Lin was more of an accessory than a part of his life. She interfered not at all with his studies, his business, or his friends, and when not engaged in housework or sewing, spent most of her time in the society of one or the other of the merchants' wives who lived in the flats and apartments around her own. She kept up the Chinese custom of taking her meals after her husband or at a separate table, and observed faithfully the rule laid down for her by her late mother-in-law: to keep a quiet tongue in the presence of her man. Sankwei, on his part, was always kind and indulgent. He bought her silk dresses, hair ornaments, fans, and sweetmeats. He ordered her favorite dishes from the Chinese restaurant. When she wished to go out with her women friends, he hired a carriage, and shortly after her advent erected behind her sleeping room a chapel for the ancestral tablet[1] and gorgeous goddess which she had brought over seas with her.

Upon the child both parents lavished affection. He was a quaint, serious little fellow, small for his age and requiring much care. Although naturally much attached to his mother, he became also very fond of his father who, more like an elder brother than a parent, delighted in playing all kinds of games with him, and whom he followed about like a little dog. Adah Charlton took a great fancy to him and sketched him in many different poses for a book on Chinese children which she was illustrating.

"He will be strong enough to go to school next year," said Sankwei to her one day. "Later on I intend to put him through an American college."

"What does your wife think of a Western training for him?" inquired the young girl.

"I have not consulted her about the matter," he answered. "A woman does not understand such things."

"A woman, Mr. Wou," declared Adah, "understands such things as well as and sometimes better than a man."

"An American woman, maybe," amended Sankwei; "but not a Chinese."

From the first Pau Lin had shown no disposition to become Americanized, and Sankwei himself had not urged it.

"I do appreciate the advantages of becoming westernized," said he to Mrs. Dean whose influence and interest in his studies in America had helped him to become what he was, "but it is not as if she had come here as I came, in her learning days. The time for learning with her is over."

One evening, upon returning from his store, he found the little Yen sobbing pitifully.

"What!" he teased, "A man—and weeping."

The boy tried to hide his face, and as he did so, the father noticed that his little hand was red and swollen. He strode into the kitchen where Pau Lin was preparing the evening meal.

"The little child who is not strong—is there anything he could do to merit the infliction of pain?" he questioned.

Pau Lin faced her husband. "Yes, I think so," said she.

"What?"

"I forbade him to speak the language of the white women, and

---

1   A tablet designating the continued presence of an ancestor, used in rituals of ancestor veneration.

he disobeyed me. He had words in that tongue with the white boy from the next street."

Sankwei was astounded.

"We are living in the white man's country," said he. "The child will have to learn the white man's language."

"Not my child," answered Pau Lin.

Sankwei turned away from her. "Come, little one," said he to his son, "we will take supper tonight at the restaurant, and afterwards Yen shall see a show."

Pau Lin laid down the dish of vegetables which she was straining and took from a hook a small wrap which she adjusted around the boy.

"Now go with thy father," said she sternly.

But the boy clung to her—to the hand which had punished him. "I will sup with you," he cried, "I will sup with you."

"Go," repeated his mother, pushing him from her. And as the two passed over the threshold, she called to the father: "Keep the wrap around the child. The night air is chill."

Late that night, while father and son were peacefully sleeping, the wife and mother arose, and lifting gently the unconscious boy, bore him into the next room where she sat down with him in a rocker.

Waking, he clasped his arms around her neck. Backwards and forwards she rocked him, passionately caressing the wounded hand and crooning and crying until he fell asleep again.

The first chastisement that the son of Wou Sankwei had received from his mother, was because he had striven to follow in the footsteps of his father and use the language of the stranger.

"You did perfectly right," said old Sien Tau the following morning, as she leaned over her balcony to speak to the wife of Wou Sankwei. "Had I again a son to rear, I should see to it that he followed not after the white people."

Sien Tau's son had married a white woman, and his children passed their grandame on the street without recognition.

"In this country, she is most happy who has no child," said Lae Choo, resting her elbow upon the shoulder of Sien Tau. "A Toy, the young daughter of Lew Wing, is as bold and free in her ways as are the white women, and her name is on all the men's tongues. What prudent man of our race would take her as wife?"

"One needs not to be born here to be made a fool of," joined in Pau Lin, appearing at another balcony door. "Think of Hum Wah. From sunrise till midnight he worked for fourteen years, then a white man came along and persuaded from him every dollar, promising to return doublefold within the moon. Many moons have risen and waned and HumWah still waits on this side of the sea for the white man and his money. Meanwhile, his father and mother, who looked long for his coming, have passed beyond returning."

"The new religion—what trouble it brings!" exclaimed Lae Choo. "My man received word yestereve that the good old mother of Chee Ping—he who was baptized a Christian at the last baptizing in the Mission around the corner—had her head secretly severed from her body by the steadfast people of the village, as soon as the news reached there.[1] 'Twas the first violent death in the records of the place. This happened to the mother of one of the boys attending the Mission corner of my street."

"No doubt, the poor old mother, having lost face, minded not so much the losing of her head," sighed Pau Lin. She gazed below her curiously. The American Chinatown held a strange fascination for the girl from the seacoast village. Streaming along the street was a motley throng made up of all nationalities. The sing-song voices of girls whom respectable merchants' wives shudder to name, were calling to one another from high balconies up shadowy alleys. A fat barber was laughing hilariously at a drunken white man who had fallen into a gutter; a withered old fellow, carrying a bird in a cage, stood at the corner entreating passersby to have a good fortune told, some children were burning punk on the curbstone. There went by a stalwart Chief of the Six Companies[2] engaged in earnest confab with a yellow-robed priest from the Joss[3] house. A Chinese dressed in the latest American style and a very blonde woman, laughing immoderately, were entering a Chinese restaurant together. Above all the hubbub of voices was heard the clang of electric cars and the jarring of heavy wheels over cobblestones.

Pau Lin raised her head and looked her thoughts at the old woman, Sien Tau.

---

1 Perhaps the most intense outbursts of Chinese anti-Christian violence (often fueled by anti-imperialist sentiment) in this period were the Tientsin Massacre of 1870 and the Boxer Uprising of 1899–1900.
2 The Six Companies, or Chinese Consolidated Benevolent Association, consisted of six associations founded (beginning in the 1850s) to facilitate immigration and protect the interests of immigrants from particular districts in China. The Six Companies provided aid, social services, employment, advice, and the adjudication of grievances to members.
3 A pidgin term derived from the Portuguese *deos* ("god"), "Joss" refers to any Chinese deity worshiped in the form of an idol in a shrine.

"Yes," nodded the dame, "'tis a mad place in which to bring up a child."

Pau Lin went back into the house, gave little Yen his noonday meal, and dressed him with care. His father was to take him out that afternoon. She questioned the boy, as she braided his queue, concerning the white women whom he visited with his father.

It was evening when they returned—Wou Sankwei and his boy. The little fellow ran up to her in high glee. "See, mother," said he, pulling off his cap, "I am like father now. I wear no queue."

The mother looked down upon him—at the little round head from which the queue, which had been her pride, no longer dangled.

"Ah!" she cried. "I am ashamed of you; I am ashamed!"

The boy stared at her, hurt and disappointed.

"Never mind, son," comforted his father. "It is all right."

Pau Lin placed the bowls of seaweed and chickens' liver before them and went back to the kitchen where her own meal was waiting. But she did not eat. She was saying within herself: "It is for the white woman he has done this; it is for the white woman!"

Later, as she laid the queue of her son within the trunk wherein lay that of his father, long since cast aside, she discovered a picture of Mrs. Dean, taken when the American woman had first become the teacher and benefactress of the youthful laundryman. She ran over with it to her husband. "Here," said she; "it is a picture of one of your white friends."

Sankwei took it from her almost reverently, "That woman," he explained, "has been to me as a mother."

"And the young woman—the one with eyes the color of blue china—is she also as a mother?" inquired Pau Lin gently.

But for all her gentleness, Wou Sankwei flushed angrily.

"Never speak of her," he cried. "Never speak of her!"

"Ha, ha, ha! Ha, ha, ha!" laughed Pau Lin. It was a soft and not unmelodious laugh, but to Wou Sankwei it sounded almost sacrilegious.

Nevertheless, he soon calmed down. Pau Lin was his wife, and to be kind to her was not only his duty but his nature. So when his little boy climbed into his lap and besought his father to pipe him a tune, he reached for his flute and called to Pau Lin to put aside work for that night. He would play her some Chinese music. And Pau Lin, whose heart and mind, undiverted by change, had been concentrated upon Wou Sankwei ever since the day she had become his wife, smothered, for the time being, the bitterness in her heart, and succumbed to the magic of her husband's playing—a magic which transported her in thought to the old Chinese days, the old Chinese days whose impression and influence ever remain with the exiled sons and daughters of China.

IV

THAT a man should take to himself two wives, or even three, if he thought proper, seemed natural and right in the eyes of Wou Pau Lin. She herself had come from a home where there were two broods of children and where her mother and her father's other wife had eaten their meals together as sisters. In that home there had not always been peace; but each woman, at least, had the satisfaction of knowing that her man did not regard or treat the other woman as her superior. To each had fallen the common lot—to bear children to the man, and the man was master of all.

But, oh! the humiliation and shame of bearing children to a man who looked up to another woman—and a woman of another race—as a being above the common uses of women. There is a jealousy of the mind more poignant than any mere animal jealousy.

When Wou Sankwei's second child was two weeks old, Adah Charlton and her aunt called to see the little one, and the young girl chatted brightly with the father and played merrily with Yen, who was growing strong and merry. The American women could not, of course, converse with the Chinese; but Adah placed beside her a bunch of beautiful flowers, pressed her hand, and looked down upon her with radiant eyes. Secure in the difference of race, in the love of many friends, and in the happiness of her chosen work, no suspicion whatever crossed her mind that the woman whose husband was her aunt's protégé tasted everything bitter because of her.

After the visitors had gone, Pau Lin, who had been watching her husband's face while the young artist was in the room, said to him:

"She can be happy who takes all and gives nothing."

"Takes all and gives nothing," echoed her husband. "What do you mean?"

"She has taken all your heart," answered Pau Lin, "but she has not given you a son. It is I who have had that task."

"You are my wife," answered Wou Sankwei. "And she—oh! how can you speak of her so? She, who is as a pure water-flower—a lily!"

He went out of the room, carrying with him a little painting of their boy, which Adah Charlton had given to him as she bade him goodbye and which he had intended showing with pride to the mother.

It was on the day that the baby died that Pau Lin first saw the little picture. It had fallen out of her husband's coat pocket when he lifted the tiny form in his arms and declared it lifeless. Even in that first moment of loss Pau Lin, stooping to pick up the portrait, had shrunk back in horror, crying: "She would cast a spell! She would cast a spell!"

She set her heel upon the face of the picture and destroyed it beyond restoration.

"You know not what you say and do," sternly rebuked Sankwei. He would have added more, but the mystery of the dead child's look forbade him.

"The loss of a son is as the loss of a limb," said he to his childless partner, as under the red glare of the lanterns they sat discussing the sad event.

"But you are not without consolation," returned Leung Tsao. "Your firstborn grows in strength and beauty."

"True," assented Wou Sankwei, his heavy thoughts becoming lighter.

And Pau Lin, in her curtained balcony overhead, drew closer her child and passionately cried:

"Sooner would I, O heart of my heart, that the light of thine eyes were also quenched, than that thou shouldst be contaminated with the wisdom of the new."

V

THE Chinese women friends of Wou Pau Lin gossiped among themselves, and their gossip reached the ears of the American woman friend of Pau Lin's husband. Since the days of her widowhood Mrs. Dean had devoted herself earnestly and wholeheartedly to the betterment of the condition and the uplifting of the young workingmen of Chinese race who came to America. Their appeal and need, as she had told her niece, was for closer acquaintance with the knowledge of the Western people, and *that* she had undertaken to give them, as far as she was able. The rewards and satisfactions of her work had been rich in some cases. Witness Wou Sankwei.

But the gossip had reached and much perturbed her. What was it that they said Wou Sankwei's wife had declared—that her little son should not go to an American school nor learn the American learning. Such bigotry and narrow-mindedness! How sad to think of! Here was a man who had benefited and profited by living in America, anxious to have his son receive the benefits of a Western education—and here was this man's wife opposing him with her ignorance and hampering him with her unreasonable jealousy.

Yes, she had heard that too. That Wou Sankwei's wife was jealous—jealous—and her husband the most moral of men, the kindest and the most generous.

"Of what is she jealous?" she questioned Adah Charlton. "Other Chinese men's wives, I have known, have had cause to be jealous, for it is true some of them are dreadfully immoral and openly support two or more wives. But not Wou Sankwei. And this little Pau Lin. She has everything that a Chinese woman could wish for."

A sudden flash of intuition came to the girl, rendering her for a moment speechless. When she did find words, she said:

"Everything that a Chinese woman could wish for, you say. Auntie, I do not believe there is any real difference between the feelings of a Chinese wife and an American wife. Sankwei is treating Pau Lin as he would treat her were he living in China. Yet it cannot be the same to her as if she were in their own country, where he would not come in contact with American women. A woman is a woman with intuitions and perceptions, whether Chinese or American, whether educated or uneducated, and Sankwei's wife must have noticed, even on the day of her arrival, her husband's manner towards us, and contrasted it with his manner towards her. I did not realize this before you told me that she was jealous. I only wish I had. Now, for all her ignorance, I can see that the poor little thing became more of an American in that one half hour on the steamer than Wou Sankwei, for all your pride in him, has become in seven years."

Mrs. Dean rested her head on her hand. She was evidently much perplexed.

"What you say may be, Adah," she replied after a while; "but even so, it is Sankwei whom I have known so long, who has my sympathies. He has much to put up with. They have drifted seven years of life apart. There is no bond of interest or sympathy between them, save the boy. Yet never the slightest hint of trouble has come to me from his own lips. Before the coming of Pau Lin, he would confide in me every little thing that worried him, as if he were my own son. Now he maintains absolute silence as to his private affairs."

"Chinese principles," observed Adah, resuming her work. "Yes, I admit Sankwei has some puzzles to solve. Naturally, when he tries to live two lives—that of a Chinese and that of an American."

"He is compelled to that," retorted Mrs. Dean. "Is it not what we teach these Chinese boys—to become Americans? And yet, they are Chinese, and must, in a sense, remain so."

Adah did not answer.

Mrs. Dean sighed. "Poor, dear children, both of them," mused she.

"I feel very low-spirited over the matter. I suppose you wouldn't care to come down town with me. I should like to have another chat with Mrs. Wing Sing."

"I shall be glad of the change," replied Adah, laying down her brushes.

Rows of lanterns suspended from many balconies shed a mellow, moonshiny radiance. On the walls and doors were splashes of red paper inscribed with hieroglyphics. In the narrow streets, booths decorated with flowers, and banners and screens painted with immense figures of josses diverted the eye; while bands of musicians in gaudy silks, shrilled and banged, piped and fluted.

Everybody seemed to be out of doors—men, women, and children—and nearly all were in holiday attire. A couple of priests, in vivid scarlet and yellow robes, were kowtowing[1] before an altar covered with a rich cloth, embroidered in white and silver. Some Chinese students from the University of California stood looking on with comprehending, half-scornful interest; three girls lavishly dressed in colored silks, with their black hair plastered back from their faces and heavily bejewelled behind, chirped and chattered in a gilded balcony above them like birds in a cage. Little children, their hands full of half-moon-shaped cakes, were pattering about, with eyes, for all the hour, as bright as stars.

Chinatown was celebrating the Harvest Moon Festival,[2] and Adah Charlton was glad that she had an opportunity to see something of the celebration before she returned East. Mrs. Dean,

---

1 Touching the ground with one's forehead as a sign of submission, homage, or worship.
2 The mid-autumn festival, held on the fifteenth day of the eighth lunar month, celebrates the end of the summer harvest. Traditions include eating mooncakes and gathering outdoors to observe the full harvest moon.

familiar with the Chinese people and the mazes of Chinatown, led her around fearlessly, pointing out this and that object of interest and explaining to her its meaning. Seeing that it was a gala night, she had abandoned her idea of calling upon the Chinese friend.

Just as they turned a corner leading up to the street where Wou Sankwei's place of business and residence was situated, a pair of little hands grasped Mrs. Dean's skirt and a delighted little voice piped: "See me! See me!" It was little Yen, resplendent in mauve colored pantaloons and embroidered vest and cap. Behind him was a tall man whom both women recognized.

"How do you happen to have Yen with you?" Adah asked.

"His father handed him over to me as a sort of guide, counsellor, and friend. The little fellow is very amusing."

"See over here," interrupted Yen. He hopped over the alley to where the priests stood by the altar. The grown people followed him.

"What is that man chanting?" asked Adah. One of the priests had mounted a table, and with arms outstretched towards the moon sailing high in the heavens, seemed to be making some sort of an invocation.

Her friend listened for some moments before replying:

"It is a sort of apotheosis of the moon. I have heard it on a like occasion in Hankow, and the Chinese *bonze*[1] who officiated gave me a translation. I almost know it by heart. May I repeat it to you?"

Mrs. Dean and Yen were examining the screen with the big josses.

"Yes, I should like to hear it," said Adah.

"Then fix your eyes upon Diana."[2]

"Dear and lovely moon, as I watch thee pursuing thy solitary course o'er the silent heavens, heart-easing thoughts steal o'er me and calm my passionate soul. Thou art so sweet, so serious, so serene, that thou causest me to forget the stormy emotions which crash like jarring discords across the harmony of life, and bringest to my memory a voice scarce ever heard amidst the warring of the world—love's low voice.

"Thou art so peaceful and so pure that it seemeth as if naught false or ignoble could dwell beneath thy gentle radiance, and that

---

1   A Buddhist monk.
2   Diana was the Roman goddess of the moon.

earnestness—even the earnestness of genius—must glow within the bosom of him on whose head thy beams fall like blessings.

"The magic of thy sympathy disburtheneth me of many sorrows, and thoughts, which, like the songs of the sweetest sylvan singer, are too dear and sacred for the careless ears of day, gush forth with unconscious eloquence when thou art the only listener.

"Dear and lovely moon, there are some who say that those who dwell in the sunlit fields of reason should fear to wander through the moonlit valley of imagination; but I, who have ever been a pilgrim and a stranger in the realm of the wise, offer to thee the homage of a heart which appreciates that thou graciously shinest—even on the fool."

"Is that really Chinese?" queried Adah.

"No doubt about it—in the main. Of course, I cannot swear to it word for word."

"I should think that there would be some reference to the fruits of the earth—the harvest. I always understood that the Chinese religion was so practical."

"Confucianism is. But the Chinese mind requires two religions. Even the most commonplace Chinese has yearnings for something above everyday life. Therefore, he combines with his Confucianism, Buddhism—or, in this country, Christianity."

"Thank you for the information. It has given me a key to the mind of a certain Chinese in whom Auntie and I are interested."

"And who is this particular Chinese in whom you are interested."

"The father of the little boy who is with us tonight."

"Wou Sankwei! Why, here he comes with Lee Tong Hay. Are you acquainted with Lee Tong Hay?"

"No, but I believe Aunt is. Plays and sings in vaudeville, doesn't he?"

"Yes he can turn himself into a German, a Scotchman, an Irishman, or an American, with the greatest ease, and is as natural in each character as he is as a Chinaman. Hello, Lee Tong Hay."

"Hello, Mr. Stimson."

While her friend was talking to the lively young Chinese who had answered his greeting, Adah went over to where Wou Sankwei stood speaking to Mrs. Dean.

"Yen begins school next week," said her aunt, drawing her arm within her own. It was time to go home.

Adah made no reply. She was settling her mind to do something quite out of the ordinary. Her aunt often called her romantic and impractical. Perhaps she was.

VI

"AUNTIE went out of town this morning," said Adah Charlton. "I 'phoned for you to come up, Sankwei, because I wished to have a personal and private talk with you."

"Any trouble, Miss Adah," inquired the young merchant. "Anything I can do for you?"

Mrs. Dean often called upon him to transact little business matters for her or to consult with him on various phases of her social and family life.

"I don't know what I would do without Sankwei's head to manage for me," she often said to her niece.

"No," replied the girl, "you do too much for us. You always have, ever since I've known you. It's a shame for us to have allowed you."

"What are you talking about, Miss Adah? Since I came to America your aunt has made this house like a home to me, and, of course, I take an interest in it and like to do anything for it that a man can. I am always happy when I come here."

"Yes, I know you are, poor old boy," said Adah to herself.

Aloud she said: "I have something to say to you which I would like you to hear. Will you listen, Sankwei?"

"Of course I will," he answered.

"Well then," went on Adah, "I asked you to come here today because I have heard that there is trouble at your house and that your wife is jealous of you."

"Would you please not talk about that, Miss Adah. It is a matter which you cannot understand."

"You promised to listen and heed. I do understand, even though I cannot speak to your wife nor find out what she feels and thinks. I know you, Sankwei, and I can see just how the trouble has arisen. As soon as I heard that your wife was jealous I knew why she was jealous."

"Why?" he queried.

"Because," she answered unflinchingly, "you are thinking far too much of other women."

"Too much of other women?" echoed Sankwei dazedly. "I did not know that."

"No, you didn't. That is why I am telling you. But you are, Sankwei. And you are becoming too Americanized. My aunt encourages you to become so, and she is a good woman, with the best and highest of motives; but we are all liable to make mistakes, and it is a mistake to try and make a Chinese man into an American—if he has a wife who is to remain as she always has been. It would be different if you were not married and were a man free to advance. But you are not."

"What am I to do then, Miss Adah? You say that I think too much of other women besides her, and that I am too much Americanized. What can I do about it now that it is so?"

"First of all you must think of your wife. She has done for you what no American woman would do—came to you to be your wife, love you and serve you without even knowing you—took you on trust altogether. You must remember that for many years she was chained in a little cottage to care for your ailing and aged mother—a hard task indeed for a young girl. You must remember that you are the only man in the world to her, and that you have always been the only one that she has ever cared for. Think of her during all the years you are here, living a lonely hard-working life—a baby and an old woman her only companions. For this, she had left all her own relations. No American woman would have sacrificed herself so.

"And, now, what has she? Only you and her housework. The white woman reads, plays, paints, attends concerts, entertainments, lectures, absorbs herself in the work she likes, and in the course of her life thinks of and cares for a great many people. She has much to make her happy besides her husband. The Chinese woman has him only."

"And her boy."

"Yes, her boy," repeated Adah Charlton, smiling in spite of herself, but lapsing into seriousness the moment after. "There's another reason for you to drop the American for a time and go back to being a Chinese. For sake of your darling little boy, you and your wife should live together kindly and cheerfully. That is much more important for his welfare than that he should go to the American school and become Americanized."

"It is my ambition to put him through both American and Chinese schools."

"But what he needs most of all is a loving mother."

"She loves him all right."

"Then why do you not love her as you should? If I were married I would not think my husband loved me very much if he preferred spending his evenings in the society of other women than in mine, and was so much more polite and deferential to other women than he was to me. Can't you understand now why your wife is jealous?"

Wou Sankwei stood up.

"Goodbye," said Adah Charlton, giving him her hand.

"Goodbye," said Wou Sankwei.

Had he been a white man, there is no doubt that Adah Charlton's little lecture would have had a contrary effect from what she meant it to have. At least, the lectured would have been somewhat cynical as to her sincerity. But Wou Sankwei was not a white man. He was a Chinese, and did not see any reason for insincerity in a matter as important as that which Adah Charlton had brought before him. He felt himself exiled from Paradise, yet it did not occur to him to question, as a white man would have done, whether the angel with the flaming sword[1] had authority for her action. Neither did he lay the blame for things gone wrong upon any woman. He simply made up his mind to make the best of what was.

VII

IT had been a peaceful week in the Wou household—the week before little Yen was to enter the American school. So peaceful indeed that Wou Sankwei had begun to think that his wife was reconciled to his wishes with regard to the boy. He whistled softly as he whittled away at a little ship he was making for him. Adah Charlton's suggestions had set coursing a train of thought which had curved around Pau Lin so closely that he had decided that, should she offer any further opposition to the boy's attending the American school, he would not insist upon it. After all, though the American language might be useful during this century, the wheel of the world would turn again, and then it might not be necessary at all. Who could tell? He came very near to expressing himself thus to Pau Lin.

And now it was the evening before the morning that little Yen was to march away to the American school. He had been excited all day over the prospect, and to calm him, his father finally told him to read aloud a little story from the Chinese book which he had given him on his first birthday in America and which he had taught him to read. Obediently the little fellow drew his stool to

---

1 See Genesis 3:24: "So he drove out the man; and he placed at the east of the garden of Eden Cherubims, and a flaming sword which turned every way, to keep the way of the tree of life."

his mother's side and read in his childish sing-song the story of an irreverent lad who came to great grief because he followed after the funeral of his grandfather and regaled himself on the crisply roasted chickens and loose-skinned oranges which were left on the grave for the feasting of the spirit.

Wou Sankwei laughed heartily over the story. It reminded him of some of his own boyish escapades. But Pau Lin stroked silently the head of the little reader, and seemed lost in reverie.

A whiff of fresh salt air blew in from the Bay. The mother shivered, and Wou Sankwei, looking up from the fastening of the boat's rigging, bade Yen close the door. As the little fellow came back to his mother's side he stumbled over her knee.

"Oh, poor mother!" he exclaimed with quaint apology. "'Twas the stupid feet, not Yen."

"So," she replied, curling her arm around his neck, "'tis always the feet. They are to the spirit as the cocoon to the butterfly. Listen, and I will sing you the song of the Happy Butterfly."

She began singing the old Chinese ditty in a fresh birdlike voice. Wou Sankwei, listening, was glad to hear her. He liked having everyone around him cheerful and happy. That had been the charm of the Dean household.

The ship was finished before the little family retired. Yen examined it, critically at first, then exultingly. Finally, he carried it away and placed it carefully in the closet where he kept his kites, balls, tops, and other treasures. "We will set sail with it tomorrow after school," said he to his father, hugging gratefully that father's arm.

Sankwei rubbed the little round head. The boy and he were great chums.

What was that sound which caused Sankwei to start from his sleep? It was just on the border land of night and day, an unusual time for Pau Lin to be up. Yet, he could hear her voice in Yen's room. He raised himself on his elbow and listened. She was softly singing a nursery song about some little squirrels and a huntsman. Sankwei wondered at her singing in that way at such an hour. From where he lay he could just perceive the child's cot and the silent child figure lying motionless in the dim light. How very motionless! In a moment Sankwei was beside it.

The empty cup with its dark dregs told the tale.

The thing he loved the best in all the world—the darling son who had crept into his heart with his joyousness and beauty—had been taken from him—by her who had given.

Sankwei reeled against the wall. The kneeling figure by the cot arose. The face of her was solemn and tender.

"He is saved," smiled she, "from the Wisdom of the New."

In grief too bitter for words the father bowed his head upon his hands.

"Why! Why!" queried Pau Lin, gazing upon him bewilderedly. "The child is happy. The butterfly mourns not o'er the shed cocoon."

Sankwei put up his shutters and wrote this note to Adah Charlton:

I have lost my boy through an accident. I am returning to China with my wife whose health requires a change.

"Its Wavering Image"

I

PAN was a half white, half Chinese girl. Her mother was dead, and Pan lived with her father who kept an Oriental Bazaar on Dupont Street.[1] All her life had Pan lived in Chinatown, and if she were different in any sense from those around her, she gave little thought to it. It was only after the coming of Mark Carson that the mystery of her nature began to trouble her.

They met at the time of the boycott of the Sam Yups by the See Yups.[2] After the heat and dust and unsavoriness of the highways and byways of Chinatown, the young reporter who had been sent to find a story, had stepped across the threshold of a cool, deep room, fragrant with the odor of dried lilies and sandalwood, and found Pan.

She did not speak to him, nor he to her. His business was with the spectacled merchant, who, with a pointed brush, was making up accounts in brown paper books and rolling balls in an abacus

---

1 Dupont Street was the busiest thoroughfare in San Francisco's China-town. After the 1906 earthquake, the city renamed it Grant Street, in an effort to clean up Chinatown's image. Locals continue to refer to Grant Street as "Dupont Gai" (Dupont Avenue) in Chinese.

2 In the late 1880s and 1890s, the See Yup Benevolent Association—whose membership consisted of workers and small businessmen—began to boycott and sometimes fight with the wealthier and primarily merchant-class Sam Yups.

box. As to Pan, she always turned from whites. With her father's people she was natural and at home; but in the presence of her mother's she felt strange and constrained, shrinking from their curious scrutiny as she would from the sharp edge of a sword.

When Mark Carson returned to the office, he asked some questions concerning the girl who had puzzled him. What was she? Chinese or white? The city editor answered him, adding: "She is an unusually bright girl, and could tell more stories about the Chinese than any other person in this city—if she would."

Mark Carson had a determined chin, clever eyes, and a tone to his voice which easily won for him the confidence of the unwary. In the reporter's room he was spoken of as "a man who would sell his soul for a story."

After Pan's first shyness had worn off, he found her bewilderingly frank and free with him; but he had all the instincts of a gentleman save one, and made no ordinary mistake about her. He was Pan's first white friend. She was born a Bohemian,[1] exempt from the conventional restrictions imposed upon either the white or Chinese woman; and the Oriental who was her father mingled with his affection for his child so great a respect for and trust in the daughter of the dead white woman, that everything she did or said was right to him. And Pan herself! A white woman might pass over an insult; a Chinese woman fail to see one. But Pan! He would be a brave man indeed who offered one to childish little Pan.

All this Mark Carson's clear eyes perceived, and with delicate tact and subtlety he taught the young girl that, all unconscious until his coming, she had lived her life alone. So well did she learn this lesson that it seemed at times as if her white self must entirely dominate and trample under foot her Chinese.

Meanwhile, in full trust and confidence, she led him about Chinatown, initiating him into the simple mystery and history of many things, for which she, being of her father's race, had a tender regard and pride. For her sake he was received as a brother by the yellow-robed priest in the joss[2] house, the Astrologer of Prospect Place, and other conservative Chinese. The Water Lily Club opened its doors to him when she knocked, and the Sublimely Pure Brothers' organization admitted him as one of its honorary members, thereby enabling him not only to see but to take part in a ceremony in which no American had ever before participated. With her by his side, he was welcomed wherever he

---

1 Someone with an unconventional, nonconformist lifestyle.
2 See p. 68, note 3.

went. Even the little Chinese women in the midst of their babies, received him with gentle smiles, and the children solemnly munched his candies and repeated nursery rhymes for his edification.

He enjoyed it all, and so did Pan. They were both young and light-hearted. And when the afternoon was spent, there was always that high room open to the stars, with its China bowls full of flowers and its big colored lanterns, shedding a mellow light.

Sometimes there was music. A Chinese band played three evenings a week in the gilded restaurant beneath them, and the louder the gongs sounded and the fiddlers fiddled, the more delighted was Pan. Just below the restaurant was her father's bazaar. Occasionally Mun You would stroll upstairs and inquire of the young couple if there was anything needed to complete their felicity, and Pan would answer: "Thou only." Pan was very proud of her Chinese father. "I would rather have a Chinese for a father than a white man," she often told Mark Carson. The last time she had said that he had asked whom she would prefer for a husband, a white man or a Chinese. And Pan, for the first time since he had known her, had no answer for him.

II

IT was a cool, quiet evening, after a hot day. A new moon was in the sky.

"How beautiful above! How unbeautiful below!" exclaimed Mark Carson involuntarily.

He and Pan had been gazing down from their open retreat into the lantern-lighted, motley-thronged street beneath them.

"Perhaps it isn't very beautiful," replied Pan, "but it is here I live. It is my home." Her voice quivered a little.

He leaned towards her suddenly and grasped her hands.

"Pan," he cried, "you do not belong here. You are white— white."

"No! no!" protested Pan.

"You are," he asserted. "You have no right to be here."

"I was born here," she answered, "and the Chinese people look upon me as their own."

"But they do not understand you," he went on. "Your real self is alien to them. What interest have they in the books you read— the thoughts you think?"

"They have an interest in me," answered faithful Pan. "Oh, do not speak in that way any more."

"But I must," the young man persisted. "Pan, don't you see that you have got to decide what you will be—Chinese or white? You cannot be both."

"Hush! Hush!" bade Pan. "I do not love you when you talk to me like that."

A little Chinese boy brought tea and saffron cakes. He was a picturesque little fellow with a quaint manner of speech. Mark Carson jested merrily with him, while Pan holding a tea-bowl between her two small hands laughed and sipped.

When they were alone again, the silver stream and the crescent moon became the objects of their study. It was a very beautiful evening.

After a while Mark Carson, his hand on Pan's shoulder, sang:

"And forever, and forever,
As long as the river flows,
As long as the heart has passions,
As long as life has woes,
The moon and its broken reflection,
And its shadows shall appear,
As the symbol of love in heaven,
And its wavering image here."[1]

Listening to that irresistible voice singing her heart away, the girl broke down and wept. She was so young and so happy.

"Look up at me," bade Mark Carson. "Oh, Pan! Pan! Those tears prove that you are white."

Pan lifted her wet face.

"Kiss me, Pan," said he. It was the first time.

Next morning Mark Carson began work on the special-feature article which he had been promising his paper for some weeks.

III

"CURSED be his ancestors," bayed Man You.

He cast a paper at his daughter's feet and left the room.

Startled by her father's unwonted passion, Pan picked up the paper, and in the clear passionless light of the afternoon read that which forever after was blotted upon her memory.

---

1 From "The Bridge" (1845), a lyric poem by the popular American poet Henry Wadsworth Longfellow. "The Bridge" was set to music by several composers during the nineteenth century.

"Betrayed! Betrayed! Betrayed to be a betrayer!"

It burnt red hot; agony unrelieved by words, unassuaged by tears.

So till evening fell. Then she stumbled up the dark stairs which led to the high room open to the stars and tried to think it out. Someone had hurt her. Who was it? She raised her eyes. There shone: "Its Wavering Image." It helped her to lucidity. He had done it. Was it unconsciously dealt—that cruel blow? Ah, well did he know that the sword which pierced her through others, would carry with it to her own heart, the pain of all those others. None knew better than he that she, whom he had called "a white girl, a white woman," would rather that her own naked body and soul had been exposed, than that things, sacred and secret to those who loved her, should be cruelly unveiled and ruthlessly spread before the ridiculing and uncomprehending foreigner. And knowing all this so well, so well, he had carelessly sung her heart away, and with her kiss upon his lips, had smilingly turned and stabbed her. She, who was of the race that remembers.

IV

MARK CARSON, back in the city after an absence of two months, thought of Pan. He would see her that very evening. Dear little Pan, pretty Pan, clever Pan, amusing Pan; Pan, who was always so frankly glad to have him come to her; so eager to hear all that he was doing; so appreciative, so inspiring, so loving. She would have forgotten that article by now. Why should a white woman care about such things? Her true self was above it all. Had he not taught her *that* during the weeks in which they had seen so much of one another? True, his last lesson had been a little harsh, and as yet he knew not how she had taken it; but even if its roughness had hurt and irritated, there was a healing balm, a wizard's oil which none knew so well as he how to apply.

But for all these soothing reflections, there was an undercurrent of feeling which caused his steps to falter on his way to Pan. He turned into Portsmouth Square[1] and took a seat on one of the benches facing the fountain erected in memory of Robert Louis

---

1 A small park in San Francisco's Chinatown named after the *USS Portsmouth*, which seized the town of Yerba Buena (present-day San Francisco) in 1846 during the US–Mexican War.

Stevenson.[1] Why had Pan failed to answer the note he had written telling her of the assignment which would keep him out of town for a couple of months and giving her his address? Would Robert Louis Stevenson have known why? Yes—and so did Mark Carson. But though Robert Louis Stevenson would have boldly answered himself the question, Mark Carson thrust it aside, arose, and pressed up the hill.

"I knew they would not blame you, Pan!"

"Yes."

"And there was no word of you, dear. I was careful about that, not only for your sake, but for mine."

Silence.

"It is mere superstition anyway. These things have got to be exposed and done away with."

Still silence.

Mark Carson felt strangely chilled. Pan was not herself tonight. She did not even look herself. He had been accustomed to seeing her in American dress. Tonight she wore the Chinese costume. But for her clear-cut features she might have been a Chinese girl. He shivered.

"Pan," he asked, "why do you wear that dress?"

Within her sleeves Pan's small hands struggled together; but her face and voice were calm.

"Because I am a Chinese woman," she answered.

"You are not," cried Mark Carson, fiercely. "You cannot say that now, Pan. You are a white woman—white. Did your kiss not promise me that?"

"A white woman!" echoed Pan her voice rising high and clear to the stars above them. "I would not be a white woman for all the world. You are a white man. And what is a promise to a white man!"

---

1   Unveiled in 1897, this monument memorializes the Scottish writer Robert Louis Stevenson's frequent visits to Portsmouth Square when he moved to San Francisco in 1879. Mark Carson's meditations may be a response to the inscription on the monument, which includes the following advice: "TO KEEP A FEW FRIENDS BUT THESE WITHOUT CAPITULATION—ABOVE ALL ON THE SAME GRIM CONDITION TO KEEP FRIENDS WITH HIMSELF HERE IS A TASK FOR ALL THAT A MAN HAS OF FORTITUDE AND DELICACY." See Appendix D4 for a recent photograph of the monument.

When she was lying low, the element of Fire having raged so fiercely within her that it had almost shriveled up the childish frame, there came to the house of Man You a little toddler who could scarcely speak. Climbing upon Pan's couch, she pressed her head upon the sick girl's bosom. The feel of that little head brought tears.

"Lo!" said the mother of the toddler. "Thou wilt bear a child thyself some day, and all the bitterness of this will pass away."

And Pan, being a Chinese woman, was comforted.

The Gift of Little Me

THE schoolroom was decorated with banners and flags wrought in various colors. Chinese lanterns swung overhead. A big, green, porcelain frog with yellow eyes squatted in the centre of the teacher's desk. Tropical and native plants: azaleas, hyacinths, palms, and Chinese lilies, filled the air with their fragrance.

It was the day before the Chinese New Year of 18— and Miss McLeod's little scholars, in the decoration of their schoolroom, had expressed their love of quaint conceits and their appreciation of the beautiful. They were all in holiday attire. There was Han Wenti in sky-hued raiment and loose, flowing sleeves, upon each of which was embroidered a yellow dragon. Han Wenti's father was the Chief of his clan in America. There was San Kee, the son of the Americanized merchant, stiff and slim in American store clothes. Little Choy, on the girls' side, proudly wore a checked limousine Mother Hubbard gown,[1] while Fei and Sie looked like humming-birds in their native costume of bright-colored silks flowered with gold.

Miss McLeod's eyes wandered over the heap of gifts piled on three chairs before her desk, and over the heads of the young givers, to where on a back seat a little fellow in blue cotton tunic and pantaloons sat swinging a pair of white-soled shoes in a "don't care for anybody" fashion.

Little Me was looked upon almost as a criminal by his schoolfellows. He was the only scholar in all the school who failed to offer at the shrine of the Teacher, and the fact that he was the

---

1 A limousine is a cloak; a Mother Hubbard gown is a long, loose-fitting, long-sleeved gown with a high neck. Missionaries often introduced the Mother Hubbard gown to indigenous populations in order to cover as much skin as possible.

son of a man who dined on no richer dish than rice and soy gravy did not palliate his offense. There were other scholars who knew not the taste of mushrooms, bamboo shoots, and sucking pigs, yet who were unceasing in their offerings of paper mats, wild flowers, pebbles, strange insects, and other gifts possessing at least a sentimental value. The truth of the matter, however, was that Little Me was neither unappreciative nor unloving. He was simply afflicted with pride. If he could not give in the princely fashion of Hom Hing and Lee Chu, the sons of the richest merchants in Chinatown, he would not give at all.

Yet if Miss McLeod, in her Scotch heart, allowed herself a favorite amongst her scholars, it was Little Me. Many a time had she incurred the displeasure of the parents of Hom Hing and Lee Chu by rejecting the oft-times valuable presents of their chubby, complacent-faced sons. She had seen Little Me's eyes cloud and his small hands draw up in his sleeves when the pattering footsteps of the braided darlings of the rich led them, with their offerings, to her desk.

"Attention, children!" said Miss McLeod; and she made a little speech in which she thanked her scholars for their tokens of appreciation and affection, but impressed upon them that she prized as much a wooden image of his own carving from a boy who had nothing more to offer, as she did an ivory or jade figure from one whose father could afford to wear gold buttons; that a lichi from the orphan Amoy was as refreshing to her as a basket of oranges from the only daughter of the owner of many fruit ranches. The greatest of all gifts was beyond price. They must remember the story she had told them at Christmas time of the giving of a darling and only Son to a loved people. All the money in the world could not have paid for that dear little boy. He was a free gift.

Little Me stopped swinging his feet in their white-soled shoes. With solemn eyes and puckered brow he meditated over this speech.

The first day of the new year was kept with much rejoicing. There were gay times under the lanterns, quaint ceremonies, and fine feasting. The flutist came out with his flute, the banjo man with his banjo, and the fiddler with his fiddle. No child but had a piece of gold or silver given to him or her, and sweetmeats, loose-skinned oranges, and watermelon seeds were scattered around galore. Strains of music enlivened the dark alleys, and "flowers" or fireworks delighted both old and young. The Literary and

Benevolent Societies brought forth those of their number whose imagination and experiences gave them the power to portray the achievements of heroes, the despair of lovers, the blessings which fall to the lot of the filial son, and the terrible fate of the unduti-ful, and while the sun went down and long after it had set, groups of fascinated youths sat listening to tales of magic and enchant-ment.

In the midst of it all Little Me wandered around in his white-soled shoes, and thought of that other story—the story of the Babe.

On the second day of the Chinese New Year, Miss McLeod, her twine bag full to overflowing with little red parcels of joy, stopped before the door of the Chee house. As there was no response to her knock, she lifted the latch and entered a darkened room. By a couch in the furthest corner of the room a woman knelt, moaning and tearful. It was Chee A Tae, Little Me's mother. Little Me's proper name was Chee Ping. Miss McLeod touched her shoulder sympathetically. The woman shuddered and the low moans became heartrending cries and sobs. Did the teacher know that her baby was stolen? Some evil spirit had witched him away. Her husband, with some friends, was search-ing for the child; but she felt sure they would find him—never. She had burnt incense to "Mother" and besought the aid of the goddess of children;[1] but her prayers would not avail, because her husband had neglected that month to send his parents cash for ginseng and broth. He had tried his luck with the Gambling Cash Tiger[2] and failed. Had he been fortunate, his parents would have received twice their usual portion, but as it was, he had lost. And now the baby, the younger brother of Little Me, was lost too.

"How did it happen?" inquired Miss McLeod.

"We were alone—the babe and I," replied the Mother. "My man was visiting and Little Me was playing in the alley. I stepped over with a bowl of boiled rice and a pot of tea for old Sien Tau. We have not much for our own mouths, but it is well to begin the New Year by being kind to those who may not see another. The babe was sleeping when I last beheld him. When I returned,

---

1 "Mother" probably references Guanyin, the Buddhist bodhisattva asso-ciated with mercy, compassion, motherhood, and the granting of chil-dren.

2 Missionaries reported that gamblers in China worshiped carved images of a tiger grasping a coin or piece of cash, hoping it would bring them luck (Doolittle and Hood, 229).

whether he was asleep, awake, in the land of the living or in the spirit world, was withheld from me. A wolf—a tiger heart—alone knew."

This was truly a case needing sympathy. Miss McLeod did her best, and after a while Chee A Tae sat up and listened with some hope for her husband's footsteps. He came at last, a tired, gaunt-looking man, wearing in the face of the holiday, the blue cotton blouse and pantaloons of a working Chinaman, and a very dilapidated American slouch hat, around which he had wound his queue.[1] He was followed into the room by several of his countrymen who cast suspicious glances at the white woman present; but, upon recognition came forward, each in turn, and saluted her in American fashion. There were several points of difference between Miss McLeod and the other white teachers of Chinatown which had won for her the special favor of her pupil's parents. One was that though it was plain to all that she loved her work and taught the children committed to her charge with the utmost patience and care, she was not a child-cuddling and caressing woman. Another, that she had taken pains to learn the Chinese language before attempting to teach her own. Thirdly, she lived in Chinatown, and made herself at home amongst its denizens.

Chee A Tae was bitterly disappointed at seeing her husband without the babe. She arose from her couch, and pulling open the door, which the men had closed behind them, pointed them out again, crying: "Go, find my son! Go, find my son!"

Chee Ping the First turned upon her resentfully. "Woman," he cried, "that he is lost is your fault. I have searched with my eyes, ears, tongue, and limbs; but one might as well look for a pin at the bottom of the ocean."

The mother began to weep pitifully. "'Tis the Gambling Cash Tiger," she sobbed. "'Twas he who caused you to forget your parents and ill fortune has followed therefor. A-ya, A-ya, A-ya. My heart is as heavy as the blackest heavens!"

"What nonsense!" exclaimed Miss McLeod, thinking it time to interfere. "The child cannot be far away. Let us all hunt and see who will find him first."

A crowd of men, women, and children had gathered outside the door, most of them in gay holiday attire. At these words of the teacher there was an assenting babel of voices, followed by a darting into passages, up stairways, and behind doors. Lanterns

1 See p. 64, note 1.

were lit for the exploration of underground cellars, stores, closets, stairways, balconies. Not a hole in the vicinity of the Chee dwelling but was penetrated by keen eyes. Rich and poor alike joined in the search, a yellow-robed priest from the joss house and one of the Chiefs of the Six Companies being conspicuously interested.

The mother, following in the footsteps of Miss McLeod, kept up a plaintive wailing. "A-ya, my young bud, my jade jewel, my peach bloom. Little hands, veined like young leaves; voice like the breath of a zephyr. Alas, the fates are against me! You are lost to your poor mother who is without resource and bound with fetters. Death would be sweet indeed; but that boon is denied."

The day wore on and evening gradually stole upon them, followed by night. The wind blew in gusts, but the moon had risen and was shining bright so that there was a kind of moonlight even in the dark alleys. The main portion of Chinatown had been thoroughly scoured, and most attention was now being given to the hills which crept up to Powell Street.[1] It was in a top story of a half-way hill tenement that Miss McLeod's room was located; a cozy little place, for all its apparently comfortless environment. When the wind began to blow bleak from the Bay, her thoughts drifted longingly to her easy chair and cheery grate fire; but only for a moment. Until the baby was found she could know no rest. The distress of these Chinese people was hers; their troubles also. Had she not adopted them as her own when kinfolk had failed her? Their grateful appreciation of the smallest service; their undemonstrative but faithful affection had been as balm to a heart wounded by the indifference and bruised by the ingratitude of those to whom she had devoted her youth, her strength, and her abilities.

Suddenly a cry was heard. Wang Hom Hing, a merchant Chinaman, who had taken command of the search party detailed to explore the upper part of Chinatown, appeared at the door of a rickety tenement—the one in which Miss McLeod had built her nest—and waved, under the lanterns, a Chinese flag, signal that the child was found.

Pell-mell the Chinese rushed towards their country's emblem. With the exception of Miss McLeod, not a single white person, not even a policeman, had been impressed into the search.

---

1 Powell Street is on the western, uphill border of San Francisco's Chinatown.

Leading the rushing crowd was Chee Ping the First; in the midst panted A Tae and her white woman friend, and in the wake of all calmly and quietly pattered Little Me. Though usually the chief object of his parents' attention, this day, or rather night, he seemed altogether forgotten.

Up several flights of stairs streamed the searchers, while from every door on the landings, men, women, and children peered out, inquiring what it all meant. Hemmed in by numbers, the teacher found herself at last blocked outside her own room.

Someone was talking loudly and excitedly. It was Wang Hom Hing, the father of her pupil of that name, and the uncle of another pupil, Lee Chu. What was he saying? The teacher strained her ears to catch his words. Gracious Heavens! He was declaring that she had stolen the child; that it lay in her room, hidden under the coverlets of her bed—positive evidence that she who, under the guise of friendship, had ingratiated herself into their hearts and homes, was in reality a secret enemy.

"Trust her no more—this McLeod, Jean," he cried. "Though her smile is as sweet as honey, her heart is like a razor."

There was an ominous silence after this speech.

Wang Hom Hing was a pompous man whose conceit had been inflated by the flattery of wily white people, who, unlike the undiplomatic Scotch woman, did discriminate between the gifts of the rich and poor. Nevertheless, as President of the Water Lily Club and Secretary of the Society of Celestial Reason, he was a man of influence in Chinatown, and this was painfully impressed upon the teacher when Chee A Tae cast upon her a shuddering glance and fell swooning into the arms of a stout countrywoman behind her.

Now, the blood of Scottish chieftains throbbed in Miss McLeod's veins; and it was this brave blood which, when all the ships in which she had stored her early hopes and dreams had one by one been lost, had borne up her soul above the stormy flood, and helped her to launch another ship in a sea both wild and strange. That ship had weathered many a gale. Should she, after steering it safely into port, allow it to founder—in harbor? Never! That ship was the safe-deposit bank for all her womanly affection and energy. It carried her Chinese work—the work in which she had found consolation, peace and happiness. Hom Hing should not wreck it without some effort on her part to save.

The intrepid woman, nerved by these thoughts, pushed through the human wall before her and reached the speaker's side. Sleeping in the midst of the tumult lay the babe, its little hand under its cheek. So pretty a picture that even in her stress and excitement she paused for a moment to wonder and admire.

Then she faced the big Chinaman in his gorgeous holiday robes, her small, slight form drawn to its fullest height, her light blue eyes ablaze.

"Wang Hom Hing," she cried. "You know you are trying to make my friends believe what you do not believe yourself! I know no more than its mother does about how the dear baby came here."

The Chinese merchant shrugged his shoulders insolently, and addressing the people again, asked them to judge for themselves. The child had been stolen. The teacher had pretended to aid in a search, yet it had been he and not she who had led the way to her room where it had been found.

Low mutterings were heard throughout the place; but after they had subsided, the white woman, looking around for a friendly face, was surprised and cheered to find many. Her spirits rose.

"How was I to know the child lay in my room?" she indignantly inquired. "I left the place in the early morning. It has been brought there since by someone unknown to me."

Wang Hom Hing laughed scornfully as he moved away, his revenge, as he thought, complete.

The father of the babe raised his son in his arms and passed him on to the mother who stood with arms outstretched. Clutching the child convulsively, she gazed with horrorstruck eyes at the teacher.

"Friends," cried the white woman, raising her voice in a last effort, "will you allow that man to turn from me your hearts? Have you not known me long enough to believe that though I cannot explain to you how the baby came to be in my room, yet I am innocent of having brought it there. A Tae"—addressing the mother—"can you believe that I would harm one hair of your baby's head?"

A Tae hesitated, her eyes full of tears. She had loved the teacher, but Wang Hom Hing had sown a poisonous seed in her superstitious mind. Miss McLeod noted her hesitation with a sinking of the heart that was almost despair.

Up hobbled a very old and very tiny woman.

"McLeod, Jean," she cried, "your gracious and noble qualities of mind and soul merit a happier New Year's Day than this. Wang Hom Hing's words cannot deceive old Sien Tau."

Ah! The Scotch woman grasped gratefully the old Chinese woman's hand. She could not speak for the tickle in her throat.

Then spake A Tae: "Teacher, forgive me," besought she.

And the teacher smiled her answer.

A number of men and women came forward, looked into the teacher's face, thanked her for past kindnesses, and expressed their confidence in her.

"McLeod, Jean," declared an old man, "you are a hundred women good."

Which was the highest compliment that Jean McLeod had ever received.

"You are wrong, mother!" said she, turning with a beaming face to old Sien Tau. "This is the happiest day I have known."

Explained the father of the babe: "The gods, seeing my unworthiness, took from me to give to you."

And Little Me, straggling to the teacher's side, piped in the language she herself had taught him:

"I have one brother. I love him all over. You say baby boy best gift, so I give him to you when my father and mother not see. Little Me give better than Lee Chu and Hom Hing."

It was some time before the tumult occasioned by Little Me's boastful but sweet confession subsided. It had been heard by all, but was understood wholly by none save the teacher.

That when no watchful eye was there to see, the baby had been carried in Little Me's sturdy arms from under the home roof to the teacher's tenement room, was made plain to everyone by the child himself. But it devolved upon Miss McLeod, in order to save her little scholar from obviously justifiable paternal wrath, to explain his reason for the kidnapping, and this she did so clearly and eloquently that the father, raising his first born to his knee, declared in English: "I proud of him. He Number One scholar," while the mother fondly smiled.

Little Me looked at the baby in his mother's lap, and then at the teacher. His eyes filled with tears.

"You not like what I give you well enough to keep him," he sobbed.

"Yes, yes," consoled Miss McLeod. "I like him so well that I put him away in my heart where I keep the baby of my story. Don't you remember? That was what the Father of the story gave the baby for. To be kept in the people's hearts after he had gone back to Him!"

"Ah, yes," responded the child, his face brightening. "You keep my brother in your heart and I keep him in the house with me and my father and mother. That best of all!"

The Story of One White Woman Who Married a Chinese

I

WHY did I marry Liu Kanghi, a Chinese? Well, in the first place, because I loved him; in the second place, because I was weary of working, struggling and fighting with the world; in the third place, because my child needed a home.

My first husband was an American fifteen years older than myself. For a few months I was very happy with him. I had been a working girl—a stenographer. A home of my own filled my heart with joy. It was a pleasure to me to wait upon James, cook him nice little dinners and suppers, read to him little pieces from the papers and magazines, and sing and play to him my little songs and melodies. And for a few months he seemed to be perfectly contented. I suppose I was a novelty to him, he having lived a bachelor existence until he was thirty-four. But it was not long before he left off smiling at my little jokes, grew restive and cross when I teased him, and when I tried to get him to listen to a story in which I was interested and longed to communicate, he would bid me not bother him. I was quick to see the change and realize that there was a gulf of differences between us. Nevertheless, I loved and was proud of him. He was considered a very bright and well-informed man, and although his parents had been uneducated working people he had himself been through the public schools. He was also an omnivorous reader of socialistic and new-thought literature. Woman suffrage was one of his particular hobbies. Whenever I had a magazine around he would pick it up and read aloud to me the columns of advice to women who were ambitious to become comrades to men and walk shoulder to shoulder with their brothers. Once I ventured to remark that much as I admired a column of men keeping step together, yet men and women thus ranked would, to my mind, make a very unbeautiful and disorderly spectacle. He frowned and answered that I did not understand him, and was too frivolous. He would often draw my attention to newspaper reports concerning women of marked business ability and enterprise. Once I told him that I did not admire clever business women, as I had usually found them, and so had other girls of my acquaintance, not nearly so kind-hearted, generous, and helpful as the humble drudges of the world—the ordinary working women. His answer to this was that I was jealous and childish.

But, in spite of his unkind remarks and evident contempt for me, I wished to please him. He was my husband and I loved him. Many an afternoon, when through with my domestic duties, did I spend in trying to acquire a knowledge of labor politics, socialism, woman suffrage, and baseball, the things in which he was most interested.

It was hard work, but I persevered until one day. It was about six months after our marriage. My husband came home a little earlier than usual, and found me engaged in trying to work out problems in subtraction and addition. He laughed sneeringly. "Give it up, Minnie," said he. "You weren't built for anything but taking care of kids. Gee! But there's a woman at our place who has a head for figures that makes her worth over a hundred dollars a month. *Her* husband would have a chance to develop himself."

This speech wounded me. I knew it was James' ambition to write a book on social reform.

The next day, unknown to my husband, I called upon the wife of the man who had employed me as stenographer before I was married, and inquired of her whether she thought I could get back my old position.

"But, my dear," she exclaimed, "your husband is receiving a good salary! Why should you work?"

I told her that my husband had in mind the writing of a book on social reform, and I wished to help him in his ambition by earning some money towards its publication.

"Social reform!" she echoed. "What sort of social reformer is he who would allow his wife to work when he is well able to support her!"

She bade me go home and think no more of an office position. I was disappointed. I said: "Oh! I wish I could earn some money for James. If I were earning money, perhaps he would not think me so stupid."

"Stupid, my dear girl! You are one of the brightest little women I know," kindly comforted Mrs. Rogers.

But I knew differently and went on to tell her of my inability to figure with my husband how much he had made on certain sales, of my lack of interest in politics, labor questions, woman suffrage, and world reformation. "Oh! I cried, "I am a narrow-minded woman. All I care for is for my husband to love me and be kind to me, for life to be pleasant and easy, and to be able to help a wee bit the poor and sick around me."

Mrs. Rogers looked very serious as she told me that there were differences of opinion as to what was meant by "narrow-mindedness," and that the majority of men had no wish to drag their wives into all their business perplexities, and found more comfort in a woman who was unlike rather than like themselves. Only that morning her husband had said to her: "I hate a woman who tries to get into every kink of a man's mind, and who must be forever at his elbow meddling with all his affairs."

I went home comforted. Perhaps after a while James would feel and see as did Mr. Rogers. Vain hope!

My child was six weeks old when I entered business life again as stenographer for Rutherford & Rutherford. My salary was fifty dollars a month—more than I had ever earned before, and James was well pleased, for he had feared that it would be difficult for me to obtain a paying place after having been out of practice for so long. This fifty dollars paid for all our living expenses, with the exception of rent, so that James would be able to put by his balance against the time when his book would be ready for publication.

He began writing his book, and Miss Moran the young woman bookkeeper at his place collaborated with him. They gave three evenings a week to the work, sometimes four. She came one evening when the baby was sick and James had gone for the doctor. She looked at the child with the curious eyes of one who neither loved nor understood children. "There is no necessity for its being sick," said she. "There must be an error somewhere." I made no answer, so she went on: "Sin, sorrow, and sickness all mean the same thing. We have no disease that we do not deserve, no trouble which we do not bring upon ourselves."

I did not argue with her. I knew that I could not; but as I looked at her standing there in the prime of her life and strength, broad-shouldered, masculine-featured, and, as it seemed to me, heartless, I disliked her more than I had ever disliked anyone before. My own father had died after suffering for many years from a terrible malady, contracted while doing his duty as a physician and surgeon. And my little innocent child! What had sin to do with its measles?

When James came in she discussed with him the baseball game which had been played that afternoon, and also a woman suffrage meeting which she had attended the evening before.

After she had gone he seemed to be quite exhilarated. "That's a great woman!" he remarked.

"I do not think so!" I answered him. "One who would take from the sorrowful and suffering their hope of a happier existence hereafter, and add to their trials on earth by branding them as objects of aversion and contempt, is not only not a great woman but, to my mind no woman at all."

He picked up a paper and walked into another room.

"What do you think now?" I cried after him.

"What would be the use of my explaining to .you?" he returned. "You wouldn't understand."

How my heart yearned over my child those days! I would sit before the typewriter and in fancy hear her crying for her mother. Poor, sick little one, watched over by a strange woman, deprived of her proper nourishment. While I took dictation from my employer I thought only of her. The result, of course, was that I lost my place. My husband showed his displeasure at this in various ways, and as the weeks went by and I was unsuccessful in obtaining another position, he became colder and more indifferent. He was neither a drinking nor an abusive man; but he could say such cruel and cutting things that I would a hundred times rather have been beaten and ill-used than compelled, as I was, to hear them. He even made me feel it a disgrace to be a woman and a mother. Once he said to me: "If you had had ambition of the right sort you would have perfected yourself in your stenography so that you could have taken cases in court. There's a little fortune in that business."

I was acquainted with a woman stenographer who reported divorce cases and who had described to me the work, so I answered: "I would rather die of hunger, my baby in my arms, then report divorce proceedings under the eyes of men in a court house."

"Other women, as good as you, have done and are doing it," he retorted.

"Other women, perhaps better than I, have done and are doing it," I replied, "but all women are not alike. I am not that kind."

"That's so," said he. "Well, they are the kind who are up to date. You are behind the times."

One evening I left James and Miss Moran engaged with their work and went across the street to see a sick friend. When I returned I let myself into the house very softly for fear of awakening the baby whom I had left sleeping. As I stood in the hall I heard my husband's voice in the sitting-room. This is what he was saying:

"I am a lonely man. There is no companionship between me and my wife."

"Nonsense!" answered Miss Moran, as I thought a little impatiently. "Look over this paragraph, please, and tell me if you do not think it would be well to have it follow after the one ending with the words 'ultimate concord,' in place of that beginning with 'These great principles.'"

"I cannot settle my mind upon the work tonight," said James in a sort of thick, tired voice. "I want to talk to you—to win your sympathy—your love."

I heard a chair pushed back. I knew Miss Moran had arisen.

"Good night!" I heard her say. "Much as I would like to see this work accomplished, I shall come no more!"

"But, my God! You cannot throw the thing up at this late date."

"I can and I will. Let me pass, sir."

"If there were no millstone around my neck, you would not say, 'Let me pass, sir,' in that tone of voice."

The next I heard was a heavy fall. Miss Moran had knocked my big husband down.

I pushed open the door. Miss Moran, cool and collected, was pulling on her gloves. James was struggling to his feet.

"Oh, Mrs. Carson!" exclaimed the former. "Your husband fell over the stool. Wasn't it stupid of him!"

James, of course, got his divorce six months after I deserted him. He did not ask for the child, and I was allowed to keep it.

II

I WAS on my way to the waterfront, the baby in my arms. I was walking quickly, for my state of mind was such that I could have borne twice my burden and not have felt it. Just as I turned down a hill which led to the docks, someone touched my arm and I heard a voice say:

"Pardon me, lady; but you have dropped your baby's shoe!"

"Oh, yes!" I answered, taking the shoe mechanically from an outstretched hand, and pushing on.

I could hear the waves lapping against the pier when the voice again fell upon my ear.

"If you go any further, lady, you will fall into the water!"

My answer was a step forward.

A strong hand was laid upon my arm and I was swung around against my will.

"Poor little baby," went on the voice, which was unusually soft for a man's. "Let me hold him!"

I surrendered my child to the voice.

"Better come over where it is light and you can see where to walk!"

I allowed myself to be led into the light.

Thus I met Liu Kanghi, the Chinese who afterwards became my husband. I followed him, obeyed him, trusted him from the very first. It never occurred to me to ask myself what manner of man was succoring me. I only knew that he was a man, and that I was being cared for as no one had ever cared for me since my father died. And my grim determination to leave a world which had been cruel to me, passed away—and in its place I experienced a strange calmness and content.

"I am going to take you to the house of a friend of mine," he said as he preceded me up the hill, the baby in his arms.

"You will not mind living with Chinese people?" he added.

An electric light under which we were passing flashed across his face.

I did not recoil—not even at first. It may have been because he was wearing American clothes, wore his hair cut, and, even to my American eyes, appeared a good-looking young man—and it may have been because of my troubles; but whatever it was I answered him, and I meant it: "I would much rather live with Chinese than Americans."

He did not ask me why, and I did not tell him until long afterwards the story of my unhappy marriage, my desertion of the man who had made it impossible for me to remain under his roof; the shame of the divorce, the averted faces of those who had been my friends; the cruelty of the world; the awful struggle for an existence for myself and child; sickness followed by despair.

The Chinese family with which he placed me were kind, simple folk. The father had been living in America for more than twenty years. The family consisted of his wife, a grown daughter, and several small sons and daughters, all of whom had been born in America. They made me very welcome and adored the baby. Liu Jusong, the father, was a working jeweler; but, because of an accident by which he had lost the use of one hand, was partially incapacitated for work. Therefore, their family depended for maintenance chiefly upon their kinsman, Liu Kanghi, the Chinese who had brought me to them.

"We love much our cousin," said one of the little girls to me one day. "He teaches us so many games and brings us toys and sweets."

As soon as I recovered from the attack of nervous prostration which laid me low for over a month after being received into the Liu home my mind began to form plans for my own and my child's maintenance. One morning I put on my hat and jacket and told Mrs. Liu I would go down town and take an application for work as a stenographer at the different typewriting offices. She pleaded with me to wait a week longer—until, as she said, "your limbs are more fortified with strength"; but I assured her that I felt myself well able to begin to do for myself, and that I was anxious to repay some little part of the expense I had been to them.

"For all we have done for you," she answered, "our cousin has paid us doublefold."

"No money can recompense your kindness to myself and child," I replied; "but if it is your cousin to whom I am indebted for board and lodging, all the greater is my anxiety to repay what I owe."

When I returned to the house that evening, tired out with my quest for work, I found Liu Kanghi tossing ball with little Fong in the front porch.

Mrs. Liu bustled out to meet me and began scolding in motherly fashion.

"Oh, why you go down town before you strong enough? See! You look all sick again!" said she.

She turned to Liu Kanghi and said something in Chinese. He threw the ball back to the boy and came toward me, his face grave and concerned.

"Please be so good as to take my cousin's advice," he urged.

"I am well enough to work now," I replied, "and I cannot sink deeper into your debt."

"You need not," said he. "I know a way by which you can quickly pay me off and earn a good living without wearing yourself out and leaving the baby all day. My cousin tells me that you can create most beautiful flowers on silk, velvet, and linen. Why not then you do some of that work for my store? I will buy all you can make."

"Oh!" I exclaimed, "I should be only too glad to do such work! But do you really think I can earn a living in that way?"

"You certainly can," was his reply. "I am requiring an embroiderer, and if you will do the work for me I will try to pay you what it is worth."

So I gladly gave up my quest for office work. I lived in the Liu Jusong house and worked for Liu Kanghi. The days, weeks, and months passed peacefully and happily. Artistic needlework had always been my favorite occupation, and when it became a source both of remuneration and pleasure, I began to feel that life was worth living, after all. I watched with complacency my child grow amongst the little Chinese children. My life's experience had taught me that the virtues do not all belong to the whites. I was interested in all that concerned the Liu household, became acquainted with all their friends, and lost altogether the prejudice against the foreigner in which I had been reared.

I had been living thus more than a year when, one afternoon as I was walking home from Liu Kanghi's store on Kearney Street,[1] a parcel of silks and floss[2] under my arm, and my little girl trudging by my side, I came face to face with James Carson.

"Well, now," said he, planting himself in front of me, "you are looking pretty well. How are you making out?"

I caught up my child and pushed past him without a word. When I reached the Liu house I was trembling in every limb, so great was my dislike and fear of the man who had been my husband.

About a week later a letter came to the house addressed to me. It read:

204 BUCHANAN STREET

DEAR MINNIE,—If you are willing to forget the past and make up, I am, too. I was surprised to see you the other day, prettier than ever and much more of a woman. Let me know your mind at an early date.

Your affectionate husband,

JAMES

I ignored this letter, but a heavy fear oppressed me. Liu Kanghi, who called the evening of the day I received it, remarked as he arose to greet me that I was looking troubled, and hoped that it was not the embroidery flowers.

---

1   Kearny Street is at the eastern border of San Francisco's Chinatown, and separates it from the financial district.
2   Thread for embroidery.

"It is the shadow from my big hat," I answered lightly. I was dressed for going down town with Mrs. Liu who was preparing her eldest daughter's trousseau.[1]

"Some day," said Liu Kanghi earnestly, "I hope that you will tell to me all that is in your heart and mind."

I found comfort in his kind face.

"If you will wait until I return, I will tell you all tonight," I answered.

Strange as it may seem, although I had known Liu Kanghi now for more than a year, I had had little talk alone with him, and all he knew about me was what he had learned from Mrs. Liu; namely, that I, was a divorced woman who, when saved from self-destruction, was homeless and starving.

That night, however, after hearing my story, he asked me to be his wife. He said: "I love you and would protect you from all trouble. Your child shall be as my own."

I replied: "I appreciate your love and kindness, but I cannot answer you just yet. Be my friend for a little while longer."

"Do you have for me the love feeling?" he asked.

"I do not know," I answered truthfully.

Another letter came. It was written in a different spirit from the first and contained a threat about the child.

There seemed but one course open to me. That was to leave my Chinese friends. I did. With much sorrow and regret I bade them goodbye, and took lodgings in a part of the city far removed from the outskirts of Chinatown where my home had been with the Lius. My little girl pined for her Chinese playmates, and I myself felt strange and lonely; but I knew that if I wished to keep my child I could no longer remain with my friends.

I still continued working for Liu Kanghi, and carried my embroidery to his store in the evening after the little one had been put to sleep. He usually escorted me back; but never asked to be allowed, and I never invited him, to visit me, or even enter the house. I was a young woman, and alone, and what I had suffered from scandal since I had left James Carson had made me wise.

It was a cold, wet evening in November when he accosted me once again. I had run over to a delicatessen store at the corner of the block where I lived. As I stepped out, his burly figure loomed up in the gloom before me. I started back with a little cry, but he grasped my arm and held it.

---

1 Set of clothing and accessories assembled by a bride in preparation for her wedding.

"Walk beside me quietly if you do not wish to attract attention," said he, "and by God, if you do, I will take the kid tonight!"

"You dare not!" I answered. "You have no right to her whatever. She is my child and I have supported her for the last two years alone."

"Alone! What will the judges say when I tell them about the Chinaman?"

"What will the judges say!" I echoed. "What can they say? Is there any disgrace in working for a Chinese merchant and receiving pay for my labor?"

"And walking in the evening with him, and living for over a year in a house for which he paid the rent. Ha! ha! ha! Ha! ha! ha!"

His laugh was low and sneering. He had evidently been making enquiries concerning the Liu family, and also watching me for some time. How a woman can loathe and hate the man she has once loved!

We were nearing my lodgings. Perhaps the child had awakened and was crying for me. I would not, however, have entered the house, had he not stopped at the door and pushed it open.

"Lead the way upstairs!" said he. "I want to see the kid."

"You shall not," I cried. In my desperation I wrenched myself from his grasp and faced him, blocking the stairs.

"If you use violence," I declared, "the lodgers will come to my assistance. They know me!"

He released my arm.

"Bah!" said he. "I've no use for the kid. It is you I'm after getting reconciled to. Don't you know, Minnie, that once your husband, always your husband? Since I saw you the other day on the street, I have been more in love with you than ever before. Suppose we forget all and begin over again!"

Though the tone of his voice had softened, my fear of him grew greater. I would have fled up the stairs had he not again laid his hand on my arm.

"Answer me, girl," said he.

And in spite of my fear, I shook off his hand and answered him: "No husband of mine are you, either legally or morally. And I have no feeling whatever for you other than contempt."

"Ah! So you have sunk!"—his expression was evil—"The oily little Chink has won you!"

I was no longer afraid of him.

"Won me!" I cried, unheeding who heard me. "Yes, honorably and like a man. And what are you that dare sneer at one like him. For all your six feet of grossness, your small soul cannot measure up to his great one. You were unwilling to protect and care for the woman who was your wife or the little child you caused to come into this world; but he succored and saved the stranger woman, treated her as a woman, with reverence and respect; gave her child a home, and made them both independent, not only of others but of himself. Now, hearing you insult him behind his back, I know, what I did not know before—that I love him, and all I have to say to you is, Go!"

And James Carson went. I heard of him again but once. That was when the papers reported his death of apoplexy while exercising at a public gymnasium.

Loving Liu Kanghi, I became his wife, and though it is true that there are many Americans who look down upon me for so becoming, I have never regretted it. No, not even when men cast upon me the glances they cast upon sporting women.[1] I accept the lot of the American wife of an humble Chinaman in America. The happiness of the man who loves me is more to me than the approval or disapproval of those who in my dark days left me to die like a dog. My Chinese husband has his faults. He is hot-tempered and, at times, arbitrary; but he is always a man, and has never sought to take away from me the privilege of being but a woman. I can lean upon and trust in him. I feel him behind me, protecting and caring for me, and that, to an ordinary woman like myself, means more than anything else.

Only when the son of Liu Kanghi lays his little head upon my bosom do I question whether I have done wisely. For my boy, the son of the Chinese man, is possessed of a childish wisdom which brings the tears to my eyes; and as he stands between his father and myself, like yet unlike us both, so will he stand in after years between his father's and his mother's people. And if there is no kindliness nor understanding between them, what will my boy's fate be?

Her Chinese Husband

Sequel to the Story of the White Woman Who Married a Chinese

NOW that Liu Kanghi is no longer with me, I feel that it will ease my heart to record some memories of him—if I can. The task,

---

1 A euphemism for prostitutes.

though calling to me, is not an easy one, so throng to my mind the invincible proofs of his love for me, the things he has said and done. My memories of him are so vivid and pertinacious, my thoughts of him so tender.

To my Chinese husband I could go with all my little troubles and perplexities; to him I could talk as women love to do at times of the past and the future, the mysteries of religion, of life and death. He was not above discussing such things with me. With him I was never strange or embarrassed. My Chinese husband was simple in his tastes. He liked to hear a good story, and though unlearned in a sense, could discriminate between the good and bad in literature. This came of his Chinese education. He told me one day that he thought the stories in the Bible were more like Chinese than American stories, and added: "If you had not told me what you have about it, I should say that it was composed by the Chinese." Music had a soothing though not a deep influence over him. It could not sway his mind, but he enjoyed it just as he did a beautiful picture. Because I was interested in fancy work, so also was he. I can see his face, looking so grave and concerned, because one day by accident I spilt some ink on a piece of embroidery I was working. If he came home in the evenings and found me tired and out of sorts, he would cook the dinner himself, and go about it in such a way that I felt that he rather enjoyed showing off his skill as a cook. The next evening, if he found everything ready, he would humorously declare himself much disappointed that I was so exceedingly well.

At such times a gray memory of James Carson would arise. How his cold anger and contempt, as exhibited on like occasions, had shriveled me up in the long ago. And then—I would fall to musing on the difference between the two men as lovers and husbands.

James Carson had been much more of an ardent lover than ever had been Liu Kanghi. Indeed it was his passion, real or feigned, which had carried me off my feet. When wooing he had constantly reproached me with being cold, unfeeling, a marble statue, and so forth; and I, poor, ignorant little girl, would wonder how it was I appeared so when I felt so differently. For I had given James Carson my first love. Upon him my life had been concentrated as it has never been concentrated upon any other. Yet—!

There was nothing feigned about my Chinese husband. Simple and sincere as he was before marriage, so was he afterwards. As my union with James Carson had meant misery, bitterness, and narrowness, so my union with Liu Kanghi meant, on the whole, happiness, health, and development. Yet the former, according to American ideas, had been an educated broad-minded man; the other, just an ordinary Chinaman.

But the ordinary Chinaman that I would show to you was the sort of man that children, birds, animals, and some women love. Every morning he would go to the window and call to his pigeons, and they would flock around him, hearing and responding to his whistling and cooing. The rooms we lived in had been his rooms ever since he had come to America. They were above his store, and large and cool. The furniture had been brought from China, but there was nothing of tinsel about it. Dark wood, almost black, carved and antique, some of the pieces set with mother-of-pearl. On one side of the inner room stood a case of books and an ancestral tablet. I have seen Liu Kanghi touch the tablet with reverence, but the faith of his fathers was not strong enough to cause him to bow before it. The elegant simplicity of these rooms had surprised me much when I was first taken to them. I looked at him: then, standing for a moment by the window, a solitary pigeon peeking in at him, perhaps wondering who had come to divert from her her friend's attention. So had he lived since he had come to this country—quietly and undisturbed—from twenty years of age to twenty-five. I felt myself an intruder. A feeling of pity for the boy—for such he seemed in his enthusiasm—arose in my breast. Why had I come to confuse his calm? Was it ordained, as he declared?

My little girl loved him better than she loved me. He took great pleasure in playing with her, curling her hair over his fingers, tying her sash, and all the simple tasks from which so many men turn aside.

Once the baby got hold of a set rat trap, and was holding it in such a way that the slightest move would have released the spring and plunged the cruel steel into her tender arms. Kanghi's eyes and mine beheld her thus at the same moment. I stood transfixed with horror. Kanghi quietly went up to the child and took from her the trap. Then he asked me to release his hand. I almost fainted when I saw it. "It was the only way," said he. We had to send for the doctor, and even as it was, came very near having a case of blood poisoning.

I have heard people say that he was a keen business man, this Liu Kanghi, and I imagine that he was. I did not, however, discuss his business with him. All I was interested in were the pretty things and the women who would come in and jest with him. He could jest too. Of course, the women did not know that I was his wife. Once a woman in rich clothes gave him her card and asked him to call upon her. After she had left he passed the card to me. I tore it up. He took those things as a matter of course, and was not affected by them. "They are a part of Chinatown life," he explained.

He was a member of the Reform Club,[1] a Chinese social club, and the Chinese Board of Trade. He liked to discuss business affairs and Chinese and American politics with his countrymen, and occasionally enjoyed an evening away from me. But I never needed to worry over him.

He had his littlenesses as well as his bignesses, had Liu Kanghi. For instance, he thought he knew better about what was good for my health and other things, purely personal, than I did myself, and if my ideas opposed or did not tally with his, he would very vigorously denounce what he called "the foolishness of women." If he admired a certain dress, he would have me wear it on every occasion possible, and did not seem to be able to understand that it was not always suitable.

"Wear the dress with the silver lines," he said to me one day somewhat authoritatively. I was attired for going out, but not as he wished to see me. I answered that the dress with the silver lines was unsuitable for a long and dusty ride on an open car.

"Never mind," said he, "whether it is unsuitable or not. I wish you to wear it."

"All right," I said. "I will wear it, but I will stay at home."

I stayed at home, and so did he.

At another time, he reproved me for certain opinions I had expressed in the presence of some of his countrymen. "You should not talk like that," said he. "They will think you are a bad woman."

My white blood rose at that, and I answered him in a way which grieves me to remember. For Kanghi had never meant to insult or hurt me. Imperious by nature, he often spoke before he thought—and he was so boyishly anxious for me to appear in the best light possible before his own people.

There were other things too: a sort of childish jealousy and suspicion which it was difficult to allay. But a woman can forgive much to a man, the sincerity and strength of whose love makes her own, though true, seem slight and mean.

---

1 A reference to the Chinese Reform Party led by Liang Qui Chao, which advocated for liberal reforms in China.

Yes, life with Liu Kanghi was not without its trials and tribulations. There was the continual uncertainty about his own life here in America, the constant irritation caused by the assumption of the white men that a white woman does not love her Chinese husband, and their actions accordingly; also sneers and offensive remarks. There was also on Liu Kanghi's side an acute consciousness that, though belonging to him as his wife, yet in a sense I was not his, but of the dominant race, which claimed, even while it professed to despise me. This consciousness betrayed itself in words and ways which filled me with a passion of pain and humiliation. "Kanghi," I would sharply say, for I had to cloak my tenderness, "do not talk to me like that. You are my superior ... I would not love you if you were not."

But in spite of all I could do or say, it was there between us: that strange, invisible—what? Was it the barrier of race—that consciousness?

Sometimes he would talk about returning to China. The thought filled me with horror. I had heard rumors of secondary wives. One afternoon the cousin of Liu Kanghi, with whom I had lived, came to see me, and showed me a letter which she had received from a little Chinese girl who had been born and brought up in America until the age of ten. The last paragraph in the letter read: "Emma and I are very sad and wish we were back in America." Kanghi's cousin explained that the father of the little girls, having no sons, had taken to himself another wife, and the new wife lived with the little girls and their mother.

That was before my little boy was born. That evening I told Kanghi that he need never expect me to go to China with him.

"You see," I began, "I look upon you as belonging to me."

He would not let me say more. After a while he said: "It is true that in China a man may and occasionally does take a secondary wife, but that custom is custom, not only because sons are denied to the first wife, but because the first wife is selected by parents and guardians before a man is hardly a man. If a Chinese marries for love, his life is a filled-up cup, and he wants no secondary wife. No, not even for sake of a son. Take, for example, me, your great husband."

I sometimes commented upon his boyish ways and appearance, which was the reason why, when he was in high spirits, he would call himself my "great husband." He was not boyish always. I have seen him, when shouldering the troubles of kinfolk, the quarrels of his clan, and other responsibilities, acting and looking like a man of twice his years.

But for all the strange marriage customs of my husband's people I considered them far more moral in their lives than the majority of Americans. I expressed myself thus to Liu Kanghi, and he replied: "The American people think higher. If only more of them lived up to what they thought, the Chinese would not be so confused in trying to follow their leadership."

If ever a man rejoiced over the birth of his child, it was Liu Kanghi. The boy was born with a veil over his face.[1] "A prophet!" cried the old mulatto Jewess who nursed me. "A prophet has come into the world."

She told this to his father when he came to look upon him, and he replied: "He is my son; that is all I care about." But he was so glad, and there was feasting and rejoicing with his Chinese friends for over two weeks. He came in one evening and found me weeping over my poor little boy. I shall never forget the expression on his face.

"Oh, shame!" he murmured, drawing my head down to his shoulder. "What is there to weep about? The child is beautiful! The feeling heart, the understanding mind is his. And we will bring him up to be proud that he is of Chinese blood; he will fear none and, after him, the name of half-breed will no longer be one of contempt."

Kanghi as a youth had attended a school in Hong Kong, and while there had made the acquaintance of several half Chinese half English lads. "They were the brightest of all," he told me, "but they lowered themselves in the eyes of the Chinese by being ashamed of their Chinese blood and ignoring it."

His theory, therefore, was that if his own son was brought up to be proud instead of ashamed of his Chinese half, the boy would become a great man.

Perhaps he was right, but he could not see as could I, an American woman, the conflict before our boy.

After the little Kanghi had passed his first month, and we had found a reliable woman to look after him, his father began to take me around with him much more than formerly, and life became very enjoyable.

---

1   Reference to a baby born with the caul or amniotic membrane around its face. While there are diverse interpretations of the meaning of the veil, Scottish and ancient Egyptian traditions associated it with prophecy. W.E.B. Du Bois, in *The Souls of Black Folk* (published by A.C. McClurg in 1903), had made the oft-quoted statement that "the Negro is ... born with a veil, and gifted with second-sight in this American world" (3).

We dined often at a Chinese restaurant kept by a friend of his, and afterwards attended theatres, concerts, and other places of entertainment. We frequently met Americans with whom he had become acquainted through business, and he would introduce them with great pride in me shining in his eyes. The little jealousies and suspicions of the first year seemed no longer to irritate him, and though I had still cause to shrink from the gaze of strangers, I know that my Chinese husband was for several years a very happy man.

Now, I have come to the end. He left home one morning, followed to the gate by the little girl and boy (we had moved to a cottage in the suburbs).

"Bring me a red ball," pleaded the little girl.

"And me too," cried the boy.

"All right, chickens," he responded, waving his hand to them.

He was brought home at night, shot through the head. There are some Chinese, just as there are some Americans, who are opposed to all progress, and who hate with a bitter hatred all who would enlighten or be enlightened.

But that I have not the heart to dwell upon. I can only remember that when they brought my Chinese husband home there were two red balls in his pocket. Such was Liu Kanghi—a man.

The Americanizing of Pau Tsu

I

WHEN Wan Hom Hing came to Seattle to start a branch of the merchant business which his firm carried on so successfully in the different ports of China, he brought with him his nephew, Wan Lin Fo, then eighteen years of age. Wan Lin Fo was a well-educated Chinese youth, with bright eyes and keen ears. In a few years' time he knew as much about the business as did any of the senior partners. Moreover, he learned to speak and write the American language with such fluency that he was never at a loss for an answer, when the white man, as was sometimes the case, sought to pose him. "All work and no play,"[1] however, is as much

---

1 "All work and no play makes Jack a dull boy" is a proverb first published in James Howell's *Proverbs in English, Italian, French, and Spanish* (1659).

against the principles of a Chinese youth as it is against those of a young American, and now and again Lin Fo would while away an evening at the Chinese Literary Club, above the Chinese restaurant, discussing with some chosen companions the works and merits of Chinese sages—and some other things. New Year's Day, or rather, Week, would also see him, business forgotten, arrayed in national costume of finest silk, and color "the blue of the sky after rain,"[1] visiting with his friends, both Chinese and American, and scattering silver and gold coin amongst the youngsters of the families visited.

It was on the occasion of one of these New Year's visits that Wan Lin Fo first made known to the family of his firm's silent American partner,[2] Thomas Raymond, that he was betrothed. It came about in this wise: One of the young ladies of the house, who was fair and frank of face and friendly and cheery in manner, observing as she handed him a cup of tea that Lin Fo's eyes wore a rather wistful expression, questioned him as to the wherefore:

"Miss Adah,"[3] replied Lin Fo, "may I tell you something?"

"Certainly, Mr. Wan," replied the girl. "You know how I enjoy hearing your tales."

"But this is no tale. Miss Adah, you have inspired in me a love—"

Adah Raymond started. Wan Lin Fo spake slowly.

"For the little girl in China to whom I am betrothed."

"Oh, Mr. Wan! That is good news. But what have I to do with it?"

"This, Miss Adah! Every time I come to this house, I see you, so good and so beautiful, dispensing tea and happiness to all around, and I think, could I have in my home and ever by my side one who is also both good and beautiful, what a felicitous life mine would be!"

"You must not flatter me, Mr. Wan!"

"All that I say is founded on my heart. But I will speak not of you. I will speak of Pau Tsu."

"Pau Tsu?"

"Yes. That is the name of my future wife. It means a pearl."

---

1 The name of a rare and highly valued shade of blue in Chinese ceramic art.

2 A silent partner has a financial share in a business but has no publicly known association with it, and/or takes no part in managing it.

3 See p. 63 for note on Adah Charlton.

"How pretty! Tell me all about her!"

"I was betrothed to Pau Tsu before leaving China. My parents adopted her to be my wife. As I remember, she had shining eyes and the good-luck color[1] was on her cheek. Her mouth was like a red vine leaf, and her eyebrows most exquisitely arched. As slender as a willow was her form, and when she spoke, her voice lilted from note to note in the sweetest melody."

Adah Raymond softly clapped her hands.

"Ah! You were even then in love with her."

"No," replied Lin Fo thoughtfully. "I was too young to be in love—sixteen years of age. Pau Tsu was thirteen. But, as I have confessed, you have caused me to remember and love her."

Adah Raymond was not a self-conscious girl, but for the life of her she could think of no reply to Lin Fo's speech.

"I am twenty-two years old now," he continued. "Pau Tsu is eighteen. Tomorrow I will write to my parents and persuade them to send her to me at the time of the spring festival.[2] My elder brother was married last year, and his wife is now under my parents' roof, so that Pau Tsu, who has been the daughter of the house for so many years, can now be spared to me."

"What a sweet little thing she must be," commented Adah Raymond.

"You will say that when you see her," proudly responded Lin Fo. "My parents say she is always happy. There is not a bird or flower or dewdrop in which she does not find some glad meaning."

"I shall be so glad to know her. Can she speak English?"

Lin Fo's face fell.

"No," he replied, "but,"—brightening—"when she comes I will have her learn to speak like you—and be like you."

II

PAU TSU came with the spring, and Wan Lin Fo was one of the happiest and proudest of bridegrooms. The tiny bride was really very pretty—even to American eyes. In her peach and plum colored robes, her little arms and hands sparkling with jewels, and her shiny black head decorated with wonderful combs and

---

1 The Chinese associate the color red with good luck.

2 The spring festival, or Chinese New Year, celebrates the first day of the first month of the lunar calendar. It is the most important traditional Chinese holiday.

pins, she appeared a bit of Eastern coloring amidst the Western lights and shades.

Lin Fo had not been forgotten, and her eyes under their downcast lids discovered him at once, as he stood awaiting her amongst a group of young Chinese merchants on the deck of the vessel.

The apartments he had prepared for her were furnished in American style, and her birdlike little figure in Oriental dress seemed rather out of place at first. It was not long, however, before she brought forth from the great box, which she had brought over seas, screens and fans, vases, panels, Chinese matting, artificial flowers and birds, and a number of exquisite carvings and pieces of antique porcelain. With these she transformed the American flat into an Oriental bower, even setting up in her sleeping-room a little chapel, enshrined in which was an image of the Goddess of Mercy,[1] two ancestral tablets, and other emblems of her faith in the Gods of her fathers.

The Misses Raymond called upon her soon after arrival, and she smiled and looked pleased. She shyly presented each girl with a Chinese cup and saucer, also a couple of antique vases, covered with whimsical pictures, which Lin Fo tried his best to explain.

The girls were delighted with the gifts, and having fallen, as they expressed themselves, in love with the little bride, invited her through her husband to attend a launch party,[2] which they intended giving the following Wednesday on Lake Washington.

Lin Fo accepted the invitation on behalf of himself and wife. He was quite at home with the Americans and, being a young man, enjoyed their rather effusive appreciation of him as an educated Chinaman. Moreover, he was of the opinion that the society of the American young ladies would benefit Pau Tsu in helping her to acquire the ways and language of the land in which he hoped to make a fortune.

Wan Lin Fo was a true son of the Middle Kingdom[3] and secretly pitied all those who were born far away from its influences; but there was much about the Americans that he admired. He also entertained sentiments of respect for a motto which hung in his room which bore the legend: "When in Rome, do as the Romans do."

---

1 Guanyin. See p. 88, note 1.
2 A party celebrating the launching of a new boat or product.
3 China.

"What is best for men is also best for women in this country," he told Pau Tsu when she wept over his suggestion that she should take some lessons in English from a white woman.

"It may be best for a man who goes out in the street," she sobbed, "to learn the new language, but of what importance is it to a woman who lives only within the house and her husband's heart?"

It was seldom, however, that she protested against the wishes of Lin Fo. As her mother-in-law had said, she was a docile, happy little creature. Moreover, she loved her husband.

But as the days and weeks went by the girl bride whose life hitherto had been spent in the quiet retirement of a Chinese home in the performance of filial duties, in embroidery work and lute playing, in sipping tea and chatting with gentle girl companions, felt very much bewildered by the novelty and stir of the new world into which she had been suddenly thrown. She could not understand, for all Lin Fo's explanations, why it was required of her to learn the strangers' language and adopt their ways. Her husband's tongue was the same as her own. So also her little maid's. It puzzled her to be always seeing this and hearing that— sights and sounds which as yet had no meaning for her. Why also was it necessary to receive visitors nearly every evening?—visitors who could neither understand nor make themselves understood by her, for all their curious smiles and stares, which she bore like a second Vashti—or rather, Esther.[1] And why, oh! why should she be constrained to eat her food with clumsy, murderous looking American implements instead of with her own elegant and easily manipulated ivory chopsticks?

Adah Raymond, who at Lin Fo's request was a frequent visitor to the house, could not fail to observe that Pau Tsu's small face grew daily smaller and thinner, and that the smile with which she invariably greeted her, though sweet, was tinged with melancholy. Her woman's instinct told her that something was wrong, but what it was the light within her failed to discover. She would reach over to Pau Tsu and take within her own firm, white hand the small, trembling fingers, pressing them lovingly and sympathetically; and the little Chinese woman would look up into the

---

1   In the biblical book of Esther, Vashti refuses to be put on display before the guests of her husband, King Ahasuerus. Convinced that men should command in their households, the king replaces Vashti with a new queen, Esther.

. beautiful face bent above hers and think to herself: "No wonder he wishes me to be like her!"

If Lin Fo happened to come in before Adah Raymond left he would engage the visitor in bright and animated conversation. They had so much of common interest to discuss, as is always the way with young people who have lived any length of time in a growing city of the West. But to Pau Tsu, pouring tea and dispensing sweetmeats, it was all Greek, or rather, all American.

"Look, my pearl, what I have brought you," said Lin Fo one afternoon as he entered his wife's apartments, followed by a messenger-boy, who deposited in the middle of the room a large cardboard box.

With murmurs of wonder Pau Tsu drew near, and the messenger-boy having withdrawn Lin Fo cut the string, and drew forth a beautiful lace evening dress and dark blue walking costume, both made in American style.

For a moment there was silence in the room. Lin Fo looked at his wife in surprise. Her face was pale and her little body was trembling, while her hands were drawn up into her sleeves.

"Why, Pau Tsu!" he exclaimed, "I thought to make you glad."

At these words the girl bent over the dress of filmy lace, and gathering the flounce in her hand smoothed it over her knee; then lifting a smiling face to her husband, replied: "Oh, you are too good, too kind to your unworthy Pau Tsu. My speech is slow, because I am overcome with happiness."

Then with exclamations of delight and admiration she lifted the dresses out of the box and laid them carefully over the couch.

"I wish you to dress like an American woman when we go out or receive," said her husband. "It is the proper thing in America to do as the Americans do. You will notice, light of my eyes, that it is only on New Year and our national holidays that I wear the costume of our country and attach a queue.[1] The wife should follow the husband in all things."

A ripple of laughter escaped Pau Tsu's lips.

"When I wear that dress," said she, touching the walking costume, "I will look like your friend, Miss Raymond."

She struck her hands together gleefully, but when her husband had gone to his business she bowed upon the floor and wept pitifully.

---

1 See p. 64, note 1. Artificial queues were common props in yellowface stage performances.

III

DURING the rainy season Pau Tsu was attacked with a very bad cough. A daughter of Southern China, the chill, moist climate of the Puget Sound winter was very hard on her delicate lungs. Lin Fo worried much over the state of her health, and meeting Adah Raymond on the street one afternoon told her of his anxiety. The kind-hearted girl immediately returned with him to the house. Pau Tsu was lying on her couch, feverish and breathing hard. The American girl felt her hands and head.

"She must have a doctor," said she, mentioning the name of her family's physician.

Pau Tsu shuddered. She understood a little English by this time.

"No! No! Not a man, not a man!" she cried.

Adah Raymond looked up at Lin Fo.

"I understand," said she. "There are several women doctors in this town. Let us send for one."

But Lin Fo's face was set.

"No!" he declared. "We are in America. Pau Tsu shall be attended to by your physician."

Adah Raymond was about to protest against this dictum[1] when the sick wife, who had also heard it, touched her hand and whispered: "I not mind now. Man all right."

So the other girl closed her lips, feeling that if the wife would not dispute her husband's will it was not her place to do so; but her heart ached with compassion as she bared Pau Tsu's chest for the stethoscope.

"It was like preparing a lamb for slaughter," she told her sister afterwards. "Pau Tsu was motionless, her eyes closed and her lips sealed, while the doctor remained; but after he had left and we two were alone she shuddered and moaned like one bereft of reason. I honestly believe that the examination was worse than death to that little Chinese woman. The modesty of generations of maternal ancestors was crucified as I rolled down the neck of her silk tunic."

It was a week after the doctor's visit, and Pau Tsu, whose cough had yielded to treatment, though she was still far from well, was playing on her lute, and whisperingly singing this little song, said to have been written on a fan which was presented to an ancient Chinese emperor by one of his wives:

---

1 An authoritative, decisive pronouncement.

"Of fresh new silk,
All snowy white,
And round as a harvest moon,
A pledge of purity and love,
A small but welcome boon.

While summer lasts,
When borne in hand,
Or folded on thy breast,
'Twill gently soothe thy burning brow,
And charm thee to thy rest.

But, oh, when Autumn winds blow chill,
And days are bleak and cold,
No longer sought, no longer loved,
'Twill lie in dust and mould.

This silken fan then deign accept,
Sad emblem of my lot,
Caressed and cherished for an hour,
Then speedily forgot."[1]

"Why so melancholy, my pearl?" asked Lin Fo, entering from the street.

"When a bird is about to die, its notes are sad," returned Pau Tsu.

"But thou art not for death—thou art for life," declared Lin Fo, drawing her towards him and gazing into a face which day by day seemed to grow finer and more transparent.

IV

A CHINESE messenger-boy ran up the street, entered the store of Wan Hom Hing & Co. and asked for the junior partner. When Lin Fo came forward he handed him a dainty, flowered missive, neatly folded and addressed. The receiver opened it and read:

---

1 An ode by Pan Chih Yu, inscribed on a fan and presented to the emperor of China. This version approximates the translation in William Alexander Parsons Martin, *The Lore of Cathay: Or, the Intellect of China* (New York: F.H. Revell, 1901), 82–83.

DEAR AND HONORED HUSBAND,—Your unworthy Pau Tsu lacks the courage to face the ordeal before her. She has, therefore, left you and prays you to obtain a divorce, as is the custom in America, so that you may be happy with the Beautiful One, who is so much your Pau Tsu's superior. This, she acknowledges, for she sees with your eyes, in which, like a star, the Beautiful One shineth. Else, why should you have your Pau Tsu follow in her footsteps? She has tried to obey your will and to be as an American woman; but now she is very weary, and the terror of what is before her has overcome.

Your stupid thorn,

PAU TSU

Mechanically Lin Fo folded the letter and thrust it within his breast pocket. A customer inquired of him the price of a lacquered tray. "I wish you good morning," he replied, reaching for his hat. The customer and clerks gaped after him as he left the store.

Out in the street, as fate would have it, he met Adah Raymond. He would have turned aside had she not spoken to him.

"Whatever is the matter with you, Mr. Wan?" she inquired. "You don't look yourself at all."

"The density of my difficulties you cannot understand," he replied, striding past her.

But Adah Raymond was persistent. She had worried lately over Pau Tsu.

"Something is wrong with your wife," she declared.

Lin Fo wheeled around.

"Do you know where she is?" he asked with quick suspicion.

"Why, no!" exclaimed the girl in surprise.

"Well, she has left me."

Adah Raymond stood incredulous for a moment, then with indignant eyes she turned upon the deserted husband.

"You deserve it!" she cried, "I have seen it for some time: your cruel, arbitrary treatment of the dearest, sweetest little soul in the world."

"I beg your pardon, Miss Adah," returned Lin Fo, "but I do not understand. Pau Tsu is heart of my heart. How then could I be cruel to her?"

"Oh, you stupid!" exclaimed the girl. "You're a Chinaman, but you're almost as stupid as an American. Your cruelty consisted in forcing Pau Tsu to be—what nature never intended her to be— an American woman; to adapt and adopt in a few months' time all our ways and customs. I saw it long ago, but as Pau Tsu was too sweet and meek to see any faults in her man I had not the heart to open her eyes—or yours. Is it not true that she has left you for this reason?"

"Yes," murmured Lin Fo. He was completely crushed. "And some other things."

"What other things?"

"She—is—afraid—of—the—doctor."

"She is!"—fiercely—"Shame upon you!"

Lin Fo began to walk on, but the girl kept by his side and continued:

"You wanted your wife to be an American woman while you remained a Chinaman. For all your clever adaptation of our American ways you are a thorough Chinaman. Do you think an American would dare treat his wife as you have treated yours?"

Wan Lin Fo made no response. He was wondering how he could ever have wished his gentle Pau Tsu to be like this angry woman. Now his Pau Tsu was gone. His anguish for the moment made him oblivious to the presence of his companion and the words she was saying. His silence softened the American girl. After all, men, even Chinamen, were nothing but big, clumsy boys, and she didn't believe in kicking a man after he was down.

"But, cheer up, you're sure to find her," said she, suddenly changing her tone. "Probably her maid has friends in Chinatown who have taken them in."

"If I find her," said Lin Fo fervently, "I will not care if she never speaks an American word, and I will take her for a trip to China, so that our son may be born in the country that Heaven loves."

"You cannot make too much amends for all she has suffered. As to Americanizing Pau Tsu—that will come in time. I am quite sure that were I transferred to your country and commanded to turn myself into a Chinese woman in the space of two or three months I would prove a sorry disappointment to whomever built their hopes upon me."

Many hours elapsed before any trace could be found of the missing one. All the known friends and acquaintances of little Pau Tsu were called upon and questioned; but if they had knowledge of the young wife's hiding place they refused to divulge it. Though Lin Fo's face was grave with an unexpressed fear, their sympathies were certainly not with him.

The seekers were about giving up the search in despair when a little boy, dangling in his hands a string of blue beads, arrested the attention of the young husband. He knew the necklace to be a gift from Pau Tsu to the maid, A-Toy. He had bought it himself. Stopping and questioning the little fellow he learned to his great joy that his wife and her maid were at the boy's home, under the care of his grandmother, who was a woman learned in herb lore.

Adah Raymond smiled in sympathy with her companion's evident great relief.

"Everything will now be all right," said she, following Lin Fo as he proceeded to the house pointed out by the lad. Arrived there, she suggested that the husband enter first and alone. She would wait a few moments.

"Miss Adah," said Lin Fo, "ten thousand times I beg your pardon, but perhaps you will come to see my wife some other time—not today?"

He hesitated, embarrassed and humiliated.

In one silent moment Adah Raymond grasped the meaning of all the morning's trouble—of all Pau Tsu's sadness.

"Lord, what fools we mortals be!"[1] she soliloquized as she walked home alone. "I ought to have known. What else could Pau Tsu have thought?—coming from a land where women have no men friends save their husbands. How she must have suffered under her smiles! Poor, brave little soul!"

In the Land of the Free

I

"SEE, Little One—the hills in the morning sun. There is thy home for years to come. It is very beautiful and thou wilt be very happy there."

The Little One looked up into his mother's face in perfect faith. He was engaged in the pleasant occupation of sucking a sweet-meat; but that did not prevent him from gurgling responsively.

"Yes, my olive bud; there is where thy father is making a fortune for thee. Thy father! Oh, wilt thou not be glad to behold his dear face. 'Twas for thee I left him."

The Little One ducked his chin sympathetically against his mother's knee. She lifted him on to her lap. He was two years old, a round, dimple-cheeked boy with bright brown eyes and a sturdy little frame.

---

1 William Shakespeare, *A Midsummer Night's Dream*, III.ii.115.

"Ah! Ah! Ah! Ooh! Ooh! Ooh!" puffed he, mocking a tugboat steaming by.

San Francisco's waterfront was lined with ships and steamers, while other craft, large and small, including a couple of white transports from the Philippines, lay at anchor here and there off shore. It was some time before the Eastern Queen could get docked, and even after that was accomplished, a lone Chinaman who had been waiting on the wharf for an hour was detained that much longer by men with the initials U.S.C. on their caps, before he could board the steamer and welcome his wife and child.

"This is thy son," announced the happy Lae Choo.

Hom Hing lifted the child, felt of his little body and limbs, gazed into his face with proud and joyous eyes; then turned inquiringly to a customs officer at his elbow.

"That's a fine boy you have there," said the man. "Where was he born?"

"In China," answered Hom Hing, swinging the Little One on his right shoulder, preparatory to leading his wife off the steamer.

"Ever been to America before?"

"No, not he," answered the father with a happy laugh.

The customs officer beckoned to another.

"This little fellow," said he, "is visiting America for the first time."

The other customs officer stroked his chin reflectively.

"Good day," said Hom Hing.

"Wait!" commanded one of the officers. "You cannot go just yet."

"What more now?" asked Hom Hing.

"I'm afraid," said the first customs officer, "that we cannot allow the boy to go ashore. There is nothing in the papers that you have shown us—your wife's papers and your own—having any bearing upon the child."

"There was no child when the papers were made out," returned Hom Hing. He spoke calmly; but there was apprehension in his eyes and in his tightening grip on his son.

"What is it? What is it?" quavered Lae Choo, who understood a little English.

The second customs officer regarded her pityingly.

"I don't like this part of the business," he muttered.

The first officer turned to Hom Hing and in an official tone of voice, said:

"Seeing that the boy has no certificate entitling him to admission to this country you will have to leave him with us."[1]

"Leave my boy!" exclaimed Hom Hing.

"Yes; he will be well taken care of, and just as soon as we can hear from Washington he will be handed over to you."

"But," protested Hom Hing, "he is my son."

"We have no proof," answered the man with a shrug of his shoulders; "and even if so we cannot let him pass without orders from the Government."

"He is my son," reiterated Hom Hing, slowly and solemnly. "I am a Chinese merchant and have been in business in San Francisco for many years. When my wife told to me one morning that she dreamed of a green tree with spreading branches and one beautiful red flower growing thereon, I answered her that I wished my son to be born in our country, and for her to prepare to go to China. My wife complied with my wish. After my son was born my mother fell sick and my wife nursed and cared for her; then my father, too, fell sick, and my wife also nursed and cared for him. For twenty moons my wife care for and nurse the old people, and when they die they bless her and my son, and I send for her to return to me. I had no fear of trouble. I was a Chinese merchant and my son was my son."

"Very good, Hom Hing," replied the first officer. "Nevertheless, we take your son."

"No, you not take him; he my son too."

It was Lae Choo. Snatching the child from his father's arms she held and covered him with her own.

The officers conferred together for a few moments; then one drew Hom Hing aside and spoke in his ear.

Resignedly Hom Hing bowed his head, then approached his wife.

"'Tis the law," said he, speaking in Chinese, "and 'twill be but for a little while—until tomorrow's sun arises."

"You, too," reproached Lae Choo in a voice eloquent with pain. But accustomed to obedience she yielded the boy to her husband, who in turn delivered him to the first officer. The Little

---

1 Under US law, Chinese residents of the merchant class were permitted to bring their children from China. However, immigration officials became more suspicious after the 1906 earthquake destroyed immigration records in San Francisco—a phenomenon that made it possible for Chinese residents to claim fictive "paper sons" in order to bring new immigrants to the US.

One protested lustily against the transfer; but his mother covered her face with her sleeve and his father silently led her away. Thus was the law of the land complied with.

II

DAY was breaking. Lae Choo, who had been awake all night dressed herself, then awoke her husband.

"'Tis the morn," she cried. "Go, bring our son."

The man rubbed his eyes and arose upon his elbow so that he could see out of the window. A pale star was visible in the sky. The petals of a lily in a bowl on the windowsill were unfurled.

"'Tis not yet time," said he, laying his head down again.

"Not yet time. Ah, all the time that I lived before yesterday is not so much as the time that has been since my little one was taken from me."

The mother threw herself down beside the bed and covered her face.

Hom Hing turned on the light, and touching his wife's bowed head with a sympathetic hand inquired if she had slept.

"Slept!" she echoed, weepingly. "Ah, how could I close my eyes with my arms empty of the little body that has filled them every night for more than twenty moons! You do not know— man—what it is to miss the feel of the little fingers and the little toes and the soft round limbs of your little one. Even in the darkness his darling eyes used to shine up to mine, and often have I fallen into slumber with his pretty babble at my ear. And now, I see him not; I touch him not; I hear him not. My baby, my little fat one!"

"Now! Now! Now!" consoled Hom Hing, patting his wife's shoulder reassuringly; "there is no need to grieve so; he will soon gladden you again. There cannot be any law that would keep a child from its mother!"

Lae Choo dried her tears.

"You are right, my husband," she meekly murmured. She arose and stepped about the apartment, setting things to rights. The box of presents she had brought for her California friends had been opened the evening before; and silks, embroideries, carved ivories, ornamental lacquer-ware, brasses, camphorwood boxes, fans, and chinaware were scattered around in confused heaps. In the midst of unpacking the thought of her child in the hands of strangers had overpowered her, and she had left everything to crawl into bed and weep.

Having arranged her gifts in order she stepped out on to the deep balcony.

The star had faded from view and there were bright streaks in the western sky. Lae Choo looked down the street and around. Beneath the flat occupied by her and her husband were quarters for a number of bachelor Chinamen, and she could hear them from where she stood, taking their early morning breakfast. Below their dining-room was her husband's grocery store. Across the way was a large restaurant. Last night it had been resplendent with gay colored lanterns and the sound of music. The rejoicings over "the completion of the moon,"[1] by Quong Sum's firstborn, had been long and loud, and had caused her to tie a handkerchief over her ears. She, a bereaved mother, had it not in her heart to rejoice with other parents. This morning the place was more in accord with her mood. It was still and quiet. The revelers had dispersed or were asleep.

A roly-poly woman in black sateen, with long pendant earrings in her ears, looked up from the street below and waved her a smiling greeting. It was her old neighbor, Kuie Hoe, the wife of the gold embosser, Mark Sing. With her was a little boy in yellow jacket and lavender pantaloons. Lae Choo remembered him as a baby. She used to like to play with him in those days when she had no child of her own. What a long time ago that seemed! She caught her breath in a sigh, and laughed instead.

"Why are you so merry?" called her husband from within.

"Because my Little One is coming home," answered Lae Choo. "I am a happy mother—a happy mother."

She pattered into the room with a smile on her face.

The noon hour had arrived. The rice was steaming in the bowls and a fragrant dish of chicken and bamboo shoots was awaiting Hom Hing. Not for one moment had Lae Choo paused to rest during the morning hours; her activity had been ceaseless. Every now and again, however, she had raised her eyes to the gilded clock on the curiously carved mantelpiece. Once, she had exclaimed:

"Why so long, oh! why so long?" Then apostrophizing herself:

---

1 A celebration occurring one month following an infant's birth. Often, the baby's name is announced and it is welcomed into the community as guests bring "lucky money" and the parents provide red dyed eggs. At the time, this ceremony was generally held only for male babies. See also Far's note on p. 204 in "Misunderstood."

"Lae Choo, be happy. The Little One is coming! The Little One is coming!" Several times she burst into tears and several times she laughed aloud.

Hom Hing entered the room; his arms hung down by his side.

"The Little One!" shrieked Lae Choo.

"They bid me call tomorrow."

With a moan the mother sank to the floor.

The noon hour passed. The dinner remained on the table.

III

THE winter rains were over: the spring had come to California, flushing the hills with green and causing an ever-changing pageant of flowers to pass over them. But there was no spring in Lae Choo's heart, for the Little One remained away from her arms. He was being kept in a mission. White women were caring for him, and though for one full moon he had pined for his mother and refused to be comforted he was now apparently happy and contented. Five moons or five months had gone by since the day he had passed with Lae Choo through the Golden Gate; but the great Government at Washington still delayed sending the answer which would return him to his parents.

Hom Hing was disconsolately rolling up and down the balls in his abacus box when a keen-faced young man stepped into his store.

"What news?" asked the Chinese merchant.

"This!" The young man brought forth a typewritten letter. Hom Hing read the words:

"Re Chinese child, alleged to be the son of Hom Hing, Chinese merchant, doing business at 425 Clay street, San Francisco.

"Same will have attention as soon as possible."

Hom Hing returned the letter, and without a word continued his manipulation of the counting machine.

"Have you anything to say?" asked the young man.

"Nothing. They have sent the same letter fifteen times before. Have you not yourself showed it to me?"

"True!" The young man eyed the Chinese merchant furtively. He had a proposition to make and he was pondering whether or not the time was opportune.

"How is your wife?" he inquired solicitously—and diplomatically.

Hom Hing shook his head mournfully.

"She seems less every day," he replied. "Her food she takes only when I bid her and her tears fall continually. She finds no pleasure in dress or flowers and cares not to see her friends. Her eyes stare all night. I think before another moon she will pass into the land of spirits."

"No!" exclaimed the young man, genuinely startled.

"If the boy not come home I lose my wife sure," continued Hom Hing with bitter sadness.

"It's not right," cried the young man indignantly. Then he made his proposition.

The Chinese father's eyes brightened exceedingly.

"Will I like you to go to Washington and make them give you the paper to restore my son?" cried he. "How can you ask when you know my heart's desire?"

"Then," said the young fellow, "I will start next week. I am anxious to see this thing through if only for the sake of your wife's peace of mind."

"I will call her. To hear what you think to do will make her glad," said Hom Hing.

He called a message to Lae Choo upstairs through a tube in the wall.

In a few moments she appeared, listless, wan, and hollow-eyed; but when her husband told her the young lawyer's suggestion she became as one electrified; her form straightened, her eyes glistened; the color flushed to her cheeks.

"Oh," she cried, turning to James Clancy, "You are a hundred man good!"

The young man felt somewhat embarrassed; his eyes shifted a little under the intense gaze of the Chinese mother.

"Well, we must get your boy for you," he responded. "Of course" turning to Hom Hing—"it will cost a little money. You can't get fellows to hurry the Government for you without gold in your pocket."

Hom Hing stared blankly for a moment. Then: "How much do you want, Mr. Clancy?" he asked quietly.

"Well, I will need at least five hundred to start with."

Hom Hing cleared his throat.

"I think I told to you the time I last paid you for writing letters for me and seeing the Custom boss here that nearly all I had was gone!"

"Oh, well then we won't talk about it, old fellow. It won't harm the boy to stay where he is, and your wife may get over it all right."

"What that you say?" quavered Lae Choo.

James Clancy looked out of the window.

"He says," explained Hom Hing in English, "that to get our boy we have to have much money."

"Money! Oh, yes."

Lae Choo nodded her head.

"I have not got the money to give him."

For a moment Lae Choo gazed wonderingly from one face to the other; then, comprehension dawning upon her, with swift anger, pointing to the lawyer, she cried: "You not one hundred man good; you just common white man."

"Yes, ma'am," returned James Clancy, bowing and smiling ironically. Hom Hing pushed his wife behind him and addressed the lawyer again: "I might try," said he, "to raise something; but five hundred—it is not possible."

"What about four?"

"I tell you I have next to nothing left and my friends are not rich."

"Very well!"

The lawyer moved leisurely toward the door, pausing on its threshold to light a cigarette.

"Stop, white man; white man, stop!"

Lae Choo, panting and terrified, had started forward and now stood beside him, clutching his sleeve excitedly.

"You say you can go to get paper to bring my Little One to me if Hom Hing give you five hundred dollars?"

The lawyer nodded carelessly; his eyes were intent upon the cigarette which would not take the fire from the match.

"Then you go get paper. If Hom Hing not can give you five hundred dollars—I give you perhaps what more that much."

She slipped a heavy gold bracelet from her wrist and held it out to the man. Mechanically he took it.

"I go get more!"

She scurried away, disappearing behind the door through which she had come.

"Oh, look here, I can't accept this," said James Clancy, walking back to Hom Hing and laying down the bracelet before him.

"It's all right," said Hom Hing, seriously, "pure China gold. My wife's parent give it to her when we married."

"But I can't take it anyway," protested the young man.

"It is all same as money. And you want money to go to Washington," replied Hom Hing in a matter of fact manner.

"See, my jade earrings—my gold buttons—my hairpins—my

comb of pearl and my rings—one, two, three, four, five rings; very good very good—all same much money. I give them all to you. You take and bring me paper for my Little One."

Lae Choo piled up her jewels before the lawyer.

Hom Hing laid a restraining hand upon her shoulder. "Not all, my wife," he said in Chinese. He selected a ring—his gift to Lae Choo when she dreamed of the tree with the red flower. The rest of the jewels he pushed toward the white man.

"Take them and sell them," said he. "They will pay your fare to Washington and bring you back with the paper."

For one moment James Clancy hesitated. He was not a sentimental man; but something within him arose against accepting such payment for his services.

"They are good, good," pleadingly asserted Lae Choo, seeing his hesitation.

Whereupon he seized the jewels, thrust them into his coat pocket, and walked rapidly away from the store.

IV

LAE CHOO followed after the missionary woman through the mission nursery school. Her heart was beating so high with happiness that she could scarcely breathe. The paper had come at last—the precious paper which gave Hom Hing and his wife the right to the possession of their own child. It was ten months now since he had been taken from them—ten months since the sun had ceased to shine for Lae Choo.

The room was filled with children—most of them wee tots, but none so wee as her own. The mission woman talked as she walked. She told Lae Choo that little Kim, as he had been named by the school, was the pet of the place, and that his little tricks and ways amused and delighted everyone. He had been rather difficult to manage at first and had cried much for his mother; "but children so soon forget, and after a month he seemed quite at home and played around as bright and happy as a bird."

"Yes," responded Lae Choo. "Oh, yes, yes!"

But she did not hear what was said to her. She was walking in a maze of anticipatory joy.

"Wait here, please," said the mission woman, placing Lae Choo in a chair. "The very youngest ones are having their breakfast."

She withdrew for a moment—it seemed like an hour to the mother—then she reappeared leading by the hand a little boy dressed in blue cotton overalls and white-soled shoes. The little boy's face was round and dimpled and his eyes were very bright.

"Little One, ah, my Little One!" cried Lae Choo.

She fell on her knees and stretched her hungry arms toward her son.

But the Little One shrunk from her and tried to hide himself in the folds of the white woman's skirt.

"Go'way, go'way!" he bade his mother.

The Chinese Lily

MERMEI lived in an upstairs room of a Chinatown dwelling-house. There were other little Chinese women living on the same floor, but Mermei never went amongst them. She was not as they were. She was a cripple. A fall had twisted her legs so that she moved around with difficulty and scarred her face so terribly that none save Lin John cared to look upon it. Lin John, her brother, was a laundryman, working for another of his countrymen. Lin John and Mermei had come to San Francisco with their parents when they were small children. Their mother had died the day she entered the foreign city, and the father the week following, both having contracted a fever on the steamer. Mermei and Lin John were then taken in charge by their father's brother, and although he was a poor man he did his best for them until called away by death.

Long before her Uncle died Mermei had met with the accident that had made her not as other girls; but that had only strengthened her brother's affection, and old Lin Wan died happy in the knowledge that Lin John would ever put Mermei before himself.

So Mermei lived in her little upstairs room, cared for by Lin John, and scarcely an evening passed that he did not call to see her. One evening, however, Lin John failed to appear, and Mermei began to feel very sad and lonely. Mermei could embroider all day in contented silence if she knew that in the evening someone would come to whom she could communicate all the thoughts that filled a small black head that knew nothing of life save what it saw from an upstairs window. Mermei's window looked down upon the street, and she would sit for hours, pressed close against it, watching those who passed below and all that took place. That day she had seen many things which she had put into her mental portfolio[1] for Lin John's edification when evening should come. Two yellow-robed priests had passed below on their way to the joss house in the next street; a little bird with a white breast had fluttered against the window pane; a man carrying an image of a Gambling Cash Tiger[2] had entered the house across the street; and six young girls of about her own age, dressed gaily as if to attend a wedding, had also passed over the same threshold.

But when nine o'clock came and no Lin John, the girl began to cry softly. She did not often shed tears, but for some reason unknown to Mermei herself, the sight of those joyous girls caused sad reflections. In the midst of her weeping a timid knock was heard. It was not Lin John. He always gave a loud rap, then entered without waiting to be bidden. Mermei hobbled to the door, pulled it open, and there, in the dim light of the hall without, beheld a young girl—the most beautiful young girl that Mermei had ever seen—and she stood there extending to Mermei a blossom from a Chinese lily plant. Mermei understood the meaning of the offered flower, and accepting it, beckoned for her visitor to follow her into her room.

What a delightful hour that was to Mermei! She forgot that she was scarred and crippled, and she and the young girl chattered out their little hearts to one another. "Lin John is dear, but one can't talk to a man, even if he is a brother, as one can to one the same as oneself," said Mermei to Sin Far—her new friend, and Sin Far, the meaning—of whose name was Pure Flower, or Chinese Lily, answered:

"Yes, indeed. The woman must be the friend of the woman, and the man the friend of the man. Is it not so in the country that Heaven loves?"

"What beneficent spirit moved you to come to my door?" asked Mermei.

"I know not," replied Sin Far, "save that I was lonely. We have but lately moved here, my sister, my sister's husband, and myself. My sister is a bride, and there is much to say between her and her husband. Therefore, in the evening, when the day's duties are done, I am alone. Several times, hearing that you were sick, I ventured to your door; but failed to knock, because always when I drew near, I heard the voice of him whom they call your brother.

---

1 Compare with the title of Eaton's/Sui Sin Far's autobiographical essay, "Leaves from the Mental Portfolio of an Eurasian" (see Appendix A1).
2 See p. 88, note 3.

Tonight, as I returned from an errand for my sister, I heard only the sound of weeping—so I hastened to my room and plucked the lily for you."

The next evening when Lin John explained how he had been obliged to work the evening before Mermei answered brightly that that was all right. She loved him just as much as ever and was just as glad to see him as ever; but if work prevented him from calling he was not to worry. She had found a friend who would cheer her loneliness.

Lin John was surprised, but glad to hear such news, and it came to pass that when he beheld Sin Far, her sweet and gentle face, her pretty drooped eyelids and arched eyebrows, he began to think of apple and peach and plum trees showering their dainty blossoms in the country that Heaven loves.

It was about four o'clock in the afternoon. Lin John, working in his laundry, paid little attention to the street uproar and the clang of the engines rushing by. He had no thought of what it meant to him and would have continued at his work undisturbed had not a boy put his head into the door and shouted:

"Lin John, the house in which your sister lives is on fire!"

The tall building was in flames when Lin John reached it. The uprising tongues licked his face as he sprung up the ladder no other man dared ascend.

"I will not go. It is best for me to die," and Mermei resisted her friend with all her puny strength.

"The ladder will not bear the weight of both of us. You are his sister," calmly replied Sin Far.

"But he loves you best. You and he can be happy together. I am not fit to live."

"May Lin John decide, Mermei?"

"Yes, Lin John may decide."

Lin John reached the casement. For one awful second he wavered. Then his eyes sought the eyes of his sister's friend.

"Come, Mermei," he called.

"Where is Sin Far?" asked Mermei when she became conscious.

"Sin Far is in the land of happy spirits."

"And I am still in this sad, dark world."

"Speak not so, little one. Your brother loves you and will protect you from the darkness."

"But you loved Sin Far better—and she loved you."

Lin John bowed his head.

"Alas!" wept Mermei. "That I should live to make others sad!"

"Nay," said Lin John, "Sin Far is happy. And I—I did my duty with her approval, aye, at her bidding. How then, little sister, can I be sad?"

The Smuggling of Tie Co

AMONGST the daring men who engage in contrabanding Chinese from Canada into the United States[1] Jack Fabian ranks as the boldest in deed, the cleverest in scheming, and the most successful in outwitting Government officers.

Uncommonly strong in person, tall and well built, with fine features and a pair of keen, steady blue eyes, gifted with a sort of rough eloquence and of much personal fascination, it is no wonder that we fellows regard him as our chief and are bound to follow where he leads. With Fabian at our head we engage in the wildest adventures and find such places of concealment for our human goods as none but those who take part in a desperate business would dare to dream of.

Jack, however, is not in search of glory—money is his object. One day when a romantic friend remarked that it was very kind of him to help the poor Chinamen over the border, a cynical smile curled his moustache.

"Kind!" he echoed. "Well, I haven't yet had time to become sentimental over the matter. It is merely a matter of dollars and cents, though, of course, to a man of my strict principles, there is a certain pleasure to be derived from getting ahead of the Government. A poor devil does now and then like to take a little out of those millionaire concerns."

It was last summer and Fabian was somewhat down on his luck. A few months previously, to the surprise of us all, he had made a blunder, which resulted in his capture by American officers, and he and his companion, together with five uncustomed[2] Chinamen, had been lodged in a county jail to await trial.

But loafing behind bars did not agree with Fabian's energetic nature, so one dark night, by means of a saw which had been given to him by a very innocent-looking visitor the day before, he

---

1 After the Chinese Exclusion Act barred working-class Chinese from migrating to the US, thousands of Chinese migrants were smuggled into the US across the Canadian and Mexican borders.

2 Not having been admitted through customs.

made good his escape, and after a long, hungry, detective-hunted tramp through woods and bushes, found himself safe in Canada.

He had had a three months' sojourn in prison, and during that time some changes had taken place in smuggling circles. Some ingenious lawyers had devised a scheme by which any young Chinaman on payment of a couple of hundred dollars could procure a father which father would swear the young Chinaman was born in America[1]—thus proving him to be an American citizen with the right to breathe United States air. And the Chinese themselves, assisted by some white men, were manufacturing certificates establishing their right to cross the border, and in that way were crossing over in large batches.

That sort of trick naturally spoiled our fellows' business, but we all know that "Yankee sharper"[2] games can hold good only for a short while; so we bided our time and waited in patience.

Not so Fabian. He became very restless and wandered around with glowering looks. He was sitting one day in a laundry, the proprietor of which had sent out many a boy through our chief's instrumentality. Indeed, Fabian is said to have "rushed over" to "Uncle Sam" himself some five hundred Celestials, and if Fabian had not been an exceedingly generous fellow he might now be a gentleman of leisure instead of an unimmortalized Rob Roy.[3]

Well, Fabian was sitting in the laundry of Chen Ting Lung & Co., telling a nice-looking young Chinaman that he was so broke that he'd be willing to take over even one man at a time.

The young Chinaman looked thoughtfully into Fabian's face. "Would you take me?" he inquired.

"Take you!" echoed Fabian. "Why, you are one of the 'bosses' here. You don't mean to say that you are hankering after a place where it would take you years to get as high up in the 'washee, washee' business as you are now?"

"Yes, I want go," replied Tie Co. "I want go to New York and I will pay you fifty dollars and all expense if you take me, and not say you take me to my partners."

---

1 Following the loss of immigration and birth records in the San Francisco earthquake and fire of 1906, thousands of Chinese "paper sons" were able to enter the US on the basis of fabricated genealogies.

2 Yankees—or natives of the New England states—were often associated with dishonest business practices; a sharper is someone who swindles or cheats others.

3 Robert Roy MacGregor was a Scottish hero and outlaw made famous by Sir Walter Scott's historical novel, *Rob Roy* (1817).

"There's no accounting for a Chinaman," muttered Fabian; but he gladly agreed to the proposal and a night was fixed.

"What is the name of the firm you are going to?" inquired the white man.

Chinamen who intend being smuggled always make arrangements with some Chinese firm in the States to receive them.

Tie Co hesitated, then mumbled something which sounded like "Quong Wo Yuen" or "Long Lo Toon," Fabian was not sure which, but did not repeat the question, not being sufficiently interested.

He left the laundry, nodding goodbye to Tie Co as he passed outside the window, and the Chinaman nodded back, a faint smile on his small, delicate face lingering until Fabian's receding form was lost to view.

It was a pleasant night on which the two men set out. Fabian had a rig waiting at the corner of the street; Tie Co, dressed in citizen's clothes, stepped into it unobserved, and the smuggler and would-be-smuggled were soon out of the city. They had a merry drive, for Fabian's liking for Tie Co was very real; he had known him for several years, and the lad's quick intelligence interested him.

The second day they left their horse at a farmhouse, where Fabian would call for it on his return trip, crossed a river in a rowboat before the sun was up, and plunged into a wood in which they would remain till evening. It was raining, but through mud and wind and rain they trudged slowly and heavily.

Tie Co paused now and then to take breath. Once Fabian remarked:

"You are not a very strong lad, Tie Co. It's a pity you have to work as you do for your living," and Tie Co had answered:

"Work velly good! No work, Tie Co die."

Fabian looked at the lad protectingly, wondering in a careless way why this Chinaman seemed to him so different from the others.

"Wouldn't you like to be back in China?" he asked.

"No," said Tie Co decidedly.

"Why?"

"I not know why," answered Tie Co.

Fabian laughed.

"Haven't you got a nice little wife at home?" he continued. "I hear you people marry very young."

"No, I no wife," asserted his companion with a choky little laugh. "I never have no wife."

"Nonsense," joked Fabian. "Why, Tie Co, think how nice it would be to have a little woman cook your rice and to love you."

"I not have wife," repeated Tie Co seriously. "I not like woman, I like man."

"You confirmed old bachelor!" ejaculated Fabian.

"I like you," said Tie Co, his boyish voice sounding clear and sweet in the wet woods. "I like you so much that I want go to New York, so you make fifty dollars. I no flend in New York."

"What!" exclaimed Fabian.

"Oh, I solly I tell you, Tie Co velly solly," and the Chinese boy shuffled on with bowed head.

"Look here, Tie Co," said Fabian; "I won't have you do this for my sake. You have been very foolish, and I don't care for your fifty dollars. I do not need it half as much as you do. Good God! how ashamed you make me feel—I who have blown in my thousands in idle pleasures cannot take the little you have slaved for. We are in New York State now. When we get out of this wood we will have to walk over a bridge which crosses a river. On the other side, not far from where we cross, there is a railway station. Instead of buying you a ticket for the city of New York I shall take train with you for Toronto."

Tie Co did not answer—he seemed to be thinking deeply. Suddenly he pointed to where some fallen trees lay.

"Two men run away behind there," cried he.

Fabian looked round them anxiously; his keen eyes seemed to pierce the gloom in his endeavor to catch a glimpse of any person; but no man was visible, and, save the dismal sighing of the wind among the trees, all was quiet.

"There's no one," he said somewhat gruffly—he was rather startled, for they were a mile over the border and he knew that the Government officers were on a sharp lookout for him, and felt, despite his strength, if any trick or surprise were attempted it would go hard with him.

"If they catch you with me it be too bad," sententiously remarked Tie Co. It seemed as if his words were in answer to Fabian's thoughts.

"But they will not catch us; so cheer up your heart, my boy," replied the latter, more heartily than he felt.

"If they come, and I not with you, they not take you and it be all lite."

"Yes," assented Fabian, wondering what his companion was thinking about.

They emerged from the woods in the dusk of the evening and were soon on the bridge crossing the river. When they were near the centre Tie Co stopped and looked into Fabian's face.

"Man come for you, I not here, man no hurt you." And with the words he whirled like a flash over the rail.

In another flash Fabian was after him. But though a first-class swimmer, the white man's efforts were of no avail, and Tie Co was borne away from him by the swift current.

Cold and dripping wet, Fabian dragged himself up the bank and found himself a prisoner.

"So your Chinaman threw himself into the river. What was that for?" asked one of the Government officers.

"I think he was out of his head," replied Fabian. And he fully believed what he uttered.

"We tracked you right through the woods," said another of the captors. "We thought once the boy caught sight of us."

Fabian remained silent.

Tie Co's body was picked up the next day. Tie Co's body, and yet not Tie Co, for Tie Co was a youth, and the body found with Tie Co's face and dressed in Tie Co's clothes was the body of a girl—a woman.

Nobody in the laundry of Chen Ting Lung & Co.—no Chinaman in Canada or New York—could explain the mystery. Tie Co had come out to Canada with a number of other youths. Though not very strong he had always been a good worker and "very smart." He had been quiet and reserved among his own countrymen; had refused to smoke tobacco or opium, and had been a regular attendant at Sunday schools and a great favorite with Mission ladies.

Fabian was released in less than a week. "No evidence against him," said the Commissioner, who was not aware that the prisoner was the man who had broken out of jail but a month before.

Fabian is now very busy; there are lots of boys taking his helping hand over the border, but none of them are like Tie Co; and sometimes, between whiles, Fabian finds himself pondering long and earnestly over the mystery of Tie Co's life—and death.

The God of Restoration

"HE that hath wine hath many friends,"[1] muttered Koan-lo the Second, as he glanced backwards into the store out of which he

---

1   Compare "The poor is hated even of his own neighbour: but the rich man hath many friends" (Proverbs 14:20).

was stepping. It was a Chinese general store, well stocked with all manner of quaint wares, and about a dozen Chinamen were sitting around; whilst in an adjoining room could be seen the recumbent forms of several smokers who were discussing business and indulging in the fascinating pipe during the intervals of conversation.

Noticeable amongst the smokers was Koan-lo the First, a tall, middle-aged Chinaman, wearing a black cap with a red button. Koan-lo the First was cousin to Koan-lo the Second, but whereas Koan-lo the Second was young and penniless, Koan-lo the First was one of the wealthiest Chinese merchants in San Francisco and a mighty man amongst the people of his name in that city, who regarded him as a father.

Koan-lo the Second had been instructed by Koan-lo the First to meet Sie, the latter's bride, who was arriving that day by steamer from China. Koan-lo the First was too busy a man to go down himself to the docks.

So Koan-lo the Second and Sie met—though not for the first time.

Five years before in a suburb of Canton City they had said to one another: "I love you."

Koan-lo the Second was an orphan and had been educated and cared for from youth upwards by Koan-lo the First.

Sie was the daughter of a slave, which will explain why she and Koan-lo the Second had had the opportunity to know one another before the latter left with his cousin for America. In China the daughters of slaves are allowed far more liberty than girls belonging to a higher class of society.

"Koan-lo, ah Koan-lo," cooed Sie softly and happily as she recognized her lover.

"Sie, my sweetest heart," returned Koan-lo the Second, his voice both glad and sad.

He saw that a mistake had been made—that Sie believed that the man who was to be her husband was himself—Koan-lo the Second. And all the love that was in him awoke, and he became dizzy thinking of what might yet be.

Could he explain that the Koan-lo who had purchased Sie for his bride, and to whom she of right belonged, was his cousin and not himself? Could he deliver to the Koan-lo who had many friends and stores of precious valuables the only friend, the only treasure he had ever possessed? And was it likely that Sie would be happy eating the rice of Koan-lo the First when she loved him, Koan-lo the Second?

Sie's little fingers crept into his. She leaned against him. "I am tired. Shall we soon rest?" said she.

"Yes, very soon, my Sie," he murmured, putting his arm around her.

"I was too glad when my father told me that you had sent for me," she whispered.

"I said: 'How good of Koan-lo to remember me all these years.'"

"And did you not remember me, my jess'mine flower?"

"Why need you ask? You know the days and nights have been filled with you."

"Having remembered me, why should you have dreamt that I might have forgotten you?"

"There is a difference. You are a man; I am a woman."

"You have been mine now for over two weeks," said Koan-lo the Second. "Do you still love me, Sie?"

"Look into mine eyes and see," she answered.

"And are you happy?"

"Happy! Yes, and this is the happiest day of all, because today my father obtains his freedom."

"How is that, Sie?"

"Why, Koan-lo, you know. Does not my father receive today the balance of the price you pay for me, and is not that, added to what you sent in advance, sufficient to purchase my father's freedom? My dear, good father—he has worked so hard all these years. He has ever been so kind to me. How glad am I to think that through me the God of Restoration[1] has decreed that he shall no longer be a slave. Yes, I am the happiest woman in the world today."

Sie kissed her husband's hand.

He drew it away and hid with it his face.

"Ah, dear husband!" cried Sie. "You are very sick."

"No, not sick," replied the miserable Koan-lo—"but, Sie, I must tell you that I am a very poor man, and we have got to leave this pretty house in the country and go to some city where I will have to work hard and you will scarcely have enough to eat."

"Kind, generous Koan-lo," answered Sie, "you have ruined yourself for my sake; you paid too high a price for me. Ah, unhappy Sie, who has pulled Koan-lo into the dust! Now let me be your servant, for gladly would I starve for your sake. I care for

---

1 Sui Sin Far may be alluding to the frequent association of God and Christ with restoration throughout the Bible.

Koan-lo, not riches."

And she fell on her knees before the young man, who raised her gently, saying:

"Sie, I am unworthy of such devotion, and your words drive a thousand spears into my heart. Hear my confession. I am your husband, but I am not the man who bought you. My cousin, Koan-lo the First, sent for you to come from China. It was he who bargained for you, and paid half the price your father asked whilst you were in Canton, and agreed to pay the balance upon sight of your face. Alas! the balance will never be paid, for as I have stolen you from my cousin, he is not bound to keep to the agreement, and your father is still a slave." Sie stood motionless, overwhelmed by the sudden and terrible news. She looked at her husband bewilderedly.

"Is it true, Koan-lo? Must my father remain a slave?" she asked.

"Yes, it is true," replied her husband. "But we have still one another, and you say you care not for poverty. So forgive me and forget your father. I forgot all for love of you."

He attempted to draw her to him, but with a pitiful cry she turned and fled.

Koan-lo the First sat smoking and meditating.

Many moons had gone by since Koan-lo the Second had betrayed the trust of Koan-lo the First, and Koan-lo the First was wondering what Koan-lo the Second was doing, and how he was living. "He had little money and was unused to working hard, and with a woman to support what will the dog do?" thought the old man. He felt injured and bitter, but towards the evening, after long smoking, his heart became softened, and he said to his pipe: "Well, well, he had a loving feeling for her, and the young I suppose must mate with the young. I think I could overlook his ungratefulness were he to come and seek forgiveness."

"Great and honored sir, the dishonored Sie kneels before you and begs you to put your foot on her head."

These words were uttered by a young Chinese girl of rare beauty who had entered the room suddenly and prostrated herself before Koan-lo the First. He looked up angrily.

"Ah, I see the false woman who made her father a liar!" he cried.

Tears fell from the downcast eyes of Sie, the kneeler.

"Good sir," said she, "ere I had become a woman or your cousin a man, we loved one another, and when we met after a long separation, we both forgot our duty. But the God of Restoration worked with my heart. I repented and now am come to you to give myself up to be your slave, to work for you until the flesh drops from my bones, if such be your desire, only asking that you will send to my father the balance of my purchase price, for he is too old and feeble to be a slave. Sir, you are known to be a more than just man. Oh, grant my request! 'Tis for my father's sake I plead. For many years he nourished me, with trouble and care; and my heart almost breaks when I think of him. Punish me for my misdeeds, dress me in rags, and feed me on the meanest food! Only let me serve you and make myself of use to you, so that I may be worth my father's freedom."

"And what of my cousin? Are you now false to him?"

"No, not false to Koan-lo, my husband—only true to my father."

"And you wish me, whom you have injured, to free your father?"

Sie's head dropped lower as she replied:

"I wish to be your slave. I wish to pay with the labor of my hands the debt I owe you and the debt I owe my father. For this I have left my husband."

Koan-lo the First arose, lifted Sie's chin with his hand, and contemplated with earnest eyes her face.

"Your heart is not all bad," he observed. Sit down and listen. I will not buy you for my slave, for in this country it is against the law to buy a woman for a slave; but I will hire you for five years to be my servant, and for that time you will do my bidding, and after that you will be free. Rest in peace concerning your father."

"May the sun ever shine on you, most gracious master!" cried Sie.

Then Koan-lo the First pointed out to her a hallway leading to a little room, which room he said she could have for her own private use while she remained with him.

Sie thanked him and was leaving his presence when the door was burst open and Koan-lo the Second, looking haggard and wild, entered. He rushed up to Sie and clutched her by the shoulder.

"You are mine!" he shouted. "I will kill you before you become another man's!"

"Cousin," said Koan-lo the First, "I wish not to have the woman to be my wife, but I claim her as my servant. She has already received her wages—her father's freedom."

Koan-lo the Second gazed bewilderedly into the faces of his wife and cousin. Then he threw up his hands and cried:

"Oh, Koan-lo, my cousin, I have been evil. Always have I envied you and carried bitter thoughts of you in my heart. Even your kindness to me in the past has provoked my ill-will, and when I have seen you surrounded by friends, I have said scornfully: 'He that hath wine hath many friends,' although I well knew the people loved you for your good heart. And Sie I have deceived. I took her to myself, knowing that she thought I was what I was not. I caused her to believe she was mine by all rights."

"So I am yours," broke in Sie tremblingly.

"So she shall be yours—when you are worthy of such a pearl and can guard and keep it," said Koan-lo the First. Then waving his cousin away from Sie, he continued:

"This is your punishment; the God of Restoration demands it. For five years you shall not see the face of Sie, your wife. Meanwhile, study, think, be honest, and work."

"Your husband comes for you today. Does the thought make you glad?" questioned Koan-lo the First.

Sie smiled and blushed.

"I shall be sorry to leave you," she replied.

"But more glad than sad," said the old man. "Sie, your husband is now a fine fellow. He has changed wonderfully during his years of probation."

"Then I shall neither know nor love him," said Sie mischievously. "Why, here he—"

"My sweet one!"

"My husband!"

"My children, take my blessing; be good and be happy. I go to my pipe, to dream of bliss if not to find it."

With these words Koan-lo the First retired.

"Is he not almost as a god?" said Sie.

"Yes," answered her husband, drawing her on to his knee. "He has been better to me than I have deserved. And you—ah, Sie, how can you care for me when you know what a bad fellow I have been?"

"Well," said Sie contentedly, "it is always our best friends who know how bad we are."

The Three Souls of Ah So Nan

I

THE sun was conquering the morning fog, dappling with gold the gray waters of San Francisco's bay, and throwing an emerald radiance over the islands around.

Close to the long line of wharves lay motionless brigs and schooners, while farther off in the harbor were ships of many nations riding at anchor.

A fishing fleet was steering in from the open sea, scudding before the wind like a flock of seabirds. All night long had the fishers toiled in the deep. Now they were returning with the results of their labor.

A young Chinese girl, watching the fleet from the beach of Fisherman's Cove, shivered in the morning air. Over her blue cotton blouse she wore no wrap; on her head, no covering. All her interest was centered in one lone boat which lagged behind the rest, being heavier freighted. The fisherman was of her own race. When his boat was beached he sprang to her side.

"O'Yam, what brings you here?" he questioned low, for the curious eyes of his fellow fishermen were on her.

"Your mother is dying," she answered.

The young man spake a few words in English to a Greek whose boat lay alongside his. The Greek answered in the same tongue. Then Fou Wang threw down his nets and, with the girl following, walked quickly along the waterfront, past the wharves, the warehouses, and the grogshops, up a zigzag hill and into the heart of Chinatown. Neither spoke until they reached their destination, a dingy three-storied building.

The young man began to ascend the stairs, the girl to follow. Fou Wang looked back and shook his head. The girl paused on the lowest step.

"May I not come?" she pleaded.

"Today is for sorrow," returned Fou Wang. "I would, for a time, forget all that belongs to the joy of life."

The girl threw her sleeve over her head and backed out of the open door.

"What is the matter?" inquired a kind voice, and a woman laid her hand upon her shoulder.

O'Yam's bosom heaved.

"Oh, Liuchi," she cried, "the mother of Fou Wang is dying, and you know what that means to me."

The woman eyed her compassionately.

"Your father, I know," said she, as she unlocked a door and led her companion into a room opening on to the street, "has long wished for an excuse to set at naught your betrothal to Fou Wang; but I am sure the lad to whom you are both sun and moon will never give him one."

She offered O'Yam some tea, but the girl pushed it aside. "You know not Fou Wang," she replied, sadly yet proudly. "He will follow his conscience, though he lose the sun, the moon, and the whole world."

A young woman thrust her head through the door.

"The mother of Fou Wang is dead," cried she.

"She was a good woman—a kind and loving mother," said Liuchi, as she gazed down upon the still features of her friend.

The young daughter of Ah So Nan burst into fresh weeping. Her pretty face was much swollen. Ah So Nan had been well loved by her children, and the falling tears were not merely waters of ceremony.

At the foot of the couch upon which the dead was laid, stood Fou Wang, his face stern and immovable, his eye solemn, yet luminous with a steadfast fire. Over his head was thrown a white cloth. From morn till eve had he stood thus, contemplating the serene countenance of his mother and vowing that nothing should be left undone which could be done to prove his filial affection and desire to comfort her spirit in the land to which it had flown. "Three years, O mother, will I give to thee and grief. Three years will I minister to the three souls,"[1] he vowed within himself, remembering how sacred to the dead woman were the customs and observances of her own country. They were also sacred to him. Living in America, in the midst of Americans and Americanized Chinese, the family of Fou Wang, with the exception of one, had clung tenaciously to the beliefs of their forefathers.

"All the living must die, and dying, return to the ground. The limbs and the flesh moulder away below, and hidden away, become the earth of the fields; but the spirit issues forth and is

---

1 Although it was customary for the Chinese to wear mourning for their parents for three years, Sui Sin Far appears to have invented the idea that this was connected to the Chinese belief that each person has three souls.

displayed on high in a condition of glorious brightness,"[1] quoted a yellow-robed priest, swinging an incense burner before a small candle-lighted altar.

It was midnight when the mourning friends of the family of Fou Wang left the chief mourner alone with his dead mother.

His sister, Fin Fan, and the girl who was his betrothed wife brushed his garments as they passed him by. The latter timidly touched his hand—an involuntary act of sympathy—but if he were conscious of that sympathy, he paid no heed to it, and his gaze never wavered from the face of the dead.

II

"MY girl, Moy Ding Fong is ready if Fou Wang is not, and you must marry this year. I have sworn you shall."

Kien Lung walked out of the room with a determined step. He was an Americanized Chinese and had little regard for what he derided as "the antiquated customs of China," save when it was to his interest to follow them. He was also a widower desirous of marrying again, but undesirous of having two women of like years, one his wife, the other his daughter, under the same roof-tree.

Left alone, O'Yam's thoughts became sorrowful, almost despairing. Six moons had gone by since Ah So Nan had passed away, yet the son of Ah So Nan had not once, during that time, spoken one word to his betrothed wife. Occasionally she had passed him on the street; but always he had gone by with uplifted countenance, and in his eyes the beauty of piety and peace. At least, so it seemed to the girl, and the thought of marriage with him had seemed almost sacrilegious. But now it had come to this. If Fou Wang adhered to his resolve to mourn three years for his mother, what would become of her? She thought of old Moy Ding Fong and shuddered. It was bitter, bitter.

There was a rapping at the door. A young girl lifted the latch and stepped in. It was Fin Fan, the sister of her betrothed.

"I have brought my embroidery work," said she, "I thought we could have a little talk before sundown when I must away to prepare the evening meal."

O'Yam, who was glad to see her visitor, brewed some fresh tea and settled down for an exchange of confidences.

---

1 From the Chinese *Book of Rites*. This translation appears in James Legge, *The Religions of China: Confucianism and Tàoism Described and Compared with Christianity* (New York: Scribner, 1881), 120–21.

"I am not going to abide by it," said Fin Fan at last. "Hom Hing is obliged to return to China two weeks hence, and with or without Fou Wang's consent I go with the man to whom my mother betrothed me."

"Without Fou Wang's consent!" echoed O'Yam.

"Yes," returned Fin Fan, snapping off a thread. "Without my honorable brother's consent."

"And your mother gone but six moons!"

O'Yam's face wore a shocked expression.

"Does the fallen leaf grieve because the green one remains on the tree?" queried Fin Fan.

"You must love Hom Hing well," murmured O'Yam—"more than Fou Wang loves me."

"Nay," returned her companion, "Fou Wang's love for you is as big as mine for Hom Hing. It is my brother's conscience alone that stands between him and you. You know that."

"He loves not me," sighed O'Yam.

"If he does not love you," returned Fin Fan, "why, when we heard that you were unwell, did he sleeplessly pace his room night after night until the news came that you were restored to health? Why does he treasure a broken fan you have cast aside?"

"Ah, well!" smiled O'Yam.

Fin Fan laughed softly.

"Fou Wang is not as other men," said she. "His conscience is an inheritance from his great-great-grandfather." Her face became pensive as she added: "It is sad to go across the sea without an elder brother's blessing."

She repeated this to Liuchi and Mai Gwi Far, the widow, whom she met on her way home.

"Why should you," inquired the latter, "when there is a way by which to obtain it?"

"How?"

"Did Ah So Nan leave no garments behind her—such garments as would well fit her three souls—and is it not always easy to delude the serious and the wise?"

"Ah!"

III

O'YAM climbed the stairs to the joss house. The desire for solitude brought her there; but when she had closed the door upon herself, she found that she was not alone. Fou Wang was there.

Before the images of the Three Wise Ones[1] he stood, silent, motionless.

"He is communing with his mother's spirit," thought O'Yam. She beheld him through a mist of tears. Love filled her whole being. She dared not move, because she was afraid he would turn and see her, and then, of course, he would go away. She would stay near him for a few moments and then retire.

The dim light of the place, the quietness in the midst of noise, the fragrance of some burning incense, soothed and calmed her. It was as if all the sorrow and despair that had overwhelmed her when her father had told her to prepare for her wedding with Moy Ding Fong had passed away. After a few moments she stepped back softly towards the door. But she was too late. Fou Wang turned and beheld her.

She fluttered like a bird until she saw that, surprised by her presence, he had forgotten death and thought only of life—of life and love. A glad, eager light shone in his eyes. He made a swift step towards her. Then—he covered his face with his hands.

"Fou Wang!" cried O'Yam, love at last overcoming superstition, "must I become the wife of Moy Ding Fong?"

"No, ah no!" he moaned.

"Then," said the girl in desperation, "take me to yourself."

Fou Wang's hands fell to his side. For a moment he looked into that pleading face—and wavered.

A little bird flew in through an open window, and perching itself upon an altar, began twittering.

Fou Wang started back, the expression on his face changing.

"A warning from the dead," he muttered, "a warning from the dead!"

An iron hand gripped O'Yam's heart. Life itself seemed to have closed upon her.

IV

IT was afternoon before evening, and the fog was rolling in from the sea. Quietness reigned in the plot of ground sacred to San Francisco's Chinese dead when Fou Wang deposited a bundle at

---

1   Three deities often personified or worshiped as idols, Fu Lu Shou represent Good Fortune, Prosperity, and Longevity. The Chinese characters for these are inscribed into every *recto* page of the first edition of *Mrs. Spring Fragrance* (see Appendix A2).

the foot of his mother's grave and prepared for the ceremony of ministering to her three souls.

The fragrance from a wall of fir trees near by stole to his nostrils as he cleared the weeds and withered leaves from his parent's resting place. As he placed the bowls of rice and chicken and the vase of incense where he was accustomed to place it, he became dimly conscious of a presence or presences behind the fir wall.

He sighed deeply. No doubt the shade of his parent was restless, because—

"Fou Wang," spake a voice, low but distinct.

The young man fell upon his knees.

"Honored Mother!" he cried.

"Fou Wang," repeated the voice, "though my name is on thy lips, O'Yam's is in thy heart."

Conscience-stricken, Fou Wang yet retained spirit enough to gasp:

"Have I not been a dutiful son? Have I not sacrificed all for thee, O Mother! Why, then, dost thou reproach me?"

"I do not reproach thee," chanted three voices, and Fou Wang, lifting his head, saw three figures emerge from behind the fir wall.

"I do not reproach thee. Thou hast been a most dutiful son, and thy offerings at my grave and in the temple have been fully appreciated. Far from reproaching thee, I am here to say to thee that the dead have regard for the living who faithfully mourn and minister to them, and to bid thee sacrifice no more until thou hast satisfied thine own heart by taking to wife the daughter of Kien Lung and given to thy sister and thy sister's husband an elder brother's blessing. Thy departed mother requires not the sacrifice of a broken heart. The fallen leaf grieves not because the green leaf still clings to the bough."

Saying this, the three figures flapped the loose sleeves of the well-known garments of Ah So Nan and faded from his vision.

For a moment Fou Wang gazed after them as if spellbound. Then he arose and rushed towards the fir wall, behind which they seemed to have vanished.

"Mother, honored parent! Come back and tell me of the new birth!" he cried.

But there was no response.

Fou Wang returned to the grave and lighted the incense. But he did not wait to see its smoke ascend. Instead he hastened to the house of Kien Lung and said to the girl who met him at the door:

"No more shall my longing for thee take the fragrance from the flowers and the light from the sun and moon."

The Prize China Baby

THE baby was the one gleam of sunshine in Fin Fan's life, and how she loved it no words can tell. When it was first born, she used to lie with her face turned to its little soft, breathing mouth and think there was nothing quite so lovely in the world as the wee pink face before her, while the touch of its tiny toes and fingers would send wonderful thrills through her whole body. Those were delightful days, but, oh, how quickly they sped. A week after the birth of the little Jessamine Flower, Fin Fan was busy winding tobacco leaves in the dark room behind her husband's factory. Winding tobacco leaves had been Fin Fan's occupation ever since she had become Chung Kee's wife, and hard and dreary work it was. Now, however, she did not mind it quite so much, for in a bunk which was built on one side of the room was a most precious bundle, and every now and then she would go over to that bunk and crow and coo to the baby therein.

But though Fin Fan prized her child so highly, Jessamine Flower's father would rather she had not been born, and considered the babe a nuisance because she took up so much of her mother's time. He would rather that Fin Fan spent the hours in winding tobacco leaves than in nursing baby. However, Fin Fan managed to do both, and by dint of getting up very early in the morning and retiring very late at night, made as much money for her husband after baby was born as she ever did before. And it was well for her that that was so, as the baby would otherwise have been taken from her and given to some other more fortunate woman. Not that Fin Fan considered herself unfortunate. Oh, no! She had been a hard-working little slave all her life, and after her mistress sold her to be wife to Chung Kee, she never dreamt of complaining, because, though a wife, she was still a slave.

When Jessamine Flower was about six months old one of the ladies of the Mission, in making her round of Chinatown, ran in to see Fin Fan and her baby.

"What a beautiful child!" exclaimed the lady. "And, oh, how cunning," she continued, noting the amulets on the little ankles and wrists, the tiny, quilted vest and gay little trousers in which Fin Fan had arrayed her treasure.

Fin Fan sat still and shyly smiled, rubbing her chin slowly against the baby's round cheek. Fin Fan was scarcely more than a child herself in years.

"Oh, I want to ask you, dear little mother," said the lady, "if you will not send your little one to the Chinese baby show which we are going to have on Christmas Eve in the Presbyterian Mission schoolroom."[1]

Fin Fan's eyes brightened.

"What you think? That my baby get a prize?" she asked hesitatingly.

"I think so, indeed," answered the lady, feeling the tiny, perfectly shaped limbs and peeping into the brightest of black eyes.

From that day until Christmas Eve, Fin Fan thought of nothing but the baby show. She would be there with her baby, and if it won a prize, why, perhaps its father might be got to regard it with more favor, so that he would not frown so blackly and mutter under his breath at the slightest cry or coo.

On the morning of Christmas Eve, Chung Kee brought into Fin Fan's room a great bundle of tobacco which he declared had to be rolled by the evening, and when it was time to start for the show, the work was not nearly finished. However, Fin Fan dressed her baby, rolled it in a shawl, and with it in her arms, stealthily left the place.

It was a bright scene that greeted her upon arrival at the Mission house. The little competitors, in the enclosure that had been arranged for them, presented a peculiarly gorgeous appearance. All had been carefully prepared for the beauty test and looked as pretty as possible, though in some cases bejewelled head dresses and voluminous silken garments almost hid the competitors. Some small figures quite blazed in gold and tinsel, and then there were solemn cherubs almost free from clothing. The majority were plump and well-formed children, and there wasn't a cross or crying baby in the forty-five. Fin Fan's baby made the forty-sixth, and it was immediately surrounded by a group of admiring ladies.

How Fin Fan's eyes danced. Her baby would get a prize, and she would never more need to fear that her husband would give it away. That terrible dread had haunted her ever since its birth. "But surely," thought the little mother, "if it gets a prize he will be so proud that he will let me keep it forever."

And Fin Fan's baby did get a prize—a shining gold bit—and Fin Fan, delighted and excited, started for home. She was so happy and proud.

---

1 Officially designated a "foreign mission" until 1925, the Presbyterian Church in San Francisco's Chinatown was founded in 1853.

Chung Kee was very angry. Fin Fan was not in her room, and the work he had given her to do that morning was lying on the table undone. He said some hard words in a soft voice, which was his way sometimes, and then told the old woman who helped the men in the factory to be ready to carry a baby to the herb doctor's wife that night. "Tell her," said he, "that my cousin, the doctor, says that she long has desired a child, and so I send her one as a Christmas present, according to American custom."

Just then came a loud knocking at the door. Chung Kee slowly unbarred it, and two men entered, bearing a stretcher upon which a covered form lay.

"Why be you come to my store?" asked Chung Kee in broken English.

The men put down their burden, and one pulled down the covering from that which lay on the stretcher and revealed an unconscious woman and a dead baby.

"It was on Jackson Street.[1] The woman was trying to run with the baby in her arms, and just as she reached the crossing a butcher's cart came around the corner. Some Chinese who knows you advised me to bring them here. Your wife and child, eh?"

Chung Kee stared speechlessly at the still faces—an awful horror in his eyes.

A curious crowd began to fill the place. A doctor was in the midst of it and elbowed his way to where Fin Fan was beginning to regain consciousness.

"Move back all of you; we want some air here!" he shouted authoritatively, and Fin Fan, roused by the loud voice, feebly raised her head, and looking straight into her husband's eyes, said:

"Chung Kee's baby got first prize. Chung Kee let Fin Fan keep baby always."

That was all. Fin Fan's eyes closed. Her head fell back beside the prize baby's—hers forever.

Lin John

IT was New Year's Eve. Lin John mused over the brightly burning fire. Through the beams of the roof the stars shone, far away in the deep night sky they shone down upon him, and he

---

1   A major street in San Francisco's Chinatown.

felt their beauty, though he had no words for it. The long braid which was wound around his head lazily uncoiled and fell down his back; his smooth young face was placid and content. Lin John was at peace with the world. Within one of his blouse sleeves lay a small bag of gold, the accumulated earnings of three years, and that gold was to release his only sister from a humiliating and secret bondage. A sense of duty done led him to dream of the To-Come. What a fortunate fellow he was to have been able to obtain profitable work, and within three years to have saved four hundred dollars! In the next three years, he might be able to establish a little business and send his sister to their parents in China to live like an honest woman. The sharp edges of his life were forgotten in the drowsy warmth and the world faded into dreamland.

The latch was softly lifted; with stealthy step a woman approached the boy and knelt beside him. By the flickering gleam of the dying fire she found that for which she searched, and hiding it in her breast swiftly and noiselessly withdrew.

Lin John arose. His spirits were light—and so were his sleeves. He reached for his bowl of rice, then set it down, and suddenly his chopsticks clattered on the floor. With hands thrust into his blouse he felt for what was not there. Thus, with bewildered eyes for a few moments. Then he uttered a low cry and his face became old and gray.

A large apartment, richly carpeted; furniture of dark and valuable wood artistically carved; ceiling decorated with beautiful Chinese ornaments and gold incense burners; walls hung from top to bottom with long bamboo panels covered with silk, on which were printed Chinese characters; tropical plants, on stands; heavy curtains draped over windows. This, in the heart of Chinatown. And in the midst of these surroundings a girl dressed in a robe of dark blue silk worn over a full skirt richly embroidered. The sleeves fell over hands glittering with rings, and shoes of light silk were on her feet. Her hair was ornamented with flowers made of jewels; she wore three or four pairs of bracelets; her jewel earrings were over an inch long.

The girl was fair to see in that her face was smooth and oval, eyes long and dark, mouth small and round, hair of jetty hue, and figure petite and graceful.

Hanging over a chair by her side was a sealskin sacque, such as is worn by fashionable American women. The girl eyed it admiringly and every few moments stroked the soft fur with caressing fingers.

"Pau Sang," she called.

A curtain was pushed aside and a heavy, broad-faced Chinese woman in blouse and trousers of black sateen[1] stood revealed.

"Look," said the beauty. "I have a cloak like the American ladies. Is it not fine?"

Pau Sang nodded. "I wonder at Moy Loy," said she. "He is not in favor with the Gambling Cash Tiger and is losing money."

"Moy Loy gave it not to me. I bought it myself."

"But from whom did you obtain the money?"

"If I let out a secret, will you lock it up?"

Pau Sang smiled grimly, and her companion, sidling closer to her, said: "I took the money from my brother—it was my money; for years he had been working to make it for me, and last week he told me that he had saved four hundred dollars to pay to Moy Loy, so that I might be free. Now, what do I want to be free for? To be poor? To have no one to buy me good dinners and pretty things—to be gay no more? Lin John meant well, but he knows little. As to me, I wanted a sealskin sacque like the fine American ladies. So two moons gone by I stole away to the country and found him asleep. I did not awaken him—and—for the first day of the New Year I had this cloak. See?"

"Heaven frowns on me," said Lin John sadly, speaking to Moy Loy. "I made the money with which to redeem my sister and I have lost it. I grieve, and I would have you say to her that for her sake, I will engage myself laboriously and conform to virtue till three more New Years have grown old, and that though I merit blame for my carelessness, yet I am faithful unto her."

And with his spade over his shoulder he shuffled away from a house, from an upper window of which a woman looked down and under her breath called "Fool!"

Tian Shan's Kindred Spirit

HAD Tian Shan been an American and China to him a forbidden country, his daring exploits and thrilling adventures would have furnished inspiration for many a newspaper and magazine article, novel, and short story. As a hero, he would certainly have

---

1 A smooth, shiny fabric resembling satin, usually made of cotton.

far outshone Dewey, Peary, or Cook.[1] Being, however, a Chinese, and the forbidden country America, he was simply recorded by the American press as "a wily Oriental, who 'by ways that are dark and tricks that are vain,'[2] is eluding the vigilance of our brave customs officers." As to his experiences, the only one who took any particular interest in them was Fin Fan.

Fin Fan was Tian Shan's kindred spirit. She was the daughter of a Canadian Chinese storekeeper and the object of much concern to both Protestant Mission ladies and good Catholic sisters.

"I like learn talk and dress like you," she would respond to attempts to bring her into the folds, "but I not want think like you. Too much discuss." And when it was urged upon her that her father was a convert—the Mission ladies declaring, to the Protestant faith, and the nuns, to the Catholic—she would calmly answer: "That so? Well, I not my father. Beside I think my father just say he Catholic (or Protestant) for sake of be amiable to you. He good-natured man and want to please you."

This independent and original stand led Fin Fan to live, as it were, in an atmosphere of outlawry even amongst her own countrywomen, for all proper Chinese females in Canada and America, unless their husbands are men of influence in their own country, conform upon request to the religion of the women of the white race.

Fin Fan sat on her father's doorstep amusing herself with a ball of yarn and a kitten. She was a pretty girl, with the delicate features, long slanting eyes, and pouting mouth of the women of Soo Chow, to which province her dead mother had belonged.

Tian Shan came along.

"Will you come for a walk around the mountain?" asked he.

"I don't know," answered Fin Fan.

"Do!" he urged.

---

1 George Dewey (1837–1917) was a US naval admiral famous for leading the Battle of Manila Bay (1898), in which the US seized control of the Philippines; Robert Edwin Peary (1856–1920) was a US explorer who, after several expeditions in the Arctic, claimed to have reached the North Pole in 1909; Captain James Cook (1728–79) was a British explorer and cartographer famous for expeditions in the Pacific Ocean in which he interacted with indigenous groups in Australia and Hawaii.

2 From Bret Harte, "Plain Language from Truthful James." See Appendix B1.

The walk around the mountain is enjoyable at all seasons, but particularly so in the fall of the year when the leaves on the trees are turning all colors, making the mount itself look like one big posy.

The air was fresh, sweet, and piny. As Tian Shan and Fin Fan walked, they chatted gaily—not so much of Tian Shan or Fin Fan as of the brilliant landscape, the sun shining through a grove of black-trunked trees with golden leaves, the squirrels that whisked past them, the birds twittering and soliloquizing over their vanishing homes, and many other objects of nature. Tian Shan's roving life had made him quite a woodsman, and Fin Fan—well, Fin Fan was his kindred spirit.

A large oak, looking like a smouldering pyre, invited them to a seat under its boughs.

After happily munching half a dozen acorns, Fin Fan requested to be told all about Tian Shan's last adventure. Every time he crossed the border, he was obliged to devise some new scheme by which to accomplish his object, and as he usually succeeded, there was always a new story to tell whenever he returned to Canada.

This time he had run across the river a mile above the Lachine Rapids[1] in an Indian war canoe, and landed in a cove surrounded by reefs, where pursuit was impossible. It had been a perilous undertaking, for he had had to make his way right through the swift current of the St. Lawrence, the turbulent rapids so near that it seemed as if indeed he must yield life to the raging cataract. But with indomitable courage he had forged ahead, the canoe, with every plunge of his paddles, rising on the swells and cutting through the whitecaps, until at last he reached the shore for which he had risked so much.

Fin Fan was thoughtful for a few moments after listening to his narration.

"Why," she queried at last, "when you can make so much more money in the States than in Canada, do you come so often to this side and endanger your life as you do when returning?"

Tian Shan was puzzled himself. He was not accustomed to analyzing the motives for his actions.

Seeing that he remained silent, Fin Fan went on:

"I think," said she, "that it is very foolish of you to keep

---

1 A series of rapids on the St. Lawrence River at the southern shore of the Island of Montreal.

running backwards and forwards from one country to another, wasting your time and accomplishing nothing."

Tian Shan dug up some soft, black earth with the heels of his boots.

"Perhaps it is," he observed.

That night Tian Shan's relish for his supper was less keen than usual, and when he laid his head upon his pillow, instead of sleeping, he could only think of Fin Fan. Fin Fan! Fin Fan! Her face was before him, her voice in his ears. The clock ticked Fin Fan; the cat purred it; a little mouse squeaked it; a night-bird sang it. He tossed about, striving to think what ailed him. With the first glimmer of morning came knowledge of his condition. He loved Fin Fan, even as the American man loves the girl he would make his wife.

Now Tian Shan, unlike most Chinese, had never saved money and, therefore, had no home to offer Fin Fan. He knew, also, that her father had his eye upon a young merchant in Montreal, who would make a very desirable son-in-law.

In the early light of the morning Tian Shan arose and wrote a letter. In this letter, which was written with a pointed brush on long yellow sheets of paper, he told Fin Fan that, as she thought it was foolish, he was going to relinquish the pleasure of running backwards and forwards across the border, for some time at least. He was possessed of a desire to save money so that he could have a wife and a home. In a year, perhaps, he would see her again.

Lee Ping could hardly believe that his daughter was seriously opposed to becoming the wife of such a good-looking, prosperous young merchant as Wong Ling. He tried to bring her to reason, but instead of yielding her will to the parental, she declared that she would take a place as a domestic to some Canadian lady with whom she had become acquainted at the Mission sooner than wed the man her father had chosen.

"Is not Wong Ling a proper man?" inquired the amazed parent.

"Whether he is proper or improper makes no difference to me," returned Fin Fan. "I will not marry him, and the law in this country is so that you cannot compel me to wed against my will."

Lee Ping's good-natured face became almost pitiful as he regarded his daughter. Only a hen who has hatched a duckling and sees it take to the water for the first time could have worn such an expression.

Fin Fan's heart softened. She was as fond of her father as he of her. Sidling up to him, she began stroking his sleeve in a coaxing fashion.

"For a little while longer I wish only to stay with you," said she.

Lee Ping shook his head, but gave in.

"You must persuade her yourself," said he to Wong Ling that evening. "We are in a country where the sacred laws and customs of China are as naught."

So Wong Ling pressed his own suit. He was not a bad-looking fellow, and knew well also how to honey his speech. Moreover, he believed in paving his way with offerings of flowers, trinkets, sweetmeats.

Fin Fan looked, listened, and accepted. Every gift that could be kept was carefully put by in a trunk which she hoped some day to take to New York. "They will help to furnish Tian Shan's home," said she.

Twelve moons had gone by since Tian Shan had begun to think of saving and once again he was writing to Fin Fan.

"I have made and I have saved," wrote he. "Shall I come for you?"

And by return mail came an answer which was not "No."

Of course, Fin Fan's heart beat high with happiness when Tian Shan walked into her father's store; but to gratify some indescribable feminine instinct she simply nodded coolly in his direction, and continued what might be called a flirtation with Wong Ling, who had that morning presented her with the first Chinese lily of the season and a box of the best preserved ginger.

Tian Shan sat himself down on a box of dried mushrooms and glowered at his would-be rival, who, unconscious of the fact that he was making a third when there was needed but a two, chattered on like a running stream. Thoughtlessly and kittenishly Fin Fan tossed a word, first to this one, and next to that; and whilst loving with all her heart one man, showed much more favor to the other.

Finally Tian Shan arose from the mushrooms and marched over to the counter.

"These yours?" he inquired of Wong Ling, indicating the lily and the box of ginger.

"Miss Fin Fan has done me the honor of accepting them," blandly replied Wong Ling.

"Very good," commented Tian Shan. He picked up the gifts and hurled them into the street.

A scene of wild disorder followed. In the midst of it the father of Fin Fan, who had been downtown, appeared at the door.

"What is the meaning of this?" he demanded.

"Oh, father, father, they are killing one another! Separate them, oh, separate them!" pleaded Fin Fan.

But her father's interference was not needed. Wong Ling swerved to one side, and falling, struck the iron foot of the stove. Tian Shan, seeing his rival unconscious, rushed out of the store.

The moon hung in the sky like a great yellow pearl and the night was beautiful and serene. But Fin Fan, miserable and unhappy, could not rest.

"All your fault! All your fault!" declared the voice of conscience.

"Fin Fan," spake a voice near to her.

Could it be? Yes, it surely was Tian Shan.

She could not refrain from a little scream.

"Sh! Sh!" bade Tian Shan. "Is he dead?"

"No," replied Fin Fan, "he is very sick, but he will recover."

"I might have been a murderer," mused Tian Shan. "As it is I am liable to arrest and imprisonment for years."

"I am the cause of all the trouble," wept Fin Fan.

Tian Shan patted her shoulder in an attempt at consolation, but a sudden footfall caused her to start away from him.

"They are hunting you!" she cried. "Go! Go!"

And Tian Shan, casting upon her one long farewell look, strode with rapid steps away.

Poor Fin Fan! She had indeed lost everyone, and added to that shame, was the secret sorrow and remorse of her own heart. All the hopes and the dreams which had filled the year that was gone were now as naught, and he, around whom they had been woven, was, because of her, a fugitive from justice, even in Canada.

One day she picked up an American newspaper which a customer had left on the counter, and, more as a habit than for any other reason, began spelling out the paragraphs.

A Chinese, who has been unlawfully breathing United States air for several years, was captured last night crossing the border, a feat which he is said to have successfully accomplished more than a dozen times during the last few years. His name is Tian Shan, and there is no doubt whatever that he will be deported to China as soon as the necessary papers can be made out.

Fin Fan lifted her head. Fresh air and light had come into her soul. Her eyes sparkled. In the closet behind her hung a suit of her father's clothes. Fin Fan was a tall and well-developed young woman.

"You are to have company," said the guard, pausing in front of Tian Shan's cage. "A boy without certificate was caught this morning by two of our men this side of Rouse's Point.[1] He has been unable to give an account of himself, so we are putting him in here with you. You will probably take the trip to China together."

Tian Shan continued reading a Chinese paper which he had been allowed to retain. He was not at all interested in the companion thrust upon him. He would have preferred to be left alone. The face of the absent one is so much easier conjured in silence and solitude. It was a foregone conclusion with Tian Shan that he would never again behold Fin Fan, and with true Chinese philosophy he had begun to reject realities and accept dreams as the stuff upon which to live. Life itself was hard, bitter, and disappointing. Only dreams are joyous and smiling.

One star after another had appeared until the heavens were patterned with twinkling lights. Through his prison bars Tian Shan gazed solemnly upon the firmament.

Some one touched his elbow. It was his fellow-prisoner. So far the boy had not intruded himself, having curled himself up in a corner of the cell and slept soundly apparently, ever since his advent.

"What do you want?" asked Tian Shan not unkindly.

"To go to China with you and to be your wife," was the softly surprising reply.

"Fin Fan!" exclaimed Tian Shan. "Fin Fan!"

The boy pulled off his cap.

"Aye," said he. "'Tis Fin Fan!"

The Sing Song Woman

I

AH OI, the Chinese actress, threw herself down on the floor of her room and, propping her chin on her hands, gazed up at the narrow strip of blue sky which could be seen through her

---

1 A fortified point at the northeastern corner of New York State, at the mouth of the Richelieu River running from Quebec into Lake Champlain.

window. She seemed to have lost her usually merry spirits. For the first time since she had left her home her thoughts were seriously with the past, and she longed with a great longing for the Chinese Sea, the boats, and the wet, blowing sands. She had been a fisherman's daughter, and many a spring had she watched the gathering of the fishing fleet to which her father's boat belonged. Well could she remember clapping her hands as the vessels steered out to sea for the season's work, her father's amongst them, looking as bright as paint could make it, and flying a neat little flag at its stern; and well could she also remember how her mother had taught her to pray to "Our Lady of Pootoo,"[1] the goddess of sailors. One does not need to be a Christian to be religious, and Ah Oi's parents had carefully instructed their daughter according to their light, and it was not their fault if their daughter was a despised actress in an American Chinatown.

The sound of footsteps outside her door seemed to chase away Ah Oi's melancholy mood, and when a girl crossed her threshold, she was gazing amusedly into the street below—a populous thoroughfare of Chinatown.

The newcomer presented a strange appearance. She was crying so hard that red paint, white powder, and carmine lip salve were all besmeared over a naturally pretty face.

Ah Oi began to laugh.

"Why, Mag-gee," said she, "how odd you look with little red rivers running over your face! What is the matter?"

"What is the matter?" echoed Mag-gee, who was a half-white girl. "The matter is that I wish that I were dead! I am to be married tonight to a Chinaman whom I have never seen, and whom I can't bear. It isn't natural that I should. I always took to other men, and never could put up with a Chinaman. I was born in America, and I'm not Chinese in looks nor in any other way. See! My eyes are blue, and there is gold in my hair; and I love potatoes and beef, and every time I eat rice it makes me sick, and so does chopped up food. He came down about a week ago and made arrangements with father, and now everything is fixed and I'm going away forever to live in China. I shall be a Chinese woman next year—I commenced to be one today, when father made me put the paint and powder on my face, and dress in Chinese clothes. Oh! I never want anyone to feel as I do. To think

---

1 Guanyin (see p. 88, note 1) is supposed to reside on the island of P'u T'o, and was among other things the deity who protected sailors.

of having to marry a Chinaman! How I hate the Chinese! And the worst of it is, loving somebody else all the while."

The girl burst into passionate sobs. The actress, who was evidently accustomed to hearing her compatriots reviled by the white and half-white denizens of Chinatown, laughed—a light, rippling laugh. Her eyes glinted mischievously.

"Since you do not like the Chinese men," said she, "why do you give yourself to one? And if you care so much for somebody else, why do you not fly to that somebody?"

Bold words for a Chinese woman to utter! But Ah Oi was not as other Chinese women, who all their lives have been sheltered by a husband or father's care.

The half-white girl stared at her companion.

"What do you mean?" she asked.

"This," said Ah Oi. The fair head and dark head drew near together; and two women passing the door heard whispers and suppressed laughter.

"Ah Oi is up to some trick," said one.

II

"The Sing Song Woman! The Sing Song Woman!" It was a wild cry of anger and surprise.

The ceremony of unveiling the bride had just been performed, and Hwuy Yen, the father of Mag-gee, and his friends, were in a state of great excitement, for the unveiled, brilliantly clothed little figure standing in the middle of the room was not the bride who was to have been; but Ah Oi, the actress, the Sing Song Woman.

Every voice but one was raised. The bridegroom, a tall, handsome man, did not understand what had happened, and could find no words to express his surprise at the uproar. But he was so newly wedded that it was not until Hwuy Yen advanced to the bride and shook his hand threateningly in her face, that he felt himself a husband, and interfered by placing himself before the girl.

"What is all this?" he inquired. "What has my wife done to merit such abuse?"

"Your wife!" scornfully ejaculated Hwuy Yen. "She is no wife of yours. You were to have married my daughter, Mag-gee. This is not my daughter; this is an impostor, an actress, a Sing Song Woman. Where is my daughter?"

Ah Oi laughed her peculiar, rippling, amused laugh. She was in no wise abashed, and, indeed, appeared to be enjoying the situation. Her bright, defiant eyes met her questioner's boldly as she answered:

"Mag-gee has gone to eat beef and potatoes with a white man. Oh, we had such a merry time making this play!"

"See how worthless a thing she is," said Hwuy Yen to the young bridegroom.

The latter regarded Ah Oi compassionately. He was a man, and perhaps a little tenderness crept into his heart for the girl towards whom so much bitterness was evinced. She was beautiful. He drew near to her.

"Can you not justify yourself?" he asked sadly.

For a moment Ah Oi gazed into his eyes—the only eyes that had looked with true kindness into hers for many a moon.

"You justify me," she replied with an upward, pleading glance.

Then Ke Leang, the bridegroom, spoke. He said: "The daughter of Hwuy Yen cared not to become my bride and has sought her happiness with another. Ah Oi, having a kind heart, helped her to that happiness, and tried to recompense me my loss by giving me herself. She has been unwise and indiscreet; but the good that is in her is more than the evil, and now that she is my wife, none shall say a word against her."

Ah Oi pulled at his sleeve.

"You give me credit for what I do not deserve," said she. "I had no kind feelings. I thought only of mischief, and I am not your wife. It is but a play like the play I shall act tomorrow."

"Hush!" bade Ke Leang. "You shall act no more. I will marry you again and take you to China."

Then something in Ah Oi's breast, which for a long time had been hard as stone, became soft and tender, and her eyes ran over with tears. "Oh, sir," said she, "it takes a heart to make a heart, and you have put one today in the bosom of a Sing Song Woman."

The Silver Leaves

THERE was a fringe of trees along an open field. They were not very tall trees, neither were they trees that flowered or fruited; but to the eyes of Ah Leen they were very beautiful. Their slender branches were covered with leaves of a light green showing a silvery under surface, and when the wind moved or tossed them, silver gleams flashed through the green in a most enchanting way.

Ah Leen stood on the other side of the road admiring the trees with the silver leaves.

A little old woman carrying a basket full of duck's eggs came happily hobbling along. She paused by the side of Ah Leen.

"Happy love!" said she. "Your eyes are as bright as jade jewels!"

Ah Leen drew a long breath. "See!" said she, "the dancing leaves."

The little old woman adjusted her blue goggles and looked up at the trees. "If only," said she, "some of that silver was up my sleeve, I would buy you a pink parasol and a folding fan."

"And if some of it were mine," answered Ah Leen, "I would give it to my baby brother." And she went on to tell the little old woman that that eve there was to be a joyful time at her father's house, for her baby brother was to have his head shaved for the first time, and everybody was coming to see it done and would give her baby brother gifts to give. She loved well her baby brother. He was so very small and so very lively, and his fingers and toes were so pink. And to think that he had lived a whole moon,[1] and she had no offering to prove the big feeling that swelled and throbbed in her little heart for him.

Ah Leen sighed very wistfully.

Just then a brisk breeze blew over the trees, and as it passed by, six of the silver leaves floated to the ground.

"Oh! Oh!" cried little Ah Leen. She pattered over to where they had fallen and picked them up.

Returning to the old woman, she displayed her treasures.

"Three for you and three for me!" she cried.

The old woman accepted the offering smilingly, and happily hobbled away. In every house she entered, she showed her silver

---

1 See p. 124, note 1 on "Completion of the Moon."

leaves, and told how she had obtained them, and every housewife that saw and heard her, bought her eggs at a double price.

At sundown, the guests with their presents began streaming into the house of Man You. Amongst them was a little old woman. She was not as well off as the other guests, but because she was the oldest of all the company, she was given the seat of honor. Ah Leen, the youngest daughter of the house, sat on a footstool at her feet. Ah Leen's eyes were very bright and her cheeks glowed. She was wearing a pair of slippers with butterfly toes, and up her little red sleeve, carefully folded in a large leaf, were three small silver leaves.

Once when the mother of Ah Leen brought a cup of tea to the little old woman, the little old woman whispered in her ear, and the mother of Ah Leen patted the head of her little daughter and smiled kindly down upon her.

Then the baby's father shaved the head of the baby, the Little Bright One. He did this very carefully, leaving a small patch of hair, the shape of a peach, in the centre of the small head. That peach-shaped patch would some day grow into a queue.[1] Ah Leen touched it lovingly with her little finger after the ceremony was over. Never had the Little Bright One seemed so dear.

The gifts were distributed after all the lanterns were lit. It was a pretty sight. The mother of the Little Bright One held him on her lap, whilst each guest, relative, or friend, in turn, laid on a table by her side his gift of silver and gold, enclosed in a bright red envelope.

The elder sister had just passed Ah Leen with her gift, when Ah Leen arose, and following after her sister to the gift-laden table, proudly deposited thereon three leaves.

"They are silver—silver," cried Ah Leen.

Nearly everybody smiled aloud; but Ah Leen's mother gently lifted the leaves and murmured in Ah Leen's ear, "They are the sweetest gift of all."

How happy felt Ah Leen! As to the old woman who sold ducks' eggs, she beamed all over her little round face, and when she went away, she left behind her a pink parasol and a folding fan.

1 See p. 64, note 1.

The Peacock Lantern

IT was such a pretty lantern—the prettiest of all the pretty lanterns that the lantern men carried. Ah Wing longed to possess it. Upon the transparent paper which covered the fine network of bamboo which enclosed the candle, was painted a picture of a benevolent prince, riding on a peacock with spreading tail. Never had Ah Wing seen such a gorgeous lantern, or one so altogether admirable.

"Honorable father," said he, "is not that a lantern of illuminating beauty, and is not thy string of cash[1] too heavy for thine honorable shoulders?"

His father laughed.

"Come hither," he bade the lantern man. "Now," said he to Ah Wing, "choose which lantern pleaseth thee best. To me all are the same."

Ah Wing pointed to the peacock lantern, and hopped about impatiently, whilst the lantern man fumbled with the wires which kept his lanterns together.

"Oh, hasten! hasten!" cried Ah Wing.

The lantern man looked into his bright little face.

"Honorable little one," said he, "would not one of the other lanterns please thee as well as this one? For indeed, I would, if I could, retain the peacock lantern. It is the one lantern of all which delights my own little lad and he is sick and cannot move from his bed."

Ah Wing's face became red.

"Why then dost thou display the lantern?" asked the father of Ah Wing.

"To draw attention to the others," answered the man. "I am very poor and it is hard for me to provide my child with rice."

The father of Ah Wing looked at his little son.

"Well?" said he.

Ah Wing's face was still red.

"I want the peacock lantern," he declared.

The father of Ah Wing brought forth his string of cash and drew therefrom more than double the price of the lantern.

"Take this," said he to the lantern man. "'Twill fill thy little sick boy's bowl with rice for many a day to come."

---

1 Standard Chinese coins, with holes in the center, were often strung together to form higher denominations.

The lantern man returned humble thanks, but while unfastening the peacock lantern from the others, his face looked very sad.

Ah Wing shifted from one foot to another.

The lantern man placed the lantern in his hand. Ah Wing stood still holding it.

"Thou hast thy heart's desire now," said his father. "Laugh and be merry."

But with the lantern man's sad face before him, Ah Wing could not laugh and be merry.

"If you please, honorable father," said he, "may I go with the honorable lantern man to see his little sick boy?"

"Yes," replied his father. "And I will go too."

When Ah Wing stood beside the bed of the little sick son of the lantern man, he said:

"I have come to see thee, because my father has bought for my pleasure the lantern which gives thee pleasure; but he has paid therefor to thy father what will buy thee food to make thee strong and well."

The little sick boy turned a very pale and very small face to Ah Wing.

"I care not," said he, "for food to make me strong and well—for strong and well I shall never be; but I would that I had the lantern for the sake of San Kee."

"And who may San Kee be?" inquired Ah Wing.

"San Kee," said the little sick boy, "is an honorable hunchback. Every evening he comes to see me and to take pleasure in my peacock lantern. It is the only thing in the world that gives poor San Kee pleasure. I would for his sake that I might have kept the peacock lantern."

"For his sake!" echoed Ah Wing.

"Yes, for his sake," answered the little sick boy. "It is so good to see him happy. It is that which makes me happy."

The tears came into Ah Wing's eyes.

"Honorable lantern man," said he, turning to the father of the little sick boy, "I wish no more for the peacock lantern. Keep it, I pray thee, for thy little sick boy. And honorable father"—he took his father's hand—"kindly buy for me at the same price as the peacock lantern one of the other beautiful lanterns belonging to the honorable lantern man."

Children of Peace[1]

I

THEY were two young people with heads hot enough and hearts true enough to believe that the world was well lost for love, and they were Chinese.

They sat beneath the shade of a cluster of tall young pines forming a perfect bower of greenness and coolness on the slope of Strawberry hill.[2] Their eyes were looking oceanwards, following a ship nearing the misty horizon. Very serious were their faces and voices. That ship, sailing from west to east, carried from each a message to his and her kin—a message which humbly but firmly set forth that they were resolved to act upon their belief and to establish a home in the new country, where they would ever pray for blessings upon the heads of those who could not see as they could see, nor hear as they could hear.

"My mother will weep when she reads," sighed the girl.

"Pau Tsu," the young man asked, "do you repent?"

"No," she replied, "but—"

She drew from her sleeve a letter written on silk paper.

The young man ran his eye over the closely penciled characters.

"'Tis very much in its tenor like what my father wrote to me," he commented.

"Not that."

Pau Tsu indicated with the tip of her pink forefinger a paragraph which read:

Are you not ashamed to confess that you love a youth who is not yet your husband? Such disgraceful boldness will surely bring upon your head the punishment you deserve. Before twelve moons go by you will be an Autumn Fan.[3]

The young man folded the missive and returned it to the girl, whose face was averted from his.

---

1 Originally published in *New England Magazine* in 1910 under the title "The Bird of Love."

2 A hill located in San Francisco's Golden Gate Park.

3 In a 1910 story in *New England Magazine* entitled "An Autumn Fan," Sui Sin Far further criticizes this image, which implies that a woman might become too old to be desirable as a wife.

"Our parents," said he, "knew not love in its springing and growing, its bud and blossom. Let us, therefore, respectfully read their angry letters, but heed them not. Shall I not love you dearer and more faithfully because you became mine at my own request and not at my father's? And Pau Tsu, be not ashamed."

The girl lifted radiant eyes.

"Listen," said she. "When you, during vacation, went on that long journey to New York, to beguile the time I wrote a play. My heroine is very sad, for the one she loves is far away and she is much tormented by enemies. They would make her ashamed of her love. But this is what she replies to one cruel taunt:

"When Memory sees his face and hears his voice,
The Bird of Love within my heart sings sweetly,
So sweetly, and so clear and jubilant,
That my little Home Bird, Sorrow,
Hides its head under its wing,
And appeareth as if dead.
Shame! Ah, speak not that word to one who loves!
For loving, all my noblest, tenderest feelings are awakened,
And I become too great to be ashamed."

"You do love me then, eh, Pau Tsu?" queried the young man.

"If it is not love, what is it?" softly answered the girl.

Happily chatting they descended the green hill. Their holiday was over. A little later Liu Venti was on the ferry-boat which leaves every half hour for the Western shore, bound for the Berkeley Hills opposite the Golden Gate, and Pau Tsu was in her room at the San Francisco Seminary,[1] where her father's ambition to make her the equal in learning of the son of Liu Jusong had placed her.

II

THE last little scholar of Pau Tsu's free class for children was pattering out of the front door when Liu Venti softly entered the schoolroom. Pau Tsu was leaning against her desk, looking rather weary. She did not hear her husband's footstep, and when he

---

1 The San Francisco Theological Seminary of the Presbyterian Church was established in 1871 and in 1892 moved to a permanent location in San Anselmo, CA.

approached her and placed his hand upon her shoulder she gave a nervous start.

"You are tired, dear one," said he, leading her towards the door where a seat was placed.

"Teacher, the leaves of a flower you gave me are withering, and mother says that is a bad omen."

The little scholar had turned back to tell her this.

"Nay," said Pau Tsu gently. "There are no bad omens. It is time for the flower to wither and die. It cannot live always."

"Poor flower!" compassionated the child.

"Not so poor!" smiled Pau Tsu. "The flower has seed from which other flowers will spring, more beautiful than itself!"

"Ah, I will tell my mother!"

The little child ran off, her queue dangling and flopping as she loped along. The teachers watched her join a group of youngsters playing on the curb in front of the quarters of the Six Companies.[1] One of the Chiefs in passing had thrown a handful of firecrackers amongst the children, and the result was a small bonfire and great glee.

It was seven years since Liu Venti and Pau Tsu had begun their work in San Francisco's Chinatown; seven years of struggle and hardship, working and waiting, living, learning, fighting, failing, loving—and conquering. The victory, to an onlooker, might have seemed small; just a modest school for adult pupils of their own race, a few white night pupils, and a free school for children. But the latter was in itself evidence that Liu Venti and Pau Tsu had not only sailed safely through the waters of poverty, but had reached a haven from which they could enjoy the blessedness of stretching out helping hands to others.

During the third year of their marriage twin sons had been born to them, and the children, long looked for and eagerly desired, were welcomed with joy and pride. But mingled with this joy and pride was much serious thought. Must their beloved sons ever remain exiles from the land of their ancestors? For their little ones Liu Venti and Pau Tsu were much more worldly than they had ever been themselves, and they could not altogether stifle a yearning to be able to bestow upon them the brightest and best that the world has to offer. Then, too, memories of childhood came thronging with their children, and filial affection reawakened. Both Liu Venti and Pau Tsu had been only children; both had been beloved and had received all the advantages which

---

1 See p. 68, note 2.

wealth in their own land could obtain; both had been the joy and pride of their homes. They might, they sometimes sadly mused, have been a little less assured in their declarations to the old folk; a little kinder, a little more considerate. It was a higher light and a stronger motive than had ever before influenced their lives which had led them to break the ties which had bound them; yet those from whom they had cut away were ignorant of such forces; at least, unable, by reason of education and environment, to comprehend them. There were days when everything seemed to taste bitter to Pau Tsu because she could not see her father and mother. And Liu's blood would tingle and his heart swell in his chest in the effort to banish from his mind the shadows of those who had cared for him before ever he had seen Pau Tsu.

"I was a little fellow of just about that age when my mother first taught me to kotow[1] to my father and run to greet him when he came into the house," said he, pointing to Little Waking Eyes, who came straggling after them, a kitten in his chubby arms.

"Oh, Liu Venti," replied Pau Tsu, "you are thinking of home—even as I. This morning I thought I heard my mother's voice, calling to me as I have so often heard her on sunny mornings in the Province of the Happy River.[2] She would flutter her fan at me in a way that was peculiarly her own. And my father! Oh, my dear father!"

"Aye," responded Liu Venti. "Our parents loved us, and the love of parents is a good thing. Here, we live in exile, and though we are happy in each other, in our children, and in the friendships which the new light has made possible for us, yet I would that our sons could be brought up in our own country and not in an American Chinatown."

He glanced comprehensively up the street as he said this. A motley throng, made up, not only of his own countrymen, but of all nationalities, was scuffling along. Two little children were eating rice out of a tin dish on a near-by door-step. The sing song voices of girls were calling to one another from high balconies up a shadowy alley. A boy, balancing a wooden tray of viands on his head, was crossing the street. The fat barber was laughing hilariously at a drunken white man who had fallen into a gutter. A withered old fellow, carrying a bird in a cage, stood at a corner

---

1 See p. 73, note 1.
2 The province of Kiang-Su in eastern China was sometimes translated as "The Country of the Happy River."

entreating passers-by to pause and have a good fortune told. A vender of dried fish and bunches of sausages held noisy possession of the corner opposite.

Liu Venti's glance travelled back to the children eating rice on the doorstep, then rested on the head of his own young son.

"And our fathers' mansions," said he, "are empty of the voices of little ones."

"Let us go home," said Pau Tsu suddenly. Liu Venti started. Pau Tsu's words echoed the wish of his own heart. But he was not as bold as she.

"How dare we?" he asked. "Have not our fathers sworn that they will never forgive us?"

"The light within me this evening," replied Pau Tsu, "reveals that our parents sorrow because they have this sworn. Oh, Liu Venti, ought we not to make our parents happy, even if we have to do so against their will?"

"I would that we could," replied Liu Venti. "But before we can approach them, there is to be overcome your father's hatred for my father and my father's hatred for thine."

A shadow crossed Pau Tsu's face. But not for long. It lifted as she softly said: "Love is stronger than hate."

Little Waking Eyes clambered upon his father's knee.

"Me too," cried Little Sleeping Eyes, following him. With chubby fists he pushed his brother to one side and mounted his father also.

Pau Tsu looked across at her husband and sons. "Oh, Liu Venti," she said, "for the sake of our children; for the sake of our parents; for the sake of a broader field of work[1] for ourselves, we are called upon to make a sacrifice!"

Three months later, Liu Venti and Pau Tsu, with mingled sorrow and hope in their hearts, bade goodbye to their little sons and sent them across the sea, offerings of love to parents of whom both son and daughter remembered nothing but love and kindness, yet from whom that son and daughter were estranged by a poisonous thing called Hate.

III

TWO little boys were playing together on a beach. One gazed across the sea with wondering eyes. A thought had come—a memory.

---

1 A common phrase used by missionaries to describe working in foreign countries.

"Where are father and mother?" he asked, turning to his brother.

The other little boy gazed bewilderedly back at him and echoed:

"Where are father and mother?"

Then the two little fellows sat down in the sand and began to talk to one another in a queer little old-fashioned way of their own. "Grandfathers and grandmothers are very good," said Little Waking Eyes.

"Very good," repeated Little Sleeping Eyes.

"They give us lots of nice things."

"Lots of nice things!"

"Balls and balloons and puff puffs and kitties."

"Balls and balloons and puff puffs and kitties."

"The puppet show is very beautiful!"

"Very beautiful!"

"And grandfathers fly kites and puff fire flowers!"

"Fly kites and puff fire flowers!"

"And grandmothers have cakes and sweeties."

"Cakes and sweeties!"

"But where are father and mother?"

Little Waking Eyes and Little Sleeping Eyes again searched each other's faces; but neither could answer the other's question. Their little mouths drooped pathetically; they propped their chubby little faces in their hands and heaved queer little sighs.

There were father and mother one time—always, always; father and mother and Sung Sung.[1] Then there was the big ship and Sung Sung only, and the big water. After the big water, grandfathers and grandmothers; and Little Waking Eyes had gone to live with one grandfather and grandmother, and Little Sleeping Eyes had gone to live with another grandfather and grandmother. And the old Sung Sung had gone away and two new Sung Sungs had come. And Little Waking Eyes and Little Sleeping Eyes had been good and had not cried at all. Had not father and mother said that grandfathers and grandmothers were just the same as fathers and mothers?

---

1 A kinship term designating an in-law paternal aunt, here used loosely to indicate a female servant. Sui Sin Far, who had limited exposure to the Chinese language, may have been extrapolating from her own experience: according to her sister, "we had only one servant that I can ever remember, a woman named Sung-Sung whom papa brought from China; but she was more like one of our family, a sort of slave" (*Me* 18).

"Just the same as fathers and mothers," repeated Little Waking Eyes to Little Sleeping Eyes, and Little Sleeping Eyes nodded his head and solemnly repeated: "Just the same as fathers and mothers."

Then all of a sudden Little Waking Eyes stood up, rubbed his fists into his eyes and shouted: "I want my father and mother; I want my father and mother!" And Little Sleeping Eyes also stood up and echoed strong and bold: "I want my father and mother; I want my father and mother."

It was the day of rebellion of the sons of Liu Venti and Pau Tsu.

When the two new Sung Sungs who had been having their fortunes told by an itinerant fortune-teller whom they had met some distance down the beach, returned to where they had left their young charges, and found them not, they were greatly perturbed and rent the air with their cries. Where could the children have gone? The beach was a lonely one, several miles from the seaport city where lived the grandparents of the children. Behind the beach, the bare land rose for a little way back up the sides and across hills to meet a forest dark and dense.

Said one Sung Sung to another, looking towards this forest: "One might as well search for a pin at the bottom of the ocean as search for the children there. Besides, it is haunted with evil spirits."

"A-ya, A-ya, A-ya!" cried the other, "Oh, what will my master and mistress say if I return home without Little Sleeping Eyes, who is the golden plum of their hearts?"

"And what will my master and mistress do to me if I enter their presence without Little Waking Eyes? I verily believe that the sun shines for them only when he is around."

For over an hour the two distracted servants walked up and down the beach, calling the names of their little charges; but there was no response.

IV

"THY grandson—the beloved of my heart, is lost, is lost! Go forth, old man, and find him."

Liu Jusong, who had just returned from the Hall, where from morn till eve he adjusted the scales of justice, stared speechlessly at the old lady who had thus accosted him. The loss of his grandson he scarcely realized; but that his humble spouse had suddenly become his superior officer, surprised him out of his dignity.

"What meaneth thy manner?" he bewilderedly inquired.

"It meaneth," returned the old lady, "that I have borne all I can bear. Thy grandson is lost through thy fault. Go, find him!"

"How my fault? Surely, thou art demented!"

"Hadst thou not hated Li Wang, Little Waking Eyes and Little Sleeping Eyes could have played together in our own grounds or within the compound of Li Wang. But this is no time to discourse on spilt plums. Go, follow Li Wang in the search for thy grandsons. I hear that he has already left for the place where the stupid thorns who had them in charge, declare they disappeared."

The old lady broke down. "Oh, my little Bright Eyes! Where art thou wandering?" she wailed. Liu Jusong regarded her sternly. "If my enemy," said he, "searcheth for my grandsons, then will not I."

With dignified step he passed out of the room. But in the hall was a child's plaything. His glance fell upon it and his expression softened. Following the servants despatched by his wife, the old mandarin[1] joined in the search for Little Waking Eyes and Little Sleeping Eyes.

Under the quiet stars they met—the two old men who had quarreled in student days and who ever since had cultivated hate for each other. The cause of their quarrel had long been forgotten; but in the fertile soil of minds irrigated with the belief that the superior man hates well and long, the seed of hate had germinated and flourished. Was it not because of that hate that their children were exiles from the homes of their fathers—those children who had met in a foreign land, and in spite of their fathers' hatred, had linked themselves in love.

They spread their fans before their faces, each pretending not to see the other, while their servants inquired: "What news of the honorable little ones?"

"No news," came the answer from each side.

The old men pondered sternly. Finally Liu Jusong said to his servants: "I will search in the forest."

"So also will I," announced Li Wang.

Liu Jusong lowered his fan. For the first time in many years he allowed his eyes to rest on the countenance of his quondam[2] friend, and that quondam friend returned his glance. But the

---

1 A high government official.
2 Former.

servant men shuddered. "It is the haunted forest," they cried. "Oh, honorable masters, venture not amongst evil spirits!"

But Li Wang laughed them to scorn, as also did Liu Jusong.

"Give me a lantern," bade Li Wang. "I will search alone since you are afraid."

He spake to his servants; but it was not his servants who answered: "Nay, not alone. Thy grandson is my grandson and mine is thine!"

"Oh, grandfather," cried Little Waking Eyes, clasping his arms around Liu Jusong's neck, "where are father and mother?"

And Little Sleeping Eyes murmured in Li Wang's ear, "I want my father and mother!"

Liu Jusong and Li Wang looked at each other. "Let us send for our children," said they.

V

"HOW many moons, Liu Venti, since our little ones went from us?" asked Pau Tsu.

She was very pale, and there was a yearning expression in her eyes.

"Nearly five," returned Liu Venti, himself stifling a sigh.

"Sometimes," said Pau Tsu, "I feel I cannot any longer bear their absence."

She drew from her bosom two little shoes, one red, one blue.

"Their first," said she. "Oh, my sons, my little sons!"

A messenger boy approached, handed Liu Venti a message, and slipped away. Liu Venti read:

May the bamboo ever wave. Son and daughter, return to your parents and your children.

LIU JUSONG,
LI WANG.

"The answer to our prayer," breathed Pau Tsu. "Oh Liu Venti, love is indeed stronger than hate!"

The Banishment of Ming and Mai

I

MANY years ago in the beautiful land of China, there lived a rich and benevolent man named Chan Ah Sin. So kind of heart was he that he could not pass through a market street without buying up all the live fish, turtles, birds, and animals that he saw, for the purpose of giving them liberty and life. The animals and birds he would set free in a cool green forest called the Forest of the Freed, and the fish and turtles he would release in a moon-loved pool called the Pool of Happy Life. He also bought up and set free all animals that were caged for show, and even remembered the reptiles.

Some centuries after this good man had passed away, one of his descendants was accused of having offended against the laws of the land, and he and all of his kin were condemned to be punished therefor. Amongst his kin were two little seventh cousins named Chan Ming and Chan Mai, who had lived very happily all their lives with a kind uncle as guardian and a good old nurse. The punishment meted out to this little boy and girl was banishment to a wild and lonely forest, which forest could only be reached by travelling up a dark and mysterious river in a small boat. The journey was long and perilous, but on the evening of the third day a black shadow loomed before Ming and Mai. This black shadow was the forest, the trees of which grew so thickly together and so close to the river's edge that their roots interlaced under the water.

The rough sailors who had taken the children from their home, beached the boat, and without setting foot to land themselves, lifted the children out, then quickly pushed away. Their faces were deathly pale, for they were mortally afraid of the forest, which was said to be inhabited by innumerable wild animals, winged and crawling things.

Ming's lip trembled. He realized that he and his little sister were now entirely alone, on the edge of a fearsome forest on the shore of a mysterious river. It seemed to the little fellow, as he thought of his dear Canton,[1] so full of bright and busy life, that he and Mai had come, not to another province, but to another world.

---

1 A Portuguese-inflected name for Guangdou province in the south of China, and also for that province's capital city, Guangzhou.

One great, big tear splashed down his cheek. Mai, turning to weep on his sleeve, saw it, checked her own tears, and slipping a little hand into his, murmured in his ear:

"Look up to the heavens, O brother. Behold, the Silver Stream floweth above us here as bright as it flowed above our own fair home." (The Chinese call the Milky Way the Silver Stream.)

While thus they stood, hand in hand, a moving thing resembling a knobby log of wood was seen in the river. Strange to say, the children felt no fear and watched it float towards them with interest. Then a watery voice was heard. "Most honorable youth and maid," it said, "go back to the woods and rest."

It was a crocodile. Swimming beside it were a silver and a gold fish, who leaped in the water and echoed the crocodile's words; and following in the wake of the trio, was a big green turtle mumbling: "To the woods, most excellent, most gracious, and most honorable."

Obediently the children turned and began to find their way among the trees. The woods were not at all rough and thorny as they had supposed they would be. They were warm and fragrant with aromatic herbs and shrubs. Moreover, the ground was covered with moss and grass, and the bushes and young trees bent themselves to allow them to pass through. But they did not wander far. They were too tired and sleepy. Choosing a comfortable place in which to rest, they lay down side by side and fell asleep.

When they awoke the sun was well up. Mai was the first to open her eyes, and seeing it shining through the trees, exclaimed: "How beautiful is the ceiling of my room!" She thought she was at home and had forgotten the river journey. But the next moment Ming raised his head and said: "The beauty you see is the sun filtering through the trees and the forest where—"

He paused, for he did not wish to alarm his little sister, and he had nearly said: "Where wild birds and beasts abound."

"Oh, dear!" exclaimed Mai in distress. She also thought of the wild birds and beasts, but like Ming, she also refrained from mentioning them.

"I am impatiently hungry," cried Ming. He eyed enviously a bright little bird hopping near. The bird had found a good, fat grasshopper for its breakfast, but when it heard Ming speak, it left the grasshopper and flew quickly away.

A moment later there was a great trampling and rustling amongst the grasses and bushes. The hearts of the children stood still. They clasped hands. Under every bush and tree, on the branches above them, in a pool near by, and close beside them, almost touching their knees, appeared a great company of living things from the animal, fish, fowl, and insect kingdoms.

It was true then—what the sailors had told them—only worse; for whereas they had expected to meet the denizens of the forest, either singly or in couples, here they were all massed together.

A tiger opened its mouth. Ming put his sister behind him and said: "Please, honorable animals, birds, and other kinds of living things, would some of you kindly retire for a few minutes. We expected to meet you, but not so many at once, and are naturally overwhelmed with the honor."

"Oh, yes, please your excellencies," quavered Mai, "or else be so kind as to give us space in which to retire ourselves, so that we may walk into the river and trouble you no more. Will we not, honorable brother?"

"Nay, sister," answered Ming. "These honorable beings have to be subdued and made to acknowledge that man is master of this forest. I am here to conquer them in fight, and am willing to take them singly, in couples, or even three at a time; but as I said before, the honor of all at once is somewhat overwhelming."

"Oh! ah!" exclaimed Mai, gazing awestruck at her brother. His words made him more terrible to her than any of the beasts of the field. Just then the tiger, who had politely waited for Ming and Mai to say their say, made a strange purring sound, loud, yet strangely soft; fierce, yet wonderfully kind. It had a surprising effect upon the children, seeming to soothe them and drive away all fear. One of little Mai's hands dropped upon the head of a leopard crouching near, whilst Ming gazed straight into the tiger's eyes and smiled as at an old friend. The tiger smiled in return, and advancing to Ming, laid himself down at his feet, the tip of his nose resting on the boy's little red shoes. Then he rolled his body around three times. Thus in turn did every other animal, bird, fish, and insect present. It took quite a time and Mai was glad that she stood behind her brother and received the obeisances by proxy.

This surprising ceremony over, the tiger sat back upon his haunches and, addressing Ming, said:

"Most valorous and honorable descendant of Chan Ah Sin the First: Your coming and the coming of your exquisite sister will cause the flowers to bloom fairer and the sun to shine brighter for us. There is, therefore, no necessity for a trial of your strength or skill with any here. Believe me, Your Highness, we were conquered many years ago—and not in fight."

"Why! How?" cried Ming.

"Why! How?" echoed Mai.

And the tiger said:

"Many years ago in the beautiful land of China, there lived a rich and benevolent man named Chan Ah Sin. So kind of heart was he that he could not pass through a market street without buying up all the live fish, turtles, birds, and animals that he saw, for the purpose of giving them liberty and life. These animals and birds he would set free in a cool green forest called the Forest of the Freed, and the fish and turtles he would release in a moon-loved pool called the Pool of Happy Life. He also bought up and set free all animals that were caged for show, and even remembered the reptiles."

The tiger paused.

"And you," observed Ming, "you, sir tiger, and your forest companions, are the descendants of the animals, fish, and turtles thus saved by Chan Ah Sin the First."

"We are, Your Excellency," replied the tiger, again prostrating himself. "The beneficent influence of Chan Ah Sin the First, extending throughout the centuries, has preserved the lives of his young descendants, Chan Ming and Chan Mai."

II

The Tiger's Farewell

MANY a moon rose and waned over the Forest of the Freed and the Moon-loved Pool of Happy Life, and Ming and Mai lived happily and contentedly amongst their strange companions. To be sure, there were times when their hearts would ache and their tears would flow for their kind uncle and good old nurse, also for their little playfellows in far-away Canton; but those times were few and far between. Full well the children knew how much brighter and better was their fate than it might have been.

One day, when they were by the river, amusing themselves with the crocodiles and turtles, the water became suddenly disturbed, and lashed and dashed the shore in a very strange manner for a river naturally calm and silent.

"Why, what can be the matter?" cried Ming.

"An honorable boat is coming," shouted a goldfish.

Ming and Mai clasped hands and trembled.

"It is the sailors," said they to one another; then stood and watched with terrified eyes a large boat sail majestically up the broad stream.

Meanwhile down from the forest had rushéd the tiger with his tigress and cubs, the leopard with his leopardess and cubs, and all the other animals with their young, and all the birds, and all the insects, and all the living things that lived in the Forest of the Freed and the Moon-loved Pool. They surrounded Ming and Mai, crouched at their feet, swarmed in the trees above their heads, and crowded one another on the beach and in the water.

The boat stopped in the middle of the stream, in front of the strip of forest thus lined with living things. There were two silk-robed men on it and a number of sailors, also an old woman carrying a gigantic parasol and a fan whose breeze fluttered the leaves in the Forest of the Freed.

When the boat stopped, the old woman cried: "Behold, I see my precious nurslings surrounded by wild beasts. A-ya, A-ya, A-ya." Her cries rent the air and Ming and Mai, seeing that the old woman was Woo Ma, their old nurse, clapped their little hands in joy.

"Come hither," they cried. "Our dear friends will welcome you. They are not wild beasts. They are elegant and accomplished superior beings."

Then one of the men in silken robes commanded the sailors to steer for the shore, and the other silk-robed man came and leaned over the side of the boat and said to the tiger and leopard:

"As I perceive, honorable beings, that you are indeed the friends of my dear nephew and niece, Chan Ming and Chan Mai, I humbly ask your permission to allow me to disembark on the shore of this river on the edge of your forest."

The tiger prostrated himself, so also did his brother animals, and all shouted:

"Welcome, O most illustrious, most benevolent, and most excellent Chan Ah Sin the Ninth."

So Mai crept into the arms of her nurse and Ming hung on to his uncle's robe, and the other silk-robed man explained how and why they had come to the Forest of the Freed and the Moon-loved Pool.

A fairy fish, a fairy duck, a fairy butterfly, and a fairy bird, who had seen the children on the river when the cruel sailors were taking them from their home, had carried the news to the peasants of the rice fields, the tea plantations, the palm and bamboo groves. Whereupon great indignation had prevailed, and the people of the province, who loved well the Chan family, arose in their might and demanded that an investigation be made into the charges against that Chan who was reputed to have broken the law, and whose relatives as well as himself had been condemned to suffer therefor. So it came to pass that the charges, which had been made by some malicious enemy of high official rank, were entirely disproved, and the edict of banishment against the Chan family recalled.

The first thought of the uncle of Ming and Mai, upon being liberated from prison, was for his little nephew and niece, and great indeed was his alarm and grief upon learning that the two tender scions of the house of Chan had been banished to a lonely forest by a haunted river, which forest and river were said to be inhabited by wild and cruel beings. Moreover, since the sailors who had taken them there, and who were the only persons who knew where the forest was situated, had been drowned in a swift rushing rapid upon their return journey, it seemed almost impossible to trace the little ones, and Chan Ah Sin the Ninth was about giving up in despair, when the fairy bird, fish, and butterfly, who had aroused the peasants, also aroused the uncle by appearing to him and telling him where the forest of banishment lay and how to reach it.

"Yes," said Chan Ah Sin the Ninth, when his friend ceased speaking, "but they did not tell me that I should find my niece and nephew so tenderly cared for. Heaven alone knows why you have been so good to my beloved children."

He bowed low to the tiger, leopard, and all the living things around him.

"Most excellent and honorable Chan Ah Sin the Ninth," replied the Tiger, prostrating himself, "we have had the pleasure and privilege of being good to these little ones, because many years ago in the beautiful land of China, your honorable ancestor, Chan Ah Sin the First, was good and kind to our forefathers."

Then arising upon his hind legs, he turned to Ming and Mai and tenderly touching them with his paws, said:

"Honorable little ones, your banishment is over, and those who roam the Forest of the Freed, and dwell in the depths of the Pool of Happy Life, will behold no more the light of your eyes. May heaven bless you and preserve you to be as good and noble ancestors to your descendants as your ancestor, Chan Ah Sin the First, was to you."

The Story of a Little Chinese Seabird

A LITTLE Chinese seabird sat in the grass which grew on a rocky island. The little Chinese seabird was very sad. Her wing was broken and all her brothers and sisters had flown away, leaving her alone. Why, oh why, had she broken her wing? Why, oh why, were brothers and sisters so?

The little Chinese seabird looked over the sea. How very beautiful its life and movement! The sea was the only consolation the little Chinese seabird had. It was always lovely and loving to the little Chinese seabird. No matter how often the white-fringed waves spent themselves for her delight, there were always more to follow. Changeably unchanged, they never deserted her nor her island home. Not so with her brothers and sisters. When she could fly with them, circle in the air, float upon the water, dive for little fish, and be happy and gay—then indeed she was one of them and they loved her. But since she had broken her wing, it was different. The little Chinese seabird shook her little head mournfully.

But what was that which the waves were bearing towards her island? The little Chinese seabird gave a quick glance, then put her little head under the wing that was not broken.

Now, what the little Chinese seabird had seen was a boat. Within the boat were three boys—and these boys were coming to the island to hunt for birds' eggs. The little Chinese seabird knew this, and her bright, wild little eyes glistened like jewels, and she shivered and shuddered as she spread herself as close to the ground as she could.

The boys beached the boat and were soon scrambling over the island, gathering all the eggs that they could find. Sometimes they passed so near to the little Chinese seabird that she thought she must surely be trampled upon, and she set her little beak tight and close so that she might make no sound, should so painful an accident occur. Once, however, when the tip of a boy's queue dangled against her head and tickled it, the little Chinese seabird forgot entirely her prudent resolve to suffer in silence, and recklessly pecked at the dangling queue. Fortunately for her, the mother who had braided the queue of the boy had neglected to tie properly the bright red cord at the end thereof. Therefore when the little Chinese seabird pecked at the braid, the effect of the peck was not to cause pain to the boy and make him turn around, as might otherwise have been the case, but to pull out of his queue the bright red cord. This, the little Chinese seabird held in her beak for quite a long time. She enjoyed glancing down at its bright red color, and was afraid to let it fall in case the boys might hear.

Meanwhile, the boys, having gathered all the eggs they could find, plotted together against the little Chinese seabird and against her brothers and sisters, and the little seabird, holding the red cord in her beak, listened with interest. For many hours after the boys had left the island, the little Chinese seabird sat meditating over what she had heard. So deeply did she meditate that she forgot all about the pain of her broken wing.

Towards evening her brothers and sisters came home and settled over the island like a wide-spreading mantle of wings.

For some time the little Chinese seabird remained perfectly still and quiet. She kept saying to herself, "Why should I care? Why should I care?" But as she did care, she suddenly let fall the bright red cord and opened and closed her beak several times.

"What is all that noise?" inquired the eldest seabird.

"Dear brother," returned the little Chinese seabird, "I hope I have not disturbed you; but is not this a very lovely night? See how radiant the moon."

"Go to sleep! Go to sleep!"

"Did you have an enjoyable flight today, brother?"

"Tiresome little bird, go to sleep, go to sleep."

It was the little Chinese seabird's eldest sister that last spoke.

"Oh, sister, is that you?" replied the little Chinese seabird. "I could see you last of the flock as you departed from our island, and I did so admire the satin white of your underwings and tail."

"Mine is whiter," chirped the youngest of all the birds.

"Go to sleep, go to sleep!" snapped the eldest brother.

"What did you have to eat today?" inquired the second brother of the little Chinese seabird.

"I had a very tasty worm porridge, dear brother," replied the little Chinese seabird. "I scooped it out of the ground beside me, because you know I dared not move any distance for fear of making worse my broken wing?"

"Your broken wing? Ah, yes, your broken wing!" murmured the second brother.

"Ah, yes, your broken wing!" faintly echoed the others.

Then they all, except the very youngest one, put their heads under their own wings, for they all, except the very youngest one, felt a little bit ashamed of themselves.

But the little Chinese seabird did not wish her brothers and sisters to feel ashamed of themselves. It embarrassed her, so she lifted up her little voice again, and said:

"But I enjoyed the day exceedingly. The sea was never so lovely nor the sky either. When I was tired of watching the waves chase each other, I could look up and watch the clouds. They sailed over the blue sky so soft and white."

"There's no fun in just watching things," said the youngest of all the birds: "we went right up into the clouds and then deep down into the waves. How we splashed and dived and swam! When I fluttered my wings after a bath in silver spray, it seemed as if a shower of jewels dropped therefrom."

"How lovely!" exclaimed the little Chinese seabird. Then she remembered that if her brothers and sisters were to have just as good a time the next day, she must tell them a story—a true one.

So she did.

After she had finished speaking, there was a great fluttering of wings, and all her brothers and sisters rose in the air above her ready for flight.

"To think," they chattered to one another, "that if we had remained an hour longer, those wicked boys would have come with lighted torches and caught us and dashed us to death against stones."

"Yes, and dressed us and salted us!"

"And dressed us and salted us!"

"And dried us!"

"And dried us!"

"And eaten us!"

"And eaten us!"

"How rude!"

"How inconsiderate!"

"How altogether uncalled for!"

"Are you quite sure?" inquired the eldest brother of the little Chinese seabird.

"See," she replied, "here is the red cord from the queue of one of the boys. I picked it out as his braid dangled against my head!"

The brothers and sisters looked at one another.

"How near they must have come to her!" exclaimed the eldest sister.

"They might have trampled her to death in a very unbecoming manner!" remarked the second.

"They will be sure to do it tonight when they search with torchlight" was the opinion of the second brother.

And the eldest brother looked sharply down upon the little Chinese seabird, and said:

"If you had not told us what these rude boys intended doing, you would not have had to die alone."

"I prefer to die alone!" proudly replied the little Chinese seabird. "It will be much pleasanter to die in quiet than with wailing screams in my ears."

"Hear her, oh, hear her!" exclaimed the second sister.

But the eldest sister, she with the satin-white under-wings and spreading tall, descended to the ground, and began pulling up some tough grass. "Come," she cried to the other birds, "let us make a strong nest for our broken-winged little sister—a nest in which we can bear away to safety one who tonight has saved our lives without thought of her own."

"We will, with pleasure," answered the other birds.

Whereupon they fluttered down and helped to build the most wonderful nest that ever was built, weaving in and out of it the bright red cord, which the little Chinese seabird had plucked out of the boy's queue. This made the nest strong enough to bear the weight of the little Chinese seabird, and when it was finished they dragged it beside her and tenderly pushed her in. Then they clutched its sides with their beaks, flapped their wings, and in a moment were soaring together far up in the sky, the little Chinese seabird with the broken wing happy as she could be in the midst of them.

What about the Cat?

"WHAT about the cat?" asked the little princess of her eldest maid.

"It is sitting on the sunny side of the garden wall, watching the butterflies. It meowed for three of the prettiest to fall into its mouth, and would you believe it, that is just what happened. A green, a blue, a pink shaded with gold, all went down pussy's red throat."

The princess smiled. "What about the cat?" she questioned her second maid.

"She is seated in your honorable father's chair of state, and your honorable father's first body-slave is scratching her back with your father's own back-scratcher, made of the purest gold and ivory."

The princess laughed outright. She pattered gracefully into another room. There she saw the youngest daughter of her foster-mother.

"What about the cat?" she asked for the third time.

"The cat! Oh, she has gone to Shinku's duck farm. The ducks love her so that when they see her, they swim to shore and embrace her with their wings. Four of them combined to make a raft and she got upon their backs and went down-stream with them. They met some of the ducklings on the way and she patted them to death with her paws. How the big ducks quacked!"

"That is a good story," quoth the princess.

She went into the garden and, seeing one of the gardeners, said: "What about the cat?"

"It is frisking somewhere under the cherry tree, but you would not know it if you saw it," replied the gardener.

"Why?" asked the princess.

"Because, Your Highness, I gave it a strong worm porridge for its dinner, and as soon as it ate it, its white fur coat became a glossy green, striped with black. It looks like a giant caterpillar, and all the little caterpillars are going to hold a festival tonight in its honor."

"Deary me! What a great cat!" exclaimed the princess.

A little further on she met one of the chamberlains of the palace. "What about the cat?" she asked.

"It is dancing in the ballroom in a dress of elegant cobwebs and a necklace of pearl rice. For partner, she has the yellow dragon in the hall, come to life, and they take such pretty steps together that all who behold them shriek in ecstasy. Three little mice hold up her train as she dances, and another sits perched on the tip of the dragon's curled tail."

At this the princess quivered like a willow tree and was obliged to seek her apartments. When there, she recovered herself, and placing a blossom on her exquisite eyebrow, commanded that all those of whom she had inquired concerning the cat should be brought before her. When they appeared she looked at them very severely and said:

"You have all told me different stories when I have asked you: 'What about the cat?' Which of these stories is true?"

No one answered. All trembled and paled.

"They are all untrue," announced the princess.

She lifted her arm and there crawled out of her sleeve her white cat. It had been there all the time.

Then the courtly chamberlain advanced towards her, kotowing[1] three times. "Princess," said he, "would a story be a story if it were true? Would you have been as well entertained this morning if, instead of our stories, we, your unworthy servants, had simply told you that the cat was up your sleeve?"

The princess lost her severity in hilarity. "Thank you, my dear servants," said she. "I appreciate your desire to amuse me."

She looked at her cat, thought of all it had done and been in the minds of her servants, and laughed like a princess again and again.

The Wild Man and the Gentle Boy[2]

"WILL you come with me?" said the Wild Man.

"With pleasure," replied the Gentle Boy.

The Wild Man took the Gentle Boy by the hand, and together they waded through rice fields, climbed tea hills, plunged through forests and at last came to a wide road, shaded on either side by large evergreen trees, with resting places made of bamboo sticks every mile or so.

"My honorable father provided these resting places for the poor carriers," said the Gentle Boy. "Here they can lay their burdens down, eat betel nuts,[3] and rest."

"Oh, ho," laughed the Wild Man. "I don't think there will be many carriers resting today. I cleared the road before I brought you."

"Indeed!" replied the Gentle Boy. "May I ask how?"

"Ate them up."

"Ah!" sighed the Gentle Boy. He felt the silence and stillness around. The very leaves had ceased to flutter, and only the soul of a bird hovered near.

The Wild Man had gigantic arms and legs and a broad, hairy chest. His mouth was exceeding large and his head was unshaved. He wore a sack of coarse linen, open in front with holes for arms. On his head was a rattan cap, besmeared with the blood of a deer.

---

1 See p. 73, note 1.

2 When first published in *Good Housekeeping* (1908), this story was subtitled "Chinese Folk Lore/Transcribed by Sui Sin Far."

3 The seed of the Areca palm tree, often chewed for its mild stimulant effects.

The Gentle Boy was small and plump; his skin was like silk and the tips of his little fingers were pink. His queue was neatly braided and interwoven with silks of many colors. He wore a peach-colored blouse and azure pantaloons, all richly embroidered, and of the finest material. The buttons on his tunic were of pure gold, and the sign of the dragon was worked on his cap. He was of the salt of the earth, a descendant of Confutze, an aristocrat of aristocrats.[1]

"Of what are you thinking?" asked the Wild Man.

"About the carriers. Did they taste good?" asked the Gentle Boy with mild curiosity.

"Yes, but there is something that will taste better, younger and tenderer, you know."

He surveyed the Gentle Boy with glistening eyes.

The Gentle Boy thought of his father's mansion, the frescoed ceilings, the chandeliers hung with pearls, the great blue vases, the dragon's smiles, the galleries of glass through which walked his mother and sisters; but most of all, he thought of his noble ancestors.

"What would Your Excellency be pleased to converse about?" he inquired after a few minutes, during which the Wild Man had been engaged in silent contemplation of the Gentle Boy's chubby cheeks.

"About good things to eat," promptly replied the Gentle Boy. "There are a great many," he dreamily observed, staring into space.

"Tell me about some of the fine dishes in your father's kitchen. It is they who have made you."

The Gentle Boy looked complacently up and down himself.

"I hope in all humility," he said, "that I do honor to my father's cook's dishes."

The Wild Man laughed so boisterously that the trees rocked.

"There is iced seaweed jelly, for one thing," began the Gentle Boy, "and a ragout of water lilies, pork and chicken dumplings with bamboo shoots, bird's-nest soup and boiled almonds, ducks' eggs one hundred years old, garnished with strips of suckling pig and heavenly fish fried in paradise oil, white balls of rice flour

---

1   See Matthew 5:13: "You are the salt of the earth. But if the salt loses its saltiness, how can it be made salty again? It is no longer good for anything, except to be thrown out and trampled underfoot"; Confucius (551–479 BCE) was a Chinese philosopher.

stuffed with sweetmeats, honey and rose-leaves, candied frogs and salted crabs, sugared seaweed and pickled stars."

He paused.

"Now, tell me," said the Wild Man, "which of all things would you like best to eat?"

The Gentle Boy's eye wandered musingly over the Wild Man's gigantic proportions, his hungry mouth, his fanglike teeth. He flipped a ladybird insect off his silken cuff and smiled at the Wild Man as he did so.

"Best of all, honorable sir," he slowly said, "I would like to eat you."

The Wild Man sat transfixed, staring at the Gentle Boy, his mouth half open, the hair standing up on his head. And to this day he sits there, on the high road to Cheang Che, a piece of petrified stone.

The Garments of the Fairies

"WHY do we never see the fairies?" asked Mermei.

"Because," replied her mother, "the fairies do not wish to be seen."

"But why, honorable mother, do they not wish to be seen?"

"Would my jade jewel wish to show herself to strangers if she wore no tunic or shoes or rosettes?"[1]

Mermei glanced down at her blue silk tunic embroidered in white and gold, at her scarlet shoes beaded at the tips so as to resemble the heads of kittens; and looking over to a mirror hung on the side of the wall where the sun shone, noted the purple rosettes in her hair and the bright butterfly's wing.

"Oh, no! honorable mother," said she, shaking her head with quite a shocked air.

"Then, when you hear the reason why the fairies do not appear to you except in your dreams, you will know that they are doing just as you would do were you in a fairy's shoes."

"A story! A story!" cried Mermei, clapping her hands and waving her fan, and Choy and Fei and Wei and Sui, who were playing battledore and shuttlecock[2] on the green, ran into the

---

1 Rosettes are rose-shaped ornaments or badges worn as accessories.
2 A game resembling badminton, where the shuttlecock is passed back and forth with the battledores, or rackets.

house and grouped themselves around Mermei and the mother. They all loved stories.

"Many, many years ago," began the mother of Mermei, "when the sun was a warm-hearted but mischievous boy, playing all kinds of pranks with fruits and flowers and growing things, and his sister, the moon, was too young to be sad and serious, the fairies met together by night. The sun, of course, was not present, and the moon had withdrawn behind a cloud. Stars alone shone in the quiet sky. By their light the fairies looked upon each other, and found themselves so fair and radiant in their robes of varied hues, all wonderfully fashioned, fringed and laced, some bright and brilliant, others, delicate and gauzy, but each and all a perfect dream of loveliness, that they danced for very joy in themselves and the garments in which they were arrayed.

"The dance being over, the queen of all sighed a fragrant sigh of happiness upon the air, and bowing to her lovely companions said:

"'Sweet sisters, the mission of the fairies is to gladden the hearts of the mortals. Let us, therefore, this night, leave behind us on the earth the exquisite garments whose hues and fashions have given us so much pleasure. And because we may not be seen uncovered, let us from henceforth be invisible.'

"'We will! We will!' cried the sister fairies. They were all good and kind of heart, and much as they loved their dainty robes, they loved better to give happiness to others.

"And that is why the fairies are invisible, and why we have the flowers."

"The flowers!" cried Mermei. "Why the flowers?"

"And the fairies' garments! Where can we find them?" asked Fei with the starry eyes.

"In the gardens, in the forests, and by the streams," answered the mother. "The flowers, dear children, are the bright-hued garments which the fairies left behind them when they flew from earth, never to return again, save invisible."

The Dreams That Failed

PING SIK and Soon Yen sat by the roadside under a spreading olive tree. They were on their way to market to sell two little pigs. With the money to be obtained from the sale of the little pigs, they were to buy caps and shoes with which to attend school.

"When I get to be a man," said Ping Sik, "I will be so great and so glorious that the Emperor will allow me to wear a three-eyed peacock feather, and whenever I walk abroad, all who meet me will bow to the ground."

"And I," said Soon Yen, "will be a great general. The reins of my steeds will be purple and scarlet, and in my cap will wave a bright blue plume."

"I shall be such a great poet and scholar," continued Ping Sik, "that the greatest university in the Middle Kingdom will present me with a vase encrusted with pearls."

"And I shall be so valiant and trustworthy that the Pearly Emperor will appoint me commander-in-chief of his army, and his enemies will tremble at the sound of my name."

"I shall wear a yellow jacket with the names of three ancestors inscribed thereon in seven colors."

"And I shall wear silk robes spun by princesses, and a cloak of throat skins of sables."

"And I shall live in a mansion of marble and gold."

"And I in halls of jadestone."

"And I will own silk and tea plantations and tens of thousands of rice farms."

"All the bamboo country shall be mine, and the rivers and sea shall be full of my fishing boats, junks, and craft of all kinds."

"People will bow down before me and cry: 'Oh, most excellent, most gracious, most beautiful!'"

"None will dare offend so mighty a man as I shall be!"

"O ho! You good-for-nothing rascals!" cried the father of Ping Sik. "What are you doing loafing under a tree when you should be speeding to market?"

"And the little pigs, where are they?" cried the father of Soon Yen.

The boys looked down at the baskets which had held the little pigs. While they had been dreaming of future glories, the young porkers had managed to scramble out of the loosely woven bamboo thatch of which the baskets were made.

The fathers of Ping Sik and Soon Yen produced canes.

"Without shoes and caps," said they, "you cannot attend school. Therefore, back to the farm and feed pigs."

Glad Yen

"I'M so glad! so glad!" shouted little Yen.

"Why?" asked Wou. "Has any one given you a gold box with jewels, or a peacock feather fan, or a coat of many colors,[1] or a purse of gold? Has your father become rich or been made a high mandarin?"[2]

Wou sighed as he put these questions. He had voiced his own longings.

"No," answered Yen, giving a hop, skip, and jump.

"Then, why are you glad?" repeated Wou.

"Why?" Yen's bright face grew brighter.

"Oh, because I have such a beautiful blue sky, such a rippling river, waterfalls that look like lace and pearls and diamonds, and sunbeams brighter and more radiant than the finest jewels. Because I have chirping insects, and flying beetles, and dear, wiggly worms—and birds, oh, such lovely birds, all colors! And some of them can sing. I have a sun and a moon and stars. And flowers? Wouldn't any one be glad at the sight of flowers?"

Wou's sad and melancholy face suddenly lighted and overflowed with smiles.

"Why," said he, "I have all these bright and beautiful things. I have the beautiful sky, and water, and birds, and flowers, too! I have the sun, and the moon, and the stars, just as you have! I never thought of that before!"

"Of course you have," replied Yen. "You have all that is mine, and I all that is yours, yet neither can take from the other!"

The Deceptive Mat

WHEN Tsin Yen was about eight years old, he and his little brother were one fine day enjoying a game of battledore and shuttlecock[3] on the green lawn, which their father had reserved as a playground for their use. The lawn was a part of a very elaborate garden laid out with many rare flowers and ferns and exquisite plants in costly porcelain jars. The whole was enclosed behind high walls.

---

1 A reference to Joseph's "coat of many colours" in Genesis 37:3, which aroused the envy of his brothers.

2 See p. 174, note 1.

3 See p. 189, note 2.

It was a very warm day and the garden gate had been left open, so that the breeze could better blow within. A man stood outside the gate, watching the boys. He carried a small parcel under his arm.

"Will not the jewel eyes of the honorable little ones deign to turn my way?" he cried at last.

Tsin Yen and Tsin Yo looked over at him.

"What is your wish, honorable sir?" asked Tsin Yen.

And the man replied: "That I may be allowed space in which to spread my mat on your green. The road outside is dusty and the insects are more lively than suits my melancholy mood."

"Spread your mat, good sir," hastily answered Tsin Yen, giving a quick glance at the small parcel, and returning to his play.

The man began quietly to unroll his bundle, Tsin Yen and Tsin Yo being too much interested in their play to pay much attention to him. But a few minutes passed, however, before the stranger touched Tsin Yen's sleeve, and bade him stand aside.

"For what reason, honorable sir?" asked Tsin Yen, much surprised.

"Did not you consent to my spreading my mat, most ingenuous son of an illustrious father?" returned the man. He pointed to his mat. Of cobweb texture and cobweb color, it already covered almost the whole green lawn, and there was a portion yet unrolled.

"How could I know that so small a bundle would make so large a mat?" exclaimed Tsin Yen protestingly.

"But you should have thought, my son," said the father of Tsin Yen, who now appeared upon the scene. "If you had thought before consenting to the spreading of the mat, you would not, this fine afternoon, be obliged to yield your playground to a stranger. However, the word of a Tsin must be made good. Stand aside, my sons."

So Tsin Yen and Tsin Yo stood aside and watched with indignant eyes the deceptive mat unrolled over the whole space where they were wont to play. When it was spread to its full capacity, the man seated himself in the middle, and remained thereon until the setting of the sun.

And that is the reason why Tsin Yen, when he became a man, always thought for three minutes before allowing any word to escape his lips.

The Heart's Desire

SHE was dainty, slender, and of waxen pallor. Her eyes were long and drooping, her eyebrows finely arched. She had the tiniest Golden Lily feet and the glossiest black hair. Her name was Li Chung O'Yam, and she lived in a sad, beautiful old palace surrounded by a sad, beautiful old garden, situated on a charming island in the middle of a lake. This lake was spanned by marble bridges, entwined with green creepers, reaching to the mainland. No boats were ever seen on its waters, but the pink lotus lily floated thereon and swans of marvellous whiteness.

Li Chung O'Yam wore priceless silks and radiant jewels. The rarest flowers bloomed for her alone. Her food and drink were of the finest flavors and served in the purest gold and silver plates and goblets. The sweetest music lulled her to sleep.

Yet Li Chung O'Yam was not happy. In the midst of the grandeur of her enchanted palace, she sighed for she knew not what.

"She is weary of being alone," said one of the attendants. And he who ruled all within the palace save Li Chung O'Yam, said: "Bring her a father!"

A portly old mandarin[1] was brought to O'Yam. She made humble obeisance, and her august father inquired ceremoniously as to the state of her health, but she sighed and was still weary.

"We have made a mistake; it is a mother she needs," said they.

A comely matron, robed in rich silks and waving a beautiful peacock feather fan, was presented to O'Yam as her mother. The lady delivered herself of much good advice and wise instruction as to deportment and speech, but O'Yam turned herself on her silken cushions and wished to say goodbye to her mother.

Then they led O'Yam into a courtyard which was profusely illuminated with brilliant lanterns and flaring torches. There were a number of little boys of about her own age dancing on stilts. One little fellow, dressed all in scarlet and flourishing a small sword, was pointed out to her as her brother. O'Yam was amused for a few moments, but in a little while she was tired of the noise and confusion.

In despair, they who lived but to please her consulted amongst themselves. O'Yam, overhearing them, said: "Trouble not your minds. I will find my own heart's ease."

---

1 See p. 174, note 1.

Then she called for her carrier dove, and had an attendant bind under its wing a note which she had written. The dove went forth and flew with the note to where a little girl named Ku Yum, with a face as round as a harvest moon, and a mouth like a red vine leaf, was hugging a cat to keep her warm and sucking her finger to prevent her from being hungry. To this little girl the dove delivered O'Yam's message, then returned to its mistress.

"Bring me my dolls and my cats, and attire me in my brightest and best," cried O'Yam.

When Ku Yum came slowly over one of the marble bridges towards the palace wherein dwelt Li Chung O'Yam, she wore a blue cotton blouse, carried a peg doll in one hand and her cat in another. O'Yam ran to greet her and brought her into the castle hall. Ku Yum looked at O'Yam, at her radiant apparel, at her cats and her dolls.

"Ah!" she exclaimed. "How beautifully you are robed! In the same colors as I. And behold, your dolls and your cats, are they not much like mine?"

"Indeed they are," replied O'Yam, lifting carefully the peg doll and patting the rough fur of Ku Yum's cat.

Then she called her people together and said to them:

"Behold, I have found my heart's desire—a little sister."

And forever after O'Yam and Ku Yum lived happily together in a glad, beautiful old palace, surrounded by a glad, beautiful old garden, on a charming little island in the middle of a lake.

The Candy That Is Not Sweet

GRANDFATHER CHAN was dozing in a big red chair. Beside him stood the baby's cradle, a thick basket held in a stout framework of wood. Inside the cradle lay the baby. He was very good and quiet and fast asleep.

The cottage door was open. On the green in front played Yen. Mother Chan, who was taking a cup of afternoon tea with a neighbor, had said to him when she bade him goodbye, "Be a good little son and take good care of the baby and your honorable grandfather."

Yen wore a scarlet silk skullcap, a gaily embroidered vest, and purple trousers. He had the roundest and smoothest of faces and the brightest of eyes. Some pretty stones which he had found heaped up in a corner of the green were affording him great delight and joy, and he was rubbing his fat little hands over them, when there arose upon the air the cry of Bo Shuie, the candy man. Yen gave a hop and a jump. In a moment he was at the corner of the street where stood the candy man, a whole hive of little folks grouped around him. Never was there such a fascinating fellow as this candy man. What a splendid big pole was that he had slung over his broad shoulders, and, oh, the baskets of sweetmeats[1] which depended from it on either side!

Yen gazed wistfully at the sugared almonds and limes, the ginger and spice cakes, and the barley sugar and cocoanut.

"I will take that, honorable candy man," said he, pointing to a twisted sugar stick of many colors.

"Cash!" said the candy man holding out his hand.

"Oh!" exclaimed Yen. He had thought only of sugar and forgotten he had no cash.

"Give it to me, honorable peddler man," said Han Yu. "I have a cash."

The peddler man transferred from his basket to the eager little hands of Han Yu the sugar stick of many colors.

Quick as his chubby legs could carry him, Yen ran back to the cottage. His grandfather was still dozing.

"Grandfather, honorable grandfather," cried Yen. But his grandfather did not hear.

Upon a hook on the wall hung a long string of cash.[2] Mother Chan had hung it there for her use when passing peddlers called.

Yen had thought to ask his grandfather to give him one of the copper coins which were strung on the string, but as his grandfather did not awaken at his call, he changed his mind. You see, he had suddenly remembered that the day before he had felt a pain, and when he had cried, his mother had said: "No more candy for Yen."

For some moments Yen stood hesitating and looking at the many copper coins on the bright red string. It hung just low enough to be reached, and Yen knew how to work the cash over the knot at the end. His mother had shown him how so that he could hand them over to her for the peddlers.

Ah, how pleasant, how good that smelt! The candy man, who carried with his baskets a tin saucepan and a little charcoal stove, had set about making candy, and the smell of the barley sugar was wafted from the corner to Yen's little nose.

---

1 Foods rich in sugar.
2 See p. 165, note 1.

Yen hesitated no longer. Grabbing the end of the string of cash, he pulled therefrom three coins, and with a hop and a jump was out in the street again.

"I will take three sticks of twisted candy of many colors," said he to the candy man.

With his three sticks of candy Yen returned to the green. He had just bitten a piece off the brightest stick of all when his eyes fell on a spinning top which his mother had given him that morning. He crunched the candy, but somehow or other it did not taste sweet.

"Yen! Yen!" called his grandfather, awaking from his sleep.

Yen ran across to him.

"Honorable grandfather," said he, "I have some beautiful candy for you!"

He put the three sticks of candy upon his grandfather's knees.

"Dear child!" exclaimed the old man, adjusting his spectacles. "How did you come to get the candy?"

Yen's little face became very red. He knew that he had done wrong, so instead of answering his grandfather, he hopped three times.

"How did you get the candy?" again inquired Grandfather Chan.

"From the candy man," said Yen, "from the candy man. Eat it, eat it."

Now Grandfather Chan was a little deaf, and taking for granted that Yen had explained the candy all right, he nibbled a little at one of the sticks, then put it down.

"Eat some more, eat all, honorable grandfather," urged Yen.

The old man laughed and shook his head.

"I cannot eat any more," said he. "The old man is not the little boy."

"But—but," puffed Yen, becoming red in the face again, "I want you to eat it, honorable grandfather."

But Grandfather Chan would not eat any more candy, and Yen began to puff and blow and talk very loud because he would not. Indeed, by the time Mother Chan returned, he was as red as a turkeycock and chattering like a little magpie.

"I do not know what is the matter with the little boy," said Grandfather Chan. "He is so vexed because I cannot eat his candy."

Mother Chan glanced at the string of cash and then at her little son's flushed face.

"I know," said she. "The candy is not sweet to him, so he would have his honorable grandfather eat it."

Yen stared at his mother. How did she know! How could she know! But he was glad that she knew, and at sundown he crept softly to her side and said, "Honorable mother, the string of cash is less then at morn, but the candy, it was not sweet."

The Inferior Man

KU YUM, the little daughter of Wen Hing, the schoolmaster, trotted into the school behind her father and crawled under his desk. From that safe retreat, her bright eyes looked out in friendly fashion upon the boys. Ku Yum was three years old and was the only little girl who had ever been in the schoolroom. Naturally, the boys were very much interested in her, and many were the covert glances bestowed upon the chubby little figure in red under the schoolmaster's desk. Now and then a little lad, after an unusually penetrating glance, would throw his sleeve over or lift his slate up to his face, and his form would quiver strangely. Well for the little lad that the schoolmaster wore glasses which somewhat clouded his vision.

The wife of Wen Hing was not very well, which was the reason why the teacher had been bringing the little Ku Yum to school with him for the last three weeks. Wen Hing, being a kind husband, thought to help his wife, who had two babies besides Ku Yum to look after.

But for all his troubled mind, the schoolmaster's sense of duty to his scholars was as keen as ever; also his sense of smell.

Suddenly he turned from the blackboard upon which he had been chalking.

"He who thinks only of good things to eat is an inferior man," and pushing back his spectacles, declared in a voice which caused his pupils to shake in their shoes:

"Some degenerate son of an honorable parent is eating unfragrant sugar."

"Unfragrant sugar! honorable sir!" exclaimed Han Wenti.

"Unfragrant sugar! honorable sir!" echoed little Yen Wing.

"Unfragrant sugar!"

"Unfragrant sugar!"

The murmur passed around the room.

"Silence!" commanded the teacher.

There was silence.

"Go Ek Ju," said the teacher, "why is thy miserable head bowed?"

"Because, O wise and just one, I am composing," answered Go Ek Ju.

"Read thy composition."

"A wild boar and a suckling pig were eating acorns from the bed of a sunken stream," shrilly declaimed Go Ek Ju.

"Enough! It can easily be perceived what thy mind is on. Canst thou look at me behind my back and declare that thou art not eating unfragrant sugar?"

"To thy illuminating back, honorable sir, I declare that I am not eating unfragrant sugar."

The teacher's brow became yet sterner.

"You, Mark Sing! Art thou the unfragrant sugar eater?"

"I know not the taste of that confection, most learned sir."

The teacher sniffed.

"Some one," he reasserted, "is eating unfragrant sugar. Whoever the miserable culprit is, let him speak now, and four strokes from the rattan[1] is all that he shall receive."

He paused. The clock ticked sixty times; but there was no response to his appeal. He lifted his rattan.

"As no guilty one," said he, "is honorable enough to acknowledge that he is dishonorably eating unfragrant sugar, I shall punish all for the offense, knowing that thereby the offender will receive justice. Go Ek Ju, come forward, and receive eight strokes from the rattan."

Go Ek Ju went forward and received the eight strokes. As he stood trembling with pain before the schoolmaster's desk, he felt a small hand grasp his foot. His lip tightened. Then he returned to his seat, sore, but undaunted, and unconfessed. In like manner also his schoolmates received the rattan.

When the fifteen aching but unrepentant scholars were copying industriously, "He who thinks only of good things to eat is an inferior man," and the schoolmaster, exhausted, had flung himself back on his seat, a little figure in red emerged from under the schoolmaster's desk and attempted to clamber on to his lap. The schoolmaster held her back.

"What! What!" he exclaimed. "What! what!" He rubbed his head in puzzled fashion. Then he lifted up the little red figure, turning its face around to the school boys. Such a chubby, happy little face as it was. Dimpled cheeks and pearly teeth showing in a gleeful smile. And the hands of the little red figure grasped two

---

1 Rattan is a type of palm whose stems were used to inflict corporal punishment.

sticky balls of red and white peppermint candy—unfragrant sugar.

"Behold!" said the teacher, with a twinkle in his spectacles, "the inferior man!"

Whereupon the boys forgot that they were aching. You see, they loved the little Ku Yum and believed that they had saved her from eight strokes of the rattan.

The Merry Blind-Man

THE little finger on Ah Yen's little left hand was very sore. Ah Yen had poked it into a hot honey tart. His honorable mother had said: "Yen, you must not touch that tart," but just as soon as his honorable mother had left the room, Yen forgot what she had said, and thrust the littlest finger of his little left hand right into the softest, sweetest, and hottest part of the tart.

Now he sat beside the window, feeling very sad and sore, for all the piece of oiled white linen which his mother had carefully wrapped around his little finger. It was a very happy-looking day. The sky was a lovely blue, trimmed with pretty, soft white clouds, and on the purple lilac tree which stood in front of his father's cottage, two little yellow eyebrows[1] were chirping to each other.

But Yen, with his sore finger, did not feel at all happy. You see, if his finger had not been sore, he could have been spinning the bright-colored top which his honorable uncle had given him the day before.

"Isn't it a lovely day, little son?" called his mother.

"I think it is a homely day," answered Yen.

"See those good little birds on the tree," said his mother.

"I don't believe they are good," replied the little boy.

"Fie, for shame!" cried his mother; and she went on with her work.

Just then an old blind-man carrying a guitar came down the street. He stopped just under the window by which Yen was seated, and leaning against the wall began thrumming away on his instrument. The tunes he played were very lively and merry. Yen looked down upon him and wondered why. The blind-man was such a very old man, and not only blind but lame, and so thin that Yen felt quite sure that he never got more than half a bowl of rice for his dinner. How was it then that he played such merry

---

1 Possibly the yellow-browed bunting, a bird that winters in China.

tunes? So merry indeed that, listening to them, Yen quite forgot to be sour and sad. The old man went on playing and Yen went on listening. After a while, the little boy smiled, then he laughed. The old man lifted his head. He could not see with his sightless eyes, but he knew that there was a little boy near to him whom he was making happy.

"Honorable great-grandfather of all the world," said Yen. "Will you please tell me why you, who are old, lame, and blind, make such merry music that everybody who hears becomes merry also?"

The old man stopped thrumming and rubbed his chin. Then he smiled around him and answered: "Why, I think, little Jewel Eyes, that the joyful music comes just because I am old, lame, and blind."

Yen looked down at his little finger.

"Do you hear what says the honorable great-grandfather of the world?" he asked.

The little finger straightened itself up. It no longer felt sore, and Yen was no longer sour and sad.

Misunderstood

THE baby was asleep. Ku Yum looked curiously at her little brother as he lay in placid slumber. His head was to be shaved for the first time that afternoon, and he was dressed for the occasion in three padded silk vests, sky-blue trousers and an embroidered cap, which was surmounted by a little gold god and a sprig of evergreen for good luck. This kept its place on his head, even in sleep. On his arms and ankles were hung many amulets and charms, and on the whole he appeared a very resplendent baby. To Ku Yum, he was simply gorgeous, and she longed to get her little arms around him and carry him to some place where she could delight in him all by herself.

Ku Yum's mind had been in a state of wonder concerning the boy, Ko Ku, ever since he had been born. Why was he so very small and so very noisy? What made his fingers and toes so pink? Why did her mother always smile and sing whenever she had the baby in her arms? Why did her father, when he came in from his vegetable garden, gaze so long at Ko Ku? Why did grandmother make so much fuss over him? And yet, why, oh why, did they give him nothing nice to eat?

The baby was sleeping very soundly. His little mouth was half open and a faint, droning sound was issuing therefrom. He had just completed his first moon and was a month old. Poor baby! that never got any rice to eat, nor nice sweet cakes. Ku Yum's heart swelled with compassion. In her hand was a delicious half-moon cake. It was the time of the harvest-moon festival[1] and Ku Yum had already eaten three. Surely the baby would like a taste. She hesitated. Would she dare, when it lay upon that silken coverlet? Ku Yum had a wholesome regard for her mother's bamboo slipper.

The window blind was torn on one side. A vagrant wind lifted it, revealing an open window. There was a way out of that window to the vegetable garden. Beyond the vegetable garden was a cool, green spot under a clump of trees; also a beautiful puddle of muddy water.

An inspiration came to Ku Yum, born of benevolence. She lifted the sleeping babe in her arms, and with hushed, panting breaths, bore him slowly and laboriously to where her soul longed to be. He opened his eyes once and gave a faint, disturbed cry, but lapsed again into dreamland.

Ku Yum laid him down on the grass, adjusted his cap, smoothed down his garments, ran her small fingers over his brows, or where his brows ought to have been, tenderly prodded his plump cheeks, and ruffled his straight hair. Little sighs of delight escaped her lips. The past and the future were as naught to her. She reveled only in the present.

For a few minutes thus: then a baby's cries filled the air. Ku Yum sat up. She remembered the cake. It had been left behind. She found a large green leaf, and placing that over the baby's mouth in the hope of mellowing its tones, cautiously wended her way back between the squash and cabbages.

All was quiet and still. It was just before sundown and it was very warm. Her mother still slept her afternoon sleep. Hastily seizing the confection, she returned to the babe, her face beaming with benevolence and the desire to do good. She pushed some morsels into the child's mouth. It closed its eyes, wrinkled its nose and gurgled; but its mouth did not seem to Ku Yum to work just as a proper mouth should under such pleasant conditions.

"Behold me! Behold me!" she cried, and herself swallowed the remainder of the cake in two mouthfuls. Ko Ku, however, did not seem to be greatly edified by the example set him. The crumbs remained, half on his tongue and half on the creases of his cheek. He still emitted explosive noises.

---

1 See p. 73, note 1.

Ku Yum sadly surveyed him.

"He doesn't know how to eat. That's why they don't give him anything," she said to herself, and having come to this logical conclusion, she set herself to benefit him in other ways than the one in which she had failed.

She found some worms and ants, which she arranged on leaves and stones, meanwhile keeping up a running commentary on their charms.

"See! This very small brown one—how many legs it has, and how fast it runs. This one is so green that I think its father and mother must have been blades of grass, don't you? And look at the wings on this worm. That one has no wings, but its belly is pretty pink. Feel how nice and slimy it is. Don't you just love slimy things that creep on their bellies, and things that fly in the air, and things with four legs? Oh, all kinds of things except grown-up things with two legs."

She inclined the baby's head so that his eyes would be on a level with her collection, but he screamed the louder for the change.

"Oh, hush thee, baby, hush thee,
And never, never fear
The bogies[1] of the dark land,
When the green bamboo is near,"

she chanted in imitation of her mother. But the baby would not be soothed.

She wrinkled her childish brow. Her little mind was perplexed. She had tried her best to amuse her brother, but her efforts seemed in vain.

Her eyes fell on the pool of muddy water. They brightened. Of all things in the world Ku Yum loved mud, real, good, clean mud. What bliss to dip her feet into that tempting pool, to feel the slow brown water oozing into her little shoes! Ku Yum had done that before and the memory thrilled her. But with that memory came another—a memory of poignant pain; the cause, a bamboo cane, which bamboo cane had been sent from China by her father's uncle, for the express purpose of helping Ku Yum to walk in the straight and narrow path laid out for a proper little Chinese girl living in Santa Barbara.

---

1 Monsters.

Still the baby cried. Ku Yum looked down on him and the cloud on her brow lifted. Ko Ku should have the exquisite pleasure of dipping his feet into that soft velvety water. There would be no bamboo cane for him. He was loved too well. Ku Yum forgot herself. Her thoughts were entirely for Ko Ku. She half dragged, half carried him to the pool. In a second his feet were immersed therein and small wiggling things were wandering up his tiny legs. He gave a little gasp and ceased crying. Ku Yum smiled. Ah! Ko Ku was happy at last! Then:

Before Ku Yum's vision flashed a large, cruel hand. Twice, thrice it appeared, after which, for a space of time, Ku Yum could see nothing but twinkling stars.

"My son! My son! the evil spirit in your sister had almost lost you to me!" cried her mother.

"That this should happen on the day of the completion of the moon, when the guests from San Francisco are arriving with the gold coins. Verily, my son, your sister is possessed of a devil," declared her father.

And her grandmother, speaking low, said: "'Tis fortunate the child is alive. But be not too hard on Ku Yum. The demon of jealousy can best be exorcised by kindness."

And the sister of Ko Ku wailed low in the grass, for there were none to understand.

NOTE—The ceremony of the "Completion of the Moon" takes place when a Chinese boy child attains to a month old. His head is then shaved for the first time amidst much rejoicing. The foundation of the babe's future fortune is laid on that day, for every guest invited to the shaving is supposed to present the baby with a gold piece, no matter how small. [Far's note]

The Little Fat One

LEE CHU and Lee Yen sat on a stone beneath the shade of a fig tree. The way to school seemed a very long way and the morning was warm, the road dusty.

"The master's new pair of goggles can see right through our heads," observed Lee Chu.

"And his new cane made Hom Wo's fingers blister yesterday," said Lee Yen.

They looked sideways at one another and sighed.

"The beach must be very cool today," said Lee Chu after a few moments.

"Ah, yes! It is not far from here." Thus Lee Yen.

"And there are many pebbles."

"Of all colors."

"Of all colors."

The two little boys turned and looked at each other.

"Our honorable parents need never know," mused one.

"No!" murmured the other. "School is so far from home. And there are five new scholars to keep the schoolmaster busy."

Yes, the beach was cool and pleasant, and the pebbles were many, and the finest in color and shape that Lee Chu and Lee Yen had ever seen. The tide washed up fresh ones every second—green, red, yellow, black, and brown; also white and transparent beauties. The boys exclaimed with delight as they gathered them. The last one spied was always the brightest sparkler.

"Here's one like fire and all the colors in the sun," cried Lee Chu.

"And this one—it is such a bright green. There never was another one like it!" declared Lee Yen.

"Ah! most beautiful!"

"Oh! most wonderful!"

And so on until they had each made an iridescent little pile. Then they sat down to rest and eat their lunch—some rice cakes which their mother had placed within their sleeves.

As they sat munching these, they became reflective. The charm of the sea and sky was on them though they knew it not.

"I think," said Lee Chu, "that these are the most beautiful pebbles that the sea has ever given to us."

"I think so too," assented Lee Yen.

"I think," again said Lee Chu, "that I will give mine to the Little Fat One."

"The Little Fat One shall also have mine," said Lee Yen. He ran his fingers through his pebbles and sighed with rapture over their glittering. Lee Chu also sighed as his eyes dwelt on the shining heap that was his.

The Little Fat One ran to greet them on his little fat legs when they returned home at sundown, and they poured their treasures into his little tunic.

"Why, where do these come from?" cried Lee Amoy, the mother, when she tried to lift the Little Fat One on to her lap and found him too heavy to raise.

Lee Chu and Lee Yen looked away.

"You bad boys!" exclaimed the mother angrily. "You have been on the beach instead of at school. When your father comes in I shall tell him to cane you."

"No, no, not bad!" contradicted the Little Fat One, scrambling after the stones which were slipping from his tunic. His mother picked up some of them, observing silently that they were particularly fine.

"They are the most beautiful pebbles that ever were seen," said Lee Chu sorrowfully. He felt sure that his mother would cast them away.

"The sea will never give up as fine again," declared Lee Yen despairingly.

"Then why did you not each keep what you found?" asked the mother.

"Because—" said Lee Chu, then looked at the Little Fat One.

"Because—" echoed Lee Yen, and also looked at the Little Fat One.

The mother's eyes softened.

"Well," said she, "for this one time we will forget the cane."

"Good! Good!" cried the Little Fat One.

A Chinese Boy-Girl

I

THE warmth was deep and all-pervading. The dust lay on the leaves of the palms and the other tropical plants that tried to flourish in the Plaza.[1] The persons of mixed nationalities lounging on the benches within and without the square appeared to be even more listless and unambitious than usual. The Italians who ran the peanut and fruit stands at the corners were doing no business to speak of. The Chinese merchants' stores in front of the Plaza looked as quiet and respectable and drowsy as such stores always do. Even the bowling alleys, billiard halls, and saloons seemed under the influence of the heat, and only a subdued clinking of glasses and roll of balls could be heard from behind the half-open doors. It was almost as hot as an August

---

1 From its first settlement around 1880 until it was displaced by the construction of Union Station in the 1930s, Los Angeles's Chinatown was located near the city's old Plaza.

day in New York City, and that is unusually sultry for Southern California.

A little Chinese girl, with bright eyes and round cheeks, attired in blue cotton garments, and wearing her long, shining hair in a braid interwoven with silks of many colors, paused beside a woman tourist who was making a sketch of the old Spanish church.[1] The tourist and the little Chinese girl were the only persons visible who did not seem to be affected by the heat. They might have been friends; but the lady, fearing for her sketch, bade the child run off. Whereupon the little thing shuffled across the Plaza, and in less than five minutes was at the door of the Los Angeles Chinatown school for children.

"Come in, little girl, and tell me what they call you," said the young American teacher, who was new to the place.

"Ku Yum be my name," was the unhesitating reply; and said Ku Yum walked into the room, seated herself complacently on an empty bench in the first row, and informed the teacher that she lived on Apablaza street,[2] that her parents were well, but her mother was dead, and her father, whose name was Ten Suie, had a wicked and tormenting spirit in his foot.

The teacher gave her a slate and pencil, and resumed the interrupted lesson by measuring with her rule ten lichis (called "Chinese nuts" by people in America) and counting them aloud.

"One, two, three, four, five, six, seven, eight, nine, ten," the baby class repeated. After having satisfied herself by dividing the lichis unequally among the babies, that they might understand the difference between a singular and a plural number, Miss Mason began a catechism on the features of the face. Nose, eyes, lips, and cheeks were properly named, but the class was mute when it came to the forehead.

"What is this?" Miss Mason repeated, posing her finger on the fore part of her head.

"Me say, me say," piped a shrill voice, and the new pupil stepped to the front, and touching the forehead of the nearest child with the tips of her fingers, christened it "one," named the next in like fashion "two," a third "three," then solemnly pronounced the fourth a "four head."

---

1 La Iglesia de Nuestra Señora Reina de los Angeles ("The Church of Our Lady Queen of the Angels")—a Catholic church founded in 1814—is the church from which Los Angeles derived its name.

2 A street in Los Angeles's old Chinatown.

Thus Ku Yum made her debut in school, and thus began the trials and tribulations of her teacher.

Ku Yum was bright and learned easily, but she seemed to be possessed with the very spirit of mischief; to obey orders was to her an impossibility, and though she entered the school a voluntary pupil, one day at least out of every week found her a truant.

"Where is Ku Yum?" Miss Mason would ask on some particularly alluring morning, and a little girl with the air of one testifying to having seen a murder committed, would reply: "She is running around with the boys." Then the rest of the class would settle themselves back in their seats like a jury that has found a prisoner guilty of some heinous offense, and, judging by the expression on their faces, were repeating a silent prayer somewhat in the strain of "O Lord, I thank thee that I am not as Ku Yum is!" For the other pupils were demure little maidens who, after once being gathered into the fold, were very willing to remain.

But if ever the teacher broke her heart over anyone it was over Ku Yum. When she first came, she took an almost unchildlike interest in the rules and regulations, even at times asking to have them repeated to her; but her study of such rules seemed only for the purpose of finding a means to break them, and that means she never failed to discover and put into effect.

After a disappearance of a day or so she would reappear, bearing a gorgeous bunch of flowers. These she would deposit on Miss Mason's desk with a little bow; and though one would have thought that the sweetness of the gift and the apparent sweetness of the giver needed but a gracious acknowledgment, something like the following conversation would ensue:

"Teacher, I plucked these flowers for you from the Garden of Heaven." (They were stolen from some park.)

"Oh, Ku Yum, whatever shall I do with you?"

"Maybe you better see my father."

"You are a naughty girl. You shall be punished. Take those flowers away."

"Teacher, the eyebrow over your little eye is very pretty."

But the child was most exasperating when visitors were present. As she was one of the brightest scholars, Miss Mason naturally expected her to reflect credit on the school at the examinations. On one occasion she requested her to say some verses which the little Chinese girl could repeat as well as any young American, and with more expression than most. Great was the teacher's chagrin when Ku Yum hung her head and said only: "Me 'shamed, me 'shamed!"

"Poor little thing," murmured the bishop's wife. "She is too shy to recite in public."

But Miss Mason, knowing that of all children Ku Yum was the least troubled with shyness, was exceedingly annoyed.

Ku Yum had been with Miss Mason about a year when she became convinced that some steps would have to be taken to discipline the child, for after school hours she simply ran wild on the streets of Chinatown, with boys for companions. She felt that she had a duty to perform towards the motherless little girl; and as the father, when apprised of the fact that his daughter was growing up in ignorance of all home duties, and, worse than that, shared the sports of boy children on the street, only shrugged his shoulders and drawled: "Too bad! Too bad!" she determined to act.

She interested in Ku Yum's case the president of the Society for the Prevention of Cruelty to Children,[1] the matron of the Rescue Home, and the most influential ministers, and the result, after a month's work, was that an order went forth from the Superior Court of the State decreeing that Ku Yum, the child of Ten Suie, should be removed from the custody of her father, and, under the auspices of the Society for the Prevention of Cruelty to Children, be put into a home for Chinese girls in San Francisco.

Her object being accomplished, strange to say, Miss Mason did not experience that peaceful content which usually follows a benevolent action. Instead, the question as to whether, after all, it was right, under the circumstances, to deprive a father of the society of his child, and a child of the love and care of a parent, disturbed her mind, morning, noon, and night. What had previously seemed her distinct duty no longer appeared so, and she began to wish with all her heart that she had not interfered in the matter.

II

KU YUM had not been seen for weeks and those who were deputed to bring her into the sheltering home were unable to find her. It was suspected that the little thing purposely kept out of the way—no difficult matter, all Chinatown being in sympathy with her and arrayed against Miss Mason. Where formerly the teacher

---

1 The California Society for the Prevention of Cruelty to Children was organized in 1876; missionaries frequently appealed to this organization to assist them in cases of suspected child abuse or enslavement.

had met with smiles and pleased greetings, she now beheld averted faces and downcast eyes, and her school had within a week dwindled from twenty-four scholars to four. Verily, though acting with the best of intentions, she had shown a lack of diplomacy.

It was about nine o'clock in the evening. She had been visiting little Lae Choo, who was lying low with typhoid fever. As she wended her way home through Chinatown, she did not feel at all easy in mind; indeed, as she passed one of the most unsavory corners and observed some men frown and mutter among themselves as they recognized her, she lost her dignity in a little run. As she stopped to take breath, she felt her skirt pulled from behind and heard a familiar little voice say:

"Teacher, be you afraid?"

"Oh, Ku Yum," she exclaimed, "is that you?" Then she added reprovingly: "Do you think it is right for a little Chinese girl to be out alone at this time of the night?"

"I be not alone," replied the little creature, and in the gloom Miss Mason could distinguish behind her two boyish figures.

She shook her head.

"Ku Yum, will you promise me that you will try to be a good little girl?" she asked.

Ku Yum answered solemnly:

"Ku Yum *never* be a good girl."

Her heart hardened. After all, it was best that the child should be placed where she would be compelled to behave herself.

"Come, see my father," said Ku Yum pleadingly.

Her voice was soft, and her expression was so subdued that the teacher could hardly believe that the moment before she had defiantly stated that she would never be a good girl. She paused irresolutely. Should she make one more appeal to the parent to make her a promise which would be a good excuse for restraining the order of the Court? Ah, if he only would, and she only could prevent the carrying out of that order!

They found Ten Suie among his curiosities, smoking a very long pipe with a very small, ivory bowl. He calmly surveyed the teacher through a pair of gold-rimmed goggles, and under such scrutiny it was hard indeed for her to broach the subject that was on her mind. However, after admiring the little carved animals, jars, vases, bronzes, dishes, pendants, charms, and snuff-boxes displayed in his handsome showcase, she took courage.

"Mr. Ten Suie," she began, "I have come to speak to you about Ku Yum."

Ten Suie laid down his pipe and leaned over the counter. Under his calm exterior some strong excitement was working, for his eyes glittered exceedingly.

"Perhaps you speak too much about Ku Yum alleady," he said. "Ku Yum be my child. I bling him up as I please. Now, teacher, I tell you something. One, two, three, four, five, seven, eight, nine years go by, I have five boy. One, two, three, four, five, six, seven years go, I have four boy. One, two, three, four, five, six years go by, I have one boy. Every year for three year evil spirit come, look at my boy, and take him. Well, one, two, three, four, five, six years go by, I see but one boy, he four year old. I say to me: Ten Suie, evil spirit be jealous. I be 'flaid he want my one boy. I dless him like one girl. Evil spirit think him one girl, and go away; no want girl."[1]

Ten Suie ceased speaking, and settled back into his seat.

For some moments Miss Mason stood uncomprehending. Then the full meaning of Ten Suie's words dawned upon her, and she turned to Ku Yum, and taking the child's little hand in hers, said:

"Goodbye, Ku Yum. Your father, by passing you off as a girl, thought to keep an evil spirit away from you; but just by that means he brought another, and one which nearly took you from him too."

"Goodbye, teacher," said Ku Yum, smiling wistfully. "I never be good girl, but perhaps I be good boy."

Pat and Pan

THEY lay there, in the entrance to the joss house,[2] sound asleep in each other's arms. Her tiny face was hidden upon his bosom and his white, upturned chin rested upon her black, rosetted[3] head.

It was that white chin which caused the passing Mission woman to pause and look again at the little pair. Yes, it was a white boy and a little Chinese girl; he, about five, she, not more than three years old.

---

1   Chinese parents sometimes dress boys as girls or give them feminine nicknames in order to trick evil spirits, who supposedly prefer to target male offspring.

2   See p. 68, note 3.

3   See p. 189, note 1.

"Whose is that boy?" asked the Mission woman of the peripatetic vender of Chinese fruits and sweetmeats.

"That boy! Oh, him is boy of Lum Yook that make the China gold ring and bracelet."

"But he is white."

"Yes, him white; but all same, China boy. His mother, she not have any white flend, and the wife of Lum Yook give her lice and tea, so when she go to the land of spilit, she give her boy to the wife of Lum Yook. Lady, you want buy lichi?"

While Anna Harrison was extracting a dime from her purse the black, rosetted head slowly turned and a tiny fist began rubbing itself into a tiny face.

"Well, chickabiddy,[1] have you had a nice nap?"

"Tjo ho! tjo ho!"[2]

The black eyes gazed solemnly and disdainfully at the stranger.

"She tell you to be good," chuckled the old man.

"Oh, you quaint little thing!"

The quaint little thing hearing herself thus apostrophized, turned herself around upon the bosom of the still sleeping boy and, reaching her arms up to his neck, buried her face again under his chin. This, of course, awakened him. He sat up and stared bewilderedly at the Mission woman.

"What is the boy's name?" she asked, noting his gray eyes and rosy skin.

His reply, though audible, was wholly unintelligible to the American woman.

"He talk only Chinese talk," said the old man.

Anna Harrison was amazed. A white boy in America talking only Chinese talk! She placed her bag of lichis beside him and was amused to see the little girl instantly lean over her companion and possess herself of it. The boy made no attempt to take it from her, and the little thing opened the bag and cautiously peeped in. What she saw evoked a chirrup of delight. Quickly she brought forth one of the browny-red fruit nuts, crushed and pulled off its soft shell. But to the surprise of the Mission woman, instead of putting it into her own mouth, she thrust the sweetish, dried pulp into that of her companion. She repeated this operation several times, then cocking her little head on one side, asked:

---

1   A term of endearment; a biddy is a small hen.
2   A rendering of Cantonese for "very good" (or perhaps, "be good").

"Ho 'm ho?[1] Is it good or bad?"

"Ho! ho!" answered the boy, removing several pits from his mouth and shaking his head to signify that he had had enough. Whereupon the little girl tasted herself of the fruit.

"Pat! Pan! Pat! Pan!" called a woman's voice, and a sleek-headed, kindly-faced matron in dark blue pantalettes and tunic, wearing double hooped gold earrings, appeared around the corner. Hearing her voice, the boy jumped up with a merry laugh and ran out into the street. The little girl more seriously and slowly followed him.

"Him mother!" informed the lichi man.

II

WHEN Anna Harrison, some months later, opened her school for white and Chinese children in Chinatown, she determined that Pat, the adopted son of Lum Yook, the Chinese jeweller, should learn to speak his mother tongue. For a white boy to grow up as a Chinese was unthinkable. The second time she saw him, it was some kind of a Chinese holiday, and he was in great glee over a row of red Chinese candles and punk[2] which he was burning on the curb of the street, in company with a number of Chinese urchins. Pat's candle was giving a brighter and bigger flame than any of the others, and he was jumping up and down with his legs doubled under him from the knees like an india-rubber ball, while Pan, from the doorstep of her father's store, applauded him in vociferous, infantile Chinese.

Miss Harrison laid her hand upon the boy's shoulder and spoke to him. It had not been very difficult for her to pick up a few Chinese phrases. Would he not like to come to her school and see some pretty pictures? Pat shook his ruddy curls and looked at Pan. Would Pan come too? Yes, Pan would. Pan's memory was good, and so were lichis and shredded cocoanut candy.

Of course Pan was too young to go to school—a mere baby; but if Pat could not be got without Pan, why then Pan must come too. Lum Yook and his wife, upon being interviewed, were quite willing to have Pat learn English. The foster-father could speak a little of the language himself; but as he used it only when in business or when speaking to Americans, Pat had not benefited thereby. However, he was more eager than otherwise to have Pat

---

1 A rendering of Cantonese for "Good, or not good?"

2 Chinese incense.

learn "the speech of his ancestors," and promised that he would encourage the little ones to practise "American" together when at home.

So Pat and Pan went to the Mission school, and for the first time in their lives suffered themselves to be divided, for Pat had to sit with the boys and tiny Pan had a little red chair near Miss Harrison, beside which were placed a number of baby toys. Pan was not supposed to learn, only to play.

But Pan did learn. In a year's time, although her talk was more broken and babyish, she had a better English vocabulary than had Pat. Moreover, she could sing hymns and recite verses in a high, shrill voice; whereas Pat, though he tried hard enough, poor little fellow, was unable to memorize even a sentence. Naturally, Pat did not like school as well as did Pan, and it was only Miss Harrison's persistent ambition for him that kept him there.

One day, when Pan was five and Pat was seven, the little girl, for the first time, came to school alone.

"Where is Pat?" asked the teacher.

"Pat, he is sick today," replied Pan.

"Sick!" echoed Miss Harrison. "Well, that is too bad. Poor Pat! What is the matter with him?"

"A big dog bite him."

That afternoon, the teacher, on her way to see the bitten Pat, beheld him up an alley busily engaged in keeping five tops spinning at one time, while several American boys stood around, loudly admiring the Chinese feat.

The next morning Pat received five strokes from a cane which Miss Harrison kept within her desk and used only on special occasions. These strokes made Pat's right hand tingle smartly; but he received them with smiling grace.

Miss Harrison then turned to five year old Pan, who had watched the caning with tearful interest.

"Pan!" said the teacher, "you have been just as naughty as Pat, and you must be punished too."

"I not stay away flom school!" protested Pan.

"No,"—severely—"you did not stay away from school; but you told me a dog had bitten Pat, and that was not true. Little girls must not say what is not true. Teacher does not like to slap Pan's hands, but she must do it, so that Pan will remember that she must not say what is not true. Come here!"

Pan, hiding her face in her sleeve, sobbingly arose.

The teacher leaned forward and pulling down the uplifted arm, took the small hand in her own and slapped it. She was about to do this a second time when Pat bounded from his seat, pushed Pan aside, and shaking his little fist in the teacher's face, dared her in a voice hoarse with passion:

"You hurt my Pan again! You hurt my Pan again!"

They were not always lovers—those two. It was aggravating to Pat, when the teacher finding he did not know his verse, would turn to Pan and say:

"Well, Pan, let us hear you."

And Pan, who was the youngest child in school and unusually small for her years, would pharisaically[1] clasp her tiny fingers and repeat word for word the verse desired to be heard.

"I hate you, Pan!" muttered Pat on one such occasion.

Happily Pan did not hear him. She was serenely singing:

"Yesu love me, t'is I know,
For the Bible tell me so."[2]

But though a little seraph in the matter of singing hymns and repeating verses, Pan, for a small Chinese girl, was very mischievous. Indeed, she was the originator of most of the mischief which Pat carried out with such spirit. Nevertheless, when Pat got into trouble, Pan, though sympathetic, always had a lecture for him. "Too bad, too bad! Why not you be good like me?" admonished she one day when he was suffering "consequences."

Pat looked down upon her with wrathful eyes.

"Why," he asked, "is bad people always so good?"

III

The child of the white woman, who had been given a babe into the arms of the wife of Lum Yook, was regarded as their own by the Chinese jeweler and his wife, and they bestowed upon him equal love and care with the little daughter who came two years after him. If Mrs. Lum Yook showed any favoritism whatever, it was to Pat. He was the first she had to her bosom; the first to gladden her heart with baby smiles and wiles; the first to call her Ah Ma; the first to love her. On his eighth birthday, she said to her husband: "The son of the white woman is the son of the white

---

1 Hypocritically self-righteous; conforming to religious practice in appearance but not in spirit.

2 First lines of a popular children's hymn written in 1859 by the American Anna B. Warner.

woman, and there are many tongues wagging because he lives under our roof. My heart is as heavy as the blackest heavens."

"Peace, my woman," answered the easygoing man. "Why should we trouble before trouble comes?"

When trouble did come it was met calmly and bravely. To the comfortably off American and wife who were to have the boy and "raise him as an American boy should be raised," they yielded him without protest. But deep in their hearts was the sense of injustice and outraged love. If it had not been for their pity for the unfortunate white girl, their care and affection for her helpless offspring, there would have been no white boy for others to "raise."

And Pat and Pan? "I will not leave my Pan! I will not leave my Pan!" shouted Pat.

"But you must!" sadly urged Lum Yook. "You are a white boy and Pan is Chinese."

"I am Chinese too! I am Chinese too!" cried Pat.

"He Chinese! He Chinese!" pleaded Pan. Her little nose was swollen with crying; her little eyes red-rimmed.

But Pat was driven away.

Pat, his schoolbooks under his arm, was walking down the hill, whistling cheerily. His roving glance down a side street was suddenly arrested.

"Gee!" he exclaimed. "If that isn't Pan! Pan, oh, Pan!" he shouted.

Pan turned. There was a shrill cry of delight, and Pan was clinging to Pat, crying: "Nice Pat! Good Pat!"

Then she pushed him away from her and scanned him from head to foot.

"Nice coat! Nice boot! How many dollars?" she queried.

Pat laughed good-humoredly. "I don't know," he answered. "Mother bought them."

"Mother!" echoed Pan. She puckered her brows for a moment.

"You are grown big, Pat," was her next remark.

"And you have grown little, Pan," retorted Pat. It was a year since they had seen one another and Pan was much smaller than any of his girl schoolfellows.

"Do you like to go to the big school?" asked Pan, noticing the books.

"I don't like it very much. But, say, Pan, I learn lots of things that you don't know anything about."

Pan eyed him wistfully. Finally she said: "O Pat! A-Toy, she die."

"A-Toy! Who is A-Toy?"

"The meow, Pat; the big gray meow! Pat, you have forgot to remember."

Pat looked across A-Toy's head and far away.

"Chinatown is very nice now," assured Pan. "Hum Lock has two trays of brass beetles in his store and Ah Ma has many flowers!"

"I would like to see the brass beetles," said Pat.

"And father's new glass case?"

"Yes."

"And Ah Ma's flowers?"

"Yes."

"Then come, Pat."

"I can't, Pan!"

"Oh!"

Again Pat was walking home from school, this time in company with some boys. Suddenly a glad little voice sounded in his ear. It was Pan's.

"Ah, Pat!" cried she joyfully. "I find you! I find you!"

"Hear the China kid!" laughed one of the boys.

Then Pat turned upon Pan. "Get away from me," he shouted. "Get away from me!"

And Pan did get away from him—just as fast as her little legs could carry her. But when she reached the foot of the hill, she looked up and shook her little head sorrowfully. "Poor Pat!" said she. "He Chinese no more; he Chinese no more!"

The Crocodile Pagoda

WHEN the father of Chung and Choy returned from the big city where lived their uncle, he brought each of his little girls a present of a pretty, painted porcelain cup and saucer. Chung's was of the blue of the sky after rain, and on the blue was painted a silver crane and a bird with a golden breast. Choy's cup was of a milky pink transparency, upon which light bouquets of flowers appeared to have been thrown; it was so beautiful in sight, form, and color that there seemed nothing in it to be improved upon. Yet was Choy discontented and envied her sister, Chung, the cup of the blue of the sky after rain. Not that she vented her feelings in any unseemly noise or word. That was not Choy's way. But for one long night and one long day after the pretty cups had been brought home, did Choy remain mute and still, refusing to eat her meals, or to move from the couch upon which she had thrown herself at sight of her sister's cup. Choy was sulking.

On the evening of the long day, little Chung, seated on her stool by her mother's side, asked her parent to tell her the story of the picture on the vase which her father had brought from the city for her mother. It was a charming little piece of china of a deep violet velvet color, fluted on top with gold like the pipes of an organ, and in the centre was a pagoda enameled thereon in gold and silver. Chung knew that there must be a story about that pagoda, for she had overheard her father tell her mother that it was the famous Crocodile Pagoda.

"There are no crocodiles in the picture. Why is it called a crocodile pagoda?" asked Chung.

"Listen, my Jes'mine Flower," replied the mother. She raised her voice, for she wished Choy, her Orchid Flower, also to hear the story.

"Once upon a time, there was big family of crocodiles that lived in a Rippling River by a beach whose sands were of gold. The young crocodiles had a merry life of it, and their father and mother were very good and kind to them. But one day, the young crocodiles wanted to climb a hill back of the beach of golden sand, and the parents, knowing that their children would perish if allowed to have their way, told them: 'Nay, nay.'

"The young crocodiles thereupon scooped a large hole in the sand and lay down therein. For half a moon they lived there, without food or drink, and when their parents cried to them to come out and sport as before in the Rippling River, they paid no attention whatever, so sadly sulky their mood.

"One day there came along a number of powerful beings, who, when they saw the golden sands of the Rippling River, exclaimed: 'How gloriously illuminating is this beach! Let us build a pagoda thereon.' They saw the hole which the young crocodiles had made, but they could not see the hole-makers at the bottom thereof. So they set to work and filled the hole, and on top thereof they built a great pagoda. That is the pagoda of the picture on the vase."

"And did the children crocodiles never get out?" asked Chung in a sad little voice.

"No, daughter," replied the mother. "After the pagoda was on top of them they began to feel very hungry and frightened. It was *so* dark. They cried to their father and mother to bring them food and find them a way to the light; but the parent crocodiles, upon seeing the pagoda arise, swam far away. They knew that they never more should see their children. And from that day till now, the young crocodiles have remained in darkness under the pagoda, shut off forever from the light of the sun and the Rippling River."

"Please, honorable mother," spake a weak little voice, "may I have some tea in my pretty, pink porcelain cup?"

Appendix A: Edith Maude Eaton/ Sui Sin Far as a Professional Writer

1. From Sui Sin Far, "Leaves from the Mental Portfolio of an Eurasian," *The Independent* (1909)

[In this candid, formally innovative memoir, Eaton/Far describes her formation as a writer, a feminist, and an advocate for the overseas Chinese by foregrounding her position as an interstitial "connecting link" between cultures and races. "Leaves" conveys how much geographical and social mobility mattered to Far's intellectual development. Her travels between Chinese and Anglo-American settlements throughout Canada, the US, and Jamaica—as well as her imaginative (as well as outwardly imposed) relationship to China—enabled Far to develop cosmopolitan views about the Chinese diaspora by drawing connections between different local events. "Leaves" also shows how important sentimentalism, Christian, and Confucian discourses were to Far's sense of herself as her "unusually large" heart, her suffering under "the cross of the Eurasian," and her Confucian sincerity combined to bolster her sympathetic defense of Chinese migrants in the Americas.]

When I look back over the years I see myself, a little child of scarcely four years of age, walking in front of my nurse, in a green English lane, and listening to her tell another of her kind that my mother is Chinese. "Oh Lord!" exclaims the informed. She turns around and scans me curiously from head to foot. Then the two women whisper together. Tho the word "Chinese" conveys very little meaning to my mind, I feel that they are talking about my father and mother and my heart swells with indignation. When we reach home I rush to my mother and try to tell her what I have heard. I am a young child. I fail to make myself intelligible. My mother does not understand, and when the nurse declares to her, "Little Miss Sui is a story-teller," my mother slaps me.

Many a long year has past over my head since that day—the day on which I first learned I was something different and apart from other children, but tho my mother has forgotten it, I have not.

I see myself again, a few years older. I am playing with another child in a garden. A girl passes by outside the gate. "Mamie," she cries to my companion. "I wouldn't speak to Sui if I were you. Her mamma is Chinese."

"I don't care," answers the little one beside me. And then to me, "Even if your mamma is Chinese, I like you better than I like Annie."

"But I don't like you," I answer, turning my back on her. It is my first conscious lie.

I am at a children's party, given by the wife of an Indian officer whose children were schoolfellows of mine. I am only six years of age, but have attended a private school for over a year, and have already learned that China is a heathen country, being civilized by England. However, for the time being, I am a merry romping child. There are quite a number of grown people present. One, a white haired old man, has his attention called to me by the hostess. He adjusts his eyeglasses and surveys me critically. "Ah, indeed!" he exclaims. "Who would have thought it at first glance. Yet now I see the difference between her and other children. What a peculiar coloring! Her mother's eyes and hair and her father's features, I presume. Very interesting little creature!"

I had been called from play for the purpose of inspection. I do not return to it. For the rest of the evening I hide myself behind a hall door and refuse to show myself until it is time to go home.

My parents have come to America. We are in Hudson City, N.Y., and we are very poor. I am out with my brother, who is ten months older than myself. We pass a Chinese store, the door of which is open. "Look!" says Charlie. "Those men in there are Chinese!" Eagerly I gaze into the long low room. With the exception of my mother, who is English bred with English ways and manner of dress, I have never seen a Chinese person. The two men within the store are uncouth specimens of their race, drest in working blouses and pantaloons with queues hanging down their backs. I recoil with a sense of shock.

"Oh, Charlie," I cry. "Are we like that?"

"Well, we're Chinese, and they're Chinese, too, so we must be!" returns my seven-year-old brother.

"Of course you are," puts in a boy who has followed us down the street, and who lives near us and has seen my mother: "Chinky, Chinky, Chinaman, yellow-face, pig-tail, rat-eater." A number of other boys and several little girls join in with him.

"Better than you," shouts my brother, facing the crowd. He is younger and smaller than any there, and I am even more insignificant than he; but my spirit revives.

"I'd rather be Chinese than anything else in the world," I scream.

They pull my hair, they tear my clothes, they scratch my face, and all but lame my brother; but the white blood in our veins fights valiantly for the Chinese half of us. When it is all over, exhausted and bedraggled, we crawl home, and report to our mother that we have "won the battle."

"Are you sure?" asks my mother doubtfully.

"Of course. They ran from us. They were frightened," returns my brother.

My mother smiles with satisfaction.

"Do you hear?" she asks my father.

"Umm," he observes, raising his eyes from his paper for an instant. My childish instinct, however, tells me that he is more interested than he appears to be.

It is tea time, but I cannot eat. Unobserved I crawl away. I do not sleep that night. I am too excited and I ache all over. Our opponents had been so very much stronger and bigger than we. Toward morning, however, I fall into a doze from which I awake myself, shouting:

"Sound the battle cry;
See the foe is nigh."[1]

My mother believes in sending us to Sunday school. She has been brought up in a Presbyterian college.

The scene of my life shifts to Eastern Canada. The sleigh which has carried us from the station stops in front of a little French Canadian hotel. Immediately we are surrounded by a number of villagers, who stare curiously at my mother as my father assists her to alight from the sleigh. Their curiosity, however, is tempered with kindness, as they watch, one after another, the little black heads of my brothers and sisters and myself emerge out of the buffalo robe, which is part of the sleigh's outfit. There are six of us, four girls and two boys; the eldest, my brother, being only seven years of age. My father and mother are still in their twenties. "Les pauvres enfants,"[2] the inhabitants murmur, as they help to carry us into the hotel. Then in lower tones: "Chinoise, Chinoise."

For some time after our arrival, whenever we children are sent for a walk, our footsteps are dogged by a number of young French and English Canadians, who amuse themselves with speculations as to whether, we being Chinese, are susceptible to pinches and hair pulling, while older persons pause and gaze upon us, very much in the same way that I have seen people gaze upon strange animals in a menagerie. Now and then we are stopt and plied with questions as to what we eat and drink, how we go to sleep, if my mother understands what my father says to her, if we sit on chairs or squat on floors, etc., etc., etc.

There are many pitched battles, of course, and we seldom leave the house without being armed for conflict. My mother takes a great inter-

---

1 First lines of a hymn by William Sherman written in 1869.

2 "The poor children" (French).

est in our battles, and usually cheers us on, tho I doubt whether she understands the depth of the troubled waters thru which her little children wade. As to my father, peace is his motto, and he deems it wisest to be blind and deaf to many things.

School days are short, but memorable. I am in the same class with my brother, my sister next to me in the class below. The little girl whose desk my sister shares shrinks close against the wall as my sister takes her place. In a little while she raises her hand.

"Please, teacher!"

"Yes, Annie."

"May I change my seat?"

"No, you may not!"

The little girl sobs. "Why should I have to sit beside a————"

Happily my sister does not seem to hear, and before long the two little girls become great friends. I have many such experiences.

My brother is remarkably bright; my sister next to me has a wonderful head for figures, and when only eight years of age helps my father with his night work accounts. My parents compare her with me. She is of sturdier build than I, and, as my father says, "Always has her wits about her." He thinks her more like my mother, who is very bright and interested in every little detail of practical life. My father tells me that I will never make half the woman that my mother is or that my sister will be. I am not as strong as my sisters, which makes me feel somewhat ashamed, for I am the eldest little girl, and more is expected of me. I have no organic disease, but the strength of my feelings seems to take from me the strength of my body. I am prostrated at times with attacks of nervous sickness. The doctor says that my heart is unusually large; but in the light of the present I know that the cross of the Eurasian bore too heavily upon my childish shoulders. I usually hide my weakness from the family until I cannot stand. I do not understand myself, and I have an idea that the others will despise me for not being as strong as they. Therefore, I like to wander away alone, either by the river or in the bush. The green fields and flowing water have a charm for me. At the age of seven, as it is today, a bird on the wing is my emblem of happiness.

I have come from a race on my mother's side which is said to be the most stolid and insensible to feeling of all races, yet I look back over the years and see myself so keenly alive to every shade of sorrow and suffering that it is almost a pain to live.

If there is any trouble in the house in the way of a difference between my father and mother, or if any child is punished, how I suffer! And when harmony is restored, heaven seems to be around me. I can be sad, but I can also be glad. My mother's screams of agony when a baby is born almost drive me wild, and long after her pangs have subsided I feel them in my own body. Sometimes it is a week before I can get to sleep after such an experience.

A debt owing by my father fills me with shame. I feel like a criminal when I pass the creditor's door. I am only ten years old. And all the while the question of nationality perplexes my little brain. Why are we what we are? I and my brothers and sisters. Why did God make us to be hooted and stared at? Papa is English, mamma is Chinese. Why couldn't we have been either one thing or the other? Why is my mother's race despised? I look into the faces of my father and mother. Is she not every bit as dear and good as he? Why? Why? She sings us the songs she learned at her English school. She tells us tales of China. Tho a child when she left her native land she remembers it well, and I am never tired of listening to the story of how she was stolen from her home. She tells us over and over again of her meeting with my father in Shanghai and the romance of their marriage. Why? Why?

I do not confide in my father and mother. They would not understand. How could they? He is English, she is Chinese. I am different to both of them—a stranger, tho their own child. "What are we?" I ask my brother. "It doesn't matter, sissy," he responds. But it does. I love poetry, particularly heroic pieces. I also love fairy tales. Stories of everyday life do not appeal to me. I dream dreams of being great and noble; my sisters and brothers also. I glory in the idea of dying at the stake and a great genie arising from the flames and declaring to those who have scorned us: "Behold, how great and glorious and noble are the Chinese people!"

My sisters are apprenticed to a dressmaker; my brother is entered in an office. I tramp around and sell my father's pictures, also some lace which I make myself. My nationality, if I had only known it at that time, helps to make sales. The ladies who are my customers call me "The Little Chinese Lace Girl." But it is a dangerous life for a very young girl. I come near to "mysteriously disappearing" many a time. The greatest temptation was in the thought of getting far away from where I was known, to where no mocking cries of "Chinese!" "Chinese!" could reach.

Whenever I have the opportunity I steal away to the library and read every book I can find on China and the Chinese. I learn that China is the oldest civilized nation on the face of the earth and a few other things. At eighteen years of age what troubles me is not that I am what I am, but that others are ignorant of my superiority. I am small, but my feelings are big—and great is my vanity.

My sisters attend dancing classes, for which they pay their own fees. In spite of covert smiles and sneers, they are glad to meet and mingle with other young folk. They are not sensitive in the sense that I am. And yet they understand. One of them tells me that she overheard a young man say to another that he would rather marry a pig than a girl with Chinese blood in her veins.

In course of time I too learn shorthand and take a position in an office. Like my sister, I teach myself, but, unlike my sister, I have neither the perseverance nor the ability to perfect myself. Besides, to a temperament like mine, it is torture to spend the hours in transcribing other people's thoughts. Therefore, altho I can always earn a moderately good salary, I do not distinguish myself in the business world as does she.

When I have been working for some years I open an office of my own. The local papers patronize me and give me a number of assignments, including most of the local Chinese reporting. I meet many Chinese persons, and when they get into trouble am often called upon to fight their battles in the papers. This I enjoy. My heart leaps for joy when I read one day an article signed by a New York Chinese in which he declares "The Chinese in America owe an everlasting debt of gratitude to Sui Sin Far for the bold stand she has taken in their defense."

The Chinaman who wrote the article seeks me out and calls upon me. He is a clever and witty man, a graduate of one of the American colleges and as well a Chinese scholar. I learn that he has an American wife and several children. I am very much interested in these children, and when I meet them my heart throbs in sympathetic tune with the tales they relate of their experiences as Eurasians. "Why did papa and mamma born us?" asks one. Why?

I also meet other Chinese men who compare favorably with the white men of my acquaintance in mind and heart qualities. Some of them are quite handsome. They have not as finely cut noses and as well developed chins as the white men, but they have smoother skins and their expression is more serene; their hands are better shaped and their voices softer.

Some little Chinese women whom I interview are very anxious to know whether I would marry a Chinaman. I do not answer No. They clap their hands delightedly, and assure me that the Chinese are much the finest and best of all men. They are, however, a little doubtful as to whether one could be persuaded to care for me, full-blooded Chinese people having a prejudice against the half white.

Fundamentally, I muse, people are all the same. My mother's race is as prejudiced as my father's. Only when the whole world becomes as one family will human beings be able to see clearly and hear distinctly. I believe that some day a great part of the world will be Eurasian. I cheer myself with the thought that I am but a pioneer. A pioneer should glory in suffering.

"You were walking with a Chinaman yesterday," accuses an acquaintance.

"Yes, what of it?"

"You ought not to. It isn't right."

"Not right to walk with one of my mother's people? Oh, indeed!"

I cannot reconcile his notion of righteousness with my own.

★★★

I am living in a little town away off on the north shore of a big lake. Next to me at the dinner table is the man for whom I work as a stenographer. There are also a couple of business men, a young girl and her mother.

Some one makes a remark about the cars full of Chinamen that past that morning. A transcontinental railway runs thru the town.

My employer shakes his rugged head. "Somehow or other," says he, "I cannot reconcile myself to the thought that the Chinese are humans like ourselves. They may have immortal souls, but their faces seem to be so utterly devoid of expression that I cannot help but doubt."

"Souls," echoes the town clerk. "Their bodies are enough for me. A Chinaman is, in my eyes, more repulsive than a nigger."

"They always give me such a creepy feeling," puts in the young girl with a laugh.

"I wouldn't have one in my house," declares my landlady.

"Now, the Japanese are different altogether. There is something bright and likeable about those men," continues Mr. K.

A miserable, cowardly feeling keeps me silent. I am in a Middle West town. If I declare what I am, every person in the place will hear about it the next day. The population is in the main made up of working folks with strong prejudices against my mother's countrymen. The prospect before me is not an enviable one—if I speak. I have no longer an ambition to die at the stake for the sake of demonstrating the greatness and nobleness of the Chinese people.

Mr. K turns to me with a kindly smile.

"What makes Miss Far so quiet?" he asks.

"I don't suppose she finds the 'washee washee men'[1] particularly interesting subjects of conversation," volunteers the young manager of the local bank.

With a great effort I raise my eyes from my plate. "Mr. K.," I say, addressing my employer, "the Chinese people may have no souls, no expression on their faces, be altogether beyond the pale of civilization, but whatever they are, I want you to understand that I am—I am a Chinese."

---

1 Derogatory term for Chinese laundrymen.

There is silence in the room for a few minutes. Then Mr. K. pushes back his plate and standing up beside me, says:

"I should not have spoken as I did. I know nothing whatever about the Chinese. It was pure prejudice. Forgive me!"

I admire Mr. K.'s moral courage in apologizing to me; he is a conscientious Christian man, but I do not remain much longer in the little town.

★★★

I am under a tropic sky,[1] meeting frequently and conversing with persons who are almost as high up in the world as birth, education and money can set them. The environment is peculiar, for I am also surrounded by a race of people, the reputed descendants of Ham, the son of Noah, whose offspring, it was prophesied, should be the servants of the sons of Shem and Japheth.[2] As I am a descendant, according to the Bible, of both Shem and Japheth, I have a perfect right to set my heel upon the Ham people; but tho I see others around me following out the Bible suggestion, it is not in my nature to be arrogant to any but those who seek to impress me with their superiority, which the poor black maid who has been assigned to me by the hotel certainly does not. My employer's wife takes me to task for this. "It is unnecessary," she says, "to thank a black person for a service."

The novelty of life in the West Indian island is not without its charm. The surroundings, people, manner of living, are so entirely different from what I have been accustomed to up North that I feel as if I were "born again." Mixing with people of fashion, and yet not of them, I am not of sufficient importance to create comment or curiosity. I am busy nearly all day and often well into the night. It is not monotonous work, but it is certainly strenuous. The planters and business men of the island take me as a matter of course and treat me with kindly courtesy. Occasionally an Englishman will warn me against the "brown boys" of the island, little dreaming that I too am of the "brown people" of the earth.

When it begins to be whispered about the place that I am not all white, some of the "sporty" people seek my acquaintance. I am small and look much younger than my years. When, however, they discover that I am a very serious and sober-minded spinster indeed, they retire quite gracefully, leaving me a few amusing reflections.

---

1 Edith Eaton worked as a reporter in Jamaica in 1896–97.

2 On the curse of Ham and the enslavement of his children to his brothers Shem and Japheth—an episode which supposedly provided biblical legitimacy to slavery and other forms of racism—see Genesis 9:20–27.

One evening a card is brought to my room. It bears the name of some naval officer. I go down to my visitor, thinking he is probably some one who, having been told that I am a reporter for the local paper, has brought me an item of news. I find him lounging in an easy chair on the veranda of the hotel—a big, blond, handsome fellow, several years younger than I.

"You are Lieutenant ———?" I inquire.

He bows and laughs a little. The laugh doesn't suit him somehow—and it doesn't suit me, either.

"If you have anything to tell me, please tell it quickly, because I'm very busy."

"Oh, you don't really mean that," he answers, with another silly and offensive laugh. "There's always plenty of time for good times. That's what I am here for. I saw you at the races the other day and twice at King's House.[1] My ship will be here for —— weeks."

"Do you wish that noted?" I ask.

"Oh, no! Why—I came just because I had an idea that you might like to know me. I would like to know you. You look such a nice little body. Say, wouldn't you like to go out for a sail this lovely night? I will tell you all about the sweet little Chinese girls I met when we were at Hong Kong. They're not so shy!"

★★★

I leave Eastern Canada for the Far West, so reduced by another attack of rheumatic fever that I only weigh eighty-four pounds. I travel on an advertising contract. It is presumed by the railway company that in some way or other I will give them full value for their transportation across the continent. I have been ordered beyond the Rockies by the doctor, who declares that I will never regain my strength in the East. Nevertheless, I am but two days in San Francisco when I start out in search of work. It is the first time that I have sought work as a stranger in a strange town. Both of the other positions away from home were secured for me by home influence. I am quite surprised to find that there is no demand for my services in San Francisco and that no one is particularly interested in me. The best I can do is to accept an offer from a railway agency to typewrite their correspondence for $5 a month. I stipulate, however, that I shall have the privilege of taking in outside work and that my hours shall be light. I am hopeful that the sale of a story or newspaper article may add to my income, and I console myself with the reflection that, considering that I still limp and bear traces of sickness, I am fortunate to secure any work at all.

---

1   The official residence of the Governor General of Jamaica.

The proprietor of one of the San Francisco papers, to whom I have a letter of introduction, suggests that I obtain some subscriptions from the people of Chinatown, that district of the city having never been canvassed. This suggestion I carry out with enthusiasm, tho I find that the Chinese merchants and people generally are inclined to regard me with suspicion. They have been imposed upon so many times by unscrupulous white people. Another drawback—save for a few phrases, I am unacquainted with my mother tongue. How, then, can I expect these people to accept me as their own countrywoman? The Americanized Chinamen actually laugh in my face when I tell them that I am of their race. However, they are not all "doubting Thomases."[1] Some little women discover that I have Chinese hair, color of eyes and complexion, also that I love rice and tea. This settles the matter for them—and for their husbands.

My Chinese instincts develop. I am no longer the little girl who shrunk against my brother at the first sight of a Chinaman. Many and many a time, when alone in a strange place, has the appearance of even a humble laundryman given me a sense of protection and made me feel quite at home. This fact of itself proves to me that prejudice can be eradicated by association.

I meet a half Chinese, half white girl. Her face is plastered with a thick white coat of paint and her eyelids and eyebrows are blackened so that the shape of her eyes and the whole expression of her face is changed. She was born in the East, and at the age of eighteen came West to answer an advertisement. Living for many years among the working class, she had heard little but abuse of the Chinese. It is not difficult, in a land like California, for a half Chinese, half white girl to pass as one of Spanish or Mexican origin. This the poor child does, tho she lives in nervous dread of being "discovered." She becomes engaged to a young man, but fears to tell him what she is, and only does so when compelled by a fearless American girl friend. This girl, who knows her origin, realizing that the truth sooner or later must be told, and better soon than late, advises the Eurasian to confide in the young man, assuring her that he loves her well enough not to allow her nationality to stand, a bar sinister,[2] between them. But the Eurasian prefers to keep her secret, and only reveals it to the man who is to be her husband when driven to bay by the American girl, who declares that if the half-breed will not tell the truth she will. When the young man hears that the girl he is engaged to has Chinese blood in her

---

1 In the book of John, Saint Thomas is skeptical of Jesus' resurrection and asks to touch his wounds.

2 A bar running from upper right to lower left on a coat of arms, traditionally to indicate an illegitimate birth.

veins, he exclaims: "Oh, what will my folks say?" But that is all. Love is stronger than prejudice with him, and neither he nor she deems it necessary to inform his "folks."

The Americans, having for many years manifested a much higher regard for the Japanese than for the Chinese, several half Chinese young men and women, thinking to advance themselves, both in a social and business sense, pass as Japanese. They continue to be known as Eurasians; but a Japanese Eurasian does not appear in the same light as a Chinese Eurasian. The unfortunate Chinese Eurasians! Are not those who compel them to thus cringe more to be blamed than they?

People, however, are not all alike. I meet white men, and women, too, who are proud to mate with those who have Chinese blood in their veins, and think it a great honor to be distinguished by the friendship of such. There are also Eurasians and Eurasians. I know of one who allowed herself to become engaged to a white man after refusing him nine times. She had discouraged him in every way possible, had warned him that she was half Chinese; that her people were poor, that every week or month she sent home a certain amount of her earnings, and that the man she married would have to do as much, if not more; also, most uncompromising truth of all, that she did not love him and never would. But the resolute and undaunted lover swore that it was a matter of indifference to him whether she was a Chinese or a Hottentot, that it would be his pleasure and privilege to allow her relations double what it was in her power to bestow, and as to not loving him—that did not matter at all. He loved her. So, because the young woman had a married mother and married sisters, who were always picking at her and gossiping over her independent manner of living, she finally consented to marry him, recording the agreement in her diary thus:

"I have promised to become the wife of —— —— on —— ——, 189–, because the world is so cruel and sneering to a single woman—and for no other reason."

Everything went smoothly until one day. The young man was driving a pair of beautiful horses and she was seated by his side, trying very hard to imagine herself in love with him, when a Chinese vegetable gardener's cart came rumbling along. The Chinaman was a jolly-looking individual in blue cotton blouse and pantaloons, his rakish looking hat being kept in place by a long queue which was pulled upward from his neck and wound around it. The young woman was suddenly possest with the spirit of mischief. "Look!" she cried, indicating the Chinaman, "there's my brother. Why don't you salute him?"

The man's face fell a little. He sank into a pensive mood. The wicked one by his side read him like an open book.

"When we are married," said she, "I intend to give a Chinese party every month."

No answer.

"As there are very few aristocratic Chinese in this city, I shall fill up with the laundrymen and vegetable farmers. I don't believe in being exclusive in democratic America, do you?"

He hadn't a grain of humor in his composition, but a sickly smile contorted his features as he replied:

"You shall do just as you please, my darling. But—but—consider a moment. Wouldn't it just be a little pleasanter for us if, after we are married, we allowed it to be presumed that you were—er—Japanese? So many of my friends have inquired of me if that is not your nationality. They would be so charmed to meet a little Japanese lady."

"Hadn't you better oblige them by finding one?"

"Why—er—what do you mean?"

"Nothing much in particular. Only—I am getting a little tired of this," taking off his ring.

"You don't mean what you say! Oh, put it back, dearest! You know I would not hurt your feelings for the world!"

"You haven't. I'm more than pleased. But I do mean what I say."

That evening, the "ungrateful" Chinese Eurasian diaried, among other things, the following:

"Joy, oh, joy! I'm free once more. Never again shall I be untrue to my own heart. Never again will I allow any one to 'hound' or 'sneer' me into matrimony."

I secure transportation to many California points. I meet some literary people, chief among whom is the editor of the magazine who took my first Chinese stories.[1] He and his wife give me a warm welcome to their ranch. They are broadminded people, whose interest in me is sincere and intelligent, not affected and vulgar. I also meet some funny people who advise me to "trade" upon my nationality. They tell me that if I wish to succeed in literature in America I should dress in Chinese costume, carry a fan in my hand, wear a pair of scarlet beaded slippers, live in New York, and come of high birth. Instead of making myself familiar with the Chinese-Americans around me, I should discourse on my spirit acquaintance with Chinese ancestors and quote in between the "Good mornings" and "How d'ye dos" of editors.

---

1 Charles Fletcher Lummis (1859–1928) was editor of the Southwestern regional magazine, *Land of Sunshine* (renamed *Out West* in 1901), in which Eaton/Sui Sin Far published numerous stories.

"Confucius, Confucius, how great is Confucius, Before Confucius, there never was Confucius, After Confucius, there never came Confucius,"[1] etc., etc., etc.,

or something like that, both illuminating and obscuring, don't you know. They forget, or perhaps they are not aware that the old Chinese sage taught "The way of sincerity is the way of heaven."[2]

My experiences as an Eurasian never cease; but people are not now as prejudiced as they have been. In the West, too, my friends are more advanced in all lines of thought than those whom I know in Eastern Canada—more genuine, more sincere, with less of the form of religion, but more of its spirit.

So I roam backward and forward across the continent. When I am East, my heart is West. When I am West, my heart is East. Before long I hope to be in China. As my life began in my father's country it may end in my mother's.

After all I have no nationality and am not anxious to claim any. Individuality is more than nationality. "You are you and I am I,"[3] says Confucius. I give my right hand to the Occidentals and my left to the Orientals, hoping that between them they will not utterly destroy the insignificant "connecting link." And that's all.

2. From Sui Sin Far, *Mrs. Spring Fragrance* (Chicago: A.C. McClurg & Co., 1912), 1

[The title page of the first edition of *Mrs. Spring Fragrance* shows how important the exotic "oriental" décor was to the book's design: every recto page is imprinted with images of flowers, birds, and the Chinese characters "Fu Lu Shou" (Good Fortune, Prosperity, Longevity). Despite the book's frequent Christian overtones, its publisher has managed to incorporate a reference to three Chinese deities (and common household "idols") into half of its pages. The inclusion of both "Sui Sin Far" and "[Edith Eaton]" on the title page reveals the artifice behind the author's Chinese pen name.]

---

1 A popular paean commemorating the ancient Chinese philosopher.
2 *The Doctrine of the Mean*, in *The Chinese Classics*, trans. James Legge, I.83.
3 *The Works of Mencius*, in *The Chinese Classics*, trans. James Legge, II.137.

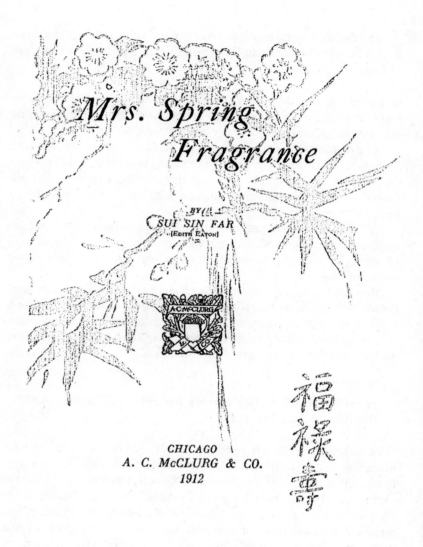

Mrs. Spring Fragrance

BY

SUI SIN FAR
(EDITH EATON)

CHICAGO
A. C. McCLURG & CO.
1912

福祿壽

3. From "The Chinese in America," *Westerner* (May 1909)

[When juxtaposed with Mrs. Spring Fragrance's desire to write a book about Americans in "The Inferior Woman," this vignette shows that Sui Sin Far recognized the limitations of sentimental fiction—which above all had to be "amusing." Here, Far suggests that the intimate proximity to Americans enjoyed by Chinese house servants and students could lead to "instructive" critical insights into American character. Instead of serving as an informant about exotic aspects of

Chinese culture, the Chinese writer in this passage reverses the ethnographic gaze and also improves it by participating actively in American society.]

A Chinese Book on Americans

"I think," said Go Ek Ju, "that when I return to China I will write a book about the American people."

"What put such an idea into your head?" I asked.

"The number of books about the Chinese by Americans," answered Go Ek Ju. "I see them in the library; they are very amusing."

"See, then, that when you write your book, it is likewise amusing."

"No," said Go Ek Ju. "My aim, when I write a book about Americans will be to make it not amusing, but interesting and instructive. The poor Americans have to content themselves with writing for amusement only because they have no means of obtaining any true knowledge of the Chinese when in China; but we Chinese in America have fine facilities for learning all about the Americans. *We go into the American houses as servants; we enter the American schools and colleges as students*; we ask questions and we think about what we hear and see. Where is there the American who will go to China and enter into the service of a Chinese family as a domestic? We have yet to hear about a band of American youths, both male and female, being admitted as students into a Chinese university."

4. From "Literary Notes," *The Independent* (15 August 1912), 388

[The following notices and reviews show how *Mrs. Spring Fragrance* was initially received by critics, and presumably by many of its readers.]

Our readers are well acquainted with the dainty stories of Chinese life written by Sui Sin Far (Miss Edith Eaton) and will be glad to know that those published in THE INDEPENDENT as well as in other periodicals have been brought together in a volume entitled *Mrs. Spring Fragrance* (McClurg; $1.40). The conflict between occidental and oriental ideas and the hardships of the American immigration laws furnish the theme for most of the tales and the reader is not only interested but has his mind widened by becoming acquainted with novel points of view.

5. Review in *Journal of Education* (31 October 1912), 468

A most delightful group of stories pertaining to the Chinese of the Pacific coast by an author who knows them intimately and writes of them appreciatively. These stories have appeared beforehand in many of our best magazines, both eastern and western, and are now presented in book form by permission of the publishers. It is a revelation to read this book. It is such an easy, almost popular thing to present the Chinaman as the "Heathen Chinee"[1] that it is gratifying to be credibly informed of quite different and most commendable features of the Chinese character by one who knows them like a book. The first story ("Mrs. Spring Fragrance") is but the initiative to the thirty-six others that follow it. It is a charming bit of composition, but no better than any of its successors. Nearly one-half the stories are juvenile, being stories commonly narrated to Chinese children. They are worthy of a recital in any nursery. Evidently "Sui Sin Far" knows the ins and outs of Chinatown in San Francisco as few know it, and she helps us to know it. The book is an elegant bit of printing also, a feature being a pictorial waterlining of every page throughout. It is unique both in text and typography.

6. "A New Note in Fiction," *New York Times* (7 July 1912), BR405

[This review from the *New York Times* clearly identifies *Mrs. Spring Fragrance*'s primary themes: intermarriage, the mixing of populations and races, and the importance (as well as the "well-nigh superhuman" difficulty) of understanding "feelings [and] sentiments" across racial lines.]

MRS. SPRING FRAGRANCE. By Sui Sin Far (Edith Eaton). A.C. McClurg & Co. $1.40.

Miss Eaton has struck a new note in American fiction. She has not struck it very surely, or with surpassing skill. But it has taken courage to strike it at all, and, to some extent, she atones for lack of artistic skill with the unusual knowledge she undoubtedly has of her theme. The thing she has tried to do is to portray for readers of the white race the lives, feelings, sentiments of the Americanized Chinese of the Pacific Coast, of those who have intermarried with them and of the children who have sprung from such unions. It is a task whose adequate doing

---

1   See Appendix B1.

would require well-nigh superhuman insight and the subtlest of methods. In some of the stories she seems not even to have tried to see inside the souls of her people, but has contented herself with the merest sketching of externals. In others, again, she has seen far and deep, and has made her account keenly interesting. Especially is this true of the analysis she makes occasionally of the character of an Americanized Chinese, of the glimpses she gives into the lives, thoughts and emotions of the Chinese women who refuse to be anything but intensely Chinese, and into the characters of the half-breed children. Particularly interesting are two stories in which an American woman is made to contrast her experiences as the wife of an American and afterward of a Chinese.

7. From Frederick Burrows, "The Uncommercial Club," *New England Magazine* (1912), 193–94

Under the daintily poetic title of "Mrs. Spring Fragrance," the McClurg Co. are bringing out a book of Chinese-American stories by Sui Sin Fan (Edith Eaton). The author knows her field with a fullness and accuracy, that tells in the minutest turns of phraseology, as well as in formal statements and descriptions. With the aid of this knowledge, and unfailing sympathy and considerable literary tact, she carries us nearer to the human heart of Chinese-American life than many of us have ever been before. As an introduction to a little-understood human group the book is as important a contribution to the brotherhood of the race as Zangwill's "Children of the Ghetto." Miss Eaton is gifted with a fine sense of humor that is as dainty and delicate as the grotesqueries of a Chinese fan. There is but small hint of a possible dark and tragic side of the story, and it is well that it is so. That phase has been overdone in many a lurid under-world tale. In Miss Eaton's book our Chinese friends have a quaint wisdom, mingled with childish simplicity and childish cunning, boundless good-nature and a prevailing right intention, that is all as human as possible.

Such a book justifies the printing press, because it brings us all nearer together. The volume is charmingly made, bound in red, the Chinese good-luck color, and printed on paper having a Chinese bamboo design under the type,—a beautiful ornament for a boudoir or library table. While this is the author's first published volume, her stories are familiar to the readers of the best magazine literature, who will welcome their collection in this permanent form. By all means make the acquaintance of her Chinese-American daintiness, "Mrs. Spring Fragrance" and with the very substantial virtues of her worthy husband.

8. Review in *The American Antiquarian and Oriental Journal* (July–September 1913), 181

[This positive review takes Sui Sin Far's novel subject matter as a point of departure for the anonymous reviewer's own theories about the inhabitants of Chinatown, the difficulty of "becom[ing] American in impulse and thought," and the disadvantageous situation of the "half-breed."]

The stories brought together in this little book have appeared in a wide range of American magazines and periodicals. They are something quite new in our literature and are intensely interesting. They are pictures of life in Chinatown—the Chinatown of San Francisco and Los Angeles and Seattle. True to life, they give an insight into the thought and feeling of the Chinese who are with us, but not of us. To what extent the stories are accounts of actual experiences we cannot say, but they are so true and so natural that they might easily be based on fact. Whether so or not, they are written by a woman who knows Chinese character intimately and appreciates the romance and tragedy of Chinatown. The Chinese who live there are in our country for a definite purpose, the accomplishment of which may be worth while, but often involves enormous humiliation and sacrifice. They are members of a proud and high-strung people, and for many of them every day and hour of their stay in this boasted land of freedom is suffering and chafing. The non-Chinese inhabitants of Chinatown are unfortunates, depraved, outcasts, and leeches, who prey upon the Chinese and take advantage of their ignorance and needs. Few of the Chinese ever become American in impulse and thought, though they may gain temporary advantage by subjecting themselves to American influences and adopting, at least in appearance, American ways. Those most Americanized, however, must now and again feel the pull of the old life, the force of old customs, the power of the old belief, and when they do the struggle is a fierce one. The half-breed American-Chinese, born in Chinatown, is an unfortunate and anomalous being, at disadvantage all along the line, heavily handicapped for life, unless he remains in Chinatown or seeks refuge in China. It is stories of these people—Chinese, outcast, and mongrel—which our author presents us. Her book is divided into two parts—Mrs. Spring Fragrance (stories for adults) and Tales of Chinese Children (juvenile stories). It surely would have been better to have divided them into two books making different appeal, but all the stories are charmingly told, with taste, fancy and sympathy. The book deserves a wide reading. It is fresh and new, different from anything else, and is pervaded by a fine spirit. It should do much to arouse sympathy through a better understanding.

Appendix B: Chinese Exclusion

1. Bret Harte, "Plain Language from Truthful James," *The Overland Monthly Magazine* (September 1870)

[A parody of Algernon Swinburne's *Atalanta in Calydon* (1865), Harte's poem was intended to satirize the anti-Chinese prejudices of Irish immigrant laborers. However, advocates for Chinese exclusion enthusiastically used this poem's description of the "heathen Chinee" to propagate anti-Chinese sentiments. When this poem became a popular and widely quoted depiction of the inscrutable character of the Chinese, Harte expressed regret that he had written it at all.]

(Table Mountain, 1870)

> Which I wish to remark,
> And my language is plain,
> That for ways that are dark
> And for tricks that are vain,
> The heathen Chinee is peculiar,
> Which the same I would rise to explain.
>
> Ah Sin was his name;
> And I shall not deny,
> In regard to the same,
> What that name might imply;
> But his smile it was pensive and childlike,
> As I frequent remarked to Bill Nye.
>
> It was August the third,
> And quite soft was the skies;
> Which it might be inferred
> That Ah Sin was likewise;
> Yet he played it that day upon William
> And me in a way I despise.
>
> Which we had a small game,
> And Ah Sin took a hand:
> It was Euchre.[1] The same

---

1 A trick-taking card game usually played with four players grouped into two pairs.

He did not understand;
But he smiled as he sat by the table,
With the smile that was childlike and bland.

Yet the cards they were stocked
In a way that I grieve,
And my feelings were shocked
At the state of Nye's sleeve,
Which was stuffed full of aces and bowers,[1]
And the same with intent to deceive.

But the hands that were played
By that heathen Chinee,
And the points that he made,
Were quite frightful to see,—
Till at last he put down a right bower,
Which the same Nye had dealt unto me.

Then I looked up at Nye,
And he gazed upon me;
And he rose with a sigh,
And said, "Can this be?
We are ruined by Chinese cheap labor,"—
And he went for that heathen Chinee.

In the scene that ensued
I did not take a hand,
But the floor it was strewed
Like the leaves on the strand
With the cards that Ah Sin had been hiding,
In the game "he did not understand."

In his sleeves, which were long,
He had twenty-four packs,—
Which was coming it strong,
Yet I state but the facts;
And we found on his nails, which were taper,
What is frequent in tapers,—that's wax.

---

1   The highest ranking trump cards in Euchre are the jacks of the trump suit
    and the other suit of the same color, referred to as the "right bower" and "left
    bower."

Which is why I remark,
And my language is plain,
That for ways that are dark
And for tricks that are vain,
The heathen Chinee is peculiar,—
Which the same I am free to maintain.

2. The Page Act of 3 March 1875, Chap 141, 18 US Stat. 477

[Passed on 3 March 1875 and named after the Republican Congressman Horace Page, the Page Act was the first federal immigration law. While its language covered persons from "China, Japan, or any Oriental country" and targeted both involuntary "coolie"[1] laborers and women suspected of being prostitutes, in practice the Page Act was most often used to bar Chinese women from immigrating. The prohibition on Asian women suspected of "lewd or immoral purposes" responds to widespread anxieties about the Chinese community's effects on morals and public health, while also blaming Chinese women for both real and imagined diseases that threatened normative American bodies. The difficulty of bringing women (in many cases even existing wives) to the US increased the gender imbalance of the US's Chinese "bachelor society" and led to alternative households which would, in turn, be viewed as further evidence of the perversity of Chinese family life.]

FORTY-THIRD CONGRESS. SESS. II. CH. 141. 1875.
CHAP. 141.—An act supplementary to the acts in relation to immigration.

Be it enacted by the Senate and House of Representatives of the United States of America in Congress assembled, That in determining whether the immigration of any subject of China, Japan, or any Oriental country, to the United States, is free and voluntary, as provided by section two thousand one hundred and sixty-two of the Revised Code, title "Immigration," it shall be the duty of the consul-general or consul of the United States residing at the port from which it is proposed to convey such subjects, in any vessels enrolled or licensed in the United States, or any port within the same, before delivering to the masters of any such vessels the permit or certificate provided for in such section, to ascertain whether such immigrant has entered into a contract or agreement for a term of service within the United States,

---

1 Frequently employed as a racial slur, the term "coolie" referred to manual laborers from Asia, often working under conditions of indentured servitude.

for lewd and immoral purposes; and if there be such contract or agreement, the said consul-general or consul shall not deliver the required permit or certificate.

SEC. 2. That if any citizen of the United States, or other person amenable to the laws of the United States shall take, or cause to be taken or transported, to or from the United States any subject of China, Japan, or any Oriental country, without their free and voluntary consent, for the purpose of holding them to a term of service, such citizen or other person shall be liable to be indicted therefor, and, on conviction of such offense, shall be punished by a fine not exceeding two thousand dollars and be imprisoned not exceeding one year; and all contracts and agreements for a term of service of such persons in the United States, whether made in advance or in pursuance of such illegal importation, and whether such importation shall have been in American or other vessels, are hereby declared void.

SEC. 3. That the importation into the United States of women for the purposes of prostitution is hereby forbidden; and all contracts and agreements in relation thereto, made in advance or in pursuance of such illegal importation and purposes, are hereby declared void; and whoever shall knowingly and willfully import, or cause any importation of, women into the United States for the purposes of prostitution, or shall knowingly or willfully hold, or attempt to hold, any woman to such purposes, in pursuance of such illegal importation and contract or agreement, shall be deemed guilty of a felony, and, on conviction thereof, shall be imprisoned not exceeding five years and pay a fine not exceeding five thousand dollars.
[...]

3. Dennis Kearney and H.L. Knight, "Appeal from California. The Chinese Invasion. Workingmen's Address," *Indianapolis Times* (28 February 1878)

[In 1877, the nativist and populist orator Dennis Kearney (1847–1907) was elected secretary of the Workingmen's Party of California. Anti-Chinese racism was, among other things, an easy way to obtain popularity and political influence. For years, Kearny spoke to audiences of dissatisfied working-class or unemployed whites who regularly gathered on a vacant sandlot near City Hall. Under his leadership, the Workingmen's Party launched both rhetorical and physical assaults against Chinese laborers, blaming them for unemployment, low wages, poor labor conditions, the dissolution of white families, and other effects of industrial capitalism. In this speech, Kearney shifts from anti-capitalist observations directed against "moneyed men" to the figure of the Chinese "coolie" or "cheap working slave" which supposedly enables the rich to maintain their power. Addresses such as this one played an important role in preparing public sentiment for immigration laws explicitly targeting the Chinese and other Asian groups.]

Our moneyed men have ruled us for the past thirty years. Under the flag of the slaveholder they hoped to destroy our liberty. Failing in that, they have rallied under the banner of the millionaire, the banker and the land monopolist, the railroad king and the false politician, to effect their purpose.

We have permitted them to become immensely rich against all sound republican policy, and they have turned upon us to sting us to death. They have seized upon the government by bribery and corruption. They have made speculation and public robbery a science. They have loaded the nation, the state, the county, and the city with debt. They have stolen the public lands. They have grasped all to themselves, and by their unprincipled greed brought a crisis of unparalleled distress on forty millions of people, who have natural resources to feed, clothe and shelter the whole human race.

Such misgovernment, such mismanagement, may challenge the whole world for intense stupidity, and would put to shame the darkest tyranny of the barbarous past.

We, here in California, feel it as well as you. We feel that the day and hour has come for the Workingmen of America to depose capital and put Labor in the Presidential chair, in the Senate and Congress, in the State House, and on the Judicial Bench. We are with you in this work. Workingmen must form a party of their own, take charge of the government, dispose gilded fraud, and put honest toil in power.

In our golden state all these evils have been intensified. Land monopoly has seized upon all the best soil in this fair land. A few men own from ten thousand to two hundred thousand acres each. The poor Laborer can find no resting place, save on the barren mountain, or in the trackless desert. Money monopoly has reached its grandest proportions. Here, in San Francisco, the palace of the millionaire looms up above the hovel of the starving poor with as wide a contrast as anywhere on earth.

To add to our misery and despair, a bloated aristocracy has sent to China—the greatest and oldest despotism in the world—for a cheap working slave. It rakes the slums of Asia to find the meanest slave on earth—the Chinese coolie—and imports him here to meet the free American in the Labor market, and still further widen the breach between the rich and the poor, still further to degrade white Labor.

These cheap slaves fill every place. Their dress is scant and cheap. Their food is rice from China. They hedge twenty in a room, ten by ten. They are whipped curs, abject in docility, mean, contemptible and obedient in all things. They have no wives, children or dependents.

They are imported by companies, controlled as serfs, worked like slaves, and at last go back to China with all their earnings. They are in every place, they seem to have no sex. Boys work, girls work; it is all alike to them.

The father of a family is met by them at every turn. Would he get work for himself? Ah! A stout Chinaman does it cheaper. Will he get a place for his oldest boy? He can not. His girl? Why, the Chinaman is in her place too! Every door is closed. He can only go to crime or suicide, his wife and daughter to prostitution, and his boys to hoodlumism and the penitentiary.

Do not believe those who call us savages, rioters, incendiaries, and outlaws. We seek our ends calmly, rationally, at the ballot box. So far good order has marked all our proceedings. But, we know how false, how inhuman, our adversaries are. We know that if gold, if fraud, if force can defeat us, they will all be used. And we have resolved that they shall not defeat us. We shall arm. We shall meet fraud and falsehood with defiance, and force with force, if need be.

We are men, and propose to live like men in this free land, without the contamination of slave labor, or die like men, if need be, in asserting the rights of our race, our country, and our families.

California must be all American or all Chinese. We are resolved that it shall be American, and are prepared to make it so. May we not rely upon your sympathy and assistance?

With great respect for the Workingman's Party of California.

Dennis Kearney, President
H.L. Knight, Secretary

4. Chinese Exclusion Act of 6 May 1882, Chap 126, 22 US Stat. 58

[Renewed and supplemented in various forms until its repeal in 1943, the Exclusion Act banned both skilled and unskilled Chinese laborers from migrating to the US. Sui Sin Far dramatized the historical conditions of immigrant detention and smuggling that resulted in stories such as "In the Land of the Free" and "The Smuggling of Tie Co." While the merchants who make up many of Sui Sin Far's characters were exempt from this exclusion, the law also introduced forms of documentation and discipline that made it difficult for Chinese to return to the US after traveling abroad, stipulating that they be accounted for along with a ship's cargo. Chinese residents of all classes were barred from naturalization and citizenship—a prohibition that legally enacted the stereotype that Chinese immigrants were disloyal and "inassimilable" to US nationality.]

Chapter 126. —An act to execute certain treaty stipulations relating to Chinese.

Preamble. Whereas, in the opinion of the Government of the United States the coming of Chinese laborers to this country endangers the good order of certain localities within the territory thereof:

Therefore,
Be it enacted by the Senate and House of Representatives of the United States of America in Congress assembled, That from and after the expiration of ninety days next after the passage of this act, and until the expiration of ten years next after the passage of this act, the coming of Chinese laborers to the United States be, and the same is hereby, suspended; and during such suspension it shall not be lawful for any Chinese laborer to come, or, having so come after the expiration of said ninety days, to remain within the United States.

SEC. 2. That the master of any vessel who shall knowingly bring within the United States on such vessel, and land or permit to be landed, any Chinese laborer, from any foreign port of place, shall be deemed guilty of a misdemeanor, and on conviction thereof shall be punished by a fine of not more than five hundred dollars for each and every such Chinese laborer so brought, and may be also imprisoned for a term not exceeding one year.

SEC. 3. That the two foregoing sections shall not apply to Chinese laborers who were in the United States on the seventeenth day of November, eighteen hundred and eighty, or who shall have come into the same before the expiration of ninety days next after the passage of this act, and who shall produce to such master before going on board such vessel, and shall produce to the collector of the port in the United States at which such vessel shall arrive, the evidence hereinafter in this act required of his being one of the laborers in this section mentioned; nor shall the two foregoing sections apply to the case of any master whose vessel, being bound to a port not within the United States by reason of being in distress or in stress of weather, or touching at any port of the United States on its voyage to any foreign port of place: Provided, That all Chinese laborers brought on such vessel shall depart with the vessel on leaving port.

SEC. 4. That for the purpose of properly identifying Chinese laborers who were in the United States on the seventeenth day of November, eighteen hundred and eighty, or who shall have come into the same before the expiration of ninety days next after the passage of this act, and in order to furnish them with the proper evidence of their right to go from and come to the United States of their free will and accord, as provided by the treaty between the United States and China dated November seventeenth, eighteen hundred and eighty, the collector of customs of the district from which any such Chinese laborer shall depart from the United States shall, in person or by deputy, go on board each vessel having on board any such Chinese laborer and cleared or about to sail from his district for a foreign port, and on such vessel make a list of all such Chinese laborers, which shall be entered in registry-books to be kept for that purpose, in which shall be stated the name, age, occupation, last place of residence, physical marks or peculiarities, and all facts necessary for the identification of each of such Chinese laborers, which books shall be safely kept in the custom-house; and every such Chinese laborer so departing from the United States shall be entitled to, and shall receive, free of any charge or cost upon application therefor, from the collector or his deputy, at the time such list is taken, a certificate, signed by the collector or his deputy and attested by his seal of office, in such form as the Secretary of the Treasury shall prescribe, which certificate shall contain a statement of the name, age, occupation, last place of residence, personal description, and fact of identification of the Chinese laborer to whom the certificate is issued, corresponding with the said list and registry in all particulars. In case any Chinese laborer after having received such certificate shall leave such vessel before her departure he shall deliver his certificate to the master of the vessel, and if such Chinese laborer shall fail to return to such vessel before her departure from port the certificate shall be delivered by the master to the collector of customs for cancellation. The certificate herein provided for shall entitle the Chinese laborer to whom the same is issued to return to and re-enter the United States upon producing and delivering the same to the collector of customs of the district at which such Chinese laborer shall seek to re-enter; and upon delivery of such certificate by such Chinese laborer to the collector of customs at the time of re-entry in the United States, said collector shall cause the same to be filed in the custom house and duly canceled.

SEC. 5. That any Chinese laborer mentioned in section four of this act being in the United States, and desiring to depart from the United States by land, shall have the right to demand and receive, free of charge or cost, a certificate of identification similar to that provided for in section four of this act to be issued to such Chinese laborers as may desire to leave the United States by water; and it is hereby made the duty of the collector of customs of the district next adjoining the foreign country to which said Chinese laborer desires to go to issue such certificate, free of charge or cost, upon application by such Chinese laborer, and to enter the same upon registry-books to be kept by him for the purpose, as provided for in section four of this act.

SEC. 6. That in order to the faithful execution of articles one and two of the treaty in this act before mentioned, every Chinese person other than a laborer who may be entitled by said treaty and this act to come within the United States, and who shall be about to come to the United States, shall be identified as so entitled by the Chinese Government in each case, such identity to be evidenced by a certificate issued under the authority of said government, which certificate shall be in the English language or (if not in the English language) accompanied by a translation into English, stating such right to come, and which certificate shall state the name, title, or official rank, if any, the age, height, and all physical peculiarities, former and present occupation or profession, and place of residence in China of the person to whom the certificate is issued and that such person is entitled conformably to the treaty in this act mentioned to come within the United States. Such certificate shall be prima-facie evidence of the fact set forth therein, and shall be produced to the collector of customs, or his deputy, of the port in the district in the United States at which the person named therein shall arrive.

SEC. 7. That any person who shall knowingly and falsely alter or substitute any name for the name written in such certificate or forge any such certificate, or knowingly utter any forged or fraudulent certificate, or falsely personate any person named in any such certificate, shall be deemed guilty of a misdemeanor; and upon conviction thereof shall be fined in a sum not exceeding one thousand dollars, and imprisoned in a penitentiary for a term of not more than five years.

SEC. 8. That the master of any vessel arriving in the United States from any foreign port or place shall, at the same time he delivers a manifest of the cargo, and if there be no cargo, then at the time of making a report of the entry of vessel pursuant to the law, in addition to the other matter required to be reported, and before landing, or permitting to land, any Chinese passengers, deliver and report to the collector of customs of the district in which such vessels shall have arrived a separate list of all Chinese passengers taken on board his vessel at any foreign port or place, and all such passengers on board the vessel at that time. Such list shall show the names of such passengers (and if accredited officers of the Chinese Government traveling on the business of that government, or their servants, with a note of such facts), and the name and other particulars, as shown by their respective certificates; and such list shall be sworn to by the master in the manner required by law in relation to the manifest of the cargo. Any willful refusal or neglect of any such master to comply with the provisions of this section shall incur the same penalties and forfeiture as are provided for a refusal or neglect to report and deliver a manifest of cargo.

SEC. 9. That before any Chinese passengers are landed from any such vessel, the collector, or his deputy, shall proceed to examine such passengers, comparing the certificates with the list and with the passengers; and no passenger shall be allowed to land in the United States from such vessel in violation of law.

[...]

SEC. 12. That no Chinese person shall be permitted to enter the United States by land without producing to the proper officer of customs the certificate in this act required of Chinese persons seeking to land from a vessel. And any Chinese person found unlawfully within the United States shall be caused to be removed therefrom to the country from whence he came, by direction of the United States, after being brought before some justice, judge, or commissioner of a court of the United States and found to be one not lawfully entitled to be or remain in the United States.

SEC. 13. That this act shall not apply to diplomatic and other officers of the Chinese Government traveling upon the business of that government, whose credentials shall be taken as equivalent to the certificate in this act mentioned, and shall exempt them and their body and household servants from the provisions of this act as to other Chinese persons.

SEC. 14. That hereafter no State court or court of the United States shall admit Chinese to citizenship; and all laws in conflict with this act are hereby repealed.

SEC. 15. That the words "Chinese laborers," whenever used in this act, shall be construed to mean both skilled and unskilled laborers and Chinese employed in mining.

5. From Samuel Gompers, *Some Reasons for Chinese Exclusion: Meat vs. Rice. American Manhood Against Asian Coolieism. Which Shall Survive?* (Washington: American Federation of Labor, 1902)

[This pamphlet by the founder and president of the American Federation of Labor is characteristic of the labor movement's nativist tendencies, and particularly its antipathy to the Chinese who—as rice eaters and predominantly unmarried men—could supposedly support themselves more cheaply than white workers with meat-eating families. The following excerpt, subtitled "Chinese Are Not Assimilative," presents a common argument about the "degenerate" offspring born to mixed-race parents. For similar reasons, the California legislature had prohibited the granting of marriage licenses to whites wishing to marry anyone of the "Negro, mulatto, or Mongolian" race in 1880. Several of Sui Sin Far's stories—along with her own parentage— feature more favorable depictions of intermarriage and mixed-race characters.]

To quote the imperial Chinese consul-general of San Francisco: They work more cheaply than whites; they live more cheaply; they send their money out of the country to China; most of them have no intention of remaining in the United States, and they do not adopt American manners, but live in colonies, and not after the American fashion.

Until this year no statute had been passed by the State forbidding their intermarriage with the whites,[1] and yet during their long residence but few intermarriages have taken place, and the offspring has been invariably degenerate. It is well established that the issue of the Caucasian and the Mongolian does not possess the virtues of either, but develops the vices of both. So physical assimilation is out of the question.

It is well known that the vast majority of the Chinese do not bring their wives with them in their immigration[2] because of their purpose to return to their native land when a competency is earned. Their practical status among us has been that of single men competing at low wages against not only men of our race, but men who have been brought up by our civilization to family life and civic duty. They pay little taxes; they support no institutions, neither school, church, nor theater; they remain steadfastly, after all these years, a permanently

---

1 In fact, intermarriage between whites and "Mongolians" had been prohibited since 1880.

2 The pamphlet makes no mention of the Page Act's effective immigration ban on working-class Chinese women.

foreign element. The purpose, no doubt, for enacting the exclusion laws for periods of ten years is due to the intention of Congress of observing the progress of these people under American institutions, and now it has been clearly demonstrated that they can not, for the deep and ineradicable reasons of race and mental organization, assimilate with our own people and be molded as are other races into strong and composite American stock.

Appendix C: Missionaries and Assimilation

1. From M.G.C. Edholm, "A Stain on the Flag," *Californian Illustrated Magazine* (1892)

[This exposé of the traffic in Chinese "slave" girls written by the US Methodist missionary Mary Grace Charlton Edholm draws an analogy between "negro American slavery" and the situation of female indentured servants and prostitutes among the American Chinese. By prohibiting the immigration of Asian women suspected of being prostitutes, barring Chinese laborers from a citizen's right to bring a spouse to the US, and prohibiting intermarriage between Caucasians and "Mongolians," federal and state laws inadvertently created the conditions for an intensified traffic in prostitutes. As with many other missionaries and journalists, Edholm's focus on spectacular scenes of physical abuse, sexual coercion, and missionary rescue loses sight of the legal creation and reinforcement of a "bachelor community."]

IT was generally supposed that slavery was abolished in the United States during the administration of Abraham Lincoln; yet, if the facts were known, as they will be to the reader of the present paper, there exists in this country, wherever the Chinese have obtained a foothold, a slavery so vile and debasing that all the horrors of negro American slavery do not begin to compare with it. [...]

[...] Young Chinese girls are often forcibly kidnapped in China, illegally landed in America, and sold to the keepers of places of ill-repute; and, of the inhuman treatment they receive, Miss Culbertson of the Presbyterian Mission[1] testifies that these cases subjoined could be multiplied a hundred fold. One little slave-girl who was being reared for a revolting life was obliged to sew from seven o'clock in the morning till one o'clock at night; and because she would fall asleep through exhaustion her ears had been cut, her hands burned, and she had been beaten and tortured frightfully. Another, who had been rescued from a life of shame, had her eyes propped open with pieces of incense wood because they would at times close wearily in sleep after sitting up through long hours. Her eyes were badly lacerated and inflamed by the treatment.

---

1 Miss Margaret Culbertson preceded Donaldina Cameron (see p. 17) as superintendent of the Presbyterian Mission Home in San Francisco's Chinatown.

The terrible condition of another little one, only eight years old, makes one's fingers burn to throttle the heartless keepers. She was brought to the Home by a white person who knew she was cruelly treated. Her body was in a fearful condition, black, blue and green in color. Her head had several cuts upon it. Her eyes and lips were much swollen, and her hands resembled pin cushions, so badly swollen were they. The Superintendent sent at once for Mr. Hunter of the Society for the Protection of Children, who said in all the years of labor for the rescue of suffering children he had never seen anything to equal this child's condition, and the woman should be arrested for cruelty. With Officer Holbrook, Miss Culbertson went and had the keeper arrested and sent to prison; but, as usual, she was bailed out by one of her countrymen for one hundred dollars.

Miss Culbertson now went to court to take out letters of guardianship, and then showed the child's body to the Judge; yet, when her keeper was tried and plead guilty she was fined the paltry sum of thirty dollars. The little girl was the slave-child of a firm on Dupont Street. The wife, a bound-footed woman, was a perfect fiend in temper. One method of punishment was to beat the little thing until she was faint, and then to catch her by the hair and drag her on the floor.

Another child had great scars and seams up and down her back and upon her limbs where she had been burned by red-hot irons and scalded with boiling water. Sometimes the tortures are so terrible and long continued that reason becomes dethroned. Sometimes their bodies are so diseased by these cruelties and privations that the best medical care in the Home and the most tender nursing cannot prevent death; but still these slave-dealers continue their horrible traffic with no punishment worthy the name.

But still worse horrors are in store for the little slave-girl as she nears womanhood; for then she is forced to a life of shame,—*the object of all Chinese slavery*; and, if she resists, all the tortures of the Inquisition are resorted to by her cruel masters till she gives herself up body and soul. [...]

2. From *Register of Inmates of Chinese Woman's Home, 933 Sacramento St., San Francisco, Cal.* (Courtesy of Department of Special Collections and University Archives, 1892–1903)

[These two case reports from the early years of the San Francisco Presbyterian Mission Home provide a sense of the different conditions from which girls were rescued (one badly beaten, the other "not happy" living with her uncle), as well as the rescue narrative's conventional trajectory from hardship and dissatisfaction to marriage and (in some cases) childbirth reported in subsequent entries.]

Chun Loie: Mar 25/92 I received word in the afternoon that a little girl about 9 yrs old living at the N/W/ Cor of Clay & Dupont Sts was being badly beaten. I got the police, went to the house and brought her to the Home. She was in a pitiable condition, two cuts from a hatchet were visible on her head—her mouth, face & hands badly swollen form [sic] the punishment she had received from her cruel mistress.

Mar 28 Rec'd letters of guardianship for Chun Loie had the woman arrested for cruelty to children. March 31st Went to the Police court with Chun Loie Judge [name illegible] fined her wicked mistress twenty five dollars.

Chun Loie grew up in the Home and remained here until Sept 20 1898 when she was married to an excellent young man, Quong [name illegible], an active member of the Congregational church. They had a beautiful wedding and went to live in rooms in the Congregational Chinese mission building.

Sept 99 Chun Loie had a baby boy greatly to their delight.

Jan 7 1898 Woon Qie

A young girl fourteen or fifteen years old, named Woon Qie, came to the Home. She is from Napa and came to San Francisco with her uncle's wife to visit her mother. She has lived with this uncle for several years her father being dead, but she is not happy in his home, thinks she has too much work to do, and is anxious to go to school. She had heard of this Home and thinks she would like to stay here. She is a cousin of Yow Ho who is one of our inmates. Yow Ho welcomed her warmly and said she had been praying that Woon Qie might come to the Home.

Her mother visited her soon after she came and gave her consent to Woon Qie's remaining in the Home. Woon Qie is of pleasing appearance and can speak a little English. Her uncle came down from Napa accompanied by a lawyer and claimed the girl as his ward but after a good deal of argument finally consented rather reluctantly to her stay.

Nov 1903 Woon Qie married Edward Park a young Chinaman who has a pretty home in Berkeley. They are very devoted & seem happy. Both are members of the Chinese Presby. (Khun Lom) Church 911 Stockton.

3. **From *Dragon Stories: The Bowl of Powfah, The Hundredth Maiden, Narratives of the Rescues and Romances of Chinese Slave Girls* (Oakland: Pacific Presbyterian Publishing Company, 1908), Unpaginated Pamphlet**

[*Dragon Stories* was a pamphlet containing two stories featuring rescue missions based at the Presbyterian Mission Home at 920 Sacramento

Street. Published by the Pacific Presbyterian Publishing Company, likely for the purposes of publicity and fundraising, *Dragon Stories* shows the process of rescuing and civilizing slave girls in the best possible light. Nevertheless, this excerpt from "The Bowl of Powfah" shows the extent to which the Chinese community and even the rescued girl herself doubt the missionary's motives, as well as the pivotal role of the police in making raids. For missionaries such as Donaldina Cameron, the ends justified the means of home invasions and police raids: as "The Hundredth Maiden" explains, rescued girls were most often "snatched in ways which were 'above the law' but with the ten points of possession, the lady and her attorney generally managed to win the legal guardianship of the slender yellow bits of womanhood. The attorney of the Home was accustomed to arm his client with ingenious papers which meant little but which bristled with seals and were calculated to impress Oriental eyes."]

[...] One day a Christian Chinese woman called at the Home and told the missionary that the day before she had been visiting in Commercial street, and, while there, had heard a great deal of the woes of a little slave girl kept by a family in the house. The child, she said, had twice attempted to kill herself, first by drinking "powfah"[1] and then by taking opium. After both attempts on her life she had been severely beaten and she was now treated more cruelly than ever. The kindly Chinese woman urged the missionary to rescue the little girl at once, giving definite directions how to find her.

The missionary telephoned at once to a "big" policeman and made arrangements for the rescue. Promptly at seven o'clock the next morning the two, with Teen Fook, the interpreter who always accompanied the missionary on her raids, started down to Commercial Street, Teen Fook excited, as usual, and eager for the fray. In a short time they reached the big tenement; the missionary and policeman secreted themselves, and Teen Fook rang the door-bell, taking her stand before the little peep-hole window. After some time this was opened and a Chinese woman peered out.

"Who is it?" asked the woman.

"A friend," Teen Fook answered.

"What do you want so early in the morning?"

"Open the door and let me in," Teen Fook answered. "I have something to tell you which I cannot out here on the stairs."

The woman opened the door cautiously, then, catching sight of the others, tried to slam it shut but Teen Fook slipped into the opening

---

1 A paste made from wood shavings, used in dressing hair.

and held the door until the missionary and policeman had rushed in. The woman ran along the hall shouting:

"Shut your doors, shut your doors! It is the Teacher-mother and the policeman." There was a general scurrying to cover.

The policeman mounted guard at the door while the missionary and Teen Fook sped after the woman. From room to room they went, along dark and narrow passages, hunting in every nook and corner for the little slave girl, but nowhere could she be found. Then they mounted guard at the door while the policeman took up the search, but without results. Once more the women went through the house. Every curtain was pulled aside, every nook and cranny searched. At last, glancing down a long passage, they saw an old curtain flutter, and a tousled head and haggard face peer out for a moment and then instantly disappear. They rushed forward and throwing back the curtain, Teen Fook pulled a mite of a child forward to the light, where they could see how thin her face was and how matted her unkempt hair. It was Ying Leen, who kicked and screamed with all her might and main, believing the dreaded white devils had her at last.

Her screams aroused the household and inmates poured from every doorway, adding their shouts to Ying Leen's cries. Some attempted to snatch the child and the battle was going against the rescuers when the policeman rushed up the stairs. Snatching up the frightened child, he threw her over his shoulder like a sack of flour and marched off down the stairs. Ying Leen screamed wildly, beating frantically on the policeman's chest with her little fists. In this way they went out on the street where a big crowd, hearing the uproar, had gathered. Windows went up and balconies filled in a moment. As they passed along Kearny street cries and excited words hurled back and forth in the crowd told all that the Mother-teacher had rescued another slave. Highbinders shouted for men to rush the policeman and take the child; others of the crowd cried, "No, let them have her."

Thus escorted, the party moved down Kearny street to the Hall of Justice, Teen Fook running by Ying Leen's side, trying to calm her by telling her that she need not be afraid for they were taking her to a beautiful home where she would have plenty to eat and where everybody would love her. But Ying Leen cried, "No, no, you are going to kill me! Let me go!"

At the Hall of Justice the police sergeant who met them said, "Well, where did you get that filthy, starved little thing? My children have a dog at home which I couldn't treat as she has been treated." The massive doors and the dark hall added new terror to Ying Leen's fears. She evidently believed that here was the torture chamber, indeed. During the hour of waiting for the police judge, Teen Fook renewed her efforts to make Ying Leen understand that she was safe. Finally

Teen Fook rolled up her sleeves and showed the slave child her own plump white arms, covered with cruel scars, and told her how her mistress had burned her to keep her awake when she herself was a little slave girl. This proof convinced Ying Leen, and soon she was crying, "Save me, save me!"

They were allowed to take the child home with them, on promising to produce her in court if proceedings were begun against them.

As they went up Sacramento street many little heads peered from the windows of the Mission Home. By the time they reached the entrance of the Home the steps were thronged with excited little maidens, eager to welcome this new sister to their midst. Ying Leen was given in charge of an older Chinese girl who took her up stairs, washed her and combed her hair and dressed her in clean new clothes. Then she was taken to a room and shown a little white bed, and told that it was hers. Ying Leen was half incredulous at first and then her joy knew no bounds. "I never had a bed before," she cried in ecstasy. Turning down the covers she gently smoothed the sheets. "They are so very, very white," she said in wonder, then she looked around her curiously. "Why do you do it? What puts it into your head to do all this for me when you never saw me before?" These forlorn little waifs almost invariably ask the same question, puzzled to know what prompts the strange kindness.

4. From Arthur H. Smith, *Chinese Characteristics* (New York: Fleming Revell & Co., 1894), 198–202

[Arthur Smith was among the most famous American missionaries of his time, and *Chinese Characteristics*, which drew on his fifty-four years of experience working as a missionary in China, became a popular and influential book for Americans (particularly missionaries) interested in Chinese "character." The following excerpt is from a chapter entitled "The Absence of Sympathy," which along with other chapters on traits such as "The Faculty of Absorbing," "The Disregard of Time," "Parasitism," "The Absence of Nerves," "The Absence of Sincerity," and "The Absence of Altruism" presented Chinese character traits as negative images of Western, Christian, and sentimental values. This excerpt expresses a view of Chinese family life that Sui Sin Far counteracted by writing sentimental stories about the Chinese.]

[...] One of the most characteristic methods in which the Chinese lack of sympathy is manifested is in the treatment which brides receive on their wedding day. They are often very young, are always timid and are naturally terror-stricken at being suddenly thrust among strangers. Customs vary widely, but there seems to be a general indifference to the feelings of the poor child thus exposed to the public gaze. In some places it is allowable for anyone who chooses to turn back the curtains of the chair and stare at her. In other regions, the unmarried girls find it a source of keen enjoyment to post themselves at a convenient position, as the bride passes, to throw upon her handfuls of hay seed or chaff, which will obstinately adhere to her carefully oiled hair for a long time. Upon her emergence from the chair, at the house of her new parents, she is subjected to the same kind of criticism as a newly bought horse, with what feelings, on her part, it is not difficult to imagine.

The whole family life of the Chinese illustrates their lack of the quality of sympathy. Not one parent in fifty has any care what his children are about, when their help is not needed in work. Few fathers have the smallest thought as to what their children are learning, if they are at school, or ever think of visiting the school-house to ascertain. This is one of many reasons why it is so common to find persons who have been years at school, who cannot read ten consecutive characters taken at random. Sometimes pupils spend two years in what is miscalled study, and do not get through the Trimetrical Classic.[1] While there are very great differences in different households, and while from the nature of the case, generalization is precarious, it is easy to see that most Chinese homes which are seen at all are by no means happy . homes. It is impossible that they should be so, for they are deficient in that unity of feeling which to us seems so essential to real home-life. A Chinese family is generally an association of individuals who are indissolubly tied together, having many of their interests the same, and many of them very different. The result is not our idea of a home, and it is not sympathy.

The deep poverty of the masses of the people of the Chinese Empire, and the terrible struggle constantly going on to secure even the barest subsistence, have familiarized them with the most pitiable exhibitions of suffering of every conceivable variety. Whatever might be the benevolent impulses of any Chinese, he is from the nature of the case wholly helpless to relieve even a thousandth part of the misery which he sees about him all the time, misery multiplied many times in any year of special distress. A thoughtful Chinese must recognize the utter futility of the means which are employed to alleviate distress, whether by individual kindness, or by government interference. All these methods, even when taken at their best, amount simply to a

---

1   A Chinese classic text probably written in the thirteenth century, which was often used to teach Confucian morality to young children. Also called the Three Character Classic, it is written in three-character verses for easy memorization.

treatment of symptoms and do absolutely nothing toward removing disease. Their operation is akin to that of societies which should distribute small pieces of ice among the victims of typhoid fever—so many ounces to each patient, with no hospitals, no dieting, no medicine and no nursing. It is not therefore strange that the Chinese are not more benevolent in practical ways, but rather, that with the total lack of system, of prevision and of supervision, benevolence continues at all. We are familiar with the phenomenon of the effect upon the most cultivated persons, of constant contact with misery which they have no power to help or to hinder, for this is illustrated in every modern war. The first sight of blood causes a sinking of the epigastric nerves,[1] and makes an indelible impression. But this soon wears away, and is succeeded by a comparative callousness, which is a perpetual surprise even to him who experiences it. In China there is always a social war, and everyone is too accustomed to its sickening effects, to give them more than a momentary attention. The instinct of relieving distress is an exotic unknown in China. A boy lying on a dunghill, in a fit, his swollen features covered with filth and flies, while the whole population of the village engage in their usual occupations in utter indifference—this is a type of wretchedness in many forms, everywhere to be seen. This represents the stage in which help might save life, if help were to be had. The dead body of a boy lying in a field, half-devoured by dogs, even now engaged in taking their horrid meal, within half a mile of where twenty people are at work in the fields, this represents the latter stages when help is forever impossible. Each of these sights, seen on a journey in one of the central provinces, is, we must repeat, typical, and a comprehension of the causes of such phenomena is a comprehension of some of the deepest needs of the Chinese people.

[...] The governor of Horian, in a memorial published in the *Peking Gazette*[2] a few years ago, showed incidentally that while there is responsibility in the eye of the law for the murder of a child by a parent, this is rendered nugatory by the provision that even if a married woman should wilfully and maliciously murder her young daughter-in-law the murderess may ransom herself by a money payment. The case reported was that in which a woman had burned the girl who was reared to become her son's wife with incense sticks, then roasted her cheeks with red-hot pincers, and finally boiled her to death with kettles full of scalding water. Other similar instances are

---

1 Nerves in the upper abdomen.
2 A regular report published by the Chinese imperial court from the eighth century until 1912 to inform the populace about memorials submitted to the emperor and imperial decisions.

referred to in the same memorial, the source of which places its authenticity beyond doubt. Such extreme barbarities are probable [sic] rare, but the cases of cruel treatment which are so aggravated as to lead to suicide, or to an attempt at suicide, are so frequent as to excite little more than passing comment. The writer is personally acquainted with many families in which these occurrences have taken place, and even while these lines are committed to paper, details of another instance are given by a mother, who wishes for sympathy in her trouble. In this case, the mother-in-law, whose family consisted only of herself, her son and her son's wife, exercised such a tyranny over the two latter, that they were never allowed to eat or to sleep together. If the son wished to please his mother, he did so by beating his wife. The latter being accused of having appropriated to her own use a skein of thread which did not belong to her, was so abused in consequence, that she threw herself into a well, whence she was rescued by her husband. Her mother brought her to the foreign home in which the mother was employed as nurse, and the daughter having passed a few days in this seclusion, remarked, with a bitter reference to her previous abode, that "it was so peaceful that it seemed like heaven!"

The woes of daughters-in-law in China should form the subject rather for a chapter than for a brief paragraph. When it is remembered that all Chinese women marry, and generally marry young, being for a considerable part of their lives under the absolute control of a mother-in-law, some faint conception may be gained of the intolerable miseries of those daughters-in-law who live in families where they are abused. Parents can do absolutely nothing to protect their married daughters, other than remonstrating with the families into which they have married, and exacting an expensive funeral, if the daughters should be actually driven to suicide. If a husband should seriously injure, or even kill his wife, he might escape all legal consequences, by representing that she was "unfilial" to his parents. Suicides of young wives are, we must repeat, excessively frequent, and in some regions scarcely a group of villages can be found where they have not recently taken place. What can be more pitiful than a mother's reproaches to a married daughter, who has attempted suicide and been rescued; "Why didn't you die when you had a chance?" [...]

5. Fred Morgan, "The Conversion of the Spider," *Daily Picayune* (1 July 1909)

[Following the murder of the white missionary Elsie Siegel—allegedly by her Chinese lover and student—cartoons such as this one questioned the civilizing project by suggesting that Chinese men had erotic motives for meeting with white schoolteachers and missionaries (See Lui, *The Chinatown Trunk Mystery*). Sui Sin Far's stories sometimes navigate connected anxieties about mixed-race relationships and the possibility of assimilating the Chinese in a way that was not merely superficial.]

6. Robert Carter, "The Real Yellow Peril," *The World* (21 June 1909)

[This cartoon suggests that "The Real Yellow Peril" is not that the US will be overrun with hordes of coolie laborers, but that Chinese Missions will become sites of potentially miscegenous proximities between well-intentioned white women and Chinese men such as the one whose figure lurks inscrutably in the doorway here.]

THE REAL YELLOW PERIL

7. Willa Cather, "The Conversion of Sum Loo," *Library* (1900)

[Possibly influenced by Mary Austin's "The Conversion of Ah Lew Sing" (1897), this early story by Willa Cather responds to the Boxer Rebellion's assaults on Western missionaries by depicting partially assimilated Chinese parents who only superficially adapt to Christian ideas. While the story's depiction of "slippery" Chinese souls may have lent credence to popular opinions about the "inscrutable" and unassimilable nature of the Chinese, Sister Hannah and Father Girrard seem just as fickle in their propensity for slipping away from their religious ideals.]

For who may know how the battle goes,
Beyond the rim of the world?
And who shall say what gods survive,
And which in the Pit are hurled?
How if a man should burn sweet smoke
And offer his prayers and tears
At the shrine of a god who had lost the fight
And been slain for a thousand years?[1]

The purport of this story is to tell how the joy at the Mission of the Heavenly Rest for the most hopeful conversion of Sum Chin and Sum Loo, his wife, was turned to weeping, and of how little Sister Hannah learned that the soul of the Oriental is a slippery thing, and hard to hold, to hold in the meshes of any creed.

Sum Chin was in those days one of the largest importers of Chinese bronzes and bric-à-brac[2] in San Francisco and a power among his own people, a convert worth a hundred of the coolie people. When he first came to the city he had gone to the Mission Sunday School for a while for the purpose of learning the tongue and picking up something of American manners. But occidental formalities are very simple to one who has mastered the complicated etiquette of southern Asia, and he soon picked up enough English for business purposes and so had fallen away from the Mission. It was not until his wife came to him, and until his little son was born that Sum Chin had regarded the mission people seriously, deeming it wise to invoke the good offices of any and all gods in the boy's behalf.

Of his conversion, or rather his concession, the people of the Heavenly Rest made great show, for besides being respected by the bankers and insurance writers, who are liberal in the matter of creed, he was well known to all the literary and artistic people of the city, both professionals and devout amateurs. Norman Girrard, the "charcoal preacher" as he was called, because he always carried a bit of crayon and sketched opportunely and inopportunely, declared that Sum Chin had the critical faculty, and that his shop was the most splendid interior in San Francisco. Girrard was a pale-eyed theological student who helped the devout deaconesses at the Mission of the Heavenly Rest in their good work, and who had vacillated between art and the Church until his whole demeanor was restless, uncertain, and indicative of a deep-seated discontent.

By some strange attraction of opposites he had got into Sum Chin's confidence as far as it is ever possible to penetrate the silent, in-

---

1 This is either Cather's own poem or from an unknown source.
2 Assorted curiosities.

scrutable inner self of the Oriental. This fateful, nervous little man found a sedative influence in the big, clean-limbed Chinaman, so smooth and calm and yellow, so content with all things finite and infinite, who could sit any number of hours in the same position without fatigue, and who once, when he saw Girrard playing tennis, had asked him how much he was paid for such terrible exertion. He liked the glowing primitive colors of Sum Chin's shop, they salved his feelings after the ugly things he saw in his mission work. On hot summer days, when the sea breeze slept, and the streets were ablaze with heat and light, he spent much time in the rear of Sum Chin's shop, where it was cool and dusky, and where the air smelt of spices and sandalwood, and the freshly opened boxes exhaled the aroma of another clime which was like an actual physical substance, and food for dreams. Those odors flashed before his eyes whole Orient landscapes, as though the ghosts of Old World cities had been sealed up in the boxes, like the djinn[1] in the Arabian bottle.

There he would sit at the side of a formidable bronze dragon with four wings, near the imported lacquered coffin which Sum Chin kept ready for the final emergency, watching the immaculate Chinaman, as he sat at an American office desk attending to his business correspondence. In his office Sum Chin wore dark purple trousers and white shoes worked with gold, and an overdress of a lighter shade of purple. He wrote with a brush which required very delicate manipulation, scraping his ink from the cake and moistening it with water, tracing the characters with remarkable neatness on the rice paper. Years afterward, when Girrard had gone over to art body and soul, and become an absinthe-drinking, lady-killing, and needlessly profane painter of Oriental subjects and marines on the other side of the water, malicious persons said that in the tortures of his early indecision he had made the acquaintance of Sum Chin's opium pipe and had weakened the underpinning of his orthodoxy, but that is exceedingly improbable.

During these long seances Girrard learned a good deal of Sum Chin's history. Sum Chin was a man of literary tastes and had begun life as a scholar. At an early age he had taken the Eminent Degree of the Flowering Talent, and was preparing for the higher Degree of the Promoted Men, when his father had committed some offense against the Imperial Government, and Sum Chin had taken his guilt upon his own head and had been forced to flee the Empire, being smuggled out of the port at Hong Kong as the body servant of a young Englishman whom he had been tutoring in the Chinese Classics. As a boy he had dwelt in Nanking, the oldest city of the oldest Empire, where the great schools are, and where the tallest pagoda in the world rears its height

---

1 Genie.

of shining porcelain. After he had taken the Eminent Degree of the Flowering Talent and been accorded an ovation by the magistrates of his town, he had grown tired of the place; tired of the rice paper books, and the masters in their black gowns, and the interminable prospect of the Seven Thousand Classics; of the distant blue mountains and the shadow of the great tower that grew longer and longer upon the yellow clay all afternoon. Then he had gone south, down the great canal on a barge with big red sails like dragons' wings. He came to Soutcheofou,[1] that is built upon the waterways of the hills of Lake Taihoo. There the air smelt always of flowers, and the bamboo thickets were green, and the canals were bright as quicksilver, and between them the waving rice fields shimmered in the sun like green watered silk. There the actors and jugglers gathered all the year round. And there the mandarins come to find concubines. For once a god loved a maiden of Soutcheofou and gave her the charms of heaven and since then the women of that city have been the most beautiful in the Middle Kingdom and have lived but to love and be loved. There Sum Chin had tarried, preparing for his second degree, when his trouble came upon him and the sacred duty of filial piety made him a fugitive.

Up to the time of his flight Sum Chin had delayed the holy duty of matrimony because the cares of paternity conflict with the meditations of the scholar, and because wives are expensive and scholars are poor. In San Francisco he had married a foreign-born Chinese girl out of Berkeley Place, but she had been sickly from the first and had borne him no children. She had lived a long time, and though she was both shrewish and indolent, it was said that her husband treated her kindly. She had been dead but a few months when the news of his father's death in Nanking, roused Sum Chin to his duty of begetting offspring who should secure repose for his own soul and his dead father's.

He was then fifty, and his choice must be made quickly. Then he bethought him of the daughter of his friend and purchasing agent, Te Wing, in Canton, whom he had visited on his last trip to China eight years before. She was but a child then, and had lain all day on a mat with her feet swathed in tight bandages,[2] but even then he had liked the little girl because her eyes were the color of jade and very bright, and her mouth was red as a flower. He used to take her costly Chinese sweetmeats and tell her stories of the five Sea Dragon Kings[3] who wear yellow armor, and of their yearly visit to the Middle Heaven, when the other gods are frightened away, and of the unicorn which

---

1 Suzhou is a city on the shores of Lake Taihu in eastern China.

2 A reference to the Chinese practice of footbinding.

3 In Chinese myth, there are five Sea Dragon Kings who occupy the center and four cardinal directions of the world.

walks abroad only when sages are born, and of the Phoenix which lays cubical eggs among the mountains, and at whose flute-like voice tigers flee. So Sum Chin wrote to Te Wing, the Cantonese merchant, and Girrard arranged the girl's admission through the ports with the Rescue Society, and the matter was accomplished.

Now a change of dwelling place, even from one village to another, is regarded as a calamity among Chinese women, and they pray to be delivered from the curse of childlessness and from long journeys. Little Te Loo must have remembered very kindly the elegant stranger who had drunk tea in her father's home and had given her sweetmeats, that she consented to cross the ocean to wed him. Yet she did this willingly, and she kept a sharp lookout for the five Sea Dragon Kings on the way, for she was quite sure that they must be friends of her husband's. She arrived in San Francisco with her many wedding gifts and her trousseau[1] done up in yellow bales bound with bamboo withers, a very silly, giggly maid, with her jade-like eyes and her flower-like mouth, and her feet like the tiny pink shells that one picks up along the seashore.

From the day of her marriage Sum Loo began devout ceremonies before the shrine of the goddess who bestows children,[2] and in a little while she had a joyful announcement to make to her husband. Then Sum Chin ceased from his desultory reading at the Seven Thousand Classics, the last remnant in him of the disappointed scholar, and began to prepare himself for weightier matters. The proper reception of a son into the world, when there are no relatives at hand, and no maternal grandmother to assist in the august and important functions, is no small responsibility, especially when the child is to have wealth and rank. In many trivial things, such as the wearing of undershirts in winter and straw hats in summer, Sum Chin had conformed to American ways, but the birth of a man's son is the most important event in his life, and he could take no chances. All ceremonials must be observed, and all must transpire as it had among his people since the years when European civilization was not even a name. Sum Loo was cheerful enough in those days, eating greedily, and admiring her trousseau, and always coaxing for new bangles and stories about the five Sea Dragon Kings. But Sum Chin was grave and preoccupied. Suppose, after all his preparations, it should be a girl, whose feet he would have to bind and for whom he would have to find a suitor, and what would it all amount to in the end? He might be too old to have other children, and a girl would not answer his purpose. Even if it were a boy he might not live to see him grow up, and his son might forget

1 See p. 102, note 1.
2 Guanyin. See p. 88, note 1.

the faith of his fathers and neglect the necessary devotions. He began to fear that he had delayed this responsibility too long.

But the child, when it came, was a boy and strong, and he heaved out his chest mightily and cried when they washed his mouth with a picture of the sun dipped in wine, the symbol of a keen intelligence. This little yellow, waxen thing was welcomed into the house of Sum Chin as a divinity, and, indeed, he looked not unlike the yellow clay gods in the temples frequented by expectant mothers. He was smooth and dark as old ivory, and his eyes were like little beads of black opium, and his nose was so diminutive that his father laughed every time he looked at it. He was called Sum Wing, and he was kept wrapped in a gorgeous piece of silk, and he lay all day long quite still, with his thumb in his mouth and his black eyes never blinking; and Girrard said he looked like an ivory image in his father's shop. Sum Wing had marked prejudices against all the important ceremonials which must be performed over all male infants. He spat out the ceremonial rice and kicked over the wine.

"Him Melican babee, I leckon," said his father in explanation of his son's disregard of the important rites. When the child kicked his mother's side so that she scolded him, Sum Chin smiled and bought her a new bracelet. When the child's cry reached him as he sat in the shop, he smiled. Often, at night, when the tiny Sum Wing slept on his mother's arm, Sum Chin would lean over in the dark to hear his son's breathing.

When the child was a month old, on a day that the priest at the joss house declared was indicated as lucky by many omens, Sum Wing's head was shaven for the first time, and that was the most important thing which had yet occurred to him.[1] Many of his father's society—which was the Society Fi, or the Guardianship of Nocturnal Vigils, a band which tried to abolish midnight "hold-ups" in Chinatown—came and brought gifts. Nine little tufts of hair were left on the back of the child's head, to indicate the number of trunks his bride would need to pack her trousseau, and nine times his father rubbed two eggs with red shells over his little pate, which eggs the members of the Society for the Guardianship of Nocturnal Vigils gravely ate, thereby pledging themselves to protect the boy, seek him if lost, and mourn for him if dead. Then a nurse was provided for Sum Wing, and his father asked Girrard to have the mission folk pray to the Jesus god for his son, and he drew a large check on his bankers for the support of the Mission. Sum Chin held that when all a man's goods are stored in one ship, he should insure it with all reputable underwriters. So, surely, when a man has but one son he should secure for him the good

1 See p. 163, note 1.

offices of all gods of any standing. For, as he would often say to Girrard, in the language of an old Taoist[1] proverb, "Have you seen your god, brother, or have I seen mine? Then why should there be any controversy between us, seeing that we are both unfortunates?"

Sum Wing was a year and a half old, and could already say wise Chinese words and play with his father's queue most intelligently, when fervent little Sister Hannah began to go to Sum Chin's house, first to see his queer little yellow baby and afterwards to save his wife's soul. Sum Loo could speak a little English by this time, and she liked to have her baby admired, and when there was lack of other amusement, she was not averse to talking about her soul. She thought the pictures of the baby Jesus god were cunning, though not so cunning as her Sum Wing, and she learned an English prayer and a hymn or two. Little Sister Hannah made great progress with Sum Lou, though she never cared to discuss theology with Sum Chin. Chinese metaphysics frightened her, and under all Sum Chin's respect for all rites and ceremonials there was a sort of passive, resigned agnosticism, a doubt older than the very beginnings of Sister Hannah's faith, and she felt incompetent to answer it. It is such an ancient doubt, that of China, and it has gradually stolen the odor from the roses and the tenderness from the breasts of the women.

The good little Sister, who should have had children of her own to bother about, became most deeply attached to Sum Wing, who loved to crumple her white headdress and pinch her plump, pink cheeks. Above all things she desired to have the child baptized, and Sum Loo was quite in the notion of it. It would be very nice to dress the child in his best clothes and take him to the Mission chapel and hold him before the preacher with many American women looking on, if only they would promise not to put enough water on him to make him sick. She coaxed Sum Chin, who could see no valid objection, since the boy would be properly instructed in the ceremonials of his own religion by the Taoist priest, and since many of his patrons were among the founders of the Mission, and it was well to be in the good books of all gods, for one never knew how things were going with the Imperial Dynasties of the other world.

So little Sum Wing was prayed, and sung, and wept over by the mission women, and a week later he fell sick and died, and the priest in the joss house chuckled maliciously. He was buried in his father's costly coffin which had come from China, and at the funeral there were many carriages and mourners and roast pigs and rice and gin in

---

1 A Chinese religious and philosophical tradition influenced by Lao Tzu's (c. 551–479 BCE) *Tao Te Ching* and emphasizing compassion, moderation, and humility.

bowls of real china, as for a grown man, for he was his father's only son.

Sum Chin, he went about with his queue unbraided and his face haggard and unshaven so that he looked like a wreck from some underground opium den, and he rent many costly garments and counted not the cost of them, for of what use is wealth to an old man who has no son? Who now would pray for the peace of his own soul or for that of his father? The voice of his old father cried out from the grave in bitterness against him, upbraiding him with his neglect to provide offspring to secure rest for his spirit. For of all unfilial crimes, childlessness is the darkest.

It was all clear enough to Sum Chin. There had been omens and omens, and he had disregarded them. And now the Jesus people had thrown cold water in his baby's face[1] and with evil incantation had killed his only son. Had not his heart stood still when the child was seized with madness and screamed when the cold water touched its face, as though demons were tearing it with red-hot pincers?—And the gods of his own people were offended and had not helped him, and the Taoist priest mocked him and grinned from the joss house across the street.

When the days of mourning were over he regained his outward composure, was scrupulous as to his dress and careful to let his nails grow long. But he avoided even the men of his own society, for these men had sons, and he hated them because the gods has prospered them. When Girrard came to his shop, Sum Chin sat writing busily with his camel's hair-brush, making neat characters on the rice paper, but he spoke no word. He maintained all his former courtesy toward the mission people, but sometimes, after they had left his shop, he would creep upstairs with ashen lips, and catching his wife's shoulder, would shake her rudely, crying between his teeth, "Jesus people, Jesus people, killee ma babee!"

As for poor Sum Loo, her life was desolated by her husband's grief. He was no longer gentle and kind. He no longer told her stories or bought her bracelets and sweetmeats. He let her go nowhere except to the joss house, he let her see no one, and roughly told her to cleanse herself from the impurities of the Foreign Devils. Still, he was a broken old man, who called upon the gods in his sleep, and she pitied him. Surely he would never have any more children, and what would her father say when he heard that she had given him no grandchildren? A poor return she made her parents for all their kindness in caring for her in her infancy when she was but a girl baby and might have been

---

1 A reference to the practice of baptism in which water is poured on the baby's head.

quietly slipped out of the world; in binding her beautiful feet when she was foolish enough to cry about it, and in giving her a good husband and a trousseau that filled many bales. Surely, too, the spirit of her husband's father would sit heavy on her stomach that she had allowed the Jesus people to kill her son. She was often very lonely without her little baby, who used to count his toes and call her by a funny name when he wanted his dinner. Then she would cry and wipe her eyes on the gorgeous raiment in which Sum Wing had been baptized.

The mission people were much concerned about Sum Loo. Since her child's death none of them had been able to gain access to the rooms above her husband's store, where she lived. Sister Hannah had again and again made valiant resolutions and set out with determination imprinted on her plump, rosy countenance, but she had never been able to get past the suave, smiling Asiatic who told her that his wife was visiting a neighbor, or had a headache, or was giving a tea party. It is impossible to contradict the polite and patent fictions of the Chinese, and Sister Hannah always went away nonplussed and berated herself for lack of courage.

One day, however, she was fortunate enough to catch sight of Sum Loo just as she was stepping into the joss house across the street, and Sister Hannah followed her into that dim, dusky place, where the air was heavy with incense. At first she could see no one at all, and she quite lost her way wandering about among the glittering tinseled gods with their offerings of meat, and rice, and wine before them. They were terrible creatures, with hoofs, and horns, and scowling faces, and the little Sister was afraid of the darkness and the heavy air of the place. Suddenly she heard a droning singsong sound, as of a chant, and, moving cautiously, she came upon Sum Loo and stood watching her in terrified amazement. Sum Loo had the copy of the New Testament in Chinese which Sister Hannah had given her husband, open before her. She sat crouching at the shrine of the goddess who bestows children and tore out the pages of the book one by one, and, carefully folding them into narrow strips, she burned them in the candles before the goddess, chanting, as she did so, one name over and over incessantly.

Sister Hannah fled weeping back to the Mission of the Heavenly Rest, and that night she wrote to withdraw the application she had sent in to the Board of Foreign Missions.

8. Wong Chin Foo, "Why Am I a Heathen?" *North American Review* 145:369 (1887), 169–79

[Part of a series including essays such as "Why Am I a Methodist?", "Why Am I a Moslem?", and "Why Am I a Free Religionist?", this essay by the Chinese-American lecturer, writer, and political activist Wong Chin Foo created some controversy when it first appeared in the *North American Review.* "Why Am I a Heathen?" was reviewed and debated in several periodicals, and directly refuted by the American Chinese writer Yan Phou Lee in "Why I Am Not a Heathen: A Rejoinder to Wong Chin Foo" (1887). More belligerent than Sui Sin Far in his critiques of missionary rhetoric, Wong explicitly links Christian evangelism with sectarianism, greed, power, hypocrisy, and the opium trade.]

MEN raised in a certain faith usually adhere to it, or drift into one of its cognates. Thus a heathen may wander from simple Confucianism into some form of Buddhism or Brahminism, just as a Christian may tire of following the Golden Rule, and adopt some special sect—one more latitudinarian or ceremonious, according to the temper of his religious conscientiousness; but the latter continues still a Christian, though a pervert; while the heathen, in Christian parlance, is still a pagan.

The main element of all religion is the moral code controlling and regulating the relations and acts of individuals towards "God, neighbor, and self"; and this intelligent "heathenism" was taught thousands of years before Christianity existed or Jewry borrowed it. Heathenism has not lost or lessened it since.

Born and raised a heathen, I learned and practiced its moral and religious code; and acting thereunder I was useful to myself and many others. My conscience was clear, and my hopes as to future life were undimmed by distracting doubt. But, when about seventeen, I was transferred to the midst of our showy Christian civilization, and at this impressible period of life Christianity presented itself to me at first under its most alluring aspects; kind Christian friends became particularly solicitous for my material and religious welfare, and I was only too willing to know the truth.

I had to take a good deal for granted as to the inspiration of the Bible—as is necessary to do—to Christianize a non-Christian mind; and I even advanced so far under the spell of my would-be soul-savers that I seriously contemplated becoming the bearer of heavenly tidings to my "benighted" heathen people.

But before qualifying for this high mission, the Christian doctrine I would teach had to be learned, and here on the threshold I was bewildered by the multiplicity of Christian sects, each one claiming a monopoly of the only and narrow road to heaven.

I looked into Presbyterianism only to retreat shudderingly from a belief in a merciless God who had long foreordained most of the helpless human race to an eternal hell. To preach such a doctrine to intelligent heathen would only raise in their minds doubts of my sanity, if they did not believe I was lying.

Then I dipped into Baptist doctrines, but found so many sects therein, of different "shells," warring over the merits of cold-water initiation and the method and time of using it, that I became disgusted with such trivialities; and the question of close communion or not, only impressed me that some were very stingy and exclusive with their bit of bread and wine, and others a little less so.

Methodism struck me as a thunder-and-lightning religion—all profession and noise. You struck it, or it struck you, like a spasm,—and so you "experienced" religion.

The Congregationalists deterred me with their starchiness and self-conscious true-goodness, and their desire only for high-toned affiliates.

Unitarianism seemed all doubt, doubting even itself.

A number of other Protestant sects based on some novelty or eccentricity—like Quakerism—I found not worth a serious study by the non-Christian. But on one point this mass of Protestant dissension cordially agreed, and that was in a united hatred of Catholicism, the older form of Christianity. And Catholicism returned with interest this animosity. It haughtily declared itself the only true Church, outside of which there was no salvation—for Protestants especially; that its chief prelate was the personal representative of God on earth, and that he was infallible. Here was religious unity, power, and authority with a vengeance. But, in chorus, my solicitous Protestant friends beseeched me not to touch Catholicism, declaring it was worse than my heathenism—in which I agreed; but the same line of argument also convinced me that Protestantism stood in the same category.

In fact, the more I studied Christianity in its various phases, and listened to the animadversions[1] of one sect upon another, the more it all seemed to me "sounding brass and tinkling cymbals."[2]

Disgusted with sectarianism, I turned to a simple study of the "inspired Bible"[3] for enlightenment.

The creation fable did not disturb me, nor the Eden incident; but some vague doubts did arise with the deluge and Noah's Ark; it seemed a reflection on a just and merciful Divinity. And I was not at all satisfied of the honesty and goodness of Jacob, or his family, or their

---

1 Censorious, critical remarks.

2 "Though I speak with the tongues of men and of angels, and have not charity, I am become as sounding brass, or a tinkling cymbal" (1 Corinthians 13:1–2).

3 The idea that all of the Bible is directly inspired by God and thus worthy of direct study.

descendants, or that there was any particular merit or reason for their being the "chosen" of God, to the detriment of the rest of mankind; for they so appreciated God's special patronage that on every occasion they ran after other gods, and had a special idolatry for the "Golden Calf,"[1] to which some Christians allege they are still devoted. That God, failing to make something out of this stiff-necked race, concluded to send his Son to redeem a few of them, and a few of the long-neglected Gentiles, is not strikingly impressive to the heathen.

It may be flattering to the Christian to know it required the crucifixion of God to save him, and that nothing less would do; but it opens up a series of inferences that makes the idea more and more incomprehensible, and more and more inconsistent with a Will, Purpose, Wisdom, and Justice thoroughly Divine.

But when I got to the New Dispensation, with its sin-forgiving business, I figuratively "went to pieces" on Christianity. The idea that, however wicked the sinner, he had the same chance of salvation, "through the Blood of the Lamb,"[2] as the most God-fearing—in fact, that the eleventh-hour man was entitled to the same heavenly compensation as the one who had labored in the Lord's vineyard from the first hour—all this was absolutely preposterous. It was not just, and God is Justice.

Applying this dogma, I began to think of my own prospects on the other side of Jordan. Suppose Dennis Kearney, the California sand-lotter,[3] should slip in and meet me there, would he not be likely to forget his heavenly songs, and howl once more: "The Chinese must go!"[4] and organize a heavenly crusade to have me and others immediately cast out into the other place?

And then the murderers, cut-throats, and thieves whose very souls had become thoroughly impregnated with their life-long crimes—these were they to become "pure as new-born babes"[5]—all within a few short hours of a death-preparation—while I, the good heathen (supposing the case), who had done naught but good to my fellow-heathen, who had spent most of my hard earnings regularly in feeding the hungry, and clothing the naked, and succoring the distressed, and

---

1 A reference to Exodus 32:4, where Aaron carves a golden calf which the Hebrews worship as an idol.

2 A reference to Revelation 7:14, where tribulation is figured as robes washed white in the blood of the Lamb.

3 On Kearney's sandlot orations, see p. 242.

4 A popular slogan of the Workingmen's Party of California and other nativist groups.

5 Reference to 1 Peter 2: "Therefore, rid yourselves of all malice and all deceit, hypocrisy, envy, and slander of every kind."

had died of yellow fever, contracted from a deserted fellow being stricken with the disease, whom no Christian would nurse, I was unmercifully consigned to hell's everlasting fire, simply because I had not heard of the glorious saving power of the Lord Jesus, or because the construction of my mind would not permit me to believe in the peculiar redeeming powers of Christ!

But, then, it was gently insinuated: "Oh, no! You heathen who had not heard of Christ will not be punished quite so severely when you die as those "'who heard the gospel and believed it not.'"

The more I read the Bible the more afraid I was to become a Christian. The idea of coming into daily or hourly contact with cold-blooded murderers, cut-throats, and other human scourges, who had had but a few moments of repentance before roaming around heaven, was abhorrent. And suppose, to this horde of shrewd, "civilized" criminals should be added the fanatic thugs of India, the pirates of China, the slavers, the cannibals, et al. Well, this was enough to shock and dismay any mild, decent soul not schooled in eccentric Christianity.

It is not only because I want to be honest, and to be sure of a heavenly home, that I choose to sign myself "Your Heathen," but because I want to be as happy as I can, in order to live longer; and I believe I can live longer here by being sincere and practical in my faith.

In the first place, my faith does not teach me predestination, nor that my life is what the gods hath long foreordained, but is what I make it myself; and naturally much of this depends on the way I live.

Unlike Christianity, "our" Church is not eager for converts; but, like Free Masonry, we think our religious doctrine strong enough to attract the seekers after light and truth to offer themselves without urging, or proselytizing efforts. It pre-eminently teaches me to mind my own business, to be contented with what I have, to possess a mind that is tranquil, and a body at ease at all times,—in a word it says: "Whatsoever ye would not that others should do unto you do ye not even so unto them."[1] We believe that if we are not able to do anybody any good, we should do nothing at all to harm them. This is better than the restless Christian doctrine of ceaseless action. Idleness is no wrong when actions fail to bring forth fruits of merit. It is these fruitless trials of one thing and another that produce so much trouble and misery in Christian society.

If my shoe factory employs 500 men, and gives me an annual profit of $10,000, why should I substitute therein machinery by the use of which I need only 100 men, thus not only throwing 400 contented,

---

1 Wong's modification of the so-called golden rule from Matthew 7:12: "Therefore all things whatsoever ye would that men should do to you, do ye even so to them: for this is the law and the prophets."

industrious men into misery, but making myself more miserable by heavier responsibilities, with possibly less profit?

We heathen believe in the happiness of a common humanity, while the Christian's only practical belief appears to be money-making (golden-calf worshiping); and there is more money to be made by being "in the swim" as a Christian than by being a heathen. Even a Christian preacher makes more money in one year than a heathen banker in two. I do not blame them for their money-making, but for their way of making it.

How many eminent Christian preachers sincerely believe in all the Christian mysteries they preach? And yet it is policy to be apparently in earnest; in fact, some are in real earnest rather from the force of habit than otherwise;—like a Bowery auctioneer who, to make trade, provides customers too—to keep up the appearance of rushing business. The more converts made, the more profit to the church, and the more wealth in the pocket of the dominie.[1]

How would the hundreds of thousands of these Christian ministers in the United States make their living if they did not bulldoze it out of the pockets of the credulous by making the "pews" believe what the "pulpit" does not?

Nor do we heathen believe in a machine way of doing good. If we find a man starving in the streets we do not wait until we find the Overseer of the Poor, nor for the unwinding of other civilized red tape before relieving the man's hunger. If a heathen sees a man fall from a tree-top, and seriously injure himself, he does not first run to a hospital for an ambulance, nor does the ambulance-man first want to know what precinct the injured man belongs to; but forthwith he is cared for and taken to the nearest shelter for other needed treatment, and when the danger is over then red tape may come in—the Christian machinery.

If we do anything charitable we do not advertise it like the Christian, nor do we suppress knowledge of the meritorious acts of others, to humor our vanity or gratify our spleen. An instance of this was conspicuous during the Memphis yellow-fever epidemic a few years ago, and when the Chinese were virulently persecuted all over the United States. Chinese merchants in China donated $40,000 at that time to the relief of plague-stricken Memphis, but the Christians quietly swallowed the sweet morsel without even a "thank you." But they did advertise it, heavily and strongly, all over the world, when they paid $137,000 to the Chinese Government as petty compensation for the massacre of 23 Chinamen by civilized American Christians, and for robbing these and other poor heathen of their earthly possessions.

---

1 Clergyman, usually in the Church of Scotland or Presbyterian Church.

In matters of charity Christians invariably let their right hand know what the left is doing, and cry it out from the housetops. The heathen is too dignified for such childish vainness.

Of course, we decline to admit all the advantages of your boasted civilization; or that the white race is the only civilized one. Its civilization is borrowed, adapted, and shaped from our older form.

China has a national history of at least 4,000 years, and had a printed history 3,500 years before a European discovered the art of type-printing. In the course of our national existence our race has passed, like others, through mythology, superstition, witchcraft, established religion, to philosophical religion. We have been "blest" with at least half a dozen religions more than any other nation. None of them were rational enough to become the abiding faith of an intelligent people; but when we began to reason we succeeded in making society better and its government more protective, and our great Reasoner, Confucius, reduced our various social and religious ideas into book form, and so perpetuated them.

China, with its teeming population of 400,000,000, is demonstration enough of the satisfactory results of this religious evolution. Where else can it be paralleled?

Call us heathen, if you will, the Chinese are still superior in social administration and social order. Among 400,000,000 of Chinese there are fewer murders and robberies in a year than there are in New York State.

True, China supports a luxurious monarch—whose every whim must be gratified; yet, withal, its people are the most lightly taxed in the world, having nothing to pay but from tilled soil, rice, and salt; and yet she has not a single dollar of national debt.

Such implicit confidence have we Chinese in our heathen politicians that we leave the matter of jurisprudence entirely in their hands; and they are able to devise the best possible laws for the preservation of life, property, and happiness, without Christian demagogism,[1] or by the cruel persecution of one class to promote the selfish interests of another; and we are so far heathenish as to no longer persecute men simply on account of race, color, or previous condition of servitude,[2] but treat them all according to their individual worth.

Though we may differ from the Christian in appearance, manners, and general ideas of civilization, we do not organize into cowardly mobs under the guise of social or political reform, to plunder and murder with impunity; and we are so far advanced in our heathenism

---

1 Gaining power and influence by arousing popular emotions and prejudices.
2 Reference to the Fifteenth Amendment, which prohibits the denial of the right to vote on the basis of these factors.

as to no longer tolerate popular feeling or religious prejudice to defeat justice or cause injustice.

We are simple enough, too, not to allow the neglect or abuse of age by youth, however mild the form. "The silent tears of age will call down the fire of heaven upon those who make them flow."[1]

"He who witnesseth a crime without preventing its commission or reporting the same to the nearest magistrate is equally responsible with the principal."

"If a stronger man assaults another who is weaker, it is the duty of the passer-by to take the weak man's part." But to Christians this would be a spectacle merely,—one to be encouraged rather than prevented.

A heathen is not allowed to marry unless he is a good citizen, moral, and capable to instruct the children he may be honored with.

"Parents are responsible for the crimes of their children." This is an axiom of the common law in Chinese heathendom.

We do not embrace our wives before our neighbor's eyes, and abuse them in the privacy of home. If we wish to fool our neighbors at all about our domestic affairs we would rather reverse the exhibition—let them think we disliked our wife, while love at home would be the warmer.

I would rather marry in the heathen fashion than in the Christian mode, because in the former instance I would take a wife for life, while in the second instance it is entirely a game of chance.

We bring up our children to be our second selves in every sense of the word. The Christian's children, like himself, are all on the lookout for No. 1, and it is a common result that the old people are badly "left" in their old age.

While traveling among the Christians one has to keep his eyes wide open; even then he has to pay dear for his comforts. In traveling in China among the pure heathen, especially in the interior, a stranger is not everybody's cow,—only good to be milked and then turned loose,—but he is the public's guest: his money is a secondary consideration.

As the heathen does not encourage labor-saving machinery, I do not have to be idle if I don't want to, and, as a result, work is more equally distributed.

If a hungry heathen steals a bowl of rice and milk, and eats it on the premises, the magistrate discharges him—as a case of necessity—like

---

1 Possibly adapted from M. Louis Jacolliot, who quotes a sacred maxim from an East Indian scripture: "The tears of a woman call down the fire of heaven on those who make them flow" (198). The sources of the "heathen" principles that follow are unknown.

self-defense. But he who knows the law and violates it, is punished more severely than he who is ignorant of it.

Christians are continually fussing about religion; they build great churches and make long prayers; and yet there is more wickedness in the neighborhood of a single church district of one thousand people in New York than among one million heathen, churchless and unsermonized.

Christian talk is long and loud about how to be good and to act charitably. It is all charity, and no fraternity—"there, dog, take your crust and be thankful!" And is it, therefore, any wonder there is more heart-breaking and suicides in the single State of New York in a year than in all China?

The difference between the heathen and the Christian is that the heathen does good for the sake of doing good. With the Christian, what little good he does he does it for immediate honor and for future reward; he lends to the Lord and wants compound interest. In fact, the Christian is the worthy heir of his religious ancestors.

The heathen does much and says little about it; the Christian does little good, but when he does he wants it in the papers and on his tombstone.

Love men for the good they do you is a practical Christian idea, not for the good you should do them as a matter of human duty. So Christians love the heathen; yes, the heathen's possessions; and in proportion to these the Christian's love grows in intensity. When the English wanted the Chinamen's gold and trade, they said they wanted "to open China for their missionaries." And opium was the chief, in fact, only, missionary they looked after, when they forced the ports open.[1] And this infamous Christian introduction among Chinamen has done more injury, social and moral, in China than all the humanitarian agencies of Christianity could remedy in 200 years. And on you, Christians, and on your greed of gold, we lay the burden of the crime resulting; of tens of millions of honest, useful men and women sent thereby to premature death after a short miserable life, besides the physical and moral prostration it entails even where it does not prematurely kill! And this great national curse was thrust on us at the points of Christian bayonets. And you wonder why we are heathen?

The only positive point Christians have impressed on heathenism is that they would sacrifice religion, honor, principle, as they do life, for—gold. And then they sanctimoniously tell the poor heathen: "You must save your soul by believing as we do!"

---

1 The British fought and won two "Opium Wars" with China (1839–42 and 1856–60) in order to force the country open to the lucrative and highly addictive drug, which traders imported from British India.

Members of my faith do not so worship gold, although they know it is a very handy thing to have in the house; but honor and principle are dearer than pelf[1] to the average heathen. But I dare say when the heathen have become sufficiently demoralized by contact with Christian civilization and its Vanity Fair of pretence, pride, and dress, they will probably be worse even than the Christian in beating their way through this wide, wicked world. Pupils are often too apt.

In public affairs, it is either niggardliness[2] that puts a premium on dishonesty, or loose extravagance for show, that encourages political debauchery and jobbery. In general, business men are lauded as great financiers who actually conspire to buy laws, place judges, control senates, corner and regulate at will the price of natural products; and, in fact, act as if the whole political and social machinery should be a lever to them to operate against the interests of the nation and people. In a heathen country such conspirators against social order and the general welfare would have short shrift.

Here in New York, the richest and the poorest city in the world, misery pines while wealth arrogantly stalks. The poor have the votes, and yet elect those who betray them for lucre to corporate and capitalistic interests; and the administration of justice—in fact, the whole system of jurisprudence—is to stimulate crime rather than prevent it. As to preventing poverty, or rendering it less intolerable, that is the most remote thought of religious and political local administration.

It is no wonder, under such circumstances and conditions, that New York is a most heavily taxed city, and the worst governed for the interests of New York. "Public office a public trust?" Rather, it is a farm to be worked, Christian-like, for all it is worth. Public spiritedness and moral worth have no value or utility in "practical" Christian politics. Such civic virtues "don't pay."

Do as we do. Give public office to the competent. Pay them well. If they are inefficient or indifferent, remove them at once. If dishonest, morally or financially, kill them as traitors.

"It is better that a child knows only what is right and what is wrong than to have a rote knowledge of all the books of the sages, and yet not know what is right and what is wrong." Collegiate education does not necessarily make a youth fit for the duties of life. And men like Lincoln, Greeley,[3] and other such Americans prove it.

"The most successful youth in life is not the most learned, but the most unblemished in conduct." So say the heathen. But here, it is

---

1 Booty or stolen wealth.
2 Stinginess.
3 Horace Greeley (1811–72) was a politician, reformer, and editor of the influential *New York Tribune*.

called smart when a boy is merely impudent to the old, and it is "smartness," and is excused by the phrase that "boys will be boys" when a boy throws a stone with malice to break some one's window, or do some injury. And parents of such a boy, while they chide, will secretly chuckle, "he's got the makings of a man in him."

It is our motto, "If we cannot bring up our children to think and do for us when we are old as we did for them when they were young, it is better not to rear them at all." But the Christian style is for children to expect their parents to do all for them, and then for the children to abandon the parents as soon as possible.

On the whole, the Christian way strikes us as decidedly an unnatural one; it is every one for himself—parents and children even. Imagine my feelings, if my own son, whom I loved better than my own life, for whom I had sacrificed all my comforts and luxury, should, through some selfish motive, go to law with me to get his share prematurely of my property, and even have me declared a lunatic, or have me arrested and imprisoned, to subserve his interest or intrigue! Is this a rare Christian case? Can it be charged against heathenism?

We heathen are a God-fearing race. Aye, we believe the whole Universe-creation—whatever exists and has existed—is of God and in God; that, figuratively, the thunder is His voice and the lightning His mighty hands; that everything we do and contemplate doing is seen and known by Him; that He has created this and other worlds to effectuate beneficent, not merciless, designs, and that all that He has done is for the steady, progressive benefit of the creatures whom He endowed with life and sensibility, and to whom as a consequence He owes and gives paternal care, and will give paternal compensation and justice; yet His voice will threaten and His mighty hand chastise those who deliberately disobey His sacred laws and their duty to their fellow man.

"Do unto others as you wish they would do unto you," or "Love your neighbor as yourself," is the great Divine law which Christians and heathen alike hold, but which the Christians ignore.

This is what keeps me the heathen I am! And I earnestly invite the Christians of America to come to Confucius.

Appendix D: Representing Chinatown

1. **W.B. Farwell, John Kunkler, E.B. Pond, "Official Map of 'Chinatown' in San Francisco" (detail) (San Francisco: Board of Supervisors Special Committee, 1885)**

[Using different colors and annotations to indicate Chinese Occupancy, Chinese Gambling Houses, Chinese Prostitution, Chinese Opium Resorts, Chinese Joss Houses, and White Prostitution, this map of San Francisco's Chinatown indicates that the City Board of Supervisors viewed the city's Chinese population as a group to be controlled, policed, and contained. The full map is available from several sources online, including the Harvard University Map Collection: http://vc.lib.harvard.edu/vc/deliver/~maps/010218358.]

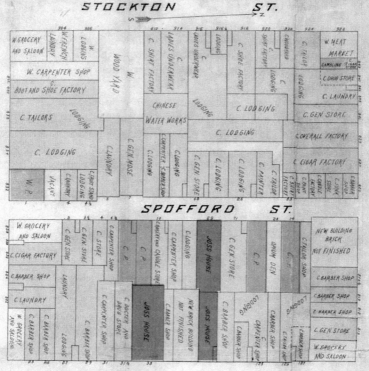

2. From Will Irwin, *Old Chinatown: A Book of Pictures by Arnold Genthe* (New York: Mitchell Kennerley, 1913), 7–8, 43–45

[A reporter and editor who spent time working in San Francisco and New York City, William Henry Irwin (1873–1948) wrote this commentary to *Old Chinatown*, a collection of Arnold Genthe's photographs of San Francisco's Chinatown prior to its destruction by the earthquake and fire of 1906. Following the earthquake, residents and entrepreneurs rebuilt Chinatown in a more exotic, Chinese-looking style in order to appeal to tourists and refute arguments that the unhygienic, dirty, and unkempt Chinese settlement should be moved to less valuable land outside the city center. Irwin's nostalgic prose commemorates the lost beauty of Chinatown's "unsanitary" buildings, streets, and alleys; however, it is important to remember that Irwin is describing not Chinatown itself but Genthe's carefully framed, cropped, sometimes posed, and in many cases doctored photographs.]

FROM the moment when you crossed the golden, dimpling bay, whose moods ran the gamut of beauty, from the moment when you sailed between those brown-and-green headlands which guarded the Gate to San Francisco, you heard always of Chinatown. It was the first thing which the guides offered to show. Whenever, in any channel of the Seven Seas, two world-wanderers met and talked about the City of Many Adventures, Chinatown ran like a thread through their reminiscences. Raised on a hill-side, it glimpsed at you from every corner of that older, more picturesque San Francisco which fell to dust and cinders in the great disaster of 1906. From the cliffs which crowned the city, one could mark it off as a somber spot, shot with contrasting patches of green and gold, in the panorama below. Its inhabitants, overflowing into the American quarters, made bright and quaint the city streets. Its exemplars of art in common things, always before the unillumined American, worked to make San Francisco the city of artists that she was. For him who came but to look and to enjoy, this was the real heart of San Francisco, this bit of the mystic, suggestive East, so modified by the West that it was neither Oriental nor yet Occidental—but just Chinatown.

It is gone now—this Old Chinatown—but in a newer and stronger San Francisco rises a newer, cleaner, more healthful Chinatown. Better for the city—O yes—and better for the Chinese, who must come to modern ways of life and health, if they are to survive among us. But where is St. Louis Alley, that tangle of sheds, doorways, irregular arcades and flaming signs which fell into the composition of such a marvelous picture? Where is the dim reach of

Ross Alley, that romantically mysterious cleft in the city's walls? Where is Fish Alley, that horror to the nose, that perfume to the eye? Where are those broken, dingy streets, in which the Chinese made art of rubbish?

[...]

COMMENCING like all Spanish towns, San Francisco clustered first about a Plaza—Portsmouth Square[1] the pioneers renamed it. On its fringes, in the days when the streets ran gold and the Vigilantes were the whole law, appeared the first modern buildings. Then, with the unaccountable, restless drift of American cities, shops and wholesale houses passed on down into the hollows and "made lands" reclaimed from the Bay marshes. The Chinese, following in, took possession of those old buildings about Portsmouth Square. An unwritten city ordinance, strictly observed by successive Boards of Supervisors, held them to an area of about eight city blocks. Old St. Mary's Church, the first Roman Catholic Cathedral, marked the southern edge of that area; and to the last day of the old city any report that the Chinese were moving south of St. Mary's drove the newspapers and the city fathers to arms. The Chinese conquest of affection never proceeded so far that the Americans wanted them for neighbors.

These eight blocks, supporting a population which varied between ten thousand and thirty thousand according to the season of the year, lay close to the very center of San Francisco, between the business district and the old palaces of Nob Hill. Wealthy citizens, walking down to their offices from the citadel of the town, used to envy the Chinese their site; the city authorities were forever starting a movement to get "dirty Chinatown" out into the suburbs, that the whites might take the Quarter back. But the Chinese owned much of the property, and paid a high rental for the rest. With their conservatism and their persistence, they stuck. They stuck even after the fire, when San Francisco, starting a dozen projects in the heroic rebound of its spirit, tried to seize the occasion to move Chinatown.

This district of old-fashioned business blocks, laid out on fine lines by the French architects who wrought before the newly-rich miners began to buy atrocities, the Chinese transformed into a semblance of a Chinese city. They added sheds, lean-tos, out-door booths, a thousand devices to extend space; they built in the eternal painted balconies of which the Chinaman is as fond as a Spaniard. Close livers by custom, they lodged twenty coolies in one abandoned law office; they

---

1 See p. 84, note 1.

even burrowed three stories underground that they might make space for winter-idle laborers, overflow of the northern canning factories. Clinging always to their native customs and dress and manners, they furnished their little stores and factories, their lodging houses, their restaurants, with the Chinese utensils of common life which were never without their touch of beauty.

So the Quarter grew into a thing like Canton and still strangely and beautifully unlike. Dirty—the Chinaman, clean about his person, inventor of the daily bath, is still terribly careless about his surroundings. Unsanitary to the last degree—Chinatown was the care and vexation of Boards of Health. But always beautiful—falling everywhere into pictures.

This beauty appealed equally to the plain citizen, who can appreciate only the picturesque, and to the artist, with his eye for composition, subtle coloring, shadowy suggestion. From every doorway flashed out a group, an arrangement, which suggested the Flemish masters. Consider that panel of a shop front in Fish Alley, which is to me the height of Dr. Genthe's collection. Such pictures glimpsed about every corner. You lifted your eyes. Perfectly arranged in coloring and line, you saw a balcony, a woman in softly gaudy robes, a window whose blackness suggested mystery. You turned to right or left; behold a pipe-bowl mender or a cobbler working with his strange Oriental tools, and behind him a vista of sheds and doorways in dim half tone, spotted with the gold and red of Chinese sign-boards. Beautiful and always mysterious—a mystery enhanced by that green-gray mist which hangs always above the Golden Gate and which softens every object exposed to the caressing winds and gentle rains of the North Pacific.

3. Photographs from *Old Chinatown: A Book of Pictures by Arnold Genthe* (New York: Mitchell Kennerley, 1913)

[Shortly after emigrating to San Francisco from Germany, Arnold Genthe (1869–1942) began photographing Chinatown, placing special emphasis on its unusual architecture, everyday street scenes, and children. Like many other photographs and popular postcards of the era, the two photographs reproduced here focus on Chinese children. Genthe's photographs often depict children who appear abandoned, threatened, or lost amid Chinatown's shadowy and untidy spaces. At times, he cropped or etched out indications of non-Chinese street traffic in Chinatown, such as white passers-by and English-language signs. The following images, titled "Cellar Doors" and "In Front of the Joss House," were taken prior to the 1906 earthquake.]

4. **Monument to Robert Louis Stevenson, Portsmouth Square, San Francisco. Photograph Courtesy of Martha Lincoln**

[When she refers to this monument to Robert Louis Stevenson in "Its Wavering Image," Far not only suggests that the white journalist Mark Carson falls short of Stevenson's moral advice but also indicates that Chinatown was a heterogeneous space with a long history of non-Chinese residents and visitors.]

5. Frank Norris, "The Third Circle," *The Wave* 16 (28 August 1897)

[Prior to writing the naturalist novels *McTeague* (1899) and *The Octopus* (1901) for which he is best known, Frank Norris (1870–1902) wrote this Gothic tale about the mysterious hidden circles and sexual perversions of Chinatown. The story capitalizes on sensationalistic notions of prostitution, opium addiction, miscegenation, and cultural contamination.]

There are more things in San Francisco's Chinatown than are dreamed of in Heaven and earth.[1] In reality there are three parts of Chinatown—the part the guides show you, the part the guides don't show you, and the part that no one ever hears of. It is with the latter part that this story has to do. There are a good many stories that might be written about this third circle[2] of Chinatown, but believe me, they never will be written—at any rate not until the "town" has been, as it were, drained off from the city, as one might drain a noisome swamp, and we shall be able to see the strange, dreadful life that wallows down there in the lowest ooze of the place—wallows and grovels there in the mud and in the dark. If you don't think this is true, ask some of the Chinese detectives (the regular squad are not to be relied on), ask them to tell you the story of the Lee On Ting affair, or ask them what was done to old Wong Sam, who thought he could break up the trade in slave girls, or why Mr. Clarence Lowney (he was a clergyman from Minnesota who believed in direct methods) is now a "dangerous" inmate of the State Asylum—ask them to tell you why Matsokura, the Japanese dentist, went back to his home lacking a face—ask them to tell you why the murderers of Little Pete will never be found, and ask them to tell you about the little slave girl, Sing Yee, or—no, on the second thought, don't ask for that story.

The tale I am to tell you now began some twenty years ago in a See Yup[3] restaurant on Waverly Place—long since torn down—where it will end I do not know. I think it is still going on. It began when young Hillegas and Miss Ten Eyck (they were from the East, and engaged to be married) found their way into the restaurant of the Seventy Moons, late in the evening of a day in March. (It was the year after the downfall of Kearney and the discomfiture of the sand-lotters.[4])

---

1 Misquotation of William Shakespeare, *Hamlet*, I.v.168–69.
2 The metaphor of numbered circles beneath circles echoes the architecture of Hell in Dante's *Inferno*.
3 See p. 80, note 2.
4 See p. 242.

"What a dear, quaint, curious old place!" exclaimed Miss Ten Eyck.

She sat down on an ebony stool with its marble seat, and let her gloved hands fall into her lap, looking about her at the huge hanging lanterns, the gilded carven screens, the lacquer work, the inlay work, the coloured glass, the dwarf oak trees growing in Satsuma[1] pots, the marquetry,[2] the painted matting, the incense jars of brass, high as a man's head, and all the grotesque jim-crackery[3] of the Orient. The restaurant was deserted at that hour. Young Hillegas pulled up a stool opposite her and leaned his elbows on the table, pushing back his hat and fumbling for a cigarette.

"Might just as well be in China itself," he commented.

"Might?" she retorted; "we are in China, Tom—a little bit of China dug out and transplanted here. Fancy all America and the Nineteenth Century just around the corner! Look! You can even see the Palace Hotel[4] from the window. See out yonder, over the roof of that temple—the Ming Yen, isn't it?—and I can actually make out Aunt Harriett's rooms."

"I say, Harry (Miss Ten Eyck's first name was Harriett) let's have some tea."

"Tom, you're a genius! Won't it be fun! Of course we must have some tea. What a lark! And you can smoke if you want to."

"This is the way one ought to see places," said Hillegas, as he lit a cigarette; "just nose around by yourself and discover things. Now, the guides never brought us here."

"No, they never did. I wonder why? Why, we just found it out by ourselves. It's ours, isn't it, Tom, dear, by right of discovery?"

At that moment Hillegas was sure that Miss Ten Eyck was quite the most beautiful girl he ever remembered to have seen. There was a daintiness about her—a certain chic trimness in her smart tailor-made gown, and the least perceptible tilt of her crisp hat that gave her the last charm. Pretty she certainly was—the fresh, vigorous, healthful prettiness only seen in certain types of unmixed American stock. All at once Hillegas reached across the table, and, taking her hand, kissed the little crumpled round of flesh that showed where her glove buttoned.

The China boy appeared to take their order, and while waiting for their tea, dried almonds, candied fruit and watermelon rinds, the pair

---

1 A Japanese porcelain.

2 Marquetry is a wooden veneer forming a decorative surface on an object or piece of furniture.

3 Showy, useless trinkets.

4 Built in 1875 (and subsequently rebuilt after the 1906 earthquake), the Palace Hotel was a large luxury hotel located several blocks from Chinatown.

wandered out upon the overhanging balcony and looked down into the darkening streets.

"There's that fortune-teller again," observed Hillegas, presently. "See—down there on the steps of the joss house?"

"Where? Oh, yes, I see."

"Let's have him up. Shall we? We'll have him tell our fortunes while we're waiting."

Hillegas called and beckoned, and at last got the fellow up into the restaurant.

"Hoh! You're no Chinaman," said he, as the fortune-teller came into the circle of the lantern-light. The other showed his brown teeth.

"Part Chinaman, part Kanaka."[1]

"Kanaka?"

"All same Honolulu. Sabe? Mother Kanaka lady—washum clothes for sailor peoples down Kaui way," and he laughed as though it were a huge joke.

"Well, say, Jim," said Hillegas; "we want you to tell our fortunes. You sabe? Tell the lady's fortune. Who she going to marry, for instance."

"No fortune—tattoo."

"Tattoo?"

"Um. All same tattoo—three, four, seven, plenty lil birds on lady's arm. Hey? You want tattoo?"

He drew a tattooing needle from his sleeve and motioned towards Miss Ten Eyck's arm.

"Tattoo my arm? What an idea! But wouldn't it be funny, Tom? Aunt Hattie's sister came back from Honolulu with the prettiest little butterfly tattooed on her finger. I've half a mind to try. And it would be so awfully queer and original."

"Let him do it on your finger, then. You never could wear evening dress if it was on your arm."

"Of course. He can tattoo something as though it was a ring, and my marquise[2] can hide it."

The Kanaka-Chinaman drew a tiny fantastic-looking butterfly on a bit of paper with a blue pencil, licked the drawing a couple of times, and wrapped it about Miss Ten Eyck's little finger—the little finger of her left hand. The removal of the wet paper left an imprint of the drawing. Then he mixed his ink in a small sea-shell, dipped his needle, and in ten minutes had finished the tattooing of a grotesque little insect, as much butterfly as anything else.

---

1 Kanakas are indigenous Hawaiians.
2 A ring with jewels set in the shape of a pointed oval.

"There," said Hillegas, when the work was done and the fortune-teller gone his way; "there you are, and it will never come out. It won't do for you now to plan a little burglary, or forge a little check, or slay a little baby for the coral round its neck, 'cause you can always be identified by that butterfly upon the little finger of your left hand."

"I'm almost sorry now I had it done. Won't it ever come out? Pshaw! Anyhow I think it's very chic," said Harriett Ten Eyck.

"I say, though!" exclaimed Hillegas, jumping up; "where's our tea and cakes and things? It's getting late. We can't wait here all evening. I'll go out and jolly that chap along."

The Chinaman to whom he had given the order was not to be found on that floor of the restaurant. Hillegas descended the stairs to the kitchen. The place seemed empty of life. On the ground floor, however, where tea and raw silk was sold, Hillegas found a Chinaman figuring up accounts by means of little balls that slid to and fro upon rods. The Chinaman was a very gorgeous-looking chap in round horn spectacles and a costume that looked like a man's nightgown, of quilted blue satin.

"I say, John," said Hillegas to this one, "I want some tea. You sabe?—up stairs—restaurant. Give China boy order—he no come. Get plenty much move on. Hey?"

The merchant turned and looked at Hillegas over his spectacles.

"Ah," he said, calmly, "I regret that you have been detained. You will, no doubt, be attended to presently. You are a stranger in China-town?"

"Ahem!—well, yes—I—we are."

"Without doubt—without doubt!" murmured the other.

"I suppose you are the proprietor?" ventured Hillegas.

"I? Oh, no! My agents have a silk house here. I believe they sub-let the upper floors to the See Yups. By the way, we have just received a consignment of India silk shawls you may be pleased to see."

He spread a pile upon the counter, and selected one that was particularly beautiful.

"Permit me," he remarked gravely, "to offer you this as a present to your good lady."

Hillegas's interest in this extraordinary Oriental was aroused. Here was a side of the Chinese life he had not seen, nor even suspected. He stayed for some little while talking to this man, whose bearing might have been that of Cicero[1] before the Senate assembled, and left him with the understanding to call upon him the next day at the Con-

---

1 Marcus Tullius Cicero (106–43 BCE) was a Roman philosopher, statesman, and orator who delivered several powerful and influential speeches before the Roman Senate.

sulate. He returned to the restaurant to find Miss Ten Eyck gone. He never saw her again. No white man ever did.

★★★

There is a certain friend of mine in San Francisco who calls himself Manning. He is a Plaza bum—that is, he sleeps all day in the old Plaza[1] (that shoal where so much human jetsam has been stranded), and during the night follows his own devices in Chinatown, one block above. Manning was at one time a deep-sea pearl diver in Oahu, and, having burst his ear drums in the business, can now blow smoke out of either ear. This accomplishment first endeared him to me, and latterly I found out that he knew more of Chinatown than is meet and right for a man to know. The other day I found Manning in the shade of the Stevenson ship, just rousing from the effects of a jag on undiluted gin, and told him, or rather recalled to him the story of Harriett Ten Eyck.

"I remember," he said, resting on an elbow and chewing grass. "It made a big noise at the time, but nothing ever came of it—nothing except a long row and the cutting down of one of Mr. Hillegas's Chinese detectives in Gambler's Alley.[2] The See Yups brought a chap over from Peking just to do the business."

"Hachet-man?" said I.

"No," answered Manning, spitting green; "he was a two-knife Kai-Gingh."

"As how?"

"Two knives—one in each hand—cross your arms and then draw 'em together, right and left, scissor-fashion—damn near slashed his man in two. He got five thousand for it. After that the detectives said they couldn't find much of a clue."

"And Miss Ten Eyck was not so much as heard from again?"

"No," answered Manning, biting his fingernails. "They took her to China, I guess, or may be up to Oregon. That sort of thing was new twenty years ago, and that's why they raised such a row, I suppose. But there are plenty of women living with Chinamen now, and nobody thinks anything about it, and they are Canton Chinamen, too—lowest kind of coolies. There's one of them up in St. Louis Place, just back of the Chinese theatre, and she's a Sheeny.[3] There's a queer team for you—the Hebrew and the Mongolian—and they've got a kid with red,

---

1 Portsmouth Square (see p. 84, note 1).
2 Ross Alley, where many of Chinatown's gaming operations were concentrated, was known as the alley of the gamblers.
3 Derogatory term for a Jew.

crinkly hair, who's a rubber in a Hammam bath.[1] Yes, it's a queer team, and there's three more white women in a slave girl joint under Ah Yee's tan room. There's where I get my opium. They can talk a little English even yet. Funny thing—one of 'em's dumb, but if you get her drunk enough she'll talk a little English to you. It's a fact! I've seen 'em do it with her often—actually get her so drunk that she can talk. Tell you what," added Manning, struggling to his feet, "I'm going up there now to get some dope. You can come along, and we'll get Sadie (Sadie's her name) we'll get Sadie full, and ask her if she ever heard about Miss Ten Eyck. They do a big business," said Manning, as we went along. "There's Ah Yeo and these three women and a policeman named Yank. They get all the yen shee—that's the cleanings of the opium pipes, you know, and make it into pills and smuggle it into the cons over at San Quentin prison[2] by means of the trusties. Why, they'll make five dollars worth of dope sell for thirty by the time it gets into the yard over at the Pen. When I was over there, I saw a chap knifed behind a jute mill for a pill as big as a pea. Ah Yee gets the stuff, the three women roll it into pills, and the policeman, Yank, gets it over to the trusties somehow. Ah Yee is independent rich by now, and the policeman's got a bank account."

"And the women?"

"Lord! They're slaves—Ah Yee's slaves! They get the swift kick most generally."

Manning and I found Sadie and her two companions four floors underneath the tan room, sitting cross-legged in a room about as big as a big trunk. I was sure they were Chinese women at first, until my eyes got accustomed to the darkness of the place. They were dressed in Chinese fashion, but I noted soon that their hair was brown and the bridges of each one's nose was high. They were rolling pills from a jar of yen shee that stood in the middle of the floor, their fingers twinkling with a rapidity that was somehow horrible to see.

Manning spoke to them briefly in Chinese while he lit a pipe, and two of them answered with the true Canton sing-song—all vowels and no consonants.

"That one's Sadie," said Manning, pointing to the third one, who remained silent the while. I turned to her. She was smoking a cigar, and from time to time spat through her teeth man-fashion. She was a dreadful-looking beast of a woman, wrinkled like a shriveled apple, her teeth quite black from nicotine, her hands bony and prehensile, like a hawk's claws—but a white woman beyond all doubt. At first Sadie

---

1 A Turkish bath.

2 The oldest penitentiary in California, founded in 1852 across the bay from San Francisco.

refused to drink, but the smell of Manning's can of gin removed her objections, and in half an hour she was hopelessly loquacious. What effect the alcohol had upon the paralysed organs of her speech I cannot say. Sober, she was tongue-tied—drunk, she could emit a series of faint bird-like twitterings that sounded like a voice heard from the bottom of a well.

"Sadie," said Manning, blowing smoke out of his ears, "what makes you live with Chinamen? You're a white girl. You got people somewhere. Why don't you get back to them?"

Sadie shook her head.

"Like um China boy better," she said, in a voice so faint we had to stoop to listen. "Ah Yee's pretty good to us—plenty to eat, plenty to smoke, and as much yen shee as we can stand. Oh, I don't complain."

"You know you can get out of this whenever you want. Why don't you make a run for it some day when you're out? Cut for the Mission House on Sacramento street[1]—they'll be good to you there."

"Oh!" said Sadie, listlessly, rolling a pill between her stained palms, "I been here so long I guess I'm kind of used to it, I've about got out of white people's ways by now. They wouldn't let me have my yen shee and my cigar, and that's about all I want nowadays. You can't eat yen shee long and care for much else, you know. Pass that gin along, will you? I'm going to faint in a minute."

"Wait a minute," said I, my hand on Manning's arm. "How long have you been living with Chinamen, Sadie?"

"Oh, I don't know. All my life, I guess. I can't remember back very far—only spots here and there. Where's that gin you promised me?"

"Only in spots?" said I; "here a little and there a little—is that it? Can you remember how you came to take up with this kind of life?"

"Sometimes I can and sometimes I can't," answered Sadie. Suddenly her head rolled upon her shoulder, her eyes closing. Manning shook her roughly:

"Let be! let be!" she exclaimed, rousing up; "I'm dead sleepy. Can't you see?"

"Wake up, and keep awake, if you can," said Manning; "this gentleman wants to ask you something."

---

1 The Occidental Board Presbyterian Mission Home, where Donaldina Cameron later served as superintendent, was established in 1875 at 920 Sacramento Street.

"Ah Yee bought her from a sailor on a junk in the Pei Ho river,"[1] put in one of the other women.

"How about that, Sadie?" I asked. "Were you ever on a junk in a China river? Hey? Try and think?"

"I don't know," she said. "Sometimes I think I was. There's lots of things I can't explain, but it's because I can't remember far enough back."

"Did you ever hear of a girl named Ten Eyck—Harriett Ten Eyck— who was stolen by Chinamen here in San Francisco a long time ago?"

There was a long silence. Sadie looked straight before her, wide-eyed, the other women rolled pills industriously, Manning looked over my shoulder at the scene, still blowing smoke through his ears; then Sadie's eyes began to close and her head to loll sideways.

"My cigar's gone out," she muttered. "You said you'd have gin for me. Ten Eyck! Ten Eyck! No, I don't remember anybody named that." Her voice failed her suddenly, then she whispered:

"Say, how did I get that on me?"

She thrust out her left hand, and I saw a butterfly tattooed on the little finger.

6. Diagram of a House in Oakland's Chinatown, in Donaldina Cameron, "The Yellow Slave Traffic" (Presbyterian Church in the USA Board of Foreign Missions, 1910), Pamphlet, 8 pp.

[This diagram shows how missionaries and reformers working to combat the trafficking of Chinese girls reproduced sensationalistic views about the deviance of Chinese families and homes. Here, a building in Oakland's Chinatown is shown with all the secretive means of entry and egress that had to be accounted for during a raid. The Chinese text advises that guards be stationed at various egresses, including a basement and several windows with street access.]

---

1 Also known as the Hai River, the Pei Ho River flows through Beijing into the Yellow Sea in eastern China.

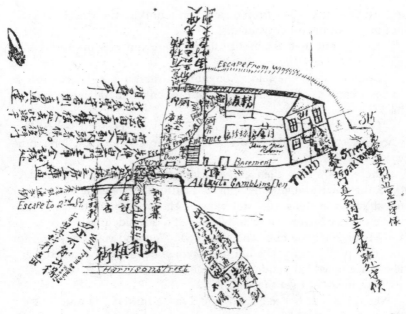

Diagram of house with secret escapes in which two slave girls were kept.

7. Sui Sin Far, "In Los Angeles' Chinatown," *Los Angeles Express* (2 October 1903)

[In 1903, Sui Sin Far wrote a series of articles about the people and cultural practices of Los Angeles's Chinatown. Unlike Gothic and anti-Chinese depictions of labyrinthine caverns and underground opium dens, Far's reports begin with Christian missions and the mission schools that represent, for her, the "brightest spot in Chinatown." Rather than emphasizing the exotic and culturally distinct aspects of Chinatown, Far dwells on evidence of assimilation in both directions: native Chinese Christian preachers, the translation of "Now I Lay Me Down to Sleep," a stringed instrument (probably the four-stringed *pipa*) that is assimilated to the term "banjo," and "excellent" Chinese foods which she heartily recommends to Caucasian readers.]

In Los Angeles the Chinese are by no means neglected by Christian home missionaries, for there are said to be nine missions in that unattractive and unsavory but interesting part of the city called Chinatown. Nearly all of these missions are in a flourishing condition. It matters not what the denomination—Methodist-Episcopal, Baptist, Presbyterian—all have their following. Four native Chinese preachers backed by American church people, gather in the flock and a Christian Chinese sermon preached to a heathen Chinese congregation can be heard every Sunday.

Attached to these missions are night schools for the Chinamen and a kindergarten for children. The brightest spot in Chinatown is this modest little hall of learning. It is run on philanthropic lines, the children being mostly gathered in from the streets by their teacher, but a few of the well-to-do Chinese merchants are glad to send their sons and daughters to learn to talk the white man's language. After once coming into the fold the little ones are quite willing to remain and become much interested in the proceedings and fond of their teacher. They are the cutest of cute things, in their coats of many colors, purple trouserettes and wooden shoes with turned-up toes.

Many of the little girls dress in American garments, but the majority wear the dress of the Chinese woman, which is the same today as centuries ago, when the first non-fabulous empress of China asked her husband to buy her a costume, which was to consist of a tunic, a pair of trousers and a divided skirt. Chinese children are bright scholars and learn quickly. They take pleasure in singing hymns. Following are the Chinese words of "Now I Lay Me Down to Sleep:"

> Tsoi Ch'ong chi ghung,
> Ka ngo fan,
> K'au shan po yau
> Chan t'al ling wan
> Wak mi ts'ang sing
> Fat in kwo shan
> K'au chu ye soo
> Tsip ngo ling wan.

At New Year and Christmas animated gatherings are held in these school rooms, which are made most inviting, Chinese lanterns being swung overhead and tables spread with all kinds of good things and beautifully decorated with plants and flowers. The flutist brings his flute, the banjo man his banjo and right merrily are visitors entertained, for all the talent of Chinatown turns out, which the little ones, like birds and butterflies, hover around.

There are several Christian Chinese families in Chinatown, noticeably the Sing family of East Commercial street. For those Chinamen who adhere to the worship of their ancestors three joss houses stand conspicuous and the smoke of the burning incense daily ascends to the nostrils of the wrathful or benevolent deities who preside. These joss houses are not so rich in draperies or carvings as are the San Francisco temples, nevertheless it took money to build them and they are well worth seeing.

Chinese restaurants are interesting. Chinese food, though rather insipid to the palate, is good and nutritious. The chief article of diet of a Chinaman, as everybody knows, is rice. It is a wholesome grain and the Chinaman cooks it cleanly and beautifully. A bowl of rice flavored with a little soy often forms the dinner of a Chinaman. Sun-dried comestibles are much used in Chinese cooking and in their soups and stews are to be detected various kinds of dried nuts, dried fish and dried vegetables. A favorite dish and a most appetizing one is small dumplings filled with minced meat and boiled in a big caldron. There is nothing on a Chinaman's table to remind one of living animals and birds—no legs, heads, limbs, wings or loins—every thing is cut up small. The Chinaman comes to the table to eat—not to work.

Shell fish stew is excellent, though it looks suspicious; so are shark fins and gelatinous preserved ducks' tongues. Balls of crab and tripe cooked to a tenderness hard to express are much favored by the Chinese, so also are prawn, ground nuts, preserved ginger and candied fruits.

Notwithstanding what is said to the contrary, the Chinese are good livers, and there are few dyspeptics among them, their food being the kind that digests easily. According to Chinese statistics there are about 4,000 Chinese in Los Angeles, including about seventy-five women and from fifty to sixty children.

Works Cited and Further Reading

Works Cited

Austin, Mary. "The Conversion of Ah Lew Sing." *Overland Monthly* 30 (October 1897): 307–12.

Cather, Willa. "The Conversion of Sum Loo." *The Library* 1 (August 1900): 4–6.

Chapman, Mary. "A 'Revolution in Ink': Sui Sin Far and Chinese Reform Discourse." *American Quarterly* 60.4 (2008): 975–1001.

Chin, Frank, et al., eds. *Aiiieeeee! An Anthology of Asian-American Writers*. New York: Penguin, 1983 [1974].

Cutter, Martha. "Empire and the Mind of the Child: Sui Sin Far's 'Tales of Chinese Children.'" *MELUS* 27.2 (Summer 2002): 31–48.

Donovan, Brian. *White Slave Crusades: Race, Gender, and Anti-Vice Activism, 1887–1917*. Urbana: U of Illinois P, 2006.

Doolittle, Justus and Edwin Paxton Hood. *Social Life of the Chinese: A Daguerreotype of Daily Life in China*. London: S. Low, Son, and Marston, 1868.

Du Bois, W.E.B. *The Souls of Black Folk: Essays and Sketches*. Chicago: A.C. McClurg & Co., 1903.

Eaton, Winnifred (Onoto Watanna). *Marion: The Story of an Artist's Model*. New York: W.J. Watt & Co., 1916.

——. *Me: A Book of Remembrance*. Jackson: UP of Mississippi, 1997.

Far, Sui Sin. "Sui Sin Far, the Half Chinese Writer, Tells of Her Career." In *Mrs. Spring Fragrance and Other Writings*. Ed. Amy Ling and Annette White-Parks. Urbana: U of Illinois P, 1995. 288–96.

Ferens, Dominika. *Edith and Winnifred Eaton: Chinatown Missions and Japanese Romances*. Urbana: U of Illinois P, 2002.

Genthe, Arnold. *As I Remember*. New York: Reynal & Hitchcock, 1936.

Jacolliot, M. Louis. *The Bible in India: Hindoo Origin of Hebrew and Christian Revelation*. London: John Camden Hotten, 1870.

James, Richard, Horatio Gottheil, and Epiphanius Wilson, eds. *Oriental Literature: The Literature of China*. New York: The Colonial Press, 1900.

Jorae, Wendy Rouse. *The Children of Chinatown: Growing Up Chinese American in San Francisco*. Chapel Hill: U of North Carolina P, 2009.

Legge, James, translator. *The Chinese Classics: A Translation*. Boston: Houghton Mifflin, 1882.

Lin, Jan. *Reconstructing Chinatown: Ethnic Enclave, Global Change.* Minneapolis: U of Minnesota P, 1998.

Lui, Mary Ting Yi. *The Chinatown Trunk Mystery: Murder, Miscegenation, and other Dangerous Encounters in Turn-of-the-Century New York City.* Princeton: Princeton UP, 2007.

McCann, Sean. "Connecting Links: The Anti-Progressivism of Sui Sin Far." *Yale Journal of Criticism* 12.1 (Spring 1999): 73–88.

Pan, Arnold. "Transnationalism at the Impasse of Race: Sui Sin Far and U.S. Imperialism." *Arizona Quarterly* 66.1 (Spring 2010): 87–114.

Pfaelzer, Jean. *Driven Out: The Forgotten War Against Chinese Americans.* New York: Random House, 2007.

Pryse, Marjorie. "Linguistic Regionalism and the Emergence of Chinese American Literature in Sui Sin Far's Mrs. Spring Fragrance." *Tamkang Review: A Quarterly of Literary and Cultural Studies* 38.1 (2007): 29–69.

Pryse, Marjorie and Judith Fetterley. *Writing Out of Place: Regionalism, Women, and American Literary Culture.* Urbana: U of Illinois P, 2003.

Shah, Nayan. *Contagious Divides: Epidemics and Race in San Francisco's Chinatown.* Berkeley: U of California P, 2001.

Song, Min Hyoung. "Sentimentalism and Sui Sin Far." *Legacy* 20.1–2 (2003): 134–52.

Further Reading

Biographical Works

Anonymous. "Edith Eaton." *The Chautauquan* 45 (July 1906): 446.

Ling, Amy. "Edith Eaton: Pioneer Chinamerican Writer and Feminist." *American Literary Realism* 16.2 (1983): 287–98.

McMullen, Lorraine. "Eaton, Edith Maud." *Dictionary of Canadian Biography Online.*

Solberg, S.E. "Sui Sin Far/Edith Eaton: The First Chinese-American Fictionist." *MELUS* 8.1 (1981): 27–39.

White-Parks, Annette. *Sui Sin Far/Edith Maude Eaton: A Literary Biography.* Urbana: U of Illinois P, 1995.

Yin, Xiao-Huang. "Between East and West: Sui Sin Far—the First Chinese American Writer." *Arizona Quarterly* 47 (1991): 49–84.

Selected Works by Sui Sin Far

For an indispensable selection of Far's journalism, sketches, and short fiction, see Amy Ling and Annette White-Parks's *Mrs. Spring Fragrance and Other Writings* (Urbana: U of Illinois P, 1995). The following is a chronological list of selected magazine stories including earlier versions of the stories Far collected in *Mrs. Spring Fragrance*. For more comprehensive, chronological bibliographies of Far's writings and letters, see White-Parks, *Sui Sin Far/Edith Maude Eaton*, 245–47 and Ferens, *Edith and Winnifred Eaton*, 201–04.

"Misunderstood: The Story of a Young Man." *Dominion Illustrated* 1 (November 1888): 314.

"Albemarle's Secret." *Dominion Illustrated* 3 (October 1889): 254.

"Spring Impressions: A Medley of Poetry and Prose." *Dominion Illustrated* 4 (June 1890): 358–59.

"Chinamen with German Wives." *Montreal Daily Star* (13 December 1895).

"Ku Yum." *Land of Sunshine* 5 (June 1896): 29–31.

"A Chinese Feud." *Land of Sunshine* 5.1 (June 1896): 236–37.

"The Story of Iso." *Lotus* 2 (August 1896): 117–19.

"A Love Story of the Orient." *Lotus* 2 (August 1896): 117–19.

"A Plea for the Chinaman: A Correspondent's Argument in His Favor." *Montreal Daily Star* (21 September 1896).

"As Others See Us." *Gall's Daily News Letter* (16 December 1896).

"The Baby Show." *Gall's Daily News Letter* (23 December 1896).

"Sweet Sin," *Land of Sunshine* 8 (April 1898): 224–25.

"The Sing-Song Woman." *Land of Sunshine* 9 (October 1898): 225–28.

"Lin John." *Land of Sunshine* 10 (January 1899): 76–77.

"A Chinese Ishmael." *Overland Monthly* 34 (July 1899): 43–49.

"The Story of Tin-A." *Land of Sunshine* 12 (December 1899): 101–03.

"The Smuggling of Tie Co." *Land of Sunshine* 13 (July 1900): 100–04.

"O Yam—A Sketch." *Land of Sunshine* 13 (November 1900): 341–43.

"The Coat of Many Colors." *Youth's Companion* 76 (April 1902): n.p.

"The Horoscope." *Out West* 19 (November 1903): 521–24.

"A Chinese Boy-Girl." *Century* 67 (April 1904): 828–31.

"Aluteh." *The Chautauquan* 42 (December 1905): 338–42.

"Woo-ma and I." *The Bohemian* 10.1 (January 1906): 66–75.

"The Puppet Show: Chinese Folk Lore." Translated by Sui Sin Far. *Good Housekeeping* 46 (February 1908): 61.

"The Wild Man and the Gentle Boy." *Good Housekeeping* 46 (February 1908): 179–80.

"What About the Cat?" *Good Housekeeping* 46 (March 1908): 290–91.

"The Heart's Desire." *Good Housekeeping* 47 (May 1908): 514–15.

"Tangled Kites." *Good Housekeeping* 47 (July 1908): 52–53.

"Ku Yum and the Butterflies." *Good Housekeeping* 48 (March 1909): 299.

"The Half Moon Cakes." *Good Housekeeping* 48 (May 1909): 584–85.

"In the Land of the Free." *Independent* 67 (September 1909): 504–08.

"Mrs. Spring Fragrance." *Hampton's* 24 (January 1910): 137–41.

"The Kitten-Headed Shoes." *Delineator* 75 (February 1910): 165.

"A White Woman Who Married a Chinaman." *The Independent* 68 (March 1910): 518–23.

"The Inferior Woman." *Hampton's* 24 (May 1910): 727–31.

"The Sugar Cane Baby." *Good Housekeeping* 50 (May 1910): 570–72.

"The Candy That is not Sweet." *Delineator* 76 (July 1910): 76.

"An Autumn Fan." *New England Magazine* 42 (August 1910): 700–02.

"Her Chinese Husband." *The Independent* 69 (August 1910): 358–61.

"The Bird of Love" [original title of "Children of Peace"]. *New England Magazine* 43 (September 1910): 25–27.

"The Persecution and Oppression of Me." *The Independent* 71 (August 1911): 421–26.

"A Love Story from the Rice Fields of China." *New England Magazine* 45 (December 1911): 343–45.

"The Moon Harp." *The Independent* 72 (May 1912): 1106.

"Chan Hen Yen, Chinese Student." *New England Magazine* 45 (June 1912): 462–66.

Scholarly Books on Edith Maude Eaton/Sui Sin Far

Ling, Amy and Annette White-Parks, eds. *Sui Sin Far, Mrs. Spring Fragrance and Other Writings.* Urbana: U of Illinois P, 1995.

Ferens, Dominika. *Edith and Winnifred Eaton: Chinatown Missions and Japanese Romances.* Urbana: U of Illinois P, 2002.

Ammons, Elizabeth. "Audacious Words: Sui Sin Far's Mrs. Spring Fragrance." *Conflicting Stories: American Women Writers at the Turn into the Twentieth Century*. New York: Oxford UP, 1992. 105–20.

Beauregard, Guy. "Reclaiming Sui Sin Far." *Re/Collecting Early Asian America: Essays in Cultural History*. Ed. Josephine Lee, Imogene L. Lim, and Yuko Matsukawa. Philadelphia: Temple UP, 2002. 340–54.

Cho, Yu-Fang. "Domesticating the Aliens Within: Sentimental Benevolence in Late Nineteenth-Century California Magazines." *American Quarterly* 61.1 (March 2009): 113–36.

——. "'Yellow Slavery,' Narratives of Rescue, and Sui Sin Far/Edith Maude Eaton's 'Lin John'" (1899). *Journal of Asian American Studies* 12.1 (February 2009): 35–63.

Chung, June Hee. "Asian Object Lessons: Orientalist Decoration in Realist Aesthetics from William Dean Howells to Sui Sin Far." *Studies in American Fiction* 36.1 (2008): 27–50.

Cutter, Martha J. "Sex, Love, Revenge, and Murder in 'Away Down in Jamaica': A Lost Short Story by Sui Sin Far (Edith Eaton)." *Legacy: A Journal of American Women Writers* 21.1 (2004): 85–89.

——. "Smuggling across the Borders of Race, Gender, and Sexuality: 'Mrs. Spring Fragrance.'" *Mixed Race Literature*. Ed. Jonathan Brennan. Stanford, CA: Stanford UP, 2002. 137–64.

——. "Sui Sin Far's Letters to Charles Lummis: Contextualizing Publication Practices for the Asian American Subject at the Turn of the Century." *American Literary Realism* 38.3 (Spring 2006): 259–75.

Dariotis, Wei Ming. "Teaching Edith Eaton/Sui Sin Far: Multiple Approaches." *Asian American Literature: Discourses and Pedagogies* 1 (2010): 70–78.

Degenhardt, Jane Hwang. "Situating the Essential Alien: Sui Sin Far's Depiction of Chinese-White Marriage and the Exclusionary Logic of Citizenship." *Modern Fiction Studies* 54.4 (Winter 2008): 654–88.

Diana, Vanessa H. "Biracial/Bicultural Identity in the Writings of Sui Sin Far." *MELUS* 26.2 (2001): 159–86.

Ferens, Dominika. "Tangled Kites: Sui Sin Far's Negotiations with Race and Readership." *Amerasia Journal* 25.2 (1999): 116–44.

Goudie, Sean. "Towards a Definition of Caribbean American Regionalism: Contesting Anglo-America's Caribbean Designs in Mary Seacole and Sui Sin Far." *American Literature* 80.2 (2008): 293–322.

Hattori, Tomo. "Model Minority Discourse and Asian American Jouis-Sense." *differences: A Journal of Feminist Cultural Studies* 11.2 (Summer 1999): 228–47.

Howard, June. "Sui Sin Far's American Words." *Comparative American Studies* 6.2 (June 2008): 144–60.

Hsu, Hsuan L. "Cultural Orphans: Domesticity, Missionaries, and China from Stowe to Sui Sin Far." *Geography and the Production of Space in Nineteenth-Century American Literature.* Cambridge: Cambridge UP, 2010. 94–128.

Leighton, Joy M. "'A Chinese Ishmael': Sui Sin Far, Writing, and Exile." *MELUS* 26.3 (2001): 3–29.

Li, Wenxin. "Sui Sin Far and the Chinese American Canon: Toward a Post-Gender-Wars Discourse." *MELUS* 29.3–4 (2004): 121–31.

Lim, Shirley Geok-lin. "Sibling Hybridities: The Case of Edith Eaton/Sui Sin Far and Winnifred Eaton/Onoto Watanna." *Life Writing* 4.1 (2007): 81–99.

Martin, Quentin E. "Sui Sin Far's Railroad Baron: A Chinese of the Future." *American Literary Realism* 29.1 (1996): 54–61.

McMullen, Lorraine. "Double Colonization: Femininity and Ethnicity in the Writings of Edith Eaton." *Crisis and Creativity in the New Literatures in English Canada.* Ed. Geoffrey Davis. Amsterdam: Rodopi Press, 1990. 141–51.

Nguyen, Viet T. "On the Origins of Asian American Literature: The Eaton Sisters and the Hybrid Body." *Race and Resistance: Literature and Politics in Asian America.* Oxford: Oxford UP, 2002. 33–60.

Patterson, Martha H. "Sui Sin Far and the Wisdom of the New." *Beyond the Gibson Girl: Reimagining the American New Woman, 1895–1915.* Urbana: U of Illinois P, 2005. 102–24.

Roh-Spaulding, Carol. "'Wavering' Images: Mixed-Race Identity in the Stories of Edith Eaton/Sui Sin Far." *Ethnicity and the American Short Story.* Ed. William E. Cain and Julia Brown. New York: Garland, 1997. 155–76.

Shih, David. "The Seduction of Origins: Sui Sin Far and the Race for Tradition." *Form and Transformation in Asian American Literature.* Ed. Xiaojing Zhou and Samina Najmi. Seattle: U of Washington P, 2005. 48–76.

Teng, Jinhua Emma. "Miscegenation and the Critique of Patriarchy in Turn-of-the-Century Fiction." *Race, Gender and Class* 4:3 (1997): 68–87.

Vogel, Todd. "Edith Eaton Plays the Chinese Water Lily." *Rewriting White: Race, Class, and Cultural Capital in Nineteenth-Century America.* New Brunswick, NJ: Rutgers UP, 2004. 10–32.

Winter, Molly. "The Multicultural Perspective of Sui Sin Far." *Amer-*